GASOLINE COWBOYS

GASOLINE COWBOYS

BAPTISM BY FIRE

Christiaan A. Lecky

atmosphere press

TABLE OF CONTENTS

Adriana took a deep breath as the video loaded up on the conference screen and straightaway bit her fingernails as the tune (made by a Japanese composer she found on the Internet a few days ago) played, closing her all-nighter of assembling the animated footage into a sensible presentation for the board meeting. Following the introductory words, the assembled footage of the animated combat test appeared on the screen. Tanks with colored radio antennas and attached hitboxes roared out of their spawn and opened fire at each other, with the camera flying above them, following registered shots or entertaining the viewers with slick angles. After a minute of nail-biting action, the camera shot up to the sky and flew over the smoke-covered battlefield, where now stationary tanks parked behind shipping containers but still aimed their cannons at each other. The fancy animation faded into black as the beat dropped. Then, as violins and brass picked up the tension, the video rewound the epic moments for the last time, with orchestral music concluding the animated spectacle.

Adriana held her breath as the video ended. She looked around the room at people taking notes and then at the TVG President to her right, who nodded and gave Adriana a thumbs up. The animated battle royale idea yielded the desired results, and Adriana allowed herself to breathe. President of the TVG, a tall man, broad in shoulders, turned towards Adriana, whose left foot shook underneath the conference table as all eyes were now on her, watching every move she made.

"Adriana, that was something! And I love it! Everyone give a round of applause to Adriana and Thomas!" The President shook hands with Adriana, who then waved around the conference room, filled to the fullest with corporate officers, their staffers, and operatives. "The new and strong opening for our upcoming Battle Royale Season Zero program for millions to see! Truly an amazing job! As I always say, only the best and brightest come to work for us!"

The conference room erupted in applause, and Adriana looked at Thomas, who sat in the last chair. He gave her a thumbs up and grinned from ear to ear. For a moment, Adriana lost him as his pale face matched the white wall behind him. The President turned towards the man in a midnight black two-piece suit, holding a tablet.

"Adriana, Thomas, I'm pleased to introduce my right hand, Mark Fletcher. Mark here will dot the i's and cross the t's. If Mark says yes, we will begin the pre-production. Everyone, we have some viewership statistics and corporate fluff to discuss next, so let's give them room to make a masterpiece!"

Mark shook hands with everyone at the door, through which other suits departed in a perfect single line. A moment later, they were left alone in the conference room, and Mark closed the door, which he held with his foot.

"Mr. Askarov, you can sit closer if you want," Mark used the door window as a mirror to ensure that his haircut was slick and then smiled, raising his hands in the air like a preacher ready to deliver the sermon to his congregation, "Let's get started, shall we?"

"Let's get started," Adriana said, and then, in the same breath, she whispered a thank you to Thomas, who prepared a chair for her.

"Okay then. Let me preface our informal talk with something important. Since TVG's integration into the Orion Network three years ago, only nine successful submissions came from outside. Now, both of you will be joining this elite group of insiders. How are you feeling?"

"I feel great." Adriana squeezed Thomas's left hand. "We're happy that this stress is finally behind us, and hopefully, a better future is ahead of us."

"Glad to hear that, and I'm sure that we'll all look fondly on this moment. You are already ahead as you built a running prototype, and the fancy animation tied the knot. Let us get to the meat and bones of this idea because I have a couple of questions." Mark placed his tablet on the table. "First question. What is your estimate of the total time it will take to finalize this production? A rough estimate, nothing more, nothing less."

"Well, we ran the numbers. The actual assembly of the tanks will consume most of the time. Adding the testing, I'm confident this will be launched by 2144. To be safe, by 2145, which gives us two years by the fastest estimate. Yes, we can deliver, but it won't be easy. It's much easier to assemble a submachine gun than a tank in 1-to-1 representation," Adriana looked at Thomas, who nodded. "Early 2145, we can launch."

"Very good. Next question. Do you want this in the simulation or a real fight?"

"If we are building this, then yeah, the real fight. We can use the simulation for training and competition. We're not compromising on our vision of realism. Our vision also follows the Orion Corp and TVG authenticity request outlined in the submission guidelines."

"Thought so too. Next point. Someone will always have a problem with your idea, and I need to ask you how ready you are to address the criticism?" Mark swiped right on the screen. "This was one of the internal observations. Allow me to read it out. The problem is not the tanks, but the era they are from. These tanks are outdated by today's standards: no night vision, ballistic computers, or other needed tools. Game

Mode has already tried the tank idea, but it didn't gain any traction. So how do we expect people to react to the riveted tracked machines shooting at each other?"

"Well, with interest. These tanks don't have night vision or thermal optics, which will be a challenge to the contestants. Also, seeing them struggle will be relatable to the audience," Adriana said, tilting her head slightly to the right. "Standard Battle Royale is a money maker, which ticks off all the boxes. Tension, underdog stories, love sometimes, and the social media craze. We will only add tanks to the formula, and the yield will be tenfold."

"If I may add, the asymmetrical combat will also be a big draw. The reason why it first failed was that all the tanks were the same—no unique bells or whistles. Our Battle Royale will remedy this problem and will allow viewers to cheer for their favorite," Thomas tapped the table with his index finger as he spoke.

"My point exactly! While I don't know much about Panzer 4 or T-34, I know that these are different names for different tanks, and I believe this is what we were looking for," Mark smiled, noting Adriana's response in bullet points. "Let's move on. How do we select contestants?"

"Standard Battle Royale takes eighty-five percent convicts and fifteen percent volunteers." Adriana tapped her thumbs. "I read somewhere that our prisons are getting overcrowded lately, so we can adjust the ratio and do a hundred percent of inmates for now. A win-win scenario for everyone."

"Such a selfless choice; I love it! Both of you were among the few insiders who, during the interview, thought of the larger picture. Thank you. Now, will there be an option to live out on the pastures?"

"I'm not following!?" Adriana looked back and forth between puzzled Thomas, who tapped his chin with his right thumb and grinning Mark.

"Aggregate details to be determined later." Mark waved

his hand. "Where will you build tanks? I assume Mr. Askarov's backyard won't be able to cope with the increased demand."

"We found a lot in Grassrange, Montana, only two hours or so away from Great Falls, providing us with everything we will need to set up the production," Thomas tossed his hat into the ring. "Purchase is finalized as we speak."

"I like your strategic thinking. Right next to TVG City of Entertainment. There is a lot of available talent on deck. Do you want full automation or hybrid? Speaking of automation, humanoids, or androids?"

"We are still optimizing the production plan, but I..." Adriana looked at Thomas and then at Mark. "The hybrid model with the sixty percent automation and forty percent of the flesh-based organisms. Is there a difference between human and andro?"

"Androids will be a better call in this case, as there aren't many spare parts for humanoids. Across the world, we are phasing them out due to high production costs and upkeep, estimating a full humanoid retirement by 2150. Some old-fashioned people still like humanoids, so I must ask. I take it as androids, then. We'll talk production numbers later." Mark tapped the tablet. "Since the entire world is in the Orion Network, we take care of the marketing costs and other expenses."

"Wow, you mean, like the entire world?" Thomas scratched his chin.

"Even the smallest island in the Pacific or loose icebergs are under Orion Network. Of course, we were able to progress the technology to the point where Martian Colonies could watch Tank Royale with a three-second delay. God bless Orion. Anyway, we will cover seventy percent of the total cost. Seeing that you are about to become two of the richest people in the world, TVG and Orion believe it is a fair ratio."

"Yeah, that is reasonable." Adriana looked at Thomas and smiled. "How else can we help?"

"You would have to move from your primary Arkansas

residence to either Great Falls or Grassrange to oversee the production and subsequent development. Can you move?"

"Already ahead of you." Adriana whistled. "Moving boxes are packed, and we are ready to go. What else, chief?"

"That is all I have. Of course, my team will follow up with you to complete the package in three to four business days. I just need you to sign here, both of you." Mark flipped his tablet around and handed a pen to Adriana first. "Ma'am, right here and right there."

Moments later, Thomas added his signature underneath Adriana's, and Mark locked the screen. Mark stretched his neck and grinned from ear to ear, flashing what Adriana assumed was a 24-karat gold watch.

"Go out and celebrate. The Tank Royale platform has been officially greenlit and will become the launch title of the TVG Battle Royale Season program, premiering on all channels and streaming media. Here at the TVG, we think about the viewer first and profit second. The best thing is that once you ride with us, it will never end."

"May it never." Adriana stood up and shook hands with Mark. "Thank you for picking us out of millions of submissions. I promise we will never compromise on our vision and deliver the best, and of course, we are not stopping there. We also have plans for battleships and aircraft, just in case."

"Pleasure is all mine. Keep an eye on her, Mr. Askarov. She is a keeper." Mark gave Thomas the same firm handshake. "I wish my girl was as active as her. If I may recommend a gourmet restaurant in Great Falls, look for Great Falls Restaurant. While the name is unassuming, to say the least, this is the oldest restaurant in town, celebrating its centennial since its founding. Currently, they have Chef Antigo in the kitchen. Anything on his list is a treat."

"Thank you for the suggestion; we'll consider it." Adriana smiled. "We'll be in touch."

———

Thomas ensured that Mark vanished in the adjacent hallway and whistled as he returned to the conference room.

"Adriana, we should go there. Adriana?" Thomas sat next to shivering Adriana, who bit her thumb. "Everything all right? Talk to me!"

"A wave of emotions just hit me in full force." Adriana took a deep breath. "We went from your backyard to national television, and now this! We are finally somebody in this world! What are the chances?!"

"Our backyard, Adriana, our. I don't know what the chances are, and I don't care." Thomas hugged her, feeling her racing heart slowly calm down. "Now, where are we going to eat?"

Adriana leaned back in the chair and took three deep breaths. Then she swung around and walked up to the window, where she gazed upon the concrete skyline of Great Falls. Thomas scratched his chin and then walked up to her, gently wrapping his right arm around her.

"What's going on here?" Thomas tapped the glass, prompting an unidentified insect to fly away.

"Tell me, how high are we?" Adriana rested her head on Thomas's right shoulder.

"If I remember correctly, this is the hundredth floor, two doors down from the President's office. Nice view." Thomas observed a VTOL cargo plane taking off from the Great Falls International Airport, built right next to the city, followed by another after twenty seconds. "Unless you took drugs, which I don't remember you taking, or any addictive medication for that matter, I don't think we are that high."

"That is not what I meant. I mean, how close to the top are we?"

"Ohm." Thomas tapped his forehead as he realized what answer Adriana was looking for. "I would say pretty high to the top of the food chain, and I'm not planning to go down any time soon. Speaking of food, where are we going to eat?"

"I'm not going down either. Savor this moment, love."

Adriana looked at Thomas. "Did you know that TVG is onboarding Benjamin Bell as the Chief Talk Host for our show?"

"Love, it doesn't matter whom they give us. It could be Bell Entertainment or some random spoony they find on the street. We were made wardens of our game now, and I will ensure that nothing compromises our vision. We worked hard to get there, and concessions were made along the way. I say, no more concessions and sacrifices!"

"And I agree! Pure artistic vision is the way forward." Adriana tapped Thomas on his right shoulder. "Thank you for standing by my side. I don't think I could have done it without you."

"Adriana, without you, this venture wouldn't go anywhere. It would sit under an improvised roof I made from a tarp and poles in my dried-up backyard. Now, I'll savor this moment with you over a glass of red wine." Thomas kissed Adriana on her forehead. "Let's get out of here. A new life, which we always wanted, is ahead of us. We'll grab it and hold on to it as long as possible!"

"Indeed. No more coupons or secondhand stores. My parents can finally travel the world and afford a new house. On top of that, we can think of how many kids we want or where to build our dream home. I have a few spots, but we'll talk later. Imagine the possibilities and new people we'll meet!" Adriana took Thomas by his bicep, and together they vanished into the hallway of tight suits and short skirts that emerged from their offices. "I think I know where we're going to eat."

"Well, tell me!"

"You'll see!" Adriana grinned from ear to ear. "You'll see, Thomas. It's a good place, trust me."

"Come on, tell me! You know I hate surprises!"

CHAPTER ONE

BLUE LINE, RED LINE

TWO YEARS LATER

"Mason, Overseer Smith wants a word!" the voice of Mike the Dispatcher crackled on the short-range radio, and Mason rolled his eyes. "Blue line ASAP!"

"I'll be there." Mason parked the truck on the side of the road and exhaled. "Do you know what they want?"

"No clue, Mason, but it is blue, not red. I'll see you tonight. The boys are excited to hit up bars in Miami. We think Brickell or Ocean Drive!"

"Likewise! And I'm the only white guy from our group who doesn't speak Spanish. Yeah, blue is good. Red is bad." Mason grinned from ear to ear. "Brickell is a good call."

Upon unstrapping himself from the worn-out seat, Mason thought: *What do they want now? I fulfill the quota all the time!* Looking into the mirror, Mason removed his hardhat and dried his short black hair from the sweat with a rag that hung behind him. When he climbed down from the cabin of the eight-wheeled cargo truck, Mason tapped the shoulder of the next man heading to take his place. Mason swept sweat from his forehead again. The blistering sun and broken air conditioning in the truck are the worst things to happen to someone in Florida. Mason gave a short nod, passing by the other workers carrying pipes and other hardware, and they saluted back. Five minutes later, he got the checkpoint.

Mason, in a reflection of a security booth, fixed his short-black hair and smiled, thinking: *What's the worst that can happen to me?*

He took a deep breath and showed the identification armband to the security guard, who scanned it and wordlessly stepped aside, allowing Mason to enter the corporate offices. Following the blue line on the ground, Mason got to the designated zone, where he was searched by the security android in a bulletproof vest. After a short scan, the machine gave a thumbs up, and Mason entered the building, removing his helmet again upon entering.

The flashing graphics on one of the many screens attracted his attention, but it was just the PSA about his work. At the same time, an energetic male voice described the Project: *Following the War, the Clean Air Project is a Corporate Initiative to make air outside breathable due to pollution and nuclear spoils. As we lost around forty percent of the worldwide trees, the Initiative divided the world into Continental Sectors, where well-compensated workers build extensive air recycling facilities. In two years, we had reconstructed air to 70 percent of the Pre-War atmosphere, but substantial upgrades and new facilities are needed to keep up as the world slowly returns to its Pre-War lives. So do your part, install a small air filter today for better sleep and brain activity for only c$35.99, and enroll in the Clean Air Initiative today to support the ongoing efforts! Orion is counting on you, and so is Mother Earth!*

All around him, people in suits and ties walked wordlessly among other operators in reflective vests and numbered hardhats in unison. Then, finally, in the corner of this never-sleeping corporate beehive, the blue line ended in front of the office, where another android stopped him. Mason handed it the badge and shook his head: *They are already tracking me everywhere I go. Is this necessary?*

"Thank you for your cooperation, Mason Knight. Overseer Smith will see you now. Note that she is not feeling well. Make it quick and return to your team."

"Understood!" Mason took the badge, and the android opened the door.

———

Overseer Smith looked up from the terminal and took a deep breath while tying her snow-white hair into a bun. She pointed at the chair, and Mason sat down, placing his hard hat on the table. A woman in her early forties, Mason never knew her first name, as during the introduction, the man in the three-piece suit introduced her as Overseer Smith.

"I'm here as requested, Overseer Smith," Mason smiled, pretending to dive into the office culture of empty smiles and wordless greetings.

"Thank you for coming on short notice. However, I must speak frankly; you are fired," Smith swung the terminal around and handed jaw-dropped Mason the pen. "Sign here, and I'll send you the rest of the paycheck for the month."

Mason stood up stunned and slowly exhaled, processing what the overseer had told him.

"If you could please speed up, I need to let go of others on top of my regular work. Please?" Smith covered her burning forehead with a frozen chill pack.

"On what grounds am I being fired?" Mason's voice whimpered. "I cannot lose this job! My brother and my aunt depend on me!"

"If you wouldn't post undesirable things on social media, I wouldn't have to go through the hassle of firing you. This is your second strike. Is it worth it to sabotage your lifeline?"

Mason stood for a few more moments before sitting down again, staring at his hard hat momentarily.

"You only suspended Jerome, who has a lot more on his plate. Why am I the only getting...."

"Don't make it harder on yourself, Mason. Jerome was picked

up by Internal Control yesterday, and I highly doubt that we will see him ever again. The same could have happened to you. So sign, take the paycheck for the month, and go home. It's not worth the fight. However," Smith looked around her, "I'll give you a bonus for saving your co-worker's life. Extra 200 as an exit bonus, plus paid fare to Pampa, Texas."

Mason couldn't believe his ears as Overseer just put a price tag on their lives, but deep inside, he knew there was no way to fight this. He stared at the hard hat, thinking: *It always catches up with you. But again, I should count my blessings. She could have called IC on me.* Mason took the pen and signed off.

"Can I at least keep the hard hat?" Mason gulped, and Overseer scratched her head as she sent in the documents.

"Your paycheck will be cleared in a couple of hours." Smith handed Mason his wish. "Good luck to you, and please, for your sake, don't stir the corporate waters. You still have a life ahead of you. Don't let Internal Control take it away."

Mason didn't even say thank you before the android dragged him out of the office and shoved him into the hallway.

"Use the red line to leave the premises," Android looked at a woman who stood next to them. "Overseer Smith will see you in a minute. She is not feeling well, so make it quick."

— — —

Awestruck, Mason got out of the building and found a lonely bench. Mason shook his head as he got seated, fighting the tears away, which watered the cushion inside his helmet that rested in his lap. He looked at his wrist tablet and declined the call. He sat under the blistering sun, staring at the dusty ground, not caring about his neck turning red or a security android standing over him with its hands folded. In his mind, voices clashed with one another. *Mason, you are a moron. Was it worth it? Just because Orion played both sides in the War, they don't get to do this. The Bill of Rights exists for a reason. There was no call to violence on my feed. I only pointed out the problems that need to be addressed, like Internal Control kicking down the doors without a warrant. In that case, amendments Four to Nine are a thing of the past. Damn me; I need to do something. Time to look for a new job, as my savings won't last that long.*

"Mason, I am ordered to escort you from the premises to collect your belongings. The Initiative has decided to pay for your ticket home. Pampa, Texas, is that correct?" Android opened his tablet and scanned Mason's face.

"Yes, that is correct." Mason dried the small tear from his right eye. "Can you give a man who just lost his job a moment?"

"Project can provide a free counseling session and rest at thirty-five percent off. Would you like to enroll?"

"No." Mason took the first step, but the android grabbed him by the collar. "What?!"

The android retracted his arm, and Mason noticed that the safety on the gun was off. The Project Guidelines required all machines to keep the safety on. The security guard waved at Mason, who shook his head. Then, as they marched across the complex, Mason took a deep breath when he realized that he barely avoided a frank reminder, but there wasn't much time to think as they got to the residential quarters.

He didn't even have to enter the area, as another android had already brought his luggage and tossed it to Mason's feet—a singular black bag, void of any markings or ownership, with a torn strap.

"If the Project missed something, it will be mailed to you. Your replacement has already arrived." Android pointed at another man being escorted into the complex, looking over his shoulder. "Please, give me your card so the identification can be scrapped. You are permitted to keep the hard hat by the request of Overseer Smith."

Mason didn't even have a chance to look at the plastic card as the android grabbed it out of his hand, scanned it, and handed it back.

"Your fare has been paid. Train to Pampa, Texas, leaves in four hours from Miami Terminal at exactly 16:55. Travel safely, and thank you for working with the Clean Air Project. Don't forget to buy the air filter for your housing unit to support this initiative."

"Thank you?" Mason took the bag and turned towards the gate. "I can find a way out myself. It's not like I worked here for two years."

"Suit yourself. The bus to Miami leaves in fifteen minutes. Have a productive day." Both androids walked away, perfectly synchronized.

———

Mason didn't move for the first five minutes, standing in the same spot, watching his livelihood disappear. He gulped and turned towards the exit. *So, this is it. I'm out. Oh, God! No, please, I can do better!* Then Mason grabbed the bag and took the first unemployed step. Passing by the gate, surrounded by the barbed wire and armed guards, Mason looked at towering facilities. He shook his head, stepped right, and found an empty bus station. The bus had already waited there, with a driver leaning against the door, smoking. He checked his watch and exhaled. *Noon. That explains it. Damn me, why me! Everyone posts, and I'm the one who catches the flak out of the entire group chat! Damn me, and damn the person!*

"Hey! Everything all right?" A voice brought Mason back to reality.

"What?" Mason stopped dead in his tracks when he realized he had passed the bus station, almost running into a lonely orange tree growing by the side of the road.

"Do you intend to walk three hours to Miami?" The bus driver flicked the cigarette on the ground. "Get in here; I have AC."

"Oh yeah, I'm sorry, Sir!" Mason jogged back and, moments

later, got seated in the front seat, sheltering his eyes from the blistering sun.

"Where are you going?" The bus driver peeked inside, and Mason opened his eyes.

"MTT." Mason looked at his wrist tablet and found a notification about the paid fare. "Miami Train Terminal Platform 3."

"Seems like nobody else is coming." The bus driver turned on the engine. "ETA one hour if it doesn't start raining and people forget how to drive."

"Thank you." Mason attached the helmet to the bag by the strap and placed it next to him.

———

Driving alongside a swamp and large rows of orange trees made Mason think about the polarity of his life, but the bumps on the road permanently derailed the thinking train. The bus driver hummed a song, and Mason took a deep breath. Then he watched another bus full of hard hats heading to the grinder. He saw himself there on his first day, looking forward to the new beginning. *The end of something always makes you reminiscent of the beginning,* Mason thought. Thirty minutes later, the bus steered right and entered the asphalt road, and in the distance, the tallest skyscrapers of the Miami skyline appeared. Mason closed his eyes again and pressed his hands against the plastic upholstery of the seat before him.

"You all right there?" Like a voice of God, the bus driver's voice echoed in the vehicle from the speakers.

"Yeah, yeah. I'm just looking for the plans for my near future, but I don't see anything."

"Do you believe in the God with the capital G?"

"I believe I do," Mason said, moving to the first seat next to the bus driver, who put down the microphone.

"Well then, there is a plan for you; you just don't see it yet." The bus driver grinned from ear to ear. "Everything will be revealed to you in time."

"I believe in God; however, I'm the maker of my destiny. He gave us free will for a reason, right?"

"That is a fair assessment. This is what I do when I'm unsure about my next steps. I stop, take a step back, and look around. It gives you a different perspective."

———

An hour later, Mason shook hands with the bus driver and stood before MTT, blistering in the cloudless day. For Mason, it looked like a collapsed skyscraper turned into a kaleidoscope, gutted by the need of the city to reimagine the glass corpse. All around him, Miami Metropolis, despite being lunchtime, kept the gears turning. Sirens, mixed shouts of Spanglish, and aggressive advertisements tailored to detail for each prospective customer. From fast hydrogen cars to space tourism, Mason felt his bank account weep at the opportunities of the twenty-second century. Mason took the bag and looked around: *Maybe it's my last time here for now, but when I save up, I'll move here. Getting a steady stream of vitamin D should be beneficial as well.*

However, Mason heard screeching brakes and an explosion, feeling a shockwave going through his body. The screaming behind him increased in intensity when he took the first step. Upon turning around, Mason immediately regretted his decision to do so when another gray bus collided with the one that just dropped him off, exploding in the hydrogen blaze of glory, engulfing its surroundings in a bright orange flame with the burning body of the bus driver flying out of the cabin.

The screaming and racket noise teleported Mason into the accident scene, finding himself in the back seat of a family SUV, driving full speed on I-10. That dusky summer day, he remembered their parents arguing in the front while he and his younger brother Ail begged their parents to stop. Then, the SUV collided with a semi-truck. Mason felt a strange tingling in his brain as his memory cut to black, and the scene changed. Mason found himself in the hospital, his head wrapped in white bandages, while he waited for his brother to be rolled out of the operating room. Then he felt more tingling, prompting his eyes to water as he returned to the real world. Outside, Mason stared at the scene, wordless or emotionless. The thousand-yard stare. He didn't know how long he had stood there; however, he found himself alone on the platform and immediately walked away as more flashing lights pulled in.

————

Mason shut the men's restroom door behind him and sat on the unopened toilet, taking three deep breaths to regain his composure. Upon reaching into his bag, Mason found the green pills awaiting him in an orange plastic box or, as he called it, the flies for the Spider, which numbed his PTSD response in situations like one just developing. On there, the handwritten note in capital letters read—one pill after every trigger, or one in the morning and one in the evening every day. After swallowing, Mason bit his right thumb, trying to focus on anything at that point, but the three knocks and shouts from outside prompted him to open the door.

"Finally!" A man in a suit shoved him aside, locked the door, and the long line moved.

"I'm sorry, man!" Mason washed his hands and entered the packed station, instinctively putting on the hard hat while he squeezed his bag.

————

He passed two Internal Control security checkpoints, the first searching him and his belongings more thoroughly than the first one. However, Mason got a short nod from one of the security officers. Mason waved back and joined another long line leading to the vending machines and small takeout windows. Standing in the line, he watched holographic projections of sales representatives talking with people and closing the deals. He watched the newest O560 Virtual Reality Rig advertisement on the large screen. *One day, I will get that. One day, I will have twenty-five thousand dollars burning a hole in my bank account.* Mason shook his head and folded his hands as he heard a woman in front of him open her new life insurance policy while the man behind him changed the shipping from standard to overnight. Two people down the line, Mason heard another man in a suit talking to his colleague on the phone.

"Hear me out. There are videos on the Old Web. Yes, they were made by Orion Corporation about this exact situation, but nobody cared about it before the War. Hey, I'm right! Go to the Old Web and watch it. It's not a conspiracy that one corporation would control the world! They even have a simulation, which is still accessible, of our day-to-day lives, and let me tell you, it isn't far away from what we are living now. Dude! Orion Corp third-partied the winner, and here we are now! One Corporation to rule them all! God is my witness!"

Mason raised his eyebrows when the security android approached and promptly escorted the protesting man away. To Mason's surprise, nobody cared or, in some cases, didn't even notice the happening. Mason looked over his shoulder, seeing that even behind him, nobody bothered or cared to comment on the situation.

———

"For your safety, wait till the light turns green. Mind the gap, and thank you for choosing Orion Highspeed Railway to bring you home, vacation, or any other venture. I repeat, for your safety...." Following two more announced delays, Mason got to the platform at exactly 18:00 and looked at the modular bullet train, which stopped behind the thick glass. The doors from the other side opened, pouring out masses that immediately spread out across the tightly packed station.

Long snake with a white base color and a United States Corporate Flag with stripes serpentine across the entire train to the last car, differentiating it from the other trains on the platform. Despite taking that same train every Friday, Mason felt a wave of patriotism around him for the first time, something he hadn't felt in a while. He looked at the wrist tablet and found his seating order: C2, Economy, Seat 28A. Mason took one last look around him and entered the bullet train, fighting his way through a tight corridor. Finally, after several collisions, four my apologies, and one go-to-hell man, Mason found his seating. With care, he stuffed the bag into the luggage compartment and got seated, feeling the white plastic keeping his back straight. He removed his hard hat and put it on his knee, staring at the numbers. Finally, for a moment, he could think about the day.

I just got fired on the pretenses of speaking out, wanting a change in the world. All I said was that constant monitoring was an invasion of privacy; well, among other things, I posted into the group chat. I correctly pointed out that Internal Control violates the Fourth Amendment by carrying out unwarranted searches and seizures. So what if they are international and part of a corporation? If you operate in the US, you follow the US laws. They are there for a reason. Bastards.

"Oh, well, that is something," Mason looked up when he heard the voice of Overseer Smith standing above him, holding her luggage and a hard hat.

Mason blinked twice and then looked away, either in shame or anger; he couldn't tell. Smith shook her head and sat opposite him, keeping her luggage under the seat. After two minutes of awkward silence, Mason relaxed his stance and looked at his former boss.

"Want to know something funny? I fired thirty people today, and I was the thirtieth."

"What?" Mason blinked. "You had to fire yourself? What pretenses?"

"I don't know if it was a cruel joke or..." Smith closed her blue eyes for a moment as she twisted her wedding ring, but Mason noticed her voice change with a bit of shakiness at the end of the sentence. "At least I went out on my own terms. At least, I think I did."

"Is everything all right?" Mason leaned forward as the suppressed anger inside him slowly faded away.

"I wish it was all right!" Smith threw her hands in the air. "While I was firing you, my husband was cremated at that moment. So now, I can watch it recorded, and the urn will be mailed to me with overnight shipping due to my husband's life insurance."

Mason's jaw dropped to the floor as the head of his former boss vanished into her shaking hands. *Oh,* was the only thought Mason formulated in his mind.

"I am sorry about your loss. But unfortunately, I know my words mean little to you now, and thoughts and prayers won't bring your husband back."

"Thank you. That means a lot to me. Yesterday, I had a family, and now, I'm sitting here, a widow with three children. All my parents and siblings are dead. Mason, you don't know what you got until it's gone. Please, for the love of God, if he even exists, don't let Internal Control take your life away. Your brother needs you. Excuse me." Smith stood up, shook her head, and vanished in the hallway, holding the black tablet in her right hand.

"Holy!" Mason said aloud, leaned back, and picked his jaw up from the floor as he realized God granted him a tiny peek into the life of one in millions.

Feeling hair standing on his hands and the Nerve Spider tickling his nervous system, Mason cogitated about the entire situation: *I don't even want to imagine what my brother would have to go through if I died.*

Mason woke up his wrist tablet from sleep and opened the STREET PAUSE Chatroom #25 or Dirty Air, a chatroom of his now former team at Clean Air. Quickly selecting the Read All function, Mason typed: *Imagine working for a Project that cleans the air for millions but refuses to help one employee going through a tough time. I was fired. This is Mason Knight signing off. PS. Brickell is a better choice than Ocean Drive. No matter what Mike says, Brickell is the one.* Then, with a singular swipe to the right, he left the group chat and put his tablet to sleep just as Smith returned.

"I hope you didn't do anything stupid while I was gone." Smith laughed and sunk into the plastic chair. "I hope you did not. I apologize; I am no longer your boss."

"It will take a moment to adjust, ma'am." Mason smiled. "It's always time that helps us."

"Do you think that is part of God's plan? Me losing my job and husband? I apologize for jumping on you like this, but you were the one with a crucifix in your pocket on the job. I don't want to attack or anything, nor offend you, and I am sorry if I did."

"No offense taken. Like you, I'm also searching for answers, as I feel the foundation of my faith shaking a bit. I have no idea, but I know he is omniscient, right? Outside of time and space? I think he accounted for this, as this is just a small step or an obstacle. I wish I could provide a concrete answer or something. Mason." Mason extended his hand, and Overseer Smith tilted her head to the right.

A moment later, she understood and shook hands. "Madison—a pleasure to meet you, Mason. Guess time will show us then. How is your brother? I know I held you longer than the week, but we were behind on the schedule."

———

Three hours from Miami to Pampa passed quickly, and Mason looked up when the train abruptly stopped at the Pampa Terminal. Compared to the colorful kaleidoscope of Miami,

Pampa Terminal was soberer in color but still humming.

"Well, Mason. It was a pleasure working with you." Madison shook hands with Mason. "Thank you for your words of encouragement and the pleasant hours spent talking with you."

"Thank you for keeping me on the payroll as long as possible. Have a safe journey." Mason was about to vanish in the hallway when Smith stopped him.

"Mason, don't throw your life away. Please!"

"I'll try." Mason grinned from ear to ear and, a moment later, emerged into the crowd heading towards the exit.

He looked over his shoulder upon hearing a whistle, and the train vanished in the blink of an eye just as another pulled into the station, and the cycle began again.

———

Emerging into the parking lot, Mason looked around, trying to remember where he had parked his four-door pickup truck. He reached into the bag and pulled out the keys. With keys in hand, Mason found the parking lot lights and remembered parking his truck underneath one. The sun slowly set, but it wasn't dark due to the long summer days. After ten minutes of searching, Mason exhaled when he found his pickup truck waiting for him, with a yellow clamp on the front wheel.

I have the permit! What the hell!? Mason kneeled to the clamp and scanned the QR code with his tablet.

Immediately, the screaming red numbers of missed payment plus fine appeared, and Mason rolled his eyes. *Hundred dollars. Well, there goes half of my bonus, which I don't have yet!* Upon paying, the clamp unlocked itself, and Mason leaned on the hood of his pickup. He folded his hands and observed the helicopter of the Internal Control hovering above the parking lot for a moment with armed operatives scanning the lot and the building. Then it flew away, and Mason got behind the wheel of his pickup and joined the exit line.

———

Twenty minutes later, Mason pulled into an empty stone driveway of a single-story suburban house hiding on the outskirts of Pampa. As he exited the truck, the door opened, and Mason smiled for real this time when his brother rolled out and waited on the porch.

"You're home early. What happened?" Ail said as Mason approached him. "Everything all right?"

"I got fired from my job. Don't tell Aunt." Mason scratched his head. "I need to figure something out fast."

"I won't tell her for at least another day. She left to see her friend in the hospital. I know you just arrived, but she left a shopping list as the fridge is empty." Ail handed Mason the sticky note. "What did you do!?"

"Let me unpack first, and then I'll go. Tell me who won the CTF. Ravens or the Crimsons?" Mason asked as he closed the door behind them and tossed the bag onto the floor.

"Crimsons, of course. The game was rigged in their favor." Ail grabbed Mason by the belt. "What happened? How did you get fired? You did everything they asked for, right?"

"I got called to the office and got fired, no explanation." Mason omitted specific facts. "Guess they didn't like me?"

"What have we become? Did you know that IC raided Mrs. Frelimo's house just three hours ago? Four vans rolled into our neighborhood, busting down the community gate. Reason? None given. Maybe the sun has finally settled, and this is a new way forward."

Mason raised his eyebrows when Ail spoke, thinking: *Something needs to be done. They cannot keep getting away with this!*

"Did you post again?" Ail tapped his thumbs. "I can tell by your slowly turning red face that you did. Mason, you must be careful! This is the second job you got fired from because of your social media posts! One more, and you are going to jail!"

"If I compromise on my values, who am I? They cannot

keep getting away with this! The Bill of Rights exists for a reason! Maybe people forgot that they have rights, but I didn't!" Mason raised his voice and immediately looked away in shame as his brother cowered in fear. "I'm sorry! It's just..."

Mason slid on the carpet and leaned his head against the wall while Ail carefully climbed down from the wheelchair and sat by Mason's side.

"Mason, I stand behind you in everything you believe. But what can we do? For now, we can only weather the storm. Mason, I cannot lose you," Ail's voice whimpered. "What would I do without you? I am all by myself most days. I watch Internal Control bust down doors and drag people away daily on TV or even here now. Please! You are the only one left who understands me after the car accident."

"All right, Ail, you're right. That was the last post. I'll take a break from social media and then find a different way of resisting. You're right, as always; I don't know how often I have to say it to myself. I'm treading on mighty thin ice." Mason looked at the flashing wrist tablet and muted all the notifications. "I cannot lose you."

"I need to finish schoolwork, so you go shopping without me. Then, we'll catch up. A lot of things have happened, good or bad. That girl I talked with, she agreed to grab a coffee with me."

"Nice!" Mason high fived Ail. "I told you; you just got to ask. Direct and to the point. Thank you for trusting me. I'll be right back."

"This time, you're right as well!" Ail laughed, infecting Mason with his smile.

———

As Mason got out of the house, another notification beeped, this time from the Pampa Bank, and he smiled when the paycheck cleared and got the bonus as well. Immediately, he sat in his small white pickup and turned on the V8 engine. He carefully placed the shopping list on the dashboard. As Mason put the truck into reverse, he heard someone knocking on the window. He widened his green eyes when his brother's face appeared. Mason rolled down the window and smiled as his brother pulled the lever on his wheelchair.

"Ail, what is the matter? You already finished?" Mason put the pickup into park and leaned out of the window.

"I realized that I'm almost done and will be waiting for you." Ail's blue eyes almost drowned Mason. "I found a new song that I want to play on your speakers."

"Sure, I'll just pull out of the driveway." Mason watched his brother steer his wheelchair away.

Mason turned his head, and a moment later he stopped the truck. He stretched his neck and got out. His white pickup stood out like a sore thumb compared to his neighbors' streamlined and clean hybrid cars. *Luckily, there is no HOA. God, I hate those people.*

"Mason! Look!" Ail pointed at the unmarked black van of Internal Control pulling into the quiet neighborhood. "That's not a good sign. They were just here!"

The van completely ignored the stop sign at the crossroads, almost running over an elderly gentleman. Mason's eyes locked with the operative in the machine-gun mount as he lowered the bulletproof screens, revealing ammunition belts with nasty long rounds.

"They don't seem to be slowing down." Mason opened the passenger door just as the van's brakes screeched next to them, and the floodgates opened.

In two seconds, Mason was on the ground, strip-searched by three masked operatives of Internal Control while the rest secured the perimeter around the driveway. Then, the officer in the ceramic battle armor with the blue armband approached them and scanned Mason's retinas. The beep came a moment later, and the officer ordered his troopers to cuff Mason while some of the doors on the nearby houses opened, and a few concerned residents peeked outside but didn't leave their residences as the operative with the machine gun swung around, scanning the surroundings.

"Mason Knight, you are under arrest. You may remain silent until the Internal Interrogation Officer notifies you of your crime. Take him to the box!" The officer stepped aside and watched Ail extending his right arm, trying to grab one of the operatives, who shoved him away.

"What happened to the Miranda Rights?" Mason said between his teeth, and one of the officers laughed. "You're required by the law to read them out to me!"

"Miranda can go to hell. Only the guilty ask for them. Oh wait, there is no such thing as Miranda Rights!" The personnel burst out laughing. "And last time we checked, you have no rights to begin with!"

The backdoor had cut off Ail's screams, and he could only watch as the van drove away. Mason saw a neighbor running out of her house through the back window, but could only guess if she helped Ail or just stood there and watched.

"We are to pick up one more and then get to site #5, where we will drop Mason. It seems like TVG is on a recruiting spree," one of the masked operatives said to the commanding officer. "Honestly, I'm considering it more and more. This pay is honestly crap compared to what I can gain in the Last Solo Standing or, hell, even Last Squad Standing."

"Why is TVG enrolling inmates? I never understood that. All that training and gear is wasted on them," CO said back and tapped the pistol holster. "One bullet is all it takes. Then we burn the bodies. Simple as that."

"It makes for a good TV. Seeing the winner I busted three

weeks ago standing on the podium, well, it brought a tear to my eye," another operative responded, tying up shoelaces on his boots. "It made my day."

"Get out of here! That really happened?" CO nudged Mason with the stock of his rifle. "You better win, Mason, if they take you! If not, we know where you live!"

"I don't think Mason will win. His beliefs will ensure he comes home in a body bag. But hey, we can visit his tombstone. But again, I do not think Mason can afford it. Or his brother."

"No parents either? How is he managing the bills?"

"Why did you have to shove my brother like that? He has done nothing to you!" Mason raised his voice. "That wasn't necessary! What could Ail have done to you in the first place! I swear to God, I break these chains and kill you!"

"He is already disabled, but he is your co-conspirator." CO shrugged his shoulders and looked at Mason, who raised his chained fists, ready to strike. "After Mason, we should tag him as well and see how he'll handle the TVG. Mason, I would advise you to save energy for the talk. And what exactly are you planning to do? You cannot even reach any of us."

Another punch, escorted by laughter, landed hard on Mason's chest, recoiling his body into the metallic wall.

"Ail has never done anything to you! I have not done anything wrong!" Mason shouted and immediately received a third punch in his face as he rattled the chains. "I hate you all! Bunch of corporate pigs! I'll never break!"

"Whoa! Language prisoner!" The Commanding Officer slapped Mason with the back of his hand. "Says the leech on our welfare system!"

"That is a lie! That is a lie! I work for a living!" Mason straightened his chest. "My taxes support you!"

"Yeah, they do. And now you get to see what those taxes get you when you misbehave!" One of the operatives injected

Mason with a blue substance, and a moment later, Mason's vision became dizzy.

In a minute, Mason's head bent forward, and a serum sent Mason into a deep sleep.

INTERNAL CONTROL

When Mason regained his vision, he found himself in the dimly lit interrogation room and immediately tried to cover his nose from the smell of the piss and someone else's dinner on the floor, but to no avail, as he was chained to the table. He rattled the chains. Then a beep echoed in the room, and an android entered, wearing the same uniform as the operatives that grabbed him from his pickup. He sat down before Mason, and his yellow eyes turned blue for several seconds. Next, Mason noticed the android's right hand resting on a black case.

"Mason Knight, born 20th of January 2120 in Miami, Florida. Moved to Pampa, Texas, shortly before the War. You were assigned to the Coast Guard and survived against all odds. You are charged with violating the Terms and Conditions, posting anti-corporate posts and videos on STREETPAUSE, with the last one logged today during your travels from Miami to Pampa quoting: Imagine working for a Project that cleans the air for millions but refuses to help one employee going through a tough time. I was fired. This is Mason Knight signing off. PS. Brickell is a better choice than Ocean Drive."

"Brickell is indeed a better choice, in my opinion," Mason coughed, "but I think that you would go for an Ocean Drive. Quite a lot of trashcans for you to meet."

"I applaud your attempt at humor, even a slur. For a cell-based organism with opposing thumbs, I expected more fight from you." Android tossed the hot potato back into Mason's lap. "The subject at hand stays the same either way you cut it. It seems like a permanent ban is the only option in your case."

"I wrote what I wrote, and I stand by what I said. So much for the truth, when one Corporation controls the narrative," Mason interrupted the android and shook his head.

"Due to your special status, Internal Control made you an offer. Do you accept a five thousand dollar fine to have your lifeline accounts unfrozen and your services reinstated?"

Mason folded his hands. "Go to hell! I am not compromising on my values. God gives me my privileges, rights, and duties, not some international corporation that believes our rights can be taken or given back at a moment's notice!"

"For your information, Orion Security Corporation is a United States-based corporation founded in Miami, Florida. Well then, to the box you go. Trust us, Mason. Our next offer won't be as good as this one." Android opened the black case and pulled out the syringe with blue liquid.

"I don't have that kind of money anyway. Go to hell!" Mason bit his tongue and looked away as the needle pierced his skin.

Then, his vision became blurry, and Mason hit the table face-first. The last words he heard: *We know.*

———

Mason rolled to his side and hit his head on the toilet stand, finding himself in a cell, dressed in a bright orange and black jumpsuit. He didn't want to open his eyes, but then, feeling that someone was with him in the cell, Mason turned around and found a brown-haired inmate staring at him. He silently sat there, observing Mason's every move under a singular lightbulb, illuminating the windowless room.

"How long was I out?" Then, using the toilet as support to stand up, Mason fell back down as his legs still felt like jelly. "And what's in this serum!?"

"I don't know, but from IC tossing you into the cell till now, I would say two minutes, three minutes. You refused the first offer, didn't you?" The inmate spoke calmly but folded his hands. "You are an idiot for not accepting that, because whatever they present you next, you'll wish you had taken that first offer."

"How do you know that?"

"Sector 2 is designed for inmates who refused the first offer. Giovanni, but call me Gio." Inmate gave Mason a hand.

"Mason. For what are you in here for?"

"I wanted more life in my corporate life. I complained three times, and I landed here. Bill of Rights? Due process? The jury of your peers? What a joke for IC." Gio sat on his bed. "A brave new world."

"That makes two of us." Mason lay on his bunkbed while Gio shook his head.

"However, there is a positive aspect in our case. TVG is on a recruiting spree for their different projects, and many inmates are getting out as our prisons are overcrowded. For life or death. Should they win, they get money and freedom."

"This is a bad choice?" Mason raised his eyebrows. "TVG?"

"Rumor has it that IC took several inmates and assessed new ammunition on them to examine the damage done to their bodies. So, yeah, it can get a lot worse. Or you could have taken a loan, paid the fine, and paid it off. You said no, and now you are here with me."

"So, why are you here if you know all these things? Why didn't you pay?"

"Let's just say my case is special." Gio grinned from ear to ear. "Also, they haven't frozen your lifeline accounts the first time. It's a ploy to get you to sign their first offer. Now, Internal froze them. If you have a family, I don't even know how they will survive without it, or even without you."

"If I compromise on my values, who am I? This is what makes me, hell, even you, different from the rest. My rights never went away."

"If you compromise for the sake of the people around you, I don't see it as bad. But every case is special, I guess. I have nobody out there waiting for me. I know that you have."

"For a man in jail, why are you smiling? Why aren't you terrified? And how do you know that I have someone waiting for me?" Mason looked at his shaking hands, which he immediately hid in the pockets of his jumpsuit.

"I have nothing to lose, unlike you. So please take my advice and accept the second offer, no matter what they say. The longer you stay, the less chance you have of surviving." Gio turned his head as he heard a whirring sound. "The untested blue injection they give you has different effects on different inmates. Some go numb, others fall asleep, and some turn violent and must be put down. You were mumbling something about your brother, Ali, Ail?"

"Ahh!" Mason covered his head as the two IC operatives entered the cell and dragged Gio away, with the third one taking several practice swings with his baton at Mason.

———

Possibly three or four hours later, but it was hard to tell; the door opened again, and two IC operatives dragged Mason to the interrogation room. Mason's eyes twitched as he got seated, and moments later another android entered the interrogation room. When he ensured Mason's cuffs were in place, he sat opposite him.

"Good evening, Mason. I hope that you were able to cool down and reconsider the offer. The fine has increased to ten thousand dollars. If you agree, you will see your brother in a couple of hours. Due to your service, we even offer you zero percent interest on the loan you will take out."

"You are a robot! Freedom or money has no value to you." Mason raised his voice.

"Yes or no answer will suffice. If you refuse, you get your last offer in eight hours, and then, should you choose to refuse our final offer, you won't see your family again."

"What time is it?"

"I fail to see how this is relevant to your answer." Android leaned back. "Based on work experience, criminals who refuse the first offer don't have a healthy family relationship. Why don't you want to see your family? Your cripple? Your aunt?"

"You shut your speaker! I will die for my brother if needed. I am not compromising on my values!" Mason rattled the chains again.

"Do you desire to bring Ail's criminal record into the negotiation?" Mason bit his tongue as the Android said it.

"His crimes are the same as mine, which aren't crimes in the first place. Objectively pointing out flaws in our system with statistics and evidence to back it up is not a crime!"

"Do you understand the Documents of Governance and their structure? What is permitted and what isn't?"

"No, I don't. Please enlighten me." Mason looked around him before answering with a slight irony.

I am going to waste his time. The least I can do in this situation.

"In that case, the rights you claim come from some mythical being in the clouds is factually wrong. The laws, rights, and duties are granted to you by the Documents of Governance, enacted by the Board of Directors of the United States, signed by the CEO of the United States, and approved by the President of North America."

"Is there anything else I need to know?" Mason imitated the android's monotone voice with exaggerated pauses. "Are you going to give me the Civics lecture? I could use some of it right now."

"I do not need to give it to you, Mason, nor will I give

you the martyrdom you seek. In that case, do you accept the offer?"

"Go to hell! You already stole forty percent of my income with theft, which you call subscriptions, which are just taxes under a new name. No, I have rights!"

"Taxation is not theft. We are providing you with services the previous government failed to deliver. In that case, Internal Control will take that as a no. Remember, if you don't take the last deal, you will never see your family again, Mason Knight." Android stood up and grabbed his pistol by the barrel. "Power without question. Authority without asking. Remember that Mason. I should send someone to beat up your brother as well."

With a singular whip, the android sent wide eyes open Mason to deep sleep.

When Mason awoke again, he found himself in the solitary cell, or 6x6x6 feet container, without light, a sense of time, or direction. Mason grunted and pressed his right hand against his burning jaw. With his left hand, he reached into the darkness, trying to latch onto anything, but the only feeling he got was cold steel.

For the first time, his determination wavered as the container rocked itself, and Mason wept. *My pride will be my downfall! I refused two offers. Why? Gio, or whatever his name was, was right. Why?! I would pay it off and be home! Mason, you moron! Ail needs me, and I need him! Am I in the wrong for wanting Internal Control to have a warrant?* The why continually echoed in the container, along with his empty stomach, as his last food, according to his foggy memory, was a King-sized Cuban sandwich at MTT and a diet lemon cola beverage. *Power without question. Authority without asking.* Mason covered his head as the haunting words of the interrogation android gripped themselves into Mason's shaken mind. *God, please, I know I wasn't perfect, but please, if I die, don't forget about my brother.* Two minutes later, torrential rain began pounding the container, prompting Mason to press his hands against his ears, screaming his lungs out. As he continued to roll back and forth from side to side, the Nerve Spider shut down Mason's body to prevent it from further damage from high octane beating heart and incoming migraine.

After an eternity, the rain finally stopped, and the shipment halted. A moment later, beeping cranes began unloading the containers, and Mason hit his head again on the cold steel.

"Please, stop! I will agree to whatever! Just let it stop!" Mason cried out to the void, but his only response was more clanging and electrical whirring sounds following his container.

———

After another three hours, at least that was Mason's time estimate, he was dragged out of the container and hosed down with cold water. Then, an android handed him a plain green T-shirt, long gray pants, and unmarked shoes. Mason raised his eyebrows when another android escorted him through a cell block, where all other inmates stared him down, dressed in orange jumpsuits. Mason gulped, and in his mind he begged the android to speed up. Mason's questions or pleas met silence and the end of the double barrel of the automatic shotgun with a drum magazine.

"One TVG contestant coming right up." Android opened a glass door and shoved Mason inside.

Inside the interrogation room, another android awaited him. Upon noticing Mason flying into the small interrogation room, he stood up, and to Mason's surprise, the android uncuffed him and invited him to sit down. However, Mason realized this android was missing ceramic battle armor from his first and second interrogators. He wore a three-piece suit instead.

"Mason Knight, please sit down; we have a lot to go over." Android moved the chair and looked at Mason. "Don't try to run or attack me. Should you try, I have an execution authority from Internal Control, and my face will be the last thing you will see."

Android watched Mason take his place and then gave a signal to the glass window.

"I'm ready to take the deal. I want to see my family again. I learned my lesson, and I won't be...."

"I am going to stop you right there. Seeing that you were a naughty boy who refused our two offers that would lead you to freedom and your brother, now I am offering you a choice of your death. Exciting right? How does it feel now? Are you going to call me a trashcan on Ocean Drive?"

Android watched Mason's heart sink deeper into his stomach, followed by a loud gasp for air.

"Please, I need to go home to my brother!" Mason's voice whimpered. "Please!"

"You had two chances, and even your temporary inmate told you to take the offer. The first option will have you thrust into the lithium mines of USAC. IC will renounce your US citizenship, and you will never see your family or friends again, but you get to keep your faith in the old man in the clouds. But, of course, it is well known that mining lithium without proper equipment comes with serious or deadly risks," Android rattled out.

"Please! I'll pay twenty thousand dollars if I must! Just let me go home!" Mason cried out, joining his hands together. "I beg of you!"

"You only have two choices, Mason. You could have got out of here yesterday."

"What is the second option?" Mason stared at the reflective table while Android nodded at the window.

"You will be enrolled in the TVG's newest addition, Tank Royale of 2145. Your chances of survival are less than one percent. If you win, your accounts will be unfrozen, apart from the financial reward that will follow. You would have to kill, which goes against your beliefs in the old man in the clouds. If you don't, your chances of survival are zero. These are your choices, Mason. Do you require a moment to think about this?"

Mason closed his eyes in defeat. "I accept the second offer."

"Excellent," the android said, and after a loud beep, Mason knew that his life was now in the hands of TVG, the largest entertainment provider in the world.

"Do I get to see my family?"

"If you win, you will see them. If you win." Android stood up and tapped the metal table. "In the meantime, your family will be placed on the Life Support Program, as you are marked the primary caregiver of your brother, Ail Knight. Diagnosed with Paraplegia following a car accident, which I have marked here as the starting point for your misbehavior."

"Who wouldn't after such an accident? When everyone rejects you, it changes your outlook on the world." Mason's face turned red as he tried to hold back tears.

The sounds of screeching tires, the explosion of the airbags, and the pierced glass made his eyes twitch, but it wasn't as severe as yesterday. Android only nodded his head.

"I can add a CMA violation to your list, but I believe you already have enough on your plate."

"What is this Tank Royale?" Mason shook his head, silencing the loud voices in his head.

"You and four other contestants will be given a World War Two-era tank and compete against other crews for the entire world to see. T-34, Panzer Hydro, or Sherman are a few names I recall from the trailers."

"Why was I given this offer?"

"Internal Control receives notices and requirements from TVG about their ongoing and upcoming events all the time, and we are happy to assist. These requirements are uploaded, and the system lists potential candidates from current inmates. You match the age, height, and weight requirements."

"So, what am I to expect?"

"Good question, Mason. You are about to find out. Do not panic when you wake up on the train with your personal belongings and no sense of direction, time, or place. Safe travels." Android opened the black case and pulled out the syringe with blue liquid.

Mason looked away and bit his tongue as the needle pierced the right side of his neck. Then, as his vision began to wobble again, he looked at the android, who gave Mason a thumbs up.

———

Mason opened his eyes and waited for his wobbly vision to adjust. He sat in one of the seating areas with other sedated inmates; however, they all lacked the orange jumpsuits. Each one had their backpack resting in the overhead compartment. Right before him, an android sat silently, tapping his knees. When he noticed Mason looking around, he touched his ear, and in a minute, two men stormed into the room.

"Who is this?"

"Mason Knight from Pampa, Texas. Violated Terms & Service of STREET PAUSE. Admitted for the Tank Royale of 2145."

"Damn, I thought that serum was strong enough to sedate him till we reach Great Falls." one of the men opened the bag and pulled out the blue serum, ready in the gun.

"Before you sedate me, is my family all right?" Mason said and looked at his barcode.

"Don't know, don't care," the man with the needle said and injected Mason, whose head fell forward.

The voices all around him had blended into one before the darkness consumed him.

"I see the problem; they must have given him a smaller dose. Where is this one coming from? You said Texas?"

"Pampa, as I said. Well, anyway, the boss says that we are to pick up the additional tanks en route, so we need to administer an extra dose for all these contestants."

"Who are you going to root for?"

"That is a good question. TVG clearly selected their favorites, so I think I'll pick one of them."

"I think I will do the same, but I want to witness some good underdog story, which TVG's favorites are not. However, mark my words; this will be the most incredible television ever. Tanks, can you believe that!?"

"Well, it is a nice spin on the Battle Royale formula. You lock the squad in the metal box on tracks with a cannon. Do they at least get night vision? Thermal optics?"

"No, they don't. Not even a ballistic computer. This is going to be fun." The second operative tapped Mason's cold forehead. "He will not make it. Mentally or physically."

"You mean the tank?" The operative closed the briefcase with the serum. "Something called Panzer 4 attracted my attention as it is a house favorite. And you know what they say? House always wins."

"I think that I will check out that T-34 they have. Looks aggressive!"

"But the T-34 isn't on the house's list." The operative stored the briefcase under the seat and held the door for his colleague. "But I can see the appeal. TVG went ham with the advertising compared to the other Battle Royales."

"Well, let's hope it will pay off. Presentation is always nice, but looking at these people, I am not sure if they deliver."

"TVG always delivers the best action and everything." The first operative exhaled. "But it has been a while since they put out something fresh. This is it!"

"You are right. I am tired of ferrying these convicts around the continental US. I want to go home."

CHAPTER THREE

COMPLEX ISSUE

The first thing that Mason heard and saw were fighter jets with a trail of colorful smoke dancing in the blue sky. Upon sitting, he found himself staring into the eyes of a masked TVG Security operative in whose goggles he saw his reflection. Then, the platform moved, and Mason realized he was sat in the truck bed. He found cuffs firmly holding his hands as he tried to stretch.

"Where am I?" Mason looked around him as they entered the backside of a complex, and the man waved to another armed security guard.

"The gasoline cowboy is finally awake. Welcome to the Main TVG Battle Royale Complex in Great Falls, Montana. It's nine o'clock in the morning. Today is Tuesday, June 8th. You are being transported to your garage. There, other team members will join you momentarily. TVG had designated you as the team leader of #28 and Commander with the Gunner position of your tank. Everything clear so far?"

"What? Commander? Gunner? Team?" Mason asked as the truck pulled into another checkpoint and was promptly allowed to enter the garages.

"Yeah, Commander and Gunner, simple as that. And this is you." The operative looked at the two-story gray garage with the number 28 painted on the door. "Your living quarters are upstairs. The first room is yours; input your name into the panel by the door. You are mandated by TVG conduct always to wear the uniform, which is in the closet. Everything else can be found on the ground floor, including the kitchen, but I recommend waiting for your teammates to break bread together. If you try to run away, you will be tasered. You'll be shot on sight and replaced if you attempt to run again."

Then, the operative reached into the pouch on his chest rig, and a moment later, Mason's cuffs fell on the floor. Mason looked around him, and his mind engaged the flight response without thinking.

"Really?!" The operative pulled out his taser just as Mason jumped from the truck and ran.

Mason was on the ground shaking in two seconds from the fifty thousand volts flowing through his body.

"Impressive that you made less than your own length. As I said," Operative turned off the taser and kneeled next to Mason, "this was your final warning. Next time, you will be shot on sight, so behave, and you might actually win. Can you behave?"

"Yes, I can!" Mason covered his head, but the operative gave him a hand.

"Good dog. Remember, you will be shot and replaced if you try this again. Do you get it?" The operative handed Mason his black backpack and tapped him on the right shoulder.

"I got it! Don't have to repeat it twice!" Mason watched the truck drive away with the operator now joining the driver, and then looked around.

Mason's eyes found the side entrance, picked up his backpack, and entered the garage with #28 silently greeting him. Scratching the back of his head, Mason noticed the lights already on as he closed the door behind him. The first thing that jumped out to him was the large Corporate American Flag hanging on the wall and the tank covered by the white tarp.

As Mason looked around, he felt an invisible hand drawing him closer to the covered war machine.

Large wooden boxes were everywhere: a yellow crane, a few chairs, and a table next to the tank. Behind it, Mason came across black drawers, and upon opening one, he found hammers, monkey wrenches, and other tools categorized in clean rows with a digital screen on the side showing what it was. For a moment, Mason smiled: *Just like the garage home, but cleaner.*

As he passed by the tank, Mason reached out, and his hand touched the slope on the side of the hull; as he moved around, he felt a steel cable and cold steel underneath. Then, as he got to the back, two boxes greeted him. *So this tank is supposed to give me freedom or death.*

Mason's eyes found a kitchen right next to the room with a large screen, chairs, and a whiteboard. However, Mason's growling stomach steered him towards the white refrigerator, which occupied the center of the kitchen. As his hand touched the handle, he remembered the words of the operative. *I should go and drop off my things.* His stomach growled again, but Mason's mind retook control and prompted Mason to climb the stairs and find the room where he would drop his backpack.

There were five bedrooms, so following orders, Mason picked the one closest to the stairs. The digital door sign greeted him, which chimed upon re-entering his name and unlocked the door for him.

Mason dropped his backpack on the bed and looked around. A nightstand, a wooden wardrobe, a chair, and a small office table with a charging station gave Mason a sense of home. There was another wooden door in the corner, and when Mason opened it, a simple bathroom greeted him. He opened the backpack and unpacked it. A few t-shirts, two pairs of work jeans, a pair of work boots, his rosary wrapped around his wrist tablet, an orange box stuffed with green pills, a small corporate bible print, and a picture of his family were all his possessions. Mason placed his wrist tablet into the charging station, opened a wardrobe, and found a green and brown overall with a tag on the hanger, which read, *Wear this at all times.*

This is an authentic Soviet Tank Great Patriotic War Uniform. Again, number 28 was present on one of his patches. He turned his head around when he heard footsteps, but shook his head and exhaled.

Moments later, Mason folded his old clothing into the backpack, which he hung in the closet, and put on the uniform. He found a mirror in the bathroom and finished his preparation with a final whirl, thinking: *Damn, I look good!* He took a deep breath and rolled up the sleeve which had covered the barcode on his left forearm. He shook his head and rolled down his sleeve. With one last look over his shoulder, Mason closed the door and went downstairs. Steering right, he found a sign next to the door: Simulation Room. With a raised eyebrow, as he was about to check it out, he heard footsteps, followed by a loud exhale and inaudible mumbling.

"Is anyone here yet? Please let me be first!" the voice echoed in the garage.

"I'm the only one so far." Mason poked out from behind the tank and noticed a young man standing before him.

With long black hair and green eyes, he stood a full head taller than Mason, but unlike Mason, his skin was almost pale. He wore denim pants, a working black shirt, and brown boots. The young man had a black backpack filled to the fullest, and he held an old green army box in his right hand.

"Team 28?" The young man attempted to salute as he noticed Mason's uniform.

"Yes. Mason, Commander, and Gunner. "Both shook hands, sizing each other briefly.

"Van Bryan, my friend, but call me Van for short. A nice android in ceramic armor told me that I was a driver. Yeah, the driver. So, this is it!" Van smiled and pointed at the covered tank. "I'm excited to be here! Where can I get such an exquisite vestment as you have?"

"What is a vestment?"

"Uniform." Van nudged Mason. "One size to rule them all."

"In your room? Didn't they tell you?"

"They did," Van grinned from ear to ear, "but I like to talk with people. You pick up on many things."

———

As Mason scratched his chin, the door to the simulation room opened, and a woman in her mid-twenties emerged, also dressed in the brown and green uniform, but unlike his overall, she wore a shirt with rolled-up sleeves and long pants. Like Mason, she wore a patch with a red 28 on her shoulder and back.

"Oh," she said and tied her long blonde hair into a bun. "Hello, guys!"

"Hello," Mason picked his jaw from the floor, unable to formulate a sentence, settling for the usual conversation starter. "How are you?"

"I am doing all right, all things considered."

"I'll be right back." Van whistled. "Someone is looking good today!"

"So, where is the last one?" the woman said, looking over Mason's right shoulder at the side entrance.

"Last one?" Mason tilted his head as he thought about her fit build. "How many of us are supposed to be here? "

"It should be four of us unless they changed it. My name is Dema."

"I'm Mason, and that is Van." Mason shook his head, catching himself checking her out.

"Pleasure to meet you." Dema smiled. "It seems like the band is completed. The last one has arrived."

Mason turned around and found a humanoid at the doorstep, peeking inside.

"TH28M reporting for duty!" The humanoid entered the garage and saluted. "Is this Team 28?"

"That's correct. Welcome," Mason invited the humanoid closer.

He seemed an older military model, as his clothing bore faded green and brown camo. Mason noticed Out of Commission written on his right arm. *Interesting. It seems like TVG indeed got everyone in here,* Mason thought as the humanoid approached him. The humanoid also carried a brown camo backpack with an attached American Flag patch.

"So, you are the team leader?" the humanoid asked Mason, who took a step back.

"I was told that, so yeah. I apologize; all of this is new to me. Why such a long designation?" Mason measured the humanoid from head to toe.

"Tactical Humanoid 28 Modernized. TH28M. I served in the former US and Corporate Army, but I was retired by force. Call me TH." Humanoid extended his hand, and Mason shook it.

"All right. We are waiting for our friend, as we should make a sort of introduction. Do you know what this is?" Dema stepped aside and pointed at the concealed war machine.

"I am sorry, but I have no idea even if I would remove the tarp." TH scanned the garage. "This place looked a lot bigger on the video. Let's unpack this machine."

"I feel that the entire squad should uncover it together." Mason pointed at the #28 patch. "You also need a uniform. I was specifically told always to wear this."

"One moment, please. It seems like I need to fetch myself some appropriate attire, then." TH grabbed his backpack and vanished upstairs while Dema strolled around the tank, her hands resting in her deep pockets.

Mason scratched his head again, thinking: *So, this is my squad. I have to say, it is an interesting bunch so far. A farmer, a service humanoid, and a girl from Eastern Europe. Well, this will be interesting. We either all win or all leave in body bags.*

Upon hearing Van sprinting downstairs, followed by TH, Mason pinched himself, and a moment later the quartet gathered around the tank.

"There are four of us, and there are five rooms upstairs. Are we missing someone?" TH was the first to break the silence.

"Well, I was told there will be four of us, but I might be wrong, and something might have changed. So, let's uncover this thing, and maybe the last person will show up," Dema said.

Mason untied the tarp, and moments later, as everyone pulled together, the eight-foot-tall, nine-foot-wide, and twenty-one-foot-long war machine revealed itself the four individuals standing before it.

Mason spotted bolted storage bins to the tank's right side, towing cable, folded antenna, handles, and the turret. There were two open round hatches on a hexagonal turret, one in the cupola. It gave a Mickey Mouse look from the front when TH opened them. The frontal plate had an additional plate welded on top of it, an open hatch, a headlight, and two hooks. As they moved around, Mason noticed seven road wheels on each side. There were two square add-ons, which were additional fuel tanks, exhausts, a back road light, and two tow hooks in the back. There was another attached road light where the barrel met the turret on the gun mantlet.

"I don't know what to say." Van touched the towing cable. "It looked larger on the promotional posters. Damn, that cannon is long. Do you think we can air dry our clothes on it? I think all of us could hang them there."

Mason already climbed on the top of the tank and opened one of the bins, where an old manual greeted him.

ДИРЕКЦИЯ БРОНЕТАНКОВЫХ ВОЙСК КРАСНОЙ АРМИИ
Для использования в сервисе.
Модернизированный Т-34-57 mod.42/43.
РУКОВОДСТВО ПО ОБСЛУЖИВАНИЮ ТАНКОВ
Народный комиссариат обороны СССР Москва 1944

Mason shook his head, expecting the words to be translated, but nothing changed after a moment of staring. Mason's hand dived deeper into the storage bin again, grabbing the same manual in English.

THE DIRECTORATE OF THE ARMORED FORCES OF
THE RED ARMY
For Service Use
T-34-57 mod.42/43 modernized
TANK SERVICE MANUAL
People's Commissariat of Defense of the U. S. S. R.
Moscow 1944

"It seems like this is T-34-57, mod.42/43 modernized. I have no idea what I just read," Mason read out the designation while his brain attempted to process the meaning behind the numbers.

He quickly scanned the pages, but nothing made sense as he got to the last page, just more tank-related jargon.

What the hell is the mil reticle? In due time, all of this will make sense. Please do.

"I think we could use an icebreaker here. So, who wants to start the introductions?" Dema looked at the group, raising her right eyebrow.

Seeing everyone silent, waiting for someone else to break the ice, Mason jumped from the tank and stood in the middle.

"All right, I'll start. I'm Mason Knight, and I come from Pampa, Texas. Well, I'm here because," Mason was torn. *Should he tell them he was forced to be here?* "I work in the Everglades, Florida, but I felt that now is the time to experience something different."

"Wow. I wish I had your balls to come here like that." Van gave Mason a short nod. "My name is Van Bryan, my friends, and I'm from Sweet Home, Oregon. Upon getting to the Complex, an android told me I was a driver. I mean, I know how to drive tracked vehicles, sort of. Anyway, I'm here because I want to open my distillery, as our family farm is going through tough times right now, and we need any dough we can get our hands on to make that bread. My father showed me how to make alcohol, and I love making it. Fun fact about me: I don't drink."

"You make alcohol, but you don't drink?" TH looked at Van. "How come?"

"There is a saying that goes, 'Never get high,' or should I say, 'Drunk on your supply.' Farming isn't easy as Corporate tries to bring us into the fold, which my family will never agree to. So, I found thirsty throats all over the West Coast, which I'm willing to supply despite Corporate hunting us down." Van looked at the woman. "And what is your story, gorgeous?"

"I am Dema, and I come from former Ukraine or Russia; it is hard to tell these days, as the place where I lived is or was always contested. The reason I am here is simple. I want a name for myself and a house. With a garden full of white orchids overlooking a calm river or lake, either one will work," Dema spoke with a slight accent, but all the more intriguing for Mason. "I was told that I am a co-driver and radio operator."

"You from Europe?" Van whistled. "Is it still that bad?"

"Since nukes buried us to the ground, half of Europe is what we call a Dark Zone. It's pretty tough out there as I was one of the lucky ones to cross the Atlantic." Dema folded her hands. "Of course, Northern and Western Europe get a priority."

"I don't even know what to say but thank you for telling us. That is so hardcore!" Van raised his eyebrows. "TH?"

"I was retired after the War, and the new and better androids replaced me. I'm here because I want to show everyone that old hardware still has it." TH made a fist with his right hand, and his eyes flashed red for a second. "The new A30s and A31s can go scrap themselves."

"I see that each of us has a noble cause to be here. But

first, I need to eat breakfast because I'm starving. Then, after we eat," Van was already at the door to the kitchen, "let's dive into this madness head-on. I have never visited the Main TVG complex before."

"I agree, but shouldn't they tell us what to do?" Dema said, and a moment later, Van opened the fridge and handed out the sandwiches, perfectly cut and wrapped in blue paper.

"Don't know, don't care," Van was already halfway through his tuna sandwich, "but I can feel that something has clicked between us."

"Slow down, tiger; some of us didn't even start eating. And what do you mean by something clicked?" Mason closed the fridge. "We all just met!"

"I can feel the chemistry between us already. But it's just my feelings, my friends. But I'm sorry, factory habits. I had short breaks, so I had to eat fast."

"What did you do?" Dema closed her eyes for a moment.

"Whatever quota was required, but mostly military-related production. After the War ended, we switched to the production for the Orion Security Battalions and Peacekeepers. On top of that, farming matters and booze, well, I'm a busy man."

"I feel like I'm not doing anything compared to you." Mason took a chunk out of the sandwich. "I'm drying up Florida swamps for air filters."

"Air filters?" TH tilted his head. "The ones repairing the ozone layer?"

"Yeah, restoring the atmosphere. If you are considering working there due to the spammed ads, don't. It's not worth it. The part about well-compensated workers is total bullshit, by the way. I apologize for the language."

"No need to apologize, Commander; we are all adults here." TH looked at Mason. "Didn't you say you live in Pampa, Texas? Why Florida? Isn't Pampa a major trading hub?"

"I earn twice as much in Florida than in Pampa, so I took the job offer, or I would end up on the Lifeline Program, making me dependent on the Orion Corp. But unfortunately, my brother's medical bills aren't cheap." Mason bit his tongue, but the word was out.

To his surprise, his teammates only nodded as a sign of understanding, and TH tapped Mason's right shoulder.

"I hope you will have enough money for your brother when we win. If not, I will give you my share." TH gave Mason a thumbs up. "Is he younger or older?"

"He is five years younger. I am twenty-five. I think my cut will be enough."

"Wow, TH. You are just going to give away your cut?" Dema tapped the table. "I mean, sure, it's your money."

"Dema, with all due respect, what I do with my money is none of your business. When we win, I will have so much excess on my hands. I made my calculations."

"Thank you, TH. This means a lot to me." Mason tapped his thumbs, trying to play it cool. "I don't know what to say."

"You already said thank you, and that is all I needed to hear." TH sent Mason a short salute. "But we need to win first."

"May I ask, why not Gamemode?" Van joined the conversation as he rolled the paper. "You can earn a quick Benjamins or Grants there."

Upon mentioning the second TVG platform, TH looked around the room, observing different reactions to the sentence. Dema expected an explanation, and Mason scratched the back of his head.

"But I can die easier. It turns out that I would have to play thirty CTF matches to make money, which I will make here." Mason finished his sandwich as well, and Van nodded. "My chances of survival are much higher here. My brother needs me alive and not six feet under."

"What is Gamemode?" Dema finished her sandwich. "I only arrived recently, and from what is in Europe, we don't have the TGV and this Battle Royale yet. But again, I haven't been there in a while, so things might have gotten better."

"TVG stands for Televised Games. Gamemode is the original TVG platform that rebooted modern entertainment. It was native to the US only, but now it's expanding worldwide. Despite the War, the need for blood and thrill only grew, and Battle Royale in all shapes and forms took over the mainstream culture," Van said without taking a breather. "You know the concept, a hundred or so people drop in, look for weapons, and only one can win. Highlander rule: there can be only one. Sometimes, there is a spin on the theme."

"So, what is the prize pool? Unfortunately, I fell asleep halfway through the terms and conditions." Dema yawned. "My apologies; it has been a long trip from Atlanta. So many stops along the way."

"First place gets six hundred thousand to share between surviving teammates. Let's say that we win, and all four of us survive; we are looking at a sure hundred fifty thousand dollars," TH spat out the data. "Does anyone want this sandwich? I am an older model which runs on battery and sun, and not on the calories."

"I'll take it if nobody else wants it." Van extended his arm, and TH handed it over.

"So, what was the name of our tank again?" Dema also finished hers.

"T-34-57 Mod.42/43 modernized something. We'll need to come up with a better name," Mason said, stretching his neck.

"I agree with Mason. It needs to be catchy, one or two words tops." Van looked around the group. "I don't have any two cents yet to add to this conversation."

"Two cents? I am not following." Dema looked at Van.

"It's a saying here in the States, nothing more than that," TH said. "What is that flash?"

THE FIRST CALL

A bright flashing light from the adjacent room with the white-board prompted Mason and his squad to surround it just as an orchestral tune played, followed by the TVG name, under-scored by the Orion. After a five-second countdown, a man in a black suit appeared on the computer screen, sitting inside what looked like a bunker. There were screens, concrete walls, old wooden chairs, and a massive black table behind, at which the anchorman sat. The man smiled, took a deep breath, and started talking.

Good morning, Gasoline Cowboys and Battle Royale Enthusiasts.

Today is Tuesday, June 8th, 2145, Day Zero. Welcome to our new TVG Battle Royale Seasons program, starting with Season Zero. I am Benjamin Bell, and I will be your host, commentator, and interviewer for this Tank Royale of 2145.

We'll keep you entertained for nine seasons full of ground-pounding action, nail-biting drama, hot love, and whatever your heart desires. But now, let me turn my attention to our Main Tank Royale of 2145 event and our contestants, who will spearhead the pilot.

I'll be here every morning, telling you what you are doing today, so contestants, always keep the computer on. For everyone else, primetime on TVG till the pilot ends!

First, before we start, there are house rules, and they will be enforced. TVG stands for fair sportsmanship, fair play, and honesty. Second, we have security patrols at the complex, watching for disturbances. If needed, they will escort you off the premises and face possible jail time. This applies to both contestants and enjoyers.

As I said, this is Day Zero of the Pilot. Feel free to explore your surroundings, get to know your fellow tankers, and try the simulations you can find in your garages. Note that the simulation will receive a substantial update in a few days, including the gear. For today, limitless options await you. In the wardrobes, you have uniforms, which you must always wear. Our field cafeteria offers breakfast from 8 to 11, lunch from 1 to 3, and dinner from 6 to 11.

As we are a branch of Battle Royale, you'll see many visitors walking around. These people are primarily here to visit the Museum of Victors or view the training for other Royale programs soon to be aired. Behave, smile, and they might cheer for you. There will be a surprise awaiting all contestants in a couple of days. All of you know what you signed up for when you signed the documents.

Now, I'll tell you about the contestants. So far, we have the most diverse group of contestants from all Battle Royale divisions, but around seventy percent are from the Corporate United States; these games are not just limited to the Americas. We have delegations from corporate Japan, South Korea, Germany, Sweden, and from down under Australia. If I forgot anyone, please don't feel left out; we welcome you to our family. Most of the tankers are between twenty and twenty-eight years old.

Benjamin took a sip of a blueish liquid and placed the can next to him on the table.

We are in the 1939-1945 era, which in history is known as World War Two. This is where tanks shone on a grand scale, and from there, these steel beasts became an essential part of any military force, so Orion Corporation and TVG, two hundred years later, decided to pay tribute to this period. Our Chief Designers, Thomas and Adriana, will talk more about behind-the-scenes soon.

Last year, in 2144, we kicked off a new Division of the already popular Battle Royale Games called Tank Royale. In March of this year, we launched the Heavy Tank Royale. Since it racked up considerable viewership, TVG gave us additional funding. Now, we are the launch title. We currently field a diverse lineup of machines so everyone can root for their favorite.

Your tanks are not just killing machines; they are a piece of history and chariots of War, so treat them with respect, and they will bring you to victory. While these are not authentic tanks from the World War Two era since none of them survived, these kits were built with the utmost mindfulness, and we worked out a few problems, but not all. Based on the scavenged data, all tanks are a hundred percent historically accurate. To make these games interesting, tankers will not fight on factory-trim tanks, but some teams have received interesting modifications or variants that will spice up the fight with a few gimmicks. Know this about your machines. Like you, they have a personality, strengths, and flaws. Name them, but nothing offensive; we will be screening them. The final deadline is due tomorrow at 12:01 PM.

In a few days, you'll go to the newly built Tank Museum for your own tour, where you'll learn more about the 1939-1945 period or be free to browse; we have an extensive data collection available. We encourage the formation of platoons as it increases your chances of survival once the real fight begins. Thank you for playing, and remember, these tanks aren't scrap metal. Don't forget to post pictures on social media to earn additional money.

I'm your host, Benjamin Bell, and this is Tank Royale.

As he finished, the screen changed to the primary desktop, awaiting further interaction, and apps called Tank Store and PR&Budget appeared. Mason played around with the computer and opened the Budget icon, revealing c$5000 in the app.

"So, what do we do now?" TH looked at Mason, who scratched his chin while clicking the apps.

Mason found dedicated windows in the PR Money App, each with unclaimed or unearned c$. Titles read Social Media Engagement, Simulations, and Donations with a note: *Use earned money to purchase items for you and your tank.*

"I would suggest trying the simulations. The hardware looks impressive, but I didn't have a chance to try them out." Dema stood up and looked at the board, where she found the table with their names and positions.

T-34-57 Mod.42/43 modernized – Team #28
Commander/Gunner – Mason
Driver – Van
Loader – TH
Radio-Operator/Co-driver – Dema

The digital sign with the *Simulation Room* was in the right corner of the garage, next to the black slide doors. There were four small cubicles with nametags, a chair, a unique black suit, goggles, gloves, and a screen to track progress. There, a note hung: *Upgrade expected in a few days.* Everything connected to the mainframe in the server room behind a glass window, and for a moment, Mason swore that he saw an outline of a human, but after looking, the space was empty with only a large humming black box. The system woke up when it registered four individuals.

"Oh wow! They have the latest O560 rigs!" Mason's jaw dropped to the floor as his hand touched the digital screen and then slid over the black and white set up with chrome lining. "I'm adding this virtual reality rig to my list."

"How much do these go for?" Dema walked up to Mason.

"Five thousand dollars for the basic version. The fully spec-out rig will cost you around twenty thousand or so. However, you can find additional hardware on the aftermarket a bit cheaper."

"On our farm, we have the O500 for learning to operate harvesters and other heavy-duty vehicles. I agree with Mason; it is something to dream about." Van put on the gloves, and Mason gave him a thumbs up.

"All right then, see you all in a bit." Dema put on the gear and sat in the chair.

———

After a short tune and a corporate logo, a menu showed up as a voice narrated his options.

Welcome to the TVG Tank Royale Simulation Training. I am Agnes, and I will be your virtual instructor. I must warn you that this simulation contains fast-flashing images and photorealism. This may cause discomfort and trigger seizures for people with photosensitive epilepsy and related abnormal neurological or post-traumatic activity. In case of an emergency, you or your teammates reach for the emergency button next to you. You have selected your position as Commander. Feel free to use your voice or press the option. Please confirm your assigned role.

"Yes! Commander," Mason almost shouted.

Commander, please say your full name.

"Mason Knight. Don't you already know that?"

Welcome, Commander Knight. Your crew is also taking their positions. Let me tell you how it will work. First, you will learn what to do in your primary position, and then I will rotate you and your crew around so you know what to do if one of your team members is out of action. You will then be placed in the tank simulation, where your skills will be assessed.

Now, you will feel itchiness on your forehead; I am extending the memory needles for better reception. These simulations were designed for military training, allowing higher retention of information. If you desire, you are qualified for everything from Pilot to Engineer once you complete these simulations. Allow me to get back to the simulation for Tank Royale of 2145. Please say your tank's name so I can load the simulation.

"T-34-57 mod.42/43 modernized."

You have selected a T-34-57 mod. 1942/43. Is that correct?

"That will be correct. So, 42/43 is a year. 1942/1943."

All right, Mason, you can sit down. Since this tank does not support the five-crew layout, you will be the tank's gunner as well. Say yes if you understand.

"Yes, I understand."

Excellent, Commander Knight. Enjoy this short video, and we will progress to the next level.

Mason looked around, wondering if his Team had the same annoying voice as he had, but her voice grew on him as Agnes spoke.

———

An hour later, the crew reunited in the tank lobby, and after Mason waited for everyone to leave the garage, he closed the door behind him.

One thing attracted Mason's attention as they pressed forward. He spotted rails and turning mechanisms spread underneath the garages on the ground. When they left their community, the gate closed behind them. People could still see through, but no access was granted to outsiders. As the four tankers explored the complex, a few drones hovered above their heads, live-streaming everything they did. Their first stop was the TVG Map Terminal, right next to the entrance.

The whole complex looked like a small city. There was a movie theater, cafeteria, library, tank museum, testing ground with an obstacle course, and tank firing range. A few miles down the road, corporate offices and studios were located. Sprinkled between them were Tank Parks.

Other teams were also present there, and Mason noticed they stuck out. All other crews were all male, all female, or humanoid crews. With a thousand pairs of eyes staring him down, Mason gulped. *They are ready to kill to win. Some of them seem like their career is killing. Wasn't war enough? And how is this God's plan? How does He tolerate this, if at all?* An android greeter awaited them as Mason and his crew made their way to the Tank Shop. Dressed up in the camo uniform and black headphones, he held the door. Before entering, Mason looked over his shoulder at the humming world as they entered one by one, with the last one being TH, who gave a short salute, and Greeter saluted back.

"Welcome to the Tank Royale Shop, where you can find anything you and your Tank desire. Tracks, pins, additional uniforms, tarps. You can have it delivered or come to pick it up. We have an all-around sale, 30% off on all items!" An announcement echoed in the shop, and Mason blinked.

Inside the Shop, Mason and his crew stood in awe. Shelves were filled with tracks, spare parts, road wheels of all shapes and sizes, armor plates, and machine guns. It felt like a warehouse; this was just the ground floor as the quartet vanished between the shelves.

"I have never seen such a shop." Dema grabbed a book and opened it to the first page. "How do we pay for this?"

"We can use the Budget money Mason discovered on the computer," TH immediately responded.

Mason stepped aside and pressed his right palm against his forehead as the new world overwhelmed him. *Mason, pull yourself together! Ail is watching me. I'm not going to win like this. Focus!*

"Wow." Van grabbed a track link and read the label barcoded so the tablet could read it. *Universal spare track link, Panzerkampfwagen Ausf IV.* Next to it, a few sealed thermite grenades stood in perfect rows.

"Seeing that you don't have your tablets or devices, please use this notebook to mark down the items you want to purchase." The TVG operator stopped by Mason and handed him the notebook and the pen. "After you are finished, please scan the list at the exit."

"Thank you?" Mason quickly collected himself, and the man walked away.

"Guys, let's go upstairs!" Dema waved her hands, grinning from ear to ear. "We are just getting started,"

After finding the escalator, Mason and his crew got to the second floor. There, as they were about to disperse, an unknown voice stopped them from behind a rack of uniforms.

"So, you are the 28s?" Mason found the noise coming from the next aisle, and for a moment, he thought he recognized the voice.

In between the camo uniforms, Mason spotted a crew of four. They had a mix of black leather helmets, scarves, and blueish uniforms to match.

"Depends on who is asking." Mason looked at the young

man, who moved his head from the gap and grinned from ear
to ear.

He seemed to be the crew leader, and his goggles made it
challenging to identify who he was, but his brown hair appeared
when he removed his headcover.

"We're your neighbors, 26, well not exactly, but pretty
close."

"So?" Mason widened his eyes as he tried to remember
where he saw the man before him.

"It is good to have a potential ally, for now. Together, we'll
have a better chance of winning, and the public will surely love
us! Do you want to join us?" The tanker looked around, and
a moment later, he and his crew joined Mason. "The Platoons
are formed as we speak, and the sooner we lock together, the
better for us because once things go south, it would be nice to
have someone in the corner with us. After you, we need one
more."

While the man in question wasn't as tall as Van, he still
commanded respect with his firm and straight composure. His
voice again sounded familiar. Mason looked away momentarily, thinking: *He is a Commander and a good one for that measure. At
least he plays it well. He already knows what to do. How can I even measure up to him or others, for that matter? But wait, what is he talking
about?*

"This year, TVG will do platoons, but the decision can
change any minute. Teams 22 and 16 are already allied, which
is ironic, considering what tanks they are fighting on."

"Why is it ironic?" Van shook his head, leading the conversation and prompting Mason to engage as the designated
team leader.

"Each tank and its crew represent a nation that fought in
World War Two, which is the theme of this Pilot Season. Do
you guys have any idea of the WW2 setting?" the tanker continued pressing, and Mason had begun suspecting that this
man knew something they didn't. "Team 16 are Germans, and

22 represent the United States."

"While we didn't learn about the sprocket wheels," Mason said, "only basics, who defeated who, and a few crucial battles, like Midway, Normandy, Bulge, and Berlin."

"Well, that counts for something. However, this knowledge won't be helpful to you. They call me Giovanni." Giovanni extended his hand, and a moment later, introductions were made.

"So, can we count on you?" Gio raised his eyebrows, and for a moment, Mason felt he recognized him, but his mind was too foggy.

"The moment Mason decides." Dema looked at his tablet and then at Mason, who tilted his head. "Are we joining?"

"Final call? Yes or no?" Giovanni looked around him. "We don't have all day."

"If it helps us, then we are looking forward to working with you." Feeling an invisible gun pointed at his head while thousands of eyes watched, Mason made a quick decision and shook hands with Giovanni.

"Excellent. We're looking forward to working with you." Giovanni gave Mason a thumbs up, and the four tankers departed in a single line.

"Also, visiting the Tank Parks will help you get a feel for this setting." Giovanni shouted as the escalator consumed him.

"All right, we are just a few hours into the day, and I learned something new." TH grabbed a helmet from the shelf and tied it around his chin. "Feels like an outdated football helmet. It's like placing a cast iron on your head."

Mason laughed and took a duffle bag, which read on its label.

Green Soviet Standard Issue Duffle Bag, 1940.

Dema finished reading the TVG Guide and looked at the digital clock on the wall. *Time for sure flies here,* Dema thought as she looked one more time at the clock to ensure she was right. She placed it back onto the shelf and wandered the store momentarily, looking for her squad, finally finding them on the third floor.

"So, what do we want to do? I don't understand this venture. We are to fight on these kit tanks?" Van looked around him. "Damn, I mean, I signed up for what I signed up for, but still."

"That is not a good thing to say out loud, but I guess you wouldn't know it anyway." They heard a thick but collected accent speaking from behind them, and as Mason turned around, he spotted a crew of four tankers.

The crew in question had stylish black and gray uniforms with matching camps. *So, it must be either Team 16 or 22,* Mason thought as he remembered Giovanni's words.

Mason correctly guessed that they are Germans based on a quick Gernglish exchange. They had blue eyes, but the taller one had a shaved head, two had black hair, and the last had dirty blond hair. All of them had a white O with #16 on their patches. One had a headset with a throat microphone, but the cable vanished behind his back.

"Who are you?" TH joined the conversation.

"We're Germany, but I'm positive that you have no idea where that is." The shaved teen moved forward, measuring Mason's team from head to toe while the rest hung back, but not far away.

Mason also measured him, but to everyone's surprise, Dema stepped forward.

"Western Europe, current Capital of the European Survivor Organization. Good thing that China mistakenly nuked it."

The German delegation stood in awe momentarily, bursting out in bitter laughter in a few seconds.

"All right, this is how we'll play the game. From one World Citizen to another, I wasn't expecting you to go that low."

"I am an American, not a World Citizen!" Dema shouted and folded her hands.

"I am sure you are. Don't worry; we'll put you out of your

misery as soon as possible. Don't forget, no step back." One of the German tankers pointed at the hovering drone and cracked his knuckles. "So, you ready to die?"

The last sentence sent shivers down Mason's spine, and for a moment his head turned as the reality check came through: *Oh Lord! I must step my game up, or I won't see my brother!* For a moment, he noticed several people vacating the store premises as fast as they could.

"Aren't we all ready to die here? We had signed the contract that make-up and fireworks would be our grave, and people would cheer us on." As Dema said this, two security androids entered the floor, shoving people aside, which, in return, got them angry looks and several middle fingers.

"All of you can trash talk elsewhere; this is a place of commerce. I recommend you leave." Both androids pointed their stun guns at Mason, but not at the German Delegation.

Everyone except Mason and the German Team flinched when androids walked around them.

"All right, we'll stop," Mason said, raising his hands.

It's a good thing that they arrived. Mason took a deep breath and silently thanked the Lord.

Behind them, the German delegation laughed. "We'll see if history will repeat itself."

"You know that you can't win. Everyone is looking for the next Stalingrad, where they would kick your ass into the stratosphere unless you freeze first," someone shouted out of nowhere, gaining everyone's attention.

"Who said that!?" The supposed leader of the German Delegation looked around, finding a tall, blue-eyed, blond-haired man in a blue uniform with large gloves hanging from his big belt with his three other crewmates in similar attire.

Upon turning, Mason spotted a number 16 on his shoulder patches while the German crew quickly collected themselves.

"Oh, we rolled over you and prepared to get rolled over again!" one of the tankers shouted. "Two can play that game.

Next time, it will be Danzig or war. You'll perish, and your sorry ass 14-TP will be your metal grave."

"We shall see soon. And it is not Danzig, but Gdańsk! Dzień dobry, skurwysyny!" Polish tanker flipped off the German crew, summoned his team with an audible command, and left the shop with bags, which one of his teammates handed him. Despite his calm composure, Mason noticed that the young man bit his tongue once the Germans mentioned the TP.

What the hell is a TP? What did they say? TP-15? 14? Mason scratched the back of his head. *Well, it seems like we are not alone in this fight.*

"I think we attracted too much attention. How about we get out of here, see those tank parks, and eat something?" Mason took the lead, and they waved goodbye to the android standing next to the main entrance, but the words of the German Delegation stayed with him.

"We just spent two hours in the Tank Shop?" Van looked at the digital clock, which hung on the top of the Tank Museum. "Damn, time flies for sure!"

———

While walking across the TVG Grounds, Mason looked over his shoulder and noticed a drone hovering over their heads like an annoying fly. The complex had slowly filled up with people, and for a moment, Mason had to fight across the tightly packed pathways. However, the blistering sun had now fully emerged from the clouds, and for a moment, Mason heard birds chirping as they sought refuge among the tall trees. Mason and his Team came across a display depicting the map of the entire TVG complex with bright red screaming letters: YOU ARE HERE.

"It seems like TVG had dedicated a small exhibition park to the unique machines of War." TH pointed at the long barrels, short barrels, fully restored, or wreckages lined up to be viewed like mechanical models on the walkway.

"All right, time to see these Tank Parks." Dema zoomed in on the display depicting a complex map and selected the first area. "Let's look at this Skink, or whatever this abomination is."

———

After a confused look and replaying the recording three times, Mason and his squad had unanimously decided to head to the cafeteria; the strange tank could wait. The Main Square of the Tank Royale Complex was now filled with people, and guided tours, marked by single-color flags, patrolled around. Other crews, tourists, and even a school field trip occupied a few tables.

As Mason looked around, he spotted that everything had a tank theme, from the gunner's chairs on which they were about to sit all the way to the buildings themselves; even the Tank Museum seemed like the factory, only missing smoking chimneys, but instead, solar panels did the job.

A TV screen showed recaps from previous seasons and the current Heavy Tank Royale, scheduled to end this week. Many languages clashed in this place, but the Japanese language stood out; since a few table baskets to Mason's right, a delegation from Asia sat and recognized the red circle on the white background. *One day, I will go to Japan.* The all-female crew had just finished their food and was about to return the plates when one of the girls looked at Mason. Her tank hat covered most of her face, but Mason could notice the long black hair on her back. Their eyes locked in the moment, but then Van waved his hand, regaining Mason's attention.

"Your turn for the food tray." Van nudged Mason with the plastic tray. "It's getting cold!"

"I'm so sorry." Mason quickly grabbed the eating utensils.

"I see that you are checking out the girls." Van smiled and

skipped Mason, who raised his hands. "Wish I could, but I have a girl waiting for me."

"I like this place. It gives me everything that I ever dreamed about. Warm food, shower, and even good clothing," Dema said as she twirled around.

Then, she took the tray and loaded it up with food. Steak, potatoes, rice, and even a can of coke landed in her tray.

"How bad is it in Europe?" Van asked. "I'm sorry for not being up to date with the current world affairs."

"Have you read any post-apocalyptic books or watched a movie about Eastern Europe? Dudes running around with AKs, gas masks, and large brown coats? That is the situation in Eastern Europe. A singular wall splits us from the West, or you know it as Western Europe that is slowly coming back to life."

"You are holding up the line." The chef opened the window and the smell of burned rice filled everyone's noses, and loud hnnnmmmm filled everyone's ears.

"We're sorry. Let's go, Team." Mason took the lead, and as they returned to their place, they found a lonely young man occupying their table.

He hadn't moved any of their belongings or the chairs, and his blue uniform seemed familiar. Mason remembered. *The Polish guy from the Tank Shop?*

"Kind sir, we have been here first. Do you mind moving?" TH initiated the conversation.

"I figured that I would find you here. Listen, I need to ask you something." The young man opened his eyes, and Mason confirmed that it was the man from the Tank Shop talking about Danzig or that other place.

"What is it?" Van brought another chair, and moments later, they got acquainted.

"Let me show you." The tanker pulled out his tablet, signed in, and waited for the file to load. "TVG just announced that they're doing platoons of three and had already adjusted several crews. We see you signed up with the 26 and wondered if we could join you? Nobody wants to be with the last team."

"This is Battle Royale, right? Rules of engagement dictate that there will be only one standing in the end." Mason folded his hands, "But I can guess everyone knows more already than we do. Have you all done this already?"

"Why platoons if we have to fight each other? Mason is right!" TH asked, and the young man shook his head.

"Let me show you the lineup so far." The young man handed his tablet to Mason, who scrolled down, and as he read out loud, he noticed on the faces of his teammates that they also had no idea what any of those words meant, but TH nodded his head when Mason read the name of their T-34. Dema scratched her head, but when she read Carro Armato, a loud huh sounded.

AC IV(17) – Australia–Team 14
Centaur Mark. III – Great Britain–Team 10
Ram II Mark. V – Canada–Team 20
Panzer IV G Hydro – Germany–Team 16
41M Turán III (75) – Hungary–Team 24
Carro Armato P26/40 – Italy–Team 26
T-34-57 Mod.42/43 – Russia–Team 28
Stridsvagn m/42 Delat Torn – Sweden–Team 12
M4A1 76W Sherman – United States–Team 22
Type 3 Chi-Nu Kai – Japan–Team 18
14TP – Poland–Team 6
Nahuel DL D3 – Argentina–Team 8

Van whistled as he first broke the stare. "What the hell is a Stridsvagn? Nahuel? Hi-Ni-Kau? Am I summoning Cthulhu with these names?"

"It's Chi-Nu Kai, meaning Imperial Year 2603 Medium tank Model 10 Prototype Improved. However, do you see the problem? Team 16, who are Germans, allied with Team 22, United States, and with Team 18, Japan, forging one of the most potent teams as their tanks are top of the line. The rest of the crews are also looking." A young man pointed at two tank crews shaking hands and asking a bystander to take a picture of them. "Must be Brits and Canadians. Where are my manners? Call me August."

"Should we join them?" Van looked at Mason, who remained silently standing the entire time. "I think we should team up. We have nothing to lose and everything to gain."

"I see Team 26 is still open." Dema pointed at the tablet. "Are they the ones who talked with us in the Shop and with whom we shook hands?"

"Yes, they are. I would suggest meeting up so all three parties can talk." August looked at his crew, which had just finished lunch. "We're about to enter a rabbit hole of madness, and it will be a good idea to have someone to stand with us."

"Count us in; we're looking for any help we can get." Mason shook hands with August, who highlighted Mason's Team in green on the tablet.

"I'll try to talk with Team 26. If I were to give you a pro tip, it would be this: spend as much time as possible in the simulations." August leaned back. "That should do it. I'll see all of you soon."

"I think we should take a picture together. A new start," Dema said, and August nodded his head.

"Picture?" Mason tilted his head.

"Yeah. Do you remember the PR App on the Computer?" Dema pointed at August's table.

"Dema is right! The announcer, Benjamin, said we should take pictures to earn extra dough!" Van looked at Mason, who nodded.

After a short pose and several flashes, Dema gave August a thumbs up.

"See you soon." TH waved off August, who vanished in the crowd.

Mason looked around the field cafeteria as they ate, taking

in the tank-themed surroundings: World War Two and the fielded tanks must have been rather interesting since they were paying tribute, but what about the first one? World War One? Were there any tanks? Did I miss the season? That is interesting! So, does that mean we'll pay tribute to the recent war in a few hundred years? It's a shame that there is nobody alive who actually fought there. I wonder, they must have some good, but possibly terrifying, stories to tell.

"Are you also admiring our surroundings? I have to say, TVG did not spare any expense to go all the way." Dema looked at Mason and nudged him, grinning from ear to ear. "Everything all right?"

"I'm fine; it just takes a moment to get a feeling for this place. I remember seeing the backstage for one of the Gamemode matches when I got a free trial for the premium TV plan. Now, we're the backstage for everyone to see."

"There are plans? Like..." Dema widened her eyes. "I have so much to learn."

"Indeed there are, Dema," TH tapped the table two times. "There is the basic plan, which restricts your channel selection to your location. Then there is a premium plan—an additional five hundred programs to watch worldwide, a 3D viewing option, behind-the-scenes features, like Mason just said, and many more. You can even send questions, which might get answered live on air. Finally, of course, there are financing options."

"I want to see more of these tanks! While the Skink was interesting, I wonder what else lurks in our parks?" Van carefully placed his silverware on the plate. "Who is ready to go?"

"What is this abomination?" Van pointed at the tank when they entered one of the enclosed smaller Tank Parks five minutes later.

A monstrosity stood on the metallic stand in the middle of the park. It seemed like someone, or something, married a different turret to the other hull, and it didn't sit right with Mason, yet there was some strange aura around it, calling everyone closer to see this piece of history. The hull had large overlapping wheels with side skirts on the top. The turret appeared to be from a separate tank, but it was hard to see on the top for further identification, but it provided enough shadow for everyone. The rear was plastered with antennas of all sizes. For a moment, Mason pondered before approaching the stand, trying to formulate his feelings, and by looking at Dema scratching the back of her head, Van blinking several times, but before he looked at TH, his eyes found Dema again. *Wow, she is hot! Oh crap, I hope she didn't notice.* Mason caught himself staring at her again and immediately looked back at the tank. He either saw a metal monster or the monument of the bygone era brought back for the enjoyment of all once again.

There was a bench and a screen with data in front of the rotating stand. A large group of tourists just left the park, leaving Mason and his team alone. He was first to wake up the idling console, and his eyes jumped out when he found the name.

"Bergepan, I'm sorry I cannot read this." Mason stood aside, and TH moved and placed his hand on the console.

Moments later, Mason rolled his eyes as TH read out the name.

"Bergepanther mit Aufgesetztem Panzerkampfwagen.IV Turm als Befehlspanzer."

"That is a mouthful. What the hell does that mean?" Dema pressed the play button, and Agnes started narrating as the tank stopped rotating.

Why convert something that is already working? You are standing in the Tank Memorial number 15 and are looking at this one off-field conversion of the legendary Panzerkampfwagen 5 or Panther in 1944. As the name implies, this is a command variant or the observation vehicle of the Panther tank family, outfitted with long and short-range radios for contact with artillery battalions, other tanks, troops, and nearby allied aircraft. The command variant didn't possess a turret, but this one had received one from the spare Panzer 4 tank. Why did this happen? We may never know why this happened due to already scarce data for researchers and historians. Feel free to take a virtual tour of this odd vehicle or continue to #16, where you can find T26E4, commonly known as a Super Pershing.

Moments later, a screen changed, and the 3D model drove into the screen from the left, awaiting further interaction. Mason smiled when the tank turned its turret around, but comically fast, like a cartoon. Then, it rocked back and forth like a rocking chair.

Benjamin was right; these tanks do have personalities. As Mason thought about it, his smile turned into a grin.

"Why does this exist? I mean, it's impressive." TH tapped the screen as he picked up the gold coin from the ground with his left hand and flipped it between his fingers. "There must be a reason, right?"

"I don't have an answer." Van looked one more time at the unpronounceable German tank. "Time to hit the road. I want to see more."

"All right, then, that was interesting. Let's see this Super Pershing?" Dema said as the breeze calmed down.

"I'm all down for exploration, but let us do one more park and then head back to the garage," Mason said. "It seems like August knew what he was talking about."

"All right, Mason, lead the way!" TH stepped aside.

"Hold on, guys!" Dema shouted, waving her hands. "Let's take a picture!"

"Picture? Didn't we just take one a few minutes ago?" TH said.

"Again!?" Van rolled his eyes. "I'm going to take more pictures here than I ever did in my life. Even my girl takes fewer pictures, which is saying something!"

"Yeah, we need money! But, from the prices I saw in the Tank Shop, pictures are just a start." Mason clapped his hands, and a moment later the four tankers lined up in front of the platform, and one of the onlookers snapped several photos.

As doors on the garage closed behind them, Mason climbed on top of the T-34 and gathered the company.

"What is it, Mason?" Dema looked up, and Mason pointed at her.

"I saw you reading the tank guide back in the Tank Shop. Would you like to share with us?"

"Oh, absolutely!" Dema coughed, and then, like a tour guide, she pointed at the tank. "What you see here is T-34-57, 1942/1943 modification. T-34 stands for this metal beast's name conceived in Soviet Russia as part of the extensive modernization program."

"So, what does the 57 mean?" Van reached out for the long barrel, barely touching the end with the tips of his fingers.

"One of the modifications was to mount a 57mm gun. Still, it achieves good penetration thanks to the long barrel, which compensates for the smaller caliber and should allow us to fight on almost equal terms against other tanks."

"Thank you for telling us." TH quickly updated his newly created database concerning World War Two tanks.

"I also read that we should start posting pictures and videos on the STREETPAUSE, so I will keep bombarding you till we are deployed." Dema grinned from ear to ear.

"So, let's do a picture then." Mason jumped down and fixed his uniform while the rest of the crew found a suitable position. "A new day, a new tank."

"But who will take the picture?" Dema said as she sat on the mudguard and fixed her hair.

"Allow me," TH climbed down and snapped a few images.

Then, Dema switched to the front camera and took several selfies. But as she finished, a trap beat remix of a song played, and Van looked away, his face turning red.

"What the hell is that?" TH looked around him.

"My ringtone. It must be Ember. One moment." Van took off, taking stairs by two while the trio tapped their thumbs.

After a minute, Van returned, and Mason tilted his head. "Who is Ember?"

"My girlfriend is not answering, even though she just called me! Anyway, who wants to sit inside?" Van had already opened the left hatch on the tank turret, moving the conversation along.

"Okay, hold on!" Dema raised her hand. "Van must sit left front, while I will sit front right. Following us is Mason on the left in the turret with TH on the right."

"All right then!" Van opened the left hatch and vanished inside.

TH waited for Dema to descend into the hull while Mason followed Van's footsteps. As everyone got to their positions, Mason quickly realized the problem. He was standing on the floor, where ammo boxes would be, with the only protection for him being a thin metal plate with rectangular cutouts. Mason shook his head as he felt goosebumps on his hands. *One shot here, and I am done. Was this a clever idea? Collect yourself and ensure that you won't get hit.* On a small panel to his right were switches for the main gun and co-axial machine gun, a light switch, drive-fly wheels for both the horizontal and vertical turret drive, and the cannon's elevation. Mason almost hit his forehead on the gunsight, which stuck out next to the gun breech. Next to him, there was a plug for the internal radio.

"Well, this is cramped, but at least my legs can fit." Van looked around and placed his hand on one of the levers as his voice echoed inside.

"How can you see from here? I have one periscope here for the machine gun!" Dema looked around like a trapped animal. "Does anyone want to switch places?"

"Was this designed on purpose or a side effect of the production?" TH looked around the garage via the vision periscope. "Well, the Computer told us that we will be moved around, but sure, Dema, we can alternate."

"Thank you. You are the best." Dema leaned back in the chair, "How bad it can get?"

Mason and TH faced similar challenges in the hexagonal turret.

"That is a crude gunsight. TH, do you think you could load the gun fast enough?" Mason blinked when he looked up, his eyes adjusting to the small light in the tank.

It would be best if you cleaned it. They look like my aunt's glasses. Or Ail's computer screen. With the right sleeve, Mason swiped up and down on the optic, and then, upon looking again, he face-palmed as he realized that there were two lenses to clear.

"Yes, I can, Commander! Mason! I believe that we have a trade-off."

"And what trade-off exactly?" Mason looked over the gun breech and tried to peek inside the cannon but gave up as his head almost got stuck.

"You always pay the price for something. Unfortunately, we are paying the price with a cramped interior and poor visibility. I wonder what we got in return?"

Mason only shrugged his shoulders. Ten minutes inside the Tank, and he wanted to get out. *I don't even want to imagine the combat conditions, and I hope my Spider will manage that. For a moment, I completely forgot that I had it. Well, the pockets on the uniform are deep enough. They cannot know.*

"All right, my friends, time to get out of this box." Mason opened the hatch and exhaled.

Looking down, he noticed Van trying to leave the tank via the open driver's hatch. He looked like a snake crawling out of a hole in the ground, escorted by inaudible cursing.

As Dema looked up, she noticed TH's eyes flashing red. Taken aback by the development, Dema screamed as the red light illuminated the cramped interior for several seconds.

"TH, you are all right up there!?" Dema punched him in the leg but to no avail.

"Everything all right down there?" Mason slid back in as TH's eyes stopped flashing and turned back to blue.

"I am so sorry." TH got his bearings together. "Everything is all right on my end!"

He quickly opened his hatch, and after he got out, he helped Dema.

"TH, what was that?" Dema joined TH. "It looked like a DEFCON 3 alert."

"It's called a Glitch, and seventy-five percent of actively deployed humanoids have it. Unfortunately, nobody can fix it for me, so I am just living with it." TH looked away as he said, "It is said that the Glitch is the reason for my sentience."

Mason stood there for a moment, thinking about the Glitch.

It definitely sounds like what I have—poor guy.

"You mean sentience like you are self-aware?" Mason tilted his head. "Like a revelation?"

"I recognize myself in the mirror. Beforehand, I just saw a humanoid. I couldn't tell the difference. After the Glitch, I see old hardware desperately trying to prove itself."

"You got this, brother." Van tapped TH on his right shoulder. "Anything we can do to help."

Mason nodded his head, and TH made a quick bow.

"Thank you all. It's unpredictable. If this were to happen to me, don't stop. Just go! It's only going to get worse from here."

"No, we're a team, and we stick together!" Mason folded his hands. "No one is leaving anyone behind, and that is an order!"

"So, what do we say to a quick tutorial session?" Dema looked at the black door leading to the Simulations.

———

After a rigorous two-hour tutorial simulation session, TH sat on a chair and stared into the void for a second while the rest of the crew stood around him in the garage, with Mason last to close the door. Then, on the wall, he noticed the time. 17:30.

"TH, what is the matter?" Dema tapped TH's shoulder. "Is it happening again?"

"I should have finished what I said before the simulation. I am not decommissioned because I am old hardware, but due to the Glitch. I am a stopgap project between the old MX20 line and the new U98, created by TH Project Agency or THPA. Another one-off project called X9, but I don't know where Orion put him. He was supposed to be my upgrade package, but the U98 line arrived faster, so there was no need to have us. THPA went under, and we ended up on the street, being replaced by androids." TH removed his green shirt, and Van spotted large red letters saying Decommissioned.

"What were your options? Did you even have any?" Van asked while Mason turned away and looked at the long barrel of the 57mm gun, feeling itchy in his nervous system as the Spider moved around.

"As a humanoid, I am considered a second or third-class citizen, so I have no rights to begin with. I was supposed to go either to the Museum, a boneyard or get a job. I saw the advertisement for Battle Royale and enlisted."

"I don't know if humanoids have feelings, but it seems like you two and the X9 were close friends," Dema said. "No offense.

"A stopgap android and a one-off prototype make an interesting duo; I will tell you that." TH turned towards Mason, who stood silently staring into the rifled barrel, and their conversion faded.

"Mason, Commander, everything all right?" TH stopped and observed Mason walking wordlessly around the tank.

On the second call, Mason shook his head.

"I apologize; I'm slowly taking these things in." A quick omission of the Spider worked. "What do we do?" Mason turned around and smiled.

"I think I should call Ember again. Maybe she will answer now. She must be worried." Van was about to vanish upstairs when TH halted him.

"Who is Ember?"

"The love of my life, one and only." Van's face turned red again, and he vanished upstairs.

"He said that Ember is his girlfriend." Dema smiled. "I almost missed it."

"Can you believe that this is just the first day!" Mason took a deep breath. "First day out of how many?"

"This day flew so fast," Dema looked at the sunset as the last orange lights gave away to the darkness, "which reminds me!"

"Don't say a picture." Mason closed his eyes momentarily.

"I am back! She is not responding again!" Van waved from the top of the staircase. "Not even text. Okay, what did I miss?"

"You're gone for a minute. Dema is about to retake a picture of us!" Mason gave a thumbs up. "Some fancy composition shots."

"Okay, it is my turn!" Van looked at Dema, who handed him the tablet. "Please and thank you! Damn right. Smile!"

Followed by the two flashes, Mason looked at his squad again. "Do we want to grab dinner?"

"I was about to say that!" Dema made a fist with her right hand.

As they walked to the entrance, Mason stayed back and looked at his barcode. *Should I be ashamed? Secret or open about it?*

"Mason, you all right?" Dema looked at Mason and smiled from ear to ear like the sun in the cartoons.

"I believe I am. I am still processing that I got here."

"This will either make us and our dreams come true or break us and send us six feet under."

"And fans love us." Van opened his tablet and showed the pictures with likes to the crew. "I wonder, why is the follower count hidden?"

"Maybe we do not have enough followers to show? There are quite a few choices for viewers." Dema scratched her chin. "But I might be wrong."

"Guys," Mason clapped his hands, "let's not worry about

how many followers we have, but how we'll fight. If we make it far, people will cheer for us no matter our prior social media following. We're fighting on the same platform, after all."

"I was never a social media guy anyway." Van flipped the tablet upside down. "But hey, I might become one today."

"So, you guys have opposing thumbs, but you post pictures on the internet and stand by for validation from someone who you never saw?" TH took the tablet into his hands. "You humans are interesting creatures. One day, I must write a research paper on you creatures who command the Earth."

CHAPTER FIVE

CRUSADING ANGEL

Mason turned on his bed for the fifth time, trying to fall asleep after a rather overwhelming first day at the Complex. After the simulations and the good night from the crew, memories of the semi colliding with the small family car, killing his parents, and paralyzing his brother hit him in full force, but it wasn't as severe as it used to be. Mason looked at the digital alarm and slowly exhaled as it showed 2350. *So I signed up for this. Well, it's still better than a lithium mine. If I run, I'll get shot and replaced. How would that even work? Can they go back and edit me out? Oh! Ail! Maybe I can call him!* Mason launched from the bed, and a moment later he called his brother, who immediately answered.

"Ail, it's Mason!" Mason lowered his voice as he turned on the lights in his room.

"Aunt almost had a heart attack when I told her what happened! I looked everywhere for you! Don't do that to me again, please. So, TVG?"

"It was either this or lithium mines in USAC." Mason fixed his pillow.

"Good call. So, what do you think?" Ail's face grinned from ear to ear. "Hello?"

"It's a different world. I tell you what; however, I believe that I can make it back home." Mason raised his eyebrows when his brother facepalmed. "What?"

"I meant Dema. All I can say is good luck to you!" Ail nodded.

"I mean, she is all right." Mason watched Ail facepalm again. "Again? What did I say?"

"Bro! What the hell is wrong with you? All right? You have a hot babe in your squad; all I hear is that she is all right. I expected more from you!"

"It's not that simple! I mean, it's..."

"Mason, you're digging yourself into a grave. Staring is all right? Come on, bro!"

"How do you know? Oh!" This time, Mason facepalmed as he remembered the drones hovering above his head.

"Good news for you, Mason. She also has been eyeballing you. Listen, I need to get going. It seems like I was able to convince that girl to come over for a night. Stay safe as much as you can, and remember, this is your shot for glory in more ways than one. However, I would prefer you to come home alive."

"Thank you! Enjoy your evening." Mason smiled, but his brother said something that sent shivers down his spine.

"I'll be watching!" The screen turned black, and Mason laid back on his pillows.

After a slow exhale, Mason thought: *Ail is correct, but I cannot let my emotions get a hold of me in this situation, especially during combat. How can I balance it out? Dema is more than all right; she is everything I ever wanted. Maybe God has finally heard my prayers. It's hard to tell, but if this is a part of God's plan, I am happy to let Him take the reins for a moment.* Mason heard someone coming to his door as he was about to pray. He immediately hid the rosary under the pillow.

"May I come in?" Dema's voice called out to Mason. "I want to talk with you in private, if I may?"

"Sure, come on in." Mason opened the door, and moments later he brought Dema a chair from his desk.

She was dressed very lightly, and Mason had to admit

that her fit body looked terrific, despite a few scars on her arms and legs. The white blanket with red stripes covering her shoulders reminded Mason of the Stripes on the original American Flag.

"Everything all right? I heard you turning on your bed for like an hour." Dema leaned forward. "And also, I want to apologize. I was insensitive to your situation when TH said he would give you his money. I am sorry. Back where I am from, I had to count every dollar I had in my wallet."

"Dema, it's all right, no hard feelings. My brother doesn't like handouts either. To come back to your previous question, not everything is all right, but I wish everything would be all right." Mason's head vanished in his arms. "How can I help?"

"It can wait. What is on your mind?" Dema said as she moved her chair closer to Mason's bed. "I am a pretty light sleeper anyway."

"Everything, Dema. My mind is on the racetrack, trying to catch up with all this madness." For a moment, Mason felt like he was visiting the psychologist, lying there on his bed while Dema listened. "Just know that you are a real trooper for standing up against the Germans. It would be best if you were the Commander, not me. Rock steady under pressure while I am still figuring this out. Hand to God."

Dema smiled and shook her head. "Comm... Uh... Mason, you were the one who kept his cool while I launched at them. I believe in you. We all believe in you. You are our only hope of surviving whatever they throw at us."

"You know what? Thank you for your encouraging words." Mason smiled as well. "Thank you."

"So, let us hear your thoughts. I can safely assume that you dislike this corporate subscription system."

"This whole corporate deal, Dema. We traded one villain for another and fought, believing that once the nuclear dust and NWO had vanished, peace would return, but no. The moment Corporate took over the world, it stayed the same, and only names changed. Taxes are called Life Subscriptions. The Bill of Rights is long gone; instead, we have Documents of Governance and Terms&Conditions. And when I came home from deployment, they thrust me into a new way of life I was never used to. I was an agent of my own life, but now, the Board of Directors, Internal Control, and Human Resources all do it for me.

"But on the other hand, Orion Group accomplished things that most governments wouldn't be able to. Everyone in the world has access to education, drinking water, and anything you can think of. I received a Vet Treatment for free and some money to kickstart my life again, but that came at the cost of my liberties. They broke my leg and then gave me the crutch." Mason focused on Dema. "But my complaining or my life situation is nothing compared to you."

"I guess so."

"Look at you! You made it here across the Atlantic. It must have been horrible to live in the Dark Zone. Constant danger, no assurance of tomorrow." Mason wanted to continue, but Dema raised her hand.

"Had its silver lining. The War and aftermath forced me to get out of my comfort zone and do things that I wouldn't usually do. I learned to survive in Eastern Europe's unforgiving wilderness and the post-war United States. I learned English, how to shoot and started somewhat believing in a higher power. I can see your rosary, which you are hiding underneath the pillow. How can you still believe that God allows all of this?" Dema touched the wooden cross, and Mason spotted a tear forming, but Dema shook it off.

"I wish I could have the answer. Look around you. Do you feel the presence of high power? I feel steel, wires, tracks, and directives, but no God. When I returned, I had a serious faith crisis." Mason looked at his rosary and handed it to Dema. "It kept me alive for all those years, so I decided to continue practicing, but the problem lies with my decision. Christians aren't supposed to kill for others' entertainment, but it was either this or a lithium mine. Yet I'll pull the trigger in the end, as my brother needs the money. Am I doomed already? Or is my salvation paved in the blood of our opponents?" Mason unintentionally squeezed Dema's hand.

To his surprise, Dema didn't mind. Instead, she covered his hand with hers for a moment before Mason retracted his.

"I really do not know an answer to your question. It was hard to find God in the Dark Zone, but now, as I reflect, there were moments where I felt his presence."

"Give me an example because, for me, it is hard to imagine such a moment. Well, I can, but you have a better idea than I do." Mason scratched his head.

"Well, one of the times I always felt his presence was after a firefight or when we fended off Scavengers. After the gunfire, you could almost miss that short silence when the injured cried out a moment later. I just lay on the ground, breathing slowly, and felt something higher, but here, I don't know. It must be that moment when I realized that I had just survived another encounter. Yeah, it had to be that. So, maybe the big man in the clouds exists after all. The big G, if you will."

Mason couldn't hold himself anymore and broke down as Dema placed her hand on Mason's forehead.

"It is all right; nobody is watching or judging you. I am here."

"Do you want to know what the most terrifying thing was I ever saw during the Assault on the Control Room?"

"That final operation that ended the War? I was one of the radio operators. You heard me or even called me. I was the Control, Overwatch, Base no.56. Sorry, I am all ears."

"First of all, I don't know how a Coast Guard ends up fighting on the frontline, but I did. When I entered the trench, I encountered a field hospital, where I found probably fifty or more heavily wounded NWO soldiers begging me to end their lives. Covered in blood mud, these men cried out for help, but there was no response. We had to press on and kill them. Laws of war? Gone in the wind the moment nuclear warheads landed on US soil." Mason looked over Dema's shoulder and then back at her.

"Look, it would be either you or them in the body bag." Dema knew that she had to switch gears. "Mason, let's talk about something else. Is there anything else?"

"T-34-57 mod.1942/3 aka our tank. I'm uncomfortable with it, but I'm not claustrophobic. I don't care how angled the plates are; it is loud, cramped, and feels like a welded coffin, just ready to bury us. Plus, Germans called a tank for simple people, and I'm not a simple man." Mason held his fist. "I am not a simple man!"

"You are not a simple man, Mason. Honestly, I do not think they were all present in the shop. Panzer Hydro supports a five-crew layout instead of four. If this T-34 brings us to victory, will it matter?"

"You are from Ukraine, right? Or somewhere from that region? From my limited knowledge of history and what I read about Eastern Europe on the Internet, tanks seem both oppressors and liberators to your people."

"I also have mixed feelings. So here, look at this." Dema handed Mason a folded photograph.

In the black-and-white picture, four young men laughed, and behind them, there was a T-34 tank with red and white markings, including the number 20.

"That looks like our tank! The long barrel, hexagonal turret! Who're these people?"

"Red Army tankers in the service of the Soviet Union in 1943. I have an old family album in my room, which I salvaged from my town's ashes." Dema looked away as she pointed at the man holding a vodka bottle. "According to my town's registry office, one of those four is my possible ancestor. So, it seems like I have tankery in my blood."

"So, how much do you know about the World War Two setting?"

"Not much; I gathered stories from memorials, which spread all over Eastern Europe, but what started it and how it ended, I have no idea, but it seems like Germans had a wild ride because some share a similar quote: For the fallen who fought against Nazi oppression. I connected a few dots. I don't know about this entire thing. I even saw a tank similar to ours."

"Dema, usually people who meet me for the first time aren't so friendly to me." Mason sat on his bed. "Thank you for listening to me."

"I barely talk with people, but you, Mason, you seem all right. I respect, even admire, that you are here for your brother. I am only here for myself."

———

As Mason and Dema talked, Van sat on the bed in his room, pulled out a picture of his girlfriend, Ember, and kissed it. *Damn, I really should get some sleep, but I am curious about this competition's setting before I close my eyes. I don't know anything about World War Two, but if it was the second one, what about the first one? I guess I'll learn tomorrow—it's time to call Ember.*

Van stood up and dialed Ember's number, but again, it went straight to voicemail. "This is Ember; I am unable to pick up your call. I will call you when I get a chance." Van shook his head and thought. *I will try again, but why won't she respond to me? I called her five times already, and she must have seen me on the TV!* Van took a deep breath and opened the door to the bathroom, but as he got to the toilet, the mirror reflection halted him. In the tired and worn-out reflection, Van couldn't believe this was him. When Van rolled up the sleeve of his uniform, the black-colored barcode appeared.

Do I really walk around like this? Looking like crap? Van, pull yourself together, win, and Ember will get her new arm, not that cheap prosthetic crap she has now, and then spend the rest for the repairs of the farm! You must win this, Van. Remember, do what Mason tells you, and we will make it to the finish line. Poor Mason, that leadership position will wear him down. Indirectly, I am happy that I am not the Commander. The burden! I should be more proactive, however, like Dema. She really stood her ground, but Mason kept it cool, almost rocksteady. His decisions can make or break us. He'll bring us home as victors in expensive cars or as losers in body bags.

———

TH had just finished the hundred one-arm push-ups and was about to do **développé** when he stopped halfway. *I should help Mason come up with the name for our tank. That is the least I can do.*

He sat at the table, pulled out the tablet, marked all notifications as read, and opened a notepad. He wrote tank names on the top, and soon, he wrote three pages of randomly generated characters. After that, TH pulled out a coin he found on the complex's ground and placed it on the table. *It has to be something that would strengthen and protect us, but what?*

TH leaned forward as his vision blurred, and he felt his right hand freeze momentarily. He touched the reboot button behind his right sound receiver for ten seconds, which should have reset the system by now, but nothing happened. Finally, on the third try, the notification All Systems Restored beeped. TH removed his shirt, opened his chest cavity, and touched the damaged battery cells. *Time is ticking for these batteries, and it is a matter of weeks before they give in. I was told that I had months to live, but now? It seems like this is my last crusade to prove that old hardware still has it. No spare parts, no oil change. Just because I am outdated, it doesn't mean I am worthless! I hope that I will see the victory, and if not, then it was a good run anyway. I have nothing to lose and everything to gain. If we win, I might be able to use my new connections to track down some spare parts.*

TH moved his head swiftly when he noticed something lurking in the shadow, but upon examination, a fly flew out, bashing its head against the window. TH nodded and opened the window, allowing the insect to vanish into the night. TH momentarily stared at the Great Falls city skyline, observing bright and flashy holographic advertisements flying around the buildings. *This is where we would go when we win—the city of TVG victors, built by the victors, for victors. I can see myself owning a penthouse on the top floor with a wardrobe of fine suits. But they might be after me! I will become paranoid, expecting someone to jump me for my wealth. Why is Corporate scared about sentient humanoids? The opportunities are endless. I guess I will find out sooner or later. Wow, this is the most I have ever thought of in my service life.*

———

As the morning of Wednesday arrived, a loud racket forced Van to jump from the bed. After he found North, Van touched the 0.50 cal ammo box and placed the picture of Ember and him inside. After a morning stretch and a quick shower, Van got dressed in his uniform and closed the door behind him. He leaned over the railing and noticed Mason sitting at the computer below while TH put the power tools back in their original places.

"What the hell is all that noise!" Van descended the stairs and noticed TH writing something on the barrel as Mason pressed the Enter as he played with the whirling power drill.

Upon hearing Van's voice almost drown in the noise, Mason placed the power drill next to him.

"Thank you! And what is TH doing?"

"Ask TH." Mason didn't look away from the screen as he said it, closing the window, from which a 3D model of the T-34 peeked out with its long barrel, surrounded by the walls of text.

"What are you doing, TH?" Van smiled as he approached the T-34.

"I'm naming our Tank. Mason, show him the others." As

TH said this, Mason grabbed the tablet and handed it to Van, who scrolled down the list.

"Hmm, oh! Damn," Van scrolled back up, "TVG is in rush, aren't they? We just got here!"

Commonwealth Platoon
*14. AC-4 17P (**Namarrkon**), 10. Centaur Mk.III (**Boudicca**), 20. Ram II late (**Peggy**)*
Power Platoon
*16. Panzer 4 G Hydrostat (**Oden**), 18 Chi-Nu-Kai (**Tomoe Gozen**), 22. M4A1 76W (**American Made**)*
All-American Platoon
*6.14TP (**Grom**), 26. P26/40 (**Da Vinci**), 28. T-34-57 mod.42/43 (**Missing, please fill ASAP**)*
Ragnarök Platoon
*12. Strv m/42 Delat Torn (**Carolus Rex**), 8. Nahuel DL D3 (**Gaucho**), 24 41M Turan III 75 (**Horthy**)*

"Who picked the name for our platoon?" Mason scratched the back of his head. "We haven't even met with everyone!"

"My guess is as good as yours. I believe that since this is the entertainment business, they need to get things to speed up. I like it, All-American." TH pointed at the Platoon name.

"These are some powerful names. What is Namarrkon?" Van touched the tablet screen, and the tank was rendered into view.

"Namarrkon is a god of lightning and storms hailing from Australia. He speaks with the thunder, so when the 76.2mm gun fires, it sounds like thunder," TH briefly explained, and Van nodded his head. "In this lineup, AC-4 has the largest gun."

"All right, so, TH, T-34-57 mod.42/43? What are the choices?"

"Good morning, all! So, what did I miss?" Dema yawned as she descended the stairs. "And what on earth was that racket!"

"TH is about to present top contenders for the name of

our tank. TH, thank you for being on top of things. I completely forgot about it." Mason tapped TH's left shoulder. "Let's hear it."

"After I finished brainstorming, I got two names. Crimson Fury and Crusading Angel."

Both Mason and Dema scratched the back of their heads simultaneously while Van walked around the tank with a loud "Hmm" escorting him around. Mason looked at the long barrel staring him down, and thought: *As much as I like Crimson Fury, the Crusading Angel is definitely better. It's like TH would know that this is my crusade as well.*

"I like Crusading Angel." Mason was first to report after a minute of silence, "Something about that name I like, but I'm not sure what."

"Same here." Dema looked at Mason, who gave her a short nod.

"I have nothing against it; it sounds perfect in my ears and has a good ring to it." Van looked at TH. "Crusading Angel. How did you decide on these two names?"

"I generated a thousand names, wrote down a hundred, and crossed out till I got to these two names. Then, a simple coin toss." As TH said this he flipped the coin and tossed it to Van, who held it against the glass roof with two fingers.

"Okay, wow. Can you also print Benjamins?" Van handed TH his coin back and vanished into the kitchen.

"Not yet." TH shook his head, prompting Mason to grin.

A moment later, a loud "Uhhh" sounded when he opened the door to the refrigerator, just as TH submitted the name.

"Hey, everything all right?" Mason shouted back. "What's happening?"

"No food or coffee. Cafeteria?" Van shut the door to the fridge and took a deep breath.

"Last time I checked, there is nothing else." Dema stood by the door, awaiting the rest of the crew.

"Dema, Dema." TH pulled out a tablet. "We just named our

tank. Shouldn't we take a picture?"

"Can we take a picture after we eat? I'm not yet presentable to the world!" Dema touched her hair.

Van rolled his eyes. "Sure."

"Let's do it quickly; I agree with Van." Mason's stomach growled.

Upon leaving the garage, Mason looked over his shoulder at the newly christened tank and smiled. *So, Crusading Angel. Protect us and lead us to victory!*

———

Gio and his crew already occupied a nearby table and waved when Mason and his band arrived. Sporting the same uniforms from yesterday, but without goggles or helmets, Mason could finally get a good look at them. However, as they approached them, Mason slowed down. *That must be Giovanni from my jail cell! I mean, that calm voice and striking eyes. It must be him!* After short introductions between the crews, Mason quickly made a mental note of their allies and momentarily measured Giovanni from head to toe.

Giovanni, the Commander; James, the Driver; Twins Adam, the Radio Operator; and Mark, the Loader. Now, where are the Gdansk people? Mason thought about it as he stood in line.

After filling their breakfast plates to the fullest, Mason watched two hydrogen golf cars hit each other, prompting the Spider to activate before the shock and unwanted memories of the car accident took over. Mason's long stare temporarily raised a few eyebrows.

"I must answer the call of nature. Be right back. But, James, keep an eye on the twins. And where the hell did they just go?" Giovanni looked at the two empty seats. "They were just here!"

"Should I go look for them?" James stood up, and Gio nodded, just as a lonely cloud covered the morning sun for a moment, providing a needed shadow from the hot Montana summer.

"Apologies again. We will be right back. Where the hell did they go? Do I need a leash?" Giovanni smiled, and Mason waved them off.

"Well then, now that they are gone, what was the most expensive purchase?" TH looked at Mason, who snapped out of the thousand-yard stare. "What were you buying?"

"Want to make a guess?" Mason shook his head.

"I don't know." Dema looked at her plate, filled with bacon and eggs. "Something related to the engine? And how did you even know what to buy?"

"No, an improved gunsight. Ten thousand credits for an upgrade. I opened the Tank Store App and found out that our tank has available upgrades, among which was improved gunsight, among other things."

"Ten thousand? Damn, inflation is real even in this closed system. What exactly was wrong with it?" Van leaned back. "How much do we have left? Did we even earn some money from yesterday?"

"Yes, with pictures, we racked up ten thousand credits, and after a few purchases, we are almost back where we started. Five thousand and spare change. If my math doesn't lie."

"What else did you buy?" Dema looked at the beans and momentarily played with her spoon.

"Tools, spare tracks, and a few other things." Mason rattled out the shopping list. "What was recommended to me by the shop."

"So, what is the problem with the old sight?" Van asked Mason. "Was there an option for a larger hatch?"

"Sadly, no option for a larger hatch. To answer your previous question, the new gun sight has a better zoom and clearer lines for tracking."

"What exactly is wrong with our tank?" Van shook his head. "It seems to be fine, well, apart from being cramped as hell."

"As I did some digging in the T-34 tank family database, we can consider ourselves lucky that we have this particular tank or, should I say, tank destroyer."

"Tank destroyer? What is the difference between a tank and a tank destroyer?" TH made a new file in his mind. "Aren't tanks supposed to destroy other tanks?"

"I'm learning as you are. So, where was I?" Mason tapped his thumbs, trying to remember where he had left off.

"That we were lucky to have this version. Please tell us, because so far, what you said convinces me that our Angel is terrible. We have a cramped interior and a smaller main gun than everyone else; I can barely see anything from my position." Dema joined Van.

"As these tanks were rushed to the frontline, the production process was simplified, which means that it should be easy to repair in the field if needed. 57mm is strong but lacks post-penetration. The cramped interior is one of the side effects of mass production and wasn't supposed to last very long. If the tank was destroyed, the crew would jump on board the next one," Mason continued talking, but Van raised his hand to stop him.

"Slow down. What the hell is post-penetration? And why wasn't it supposed to last very long? That is not good!"

"So why is the turret so cramped? Did you do some research on that as well?" TH folded his hands. "Is this also by design?"

"One by one, please! Post penetration is what a shell does to the tank once it penetrates its armor. As I said, these tanks were rushed and simplified, so there isn't much to them. To answer your question, TH, the reason why I said that we're lucky in having this tank is that the turret was so cramped on the early models. It was because they were originally designed to handle the 45mm gun. Due to the need to give these tanks a bigger gun, the caliber was raised to 76mm, which made the turret more cramped as the bigger breech took up space inside. A few new turrets were introduced to combat this problem, the most common being the hexagonal one, which we have, but ventilation is still not as good. However, our gun breech is much smaller and in the redesigned turret, giving us breathing room, with smaller ammunition taking up less storage space. The T-34-85 modification, which allowed the installation of the larger turret with a bigger gun, came with the fifth tanker, who took over the Gunner role, easing the stress of double duty."

Mason could see on his gasoline cowboys that they doubted the green beast parked in the garage. Van shook his head and slowly exhaled, while Dema's face vanished in her arms, mumbling something inaudible. TH tapped his forehead and looked at Mason with the look *Come on! We are waiting!* Dema was the first to speak after the long silence.

"All right, everyone, listen, listen! I can tell we are unhappy as we learn more about this machine. So, since you are Commander, tell us the pros and cons of Crusading Angel so we can learn how to work with it." Dema clapped her hands. "And also, where did you learn all of this?"

"I woke up a bit earlier and did some digging. Tank Shop has direct links to the Museum, so I began reading. As the Commander, I need to know what I'm getting myself into. All right, disadvantages first. A smaller caliber gun with a small post-penetration effect, bad turret visibility, and my double duty as commander/gunner will be a problem. Our interior is cramped, and we'll hear the engine more than ourselves. The tank itself wasn't meant to last long, and data shows that they accounted, on average, for around two hundred hours of service life or 150 miles, give or take. The large tubes inside the Angel are the suspension springs, which take up additional space, and I and TH are standing on top of the shell storage. Should I continue?" Mason felt his heartbeat increase.

I should have opened with the advantages first. Mason cursed between his teeth.

"Now tell us the advantages of our Angel compared to

other tanks." Dema smiled as she came to the rescue, brightening Mason's doom and gloom.

"Where to start? I think we're the only tank with strong sloped armor around the hull, including the back, which protects us and the engine compartment. We're very mobile and have one of the best off-road capabilities due to the large wheels, which act like a stabilizer, so I should be able to fire more accurately on the move. We can punch through most of the other tanks, and with smaller shells comes a faster reload rate. That's pretty much it." Mason leaned back in his chair and took a long sip from the water bottle.

"I think we can make this work. No, we will make it work! We can win this. Who is with me!" Dema raised her hand.

"I am," TH said.

"Now that I am looking at it, we have a fighting chance." Van hesitated at first, but then he raised his hand as well.

"It'll be an uphill battle, but we can win it." Mason smiled. "It'll be up to us to be the best!"

"So, what is a plan for now?" TH collected the plates and was about to leave when his right eye flashed red for a brief but noticeable moment.

Van looked at the lonely cloud slowly sailing across the empty blue sky as the sun rose, its bright light soon shining into Mason's face.

"I just remembered something that can help us. Apparently," Dema said faster than Mason, who was about to continue talking, "the Italian tank P, something slash 40, was influenced by our design, or so I read in the program. So that must account for something!"

"But they're with us!" TH tilted his head. "Right?"

"It's just something to know. I don't know how useful this knowledge is, but hey." Dema smiled and looked at Mason, giving her a thumbs up.

TH nodded. "Good observation, Dema!"

"Just doing my job. You said something first, but I jumped

in. Sorry," Dema said.

"No worries, I forgot what I wanted to ask." TH shook his head. "I think I got my answer."

Out of nowhere, the smooth voice of Benjamin Bell filled the cafeteria, and in a minute, on the large screen next to the cafeteria, his face appeared. The camera slowly zoomed out, and he clapped his hands a moment later.

"Still the same suit from yesterday," Dema commented. "Wouldn't it be more appropriate for him to have a uniform?"

"The entertainment is a business, "Mason slowly exhaled. "But I agree with Dema. He could at least have different colors than gray."

"Well, I don't think he has much of a choice. From my corporate work experience, everyone must be neat and uptight," TH said, shaking his head. "One misstep and they fly out of the window."

"Can they at least get a veteran to talk with us?" Van facepalmed as he realized the problem with his question. "That's right, they can't because they are all dead."

"It is a shame. I heard many interesting stories from that conflict," Dema said calmly.

TANKS AND TANKERS

Good morning, Gasoline Cowboys.

My name is Benjamin Bell, and today is Wednesday, June 9th, 2145.

I hope you enjoyed your Day Zero; I must say, shots were already fired. Before I tell you what you are doing today, I'll bring you some news so you don't feel that you are missing out. Our Tank Royale has already reached five hundred million viewers on the first day, and I am not surprised since there are some boring programs on TV right now.

Today, you'll be assigned a specific time slot when you visit the Tank Museum, where you'll learn how World War Two shaped the tanks you'll be fighting on. It will be only your platoon and the Curator for the personalized and private tour, but feel free to visit the Museum at any time. Commonwealth Platoon should report to the Tank Museum at 11:00 AM, which is in thirty minutes. Power Platoon will report at noon, Ragnarök Platoon will report at 15:00, and finally, All-American Platoon will report at 18:00.

While you're waiting, do something useful. Learn how to adjust the track tension. Take your war machine for a spin. Finish the simulation tutorial and go to the virtual battlefield. Don't forget to post your videos and pictures so you can earn money to buy things to survive. In two days, you'll participate in the first fully operational match against other players, so utilize the simulation training to the fullest. My name is Benjamin Bell, and this is Tank Royale.

Before I go, today is the Heavyweight Champions' final duel, so we will be switching immediately. The showdown is as expected between the

German King Tiger and IS-2 mod. 44. May the best crew win!

"That thing is massive! Look!" Dema said as the screen automatically changed to the live urban battle.

The camera slowly rose from the ground and focused on a massive tank that just rolled out from the ruins of the building and rising dust clouds, crushing everything in its path with its overlapping but not interleaved rubber-rimmed road-wheels, its engine howling at the viewers. The war machine with the long gun sticking out of the turret scraped its left side against the building as it hugged the wall. A tanker with binoculars scanned his surroundings from the commander's cupola, leaning onto the railing, and immediately shut the hatch behind him. Soon, the epic orchestral music began playing, sending shivers down Mason's spine.

"Indeed, it is! My eardrums are about to explode." Van's eyes fixated on the screen, and moments later a familiar voice cut through the loud engine.

"Don't get excited, Dema. You are looking at the seventy-five-ton German War machine called Tiger 2 or the King Tiger," Giovanni said as the tank stopped for a moment, "or for the people like me, Panzerkampfwagen Tiger Ausf. B."

"Can you tell us more?" Mason's voice drowned as the tank's engine roared again.

"How can you even stop that thing? This is what we are going up against? My Lord!" Van flinched when the King Tiger fired, and the camera followed the shell bouncing off the wall.

"Look how slow it is going, even on the asphalt road. It has an underpowered engine and transmission, which struggles to move it forward at the desired speed, and it can call quits any minute. Despite what I just said, King Tiger can still make a solid forty miles an hour, which is impressive for its weight. It's like seeing a linebacker sprinting. It wasn't meant to do it, but it has to." Giovanni smiled when Van laughed and gave him a thumbs up. "As with each tank, sides and rear are not as strongly armored, but it can still eat a lot of punishment. The tank definitely saw better days. Just look at those dents left after the bounced or non-pierced rounds."

"So, who are they facing?" Mason said as the camera quickly switched to the green tank, covered by the old iron beds.

"An IS-2. or JS-2 mod.44, however you feel like calling it." Then, without looking at the TV, Giovanni said, "This is the final round, and I wished Super Pershing would make it. Next time, I guess."

"Super Pershing? Like the one in the Tank Park?" Dema shouted, but to no avail, as the clanging sound of the bouncing round filled everyone's ears.

"What is the difference between the IS and JS?" TH created a new file in his mind and stored it in the Tank Royale folder.

Like King Tiger, the IS-2 held the T-shaped junction down, and one of the crew members controlled the heavy-caliber machine gun mounted on the tank's cupola, guarding the crossing.

It seemed like they lost sight of the King Tiger as the cloud of smoke appeared, and the Tiger was gone. *How could it disappear? Can they hear it?* Mason thought to himself as he watched IS-2 slowly reverse back from the junction.

"It all comes down to how you pronounce Joseph Stalin's name. If you say, Ioseb Stalin, it's IS. If Joseb, it's JS," James replied. "That was the clever usage of the smoke grenades. Applying pressure where they can."

As Giovanni continued explaining, the King Tiger turned right and entered the parallel street where he would turn right and find the surprise. Everyone in the cafeteria held their breaths as the King Tiger approached the junction, with its turret rotated and ready to fire. A few people gasped when Tiger 2 fired at the unsuspecting IS-2, whose barrel still faced forward, awaiting the King Tiger to appear from the smoke.

The Soviet tank exploded, creating a firework from the detonated ammo. Moments later, Benjamin Bell started talking, but Mason turned away from the screen as he did a sign of a cross. *They went out in a blaze of glory.*

"I think Tiger 2 was overkill and that Tiger 1 would be more fitting, but who am I to talk?" James reminded everyone of his presence.

"I agree with you, James." Gio gave him a thumbs up and then said between his teeth, "Godspeed, Alexander."

"Was this real or the simulation?" Dema looked around her, but the silence confirmed her fears.

Mason raised his eyebrows when Dema bent over and turned her head around, looking for a discrete place to dispose of her breakfast. She found nearby bathrooms, to which she immediately sprinted and shut the door behind her.

"Gotta have the iron stomach and nerves of steel." Giovanni looked at the bathrooms and sat down, followed by the rest of the cafeteria, as the commercials came on. "One mistake, and you're in the body bag. You saw it right there!"

"All right, I think all of us understood. Does the simulation allow you to link up with other teams?" Mason turned his chair towards Gio as his neck began to hurt.

"They do, once you pass the tutorial, which teaches you what to do in your position." Giovanni was about to leave when he halted himself. "What do you guys think of our Polish crew?"

Giovanni looked around him. "They haven't shown up, which worries me. Being down a tank isn't a good idea, especially against the Power Platoon."

"The truth is that they approached us, but I cannot say anything without solid evidence. We'll keep it in mind; thank you for telling us." Mason shook hands with Giovanni, who summoned his crew and left.

"So, what do we need to work on first?" TH turned towards his crew.

"Well, we'll need to know how to service our tank in the field, like repairing tracks and quick fixes all around. Simulations are in order, and we can take our Angel for the flight. In the evening, we shall see the Tank Museum." Dema finished planning the day.

"Or how about we do simulations now? We still have to finish the tutorial." Van raised his hand. "And then let's shoot at each other. In simulation, of course."

"That is a good point." Mason stood silent for a moment. "All right, everyone to the simulations!"

———

After leaving the field cafeteria, Mason let his crew get ahead of him and vanished into one of the tank parks; however, he ran into Giovanni, who folded his hands.

"Well, we meet again," Giovanni opened the conversation, emphasizing again, "I'm happy that you took the deal."

"It was either this or lithium mines in USAC. Did you get the same offer or something else due to your special status? And how on Earth do you know about these tanks?" Mason immediately pressed Gio against the metaphorical wall.

"One question at the time, Mason. I got the same offer as you, but with some twist. I'm to ensure that you and your crew know what to do in order to perform for the big screen. If we even get to that point in the first place."

Mason thought about what Gio had just said to him. He took a step back and tilted his head.

"So, is this a part of a larger plan?" After a moment of silence, Mason said, "Something I'm unaware of?"

"I was only told what I'm to do, but I don't know how or if I even would have a chance to do it. However, I will try. I believe you'll not disclose to anyone that we are both TVG prisoners. Let's just say that revealing this information won't help us." Giovanni extended his hand. "A lesson in return for discretion. Can I count on you?"

"Yes, you can." Mason immediately shook it. "So, what is the first lesson?"

"Finish the tutorial, and then we'll engage in a one-on-one combat session. Don't wander too long; there are many things to learn." Gio grinned ear to ear and walked away.

———

Mason blinked two times, but Gio was long gone. He scratched the back of his head as he thought. *Okay, Mason, this doesn't seem so bad after all. Let's not think about death yet.* His hands touched the screen, and Mason sat on the warm wooden bench, finding shadow underneath the platform from the afternoon sun. His eyes laid on the machine of war, listening to Agnes talking about it.

Carro Armato M Celere Sahariano, or Fiat M16/43, was a needed WW2 Italian Tank that never had a chance to arrive at the battlefield. From already scarce resources, TVG and Askarov contractors only know that it was designed to counter the British Crusader tanks in Northern Africa, hence the Sahariano or Saharan, named after a rather unforgiving largest desert in the world. We are still searching Italy for more data, so stay tuned.

Damn, she is indeed everywhere! Mason looked around him. *Is she listening to me right now?*

Mason stared at the tank momentarily, then snapped himself out of the stare. Immediately, he silently whispered a prayer, but then his mind turned 180 and stopped at the issue at hand.

How was I so naïve? I saw it right there! Kaboom! One mistake and nobody will hear from us ever again. How can I win this? Pull yourself together; Ail and the world are watching!

"Everything all right? Are you also trying to process how wide this Sahariano is?" a male voice brought Mason back to reality.

"No, I just wondered if this idea was a good call." Mason looked up and found a man attempting to initiate a conversation. "Yes, it is wide. I wonder why?"

"They call me Harper, a fellow brother in arms." the young man tipped off his hat, and Mason noticed a number 14 on his uniform. "Respect, brother! Volunteer to fight for millions to see! I mean, wow!"

"Mason. Are you from Australia? Your accent." Mason invited Harper to sit down, and he accepted the offer.

"Oy am frawm Sydney, mate, not like the rest of my crew," Harper cranked his accent to eleven.

"Excuse me?"

"I am from Sydney, my friend. Tell me, what brings you here?"

"Oh, the thrill of the adventure, I guess, which I'm definitely not regretting right now." Mason bitterly smiled, concealing the reality. "My brother and my aunt depend on me in every sense of the word. So, what brings you here?"

"This place feels so stiff, like all these people are just robots with human skin on them. Or androids? Something like that. Pardon my rambling, Mason. You know, prospects of glory, a better life. I am from the middle of nowhere or, as you know it, the Outback. Yet, the American Dream endures."

"I guess you're right. Unfortunately, there aren't many ways to climb the social ladder nowadays." Mason looked at the tank and then back at Harper. "And I could never imagine that I would go down this path."

"I'll shoot straight with you, Mason, as you seem to be a gentleman. I am a prisoner." Harper rolled up his sleeve, and Mason noticed the black lines on Harper's left forearm. "I spoke up and got arrested, those cunts. As my ancestors were shipped to Australia, I was sent to the UK. There, I got an offer I couldn't refuse, and, well, I ended up here. Anyway, I need to get going; the Namarrkon will require a blood sacrifice to win."

"Wow, I'm lost for words." Mason scratched the back of his head. "How can you be so open about it?"

"I have nothing to lose. The man with nothing to lose is

your most dangerous opponent. He can only gain. I have to get going, mate. Good luck." Harper smiled, tipped his brown hat, and left Mason to his thoughts.

———

In the garage of Team #26, Gio was about to climb into the P26/40 when James joined him. Shortest of the crew, but with the biggest smile on his face, James folded his hands.

"Gio, do you think we have a chance to win?" James coughed, attracting Gio's attention.

"Of course we do, James. While it didn't work out last time, this is our shot for glory." Gio gave James a hand, and a moment later they sat on the turret, with Gio leaning against the roof-mounted machine gun.

"Gio, listen. I drove under your command ever since we first met. Trials, Exhibition Match, private showcases. However, I feel that this is different." James looked at the goosebumps on his hands. "My thoughts are all over the place. I am still replaying the kill shot from the TV. There is no way that Alexander made it. This is it, the real deal!"

"He is in the hospital right now, but that is all I could gather. But, James, we have the upper hand. We know what to do, while most crews don't. Well, it's us and the House. Our friends who we have to kill now to make it to the finish line."

"Klemens and his German Americans do, and so do Zanai and his token crew. But, poor man, he got shafted by the TVG the hardest," James said and slowly exhaled while Gio looked at his barcode. "They jacked prices for us, but not for them. I saw it in the shop. I bought a field cap to test my theory. Their cap costs five dollars rounded up to the nearest dollar. Mine was twenty dollars. I don't even want to imagine what else TVG will do to us."

"So what? We're not going to give them that satisfaction. Yes, they control the prices, but not live ammunition and where we point it." Gio also rolled up his sleeve. "A reminder, huh?"

"A reminder that this once would be considered a crime against humanity. But I guess this is the way forward. Gio, I'm confident that Mason and his squad will hold their ground, but our Polish allies, I am not so sure." James shook his head. "We're way behind."

"Because that is what they want from me, and I'm not giving them an inch. They want me to kill, sure, I will, but that's it." Gio watched the twins emerge from their rooms. "Did you know that by the Italian classification, this is a heavy tank, but for everyone else, it is a medium?"

"I didn't know that; thank you for telling me. Although I have to say, our Da Vinci looks like a T-34 for some reason." James pulled out his tablet, and two models rendered into the view. "Sloped armor all around, cramped interior, to name a few things."

"So what, James? TVG gave us lemons, and we will weaponize them." Gio stood up as the twins approached. "All of you are safe in my hands. I'll promise to bring you all home."

"I wish I could share your confidence, but I just don't know. I feel that the game is rigged from the start." James climbed down the tank's side.

"It might be, but if I hit first, we can win, right?" Although Gio smiled again, his sure voice slowly faded. "The game is always rigged; live shots aren't. I'll ask Mason if they have finished the tutorial yet. I need to blow something up."

"Likewise." James grinned from ear to ear. "Likewise. How about we blow them up?"

"Dema, where did you put that track pin?" Van stood up, looking for the long black pin, which would keep the five hundred millimeters wide track together, but Dema only shrugged her shoulders.

After Van and Dema completed the half-hour external repairs section, Mason and TH sat in the simulation room, firing and repairing away. Sometimes, a curse or a shout of joy and excitement echoed into the main garage.

"Look under your boot; you are standing on it!" Dema pointed, and Van exhaled when he picked up the track pin.

"I am blind." Van laughed, reached out for the hammer, and hammered the pin back into its place.

After a loud cranking sound and a few curse words, Van watched the idler wheel move to the correct position, but with a corner of his left eye, he caught Dema leaning against the tank, taking deep breaths.

"How are you feeling?" Van carefully approached her, gently smiling. "The match, right?"

"When I saw the ads, I thought this would be a simulation, and I believed that until that JS, IS whatever the name of that green tank is, blew up sky high. For a frame, I saw a dead body flying out of the hatch."

"Dema, my partner in crime, Mason will make sure that we'll come home in a limousine and not a body bag." Van looked at the long barrel above their heads. "While I'm still not comfortable with this Angel, I can see our shot at the glory. My father used to say even the worst tool is useful for something or someone, for that matter. Thanks, Dad!"

"Well, the good thing is that we only have to fight one battle, right?" Dema sat down on the spare roadwheel. "But I feel that I won't get to know everyone."

"Let them go face down if they must die; it will make it easier to say goodbye, Dema. I hoped you would know that since you are the one from the Dark Zone."

"This took a dark turn, Van. What the hell?" Dema felt her heartbeat increase. "What type of world outlook is that?"

"I was conditioned like this: You don't have to make an emotional connection with everyone you meet, only those who matter. If you don't have an emotional relationship with something or someone and something happens, it will not hurt you, and you won't care. However, if you know them or it, it will break you, which is why you let them go face down," Van said to Dema like a veteran soldier to the rookie who just got drafted. "Dema, you know this, and so do I."

"I didn't want to say it out loud." Dema shook her head. "Thank you for the words of encouragement. It could have been a lot worse, I guess."

"So, will we hit the firing range and obstacle track?" Mason climbed on board and opened the hatch, followed by TH, who gently closed the door to the simulation room.

"Fresh out of the tutorial, let us dive into the real combat. What could possibly go wrong?" Van attempted to climb inside the tank via the driver's hatch, but after a loud curse and pounding of the frontal plate, he asked Mason to wait.

"Also, my people, Gio and his crew have challenged us to a 1v1 duel later. Let's smoke them!"

"Hell yeah, brother!" Van shouted. "We'll kick their asses! Wait, they are our allies, right?"

"I agree!" Dema's voice echoed in the tank while TH tapped the back of his head.

"They seem to know what they are doing. But yeah!" TH looked at Mason, who gave him a thumbs up.

Moments later, exhaust smoke filled the garage as T-34 backed out and turned left towards the firing range but came to an abrupt halt.

"Van! What's happening?!" Mason shouted into the microphone, adjusting his seat in the process.

"I missed the gear change. Sorry!" Van's slow exhale filled everyone's headphones. "Sorry!"

A moment later, Van steered the tank to avoid the bench and continued onward toward the designated zone, marked by a road sign.

Each Platoon had an obstacle course and firing range right in their backyard. As Van pulled into the box, a transparent wall blocked the crew, and Agnes's voice filled the air.

Welcome to the firing range. TVG Rule #256: Contestants are not permitted to store live ammunition in their garages to prevent detonations or fights reserved for the arena. Please do not attempt to fire at the wall. If you run out, ask for more. You will be given ammunition in just a moment, but note this. The combat conditions will heavily influence your reload speed and aiming capabilities, so do not use clocked times in this range in the fight. Now, you are presented with several armor plates varying in size, thickness, and angle at varied distances. This is to show you how your round will behave in the real world. Now, fire away!

Two drones dropped three ammo boxes into a box, prompting Mason and TH to jump out. Outside of the firing range, several onlookers observed the tankers either with binoculars or large tablet screens. TH gave them a thumbs up, which was rewarded with applause and several flashes.

Well, we are the entertainers. Let's entertain them! Mason looked at the crowd before he climbed back in.

He also gave them a thumbs up and then looked at TH.

"So, what a gorgeous morning to send some rounds down the range!" TH grabbed the first box and opened it.

Three shells greeted him, each with a different colored ring around them.

"TH load up!" Mason closed his hatch behind him, and as he sat, his foot found the foot trigger.

You have just finished the tutorial. Let's get cracking! Mason thought as he pressed his face against the gunsight, and his hands rested on the two drive-fly wheels for horizontal and vertical turret drive.

"Yes, Commander! One armor-piercing shell ready to fire!" TH rammed the shell into the breech.

Mason took a deep breath and looked through the sight, his hands cranking the flywheels, aiming the long cannon at the closest plate.

"Away!" Mason shouted, and TH observed the breech recoil right before his eyes. "Next target!"

"Up!" in three seconds, TH shouted, kicking the ejected shell to the side.

Okay, the further one. Mason adjusted the sight's position and fired. For a second, he observed the shell hit the dirt in front of the steel plate.

"What? I aimed right at the target!" Mason launched from the hatch and stared down the range. "What did I do wrong?!"

While you had aimed at the target, you forgot to account for the range, thus missing the shot. Next time, try to aim the crosshair slightly above the designated target.

"Oh! That makes sense!" As Agnes explained, Mason tapped his thumb against his chin. "Yeah, that makes sense! TH! Load it!"

"Up and ready to go!" the response came seconds later.

Following the advice, Mason adjusted the sight, aiming slightly above the target.

"Away!" Mason pressed the foot trigger and observed the shell hit the plate center mass.

"Nice hit!" Dema shouted. "Again!"

As an hour flew by, Van was ready to hit the first gear when another tank parked in the nearby box, and a moment later, the tank opened fire.

An American Flag hung from the tank's turret, but Mason noticed Pre-War Americana waving in the wind upon closer examination. The long barrel with a muzzle brake swung right, and soon the crew members jumped out and began loading the tank with the provided ammo.

"Hey! Why do they get more ammo per box than we do?" TH zoomed in on one of the boxes, "Are you guys seeing this?"

"What?" Mason sat beside TH and raised his eyebrow when he noticed what TH pointed at.

"Maybe we forgot to buy that perk at the store?" Dema scratched her head. "But it is weird indeed!"

"My friends, there is something fishy going on. Remember

our encounter with that aggressive crew in the Tank Shop?"

"Yeah. What about it?" Mason turned towards Van. "Please explain."

"You see, when the situation was about to blow up, we got swarmed by the security, right? We all remember that. However, they only aimed their stun guns at us, not them. Now, correct me if I'm wrong, but wouldn't they aim at both sides?"

Mason was the first to break the three-minute silence as the rest of the crew still processed what Van said.

"Now that you mention it, they only aimed their guns at us!"

"Damn! So, what can we do about it?" Dema said. "Do you think there are more of these occurrences we missed?"

"August, do you have a moment?" Zasada waved at August, whose head had just appeared from the 14TP.

Compared to other medium tanks, 14TP seemed to be a strange oddity. Nevertheless, the closest tank could compare the Centaur and T-34, as they shared the large roadwheels set up.

"For you, my friend, I always do. What is the matter?"

"Prices went up again." Zasada tapped the screen. "The price of our machine gun went from five hundred to a thousand out of the blue!"

"What?!" August joined Zasada and tapped the computer screen. "Why? Maybe it's a glitch or something. I'll call support."

Five minutes later, as August hung up, his mood didn't improve. August tossed his tablet next to the computer and sank into the plastic monobloc chair.

"So, what is it?" Zasada tapped his thumbs. "Well?"

"It's not a glitch. These are the new prices,"

"It feels like this is stacked against us. I bet you that the Power Platoon has their prices discounted! Mark my words; they want us to fail!"

"That might be the case; however, even if this was rigged, they cannot have all the tanks to lose at once because then there won't be any show to watch. They learned from the Interwar Exhibition Match."

"So, we are the black sheep?"

"Not at all. Do you know what puzzles me, however? Why are the United States, Germany, and Japan on the same team? This is not a Cold War theme. And why are we with Italians and Soviets? Only Commonwealth Platoon makes sense as Canada, Britain, and Australia are together. Apparently, no New Zealand." August looked at Zasada. "I'm going crazy or what?"

"You know..." The siren noises from outside drowned Zasada's chances of answering.

Moments later, heavily armored guards stormed the garage, guns raised.

"Please, do not resist. Internal Control wants to talk." The officer redirected his men, and August and his crew were dragged into unmarked cars and driven away.

"What just happened? Hey!" Gio shouted at the leaving unmarked vans, turning towards his stunned teammates. "What the hell? Everyone! We have a problem!"

A moment later, Gio's team rushed inside, but they only found the 14TP and a black bulldog barking in the morning sun

"Hey buddy, come here." Gio kneeled, and a moment later, the black bulldog lay next to him. "What happened here?"

Gio petted him, and the dog barked again.

"Well, Sharik," Gio read the name on the collar. "James, how we look?"

"All their stuff is here, but I don't get it," James shouted from upstairs.

"Wow." Gio stood up and stretched his neck. "Where are Mason and his band of merry tankers?"

"They went to shooting range but should be back any

moment. So, what do we do?" James sat next to Sharik. "How are you doing?"

"The best thing we can do now is to wait for Mason and then see where the new road will take us. Where are the twins?" Gio looked around the garage again. "I just woke up!"

"Didn't we all? Did you see prices this morning?" James cracked his knuckles. "They went up across the board."

"Well, well, well. Inflation, I guess?"

———

"Good late morning." TH entered Gio's garage forty minutes later, followed by the rest of Team #28. "Did you guys meet our new friends yet? We were about to head there and properly introduce ourselves. We should do that simulation together! Let's not single them out."

"Don't even bother." Gio watched TH look around the garage. "They were taken away in unmarked vans. So, you guys didn't hear the siren?"

"Well, we were looking at the TOG II." Dema stopped laughing halfway, and even Mason began paying attention. "What a wiener. So, what do we do now?"

"I don't know," Gio shrugged his shoulders, "simulations, I guess?"

"Did you check everywhere?" Mason sat down on the chair, holding his head. "This is terrible!"

"I still cannot believe this!" Van stepped aside and howled at the sky. "One crew down. We're so screwed! Can we even win this!?"

"If we put our mind into it, we can," James climbed down from the tank, "and we'll win. I know one thing for sure, and that is that we are not losing."

"I appreciate your enthusiasm, James, but math won't let go. Our firepower and any other tactical advantage had been cut by 1/3. We are outnumbered and outgunned." TH looked at James, and Dema bit her tongue.

"Come on, vacuum cleaner, trying to suck up the little positives we have left here! I'm trying to keep the faith." James folded his hands. "Have faith, machine! Don't be a buzzkill! That's the last thing we need in this doom and gloom. We have been kicked in the stomach, but we can still stand up and win!"

"Don't you call me a vacuum cleaner!" TH grabbed James by the collar and pressed him against the wall. "Don't you ever call me that! Did I call you a meat shield? No, you son of the monkey, as I don't see a difference between you and that animal in the zoo!"

It took a moment for everyone to process what had just happened, but luckily Mason was the first to act.

"All right, break it up, both of you." Mason stepped into the middle. "TH! Let go!"

"James, apologize!" Gio said in a calm but commanding voice. "We cannot afford to have a division now!"

"Apologies for calling you a vacuum cleaner. I'm just trying to survive! I have a life outside of these games!" James attempted to push TH away, but to no avail as the grip tightened. "A little morale boost can go a long way!"

"Apologies accepted. Likewise, I'm sorry for calling you an animal." TH released James, who shook his head.

"Peace?" James extended his hand, and TH shook.

"Peace."

"I agree with James. Yes, we have a setback, but we can work with it. Did someone say simulations?" Van was already at the door. "See you soon."

———

"Agnes, we would like to 1v1 our allies." Mason waited for everyone else to put on their gear before summoning the always-listening AI.

"Commander Knight, Team 26 is ready to go. Commander Smith has decided to have you pick the arena. In front of you, you should see the selection...."

As Agnes spoke, Mason swiped left and right, up and down across different battlefields, trying to make up his mind. Ranging from vast deserts to tightly packed urban streets, Mason blinked three times before closing his eyes and randomly selecting the arena.

"Excellent choice. A bombed city with many openings to ambush your opponent. There will be three rounds played. The winner gets twenty-five thousand dollars to their budget. Good luck!" Agnes said, and in three seconds, Mason found himself staring through the gunsight as the large white numbers counted down from 5.

"All right then! Let's wallop them!" Mason said as the Crusading Angel rolled out of the spawn zone.

"Van, keep it steady. Dema, get ready. TH, load AP." Mason showed TH his left palm.

The round sat in the breech in two seconds, ready to go. Mason continued scanning his surroundings as the Angel slowed down. Mason checked the ruins around him, but Gio and his tank were nowhere in sight. A minute later, just as the Crusading Angel entered the crossroads, Mason's screen turned black, and an explosion echoed in everyone's headphones. Then, on the black screen, a singular sentence appeared. *Don't forget to use vision slits on your commander's cupola.*

"What just happened?" Dema's voice cracked in Mason's headphones.

"We died," Van replied just as the screen showed the scoreboard. "They ambushed us!"

"Where were they?" TH said, and Mason slowly exhaled.

That was fast! What the hell! Okay, Mason, pull yourself together. Two can play that game. Mason grunted.

"Round two! Good luck," Agnes said as the arena rendered the Crusading Angel back into the spawn point.

Born in factories, delivered by engineers, immune to the bullets of the regular soldier, the tank, the future of warfare. An old female voice greeted Mason and his crew as they entered the lobby four hours later, and already the first tank had jumped on them. Long tracks were situated all around its hexagonal hull, and it seemed to have a low center of gravity, but Mason had no idea why. Behind the steel beast, a few similar tanks appeared, each with different weapons. Light in the building was toned down, giving it a factory look. Mason looked at the clock on the wall, showing exactly 18:00. Then, he looked over his shoulder, expecting Gio and his crew to walk through the door, but the only thing he could see was a lazy fly crawling on the spotless glass door.

Woa! Woa! What are these!? Who made this? Mason thought as he read the sign. Mark I Male.

Suddenly, a door on the front tank opened, and a man walked out. Blue eyes and a long white beard of wisdom measured the contestants. A loud cough and the smell of alcohol escorted him.

"Welcome to the Tank Museum, All-Americans. My name is William Black, and I am the Curator of this Museum." William coughed and took the lead, and a moment later, he stopped by the statue of the general holding a French Flag.

"Where is Gio's crew?" TH looked around him. "They should have been here!"

"Well, we don't have time for that. TVG is changing the schedule," William replied. "We don't have much time?"

"Who is this man anyway?" While looking at the main entrance, Dema raised the second question and pointed at the statue.

"This is Jean Baptiste Eugene Estienne or the Father of the French Tank Force. Mostly forgotten by the history books." William took a deep breath and in almost perfect french, he rattled out, "Messieurs, la victoire appartiendra dans cette guerre à celui des deux belligérants qui parviendra le premier à placer un canon de 75 sur une voiture capable de se mouvoir en tout terrain. Or in English: Gentlemen, the victory in this war will belong to which of the two belligerents will be the first to place a gun of 75 on a vehicle able to be driven on all-terrain,"

"What does that mean?" Mason looked at TH and then back at the curator.

"While the British are first to build the tank and engage with Imperial German forces at Villers-Bretonneux, the first tank on tank engagement in the world during World War One, it was this gentleman who realized that if the vehicle or tank were to mount the 75mm field gun, that side would truly win the war as he foresaw the future technological advancements. This kickstarted an arms race that continues today." William clapped his hands and waited for the crew to enter the second hallway.

Unlike the first part of World War One, these hallways were filled to the brim with all kinds of tracked vehicles, ranging from tanks to tank destroyers. Several cannons sat on the display in the corner where William headed, menacingly aiming at the visitors. There again, Dema caught Mason staring into the distance, but only briefly.

"Now, listen, since this will be important for you to understand. Why 75mm cannon? Does anyone want to make a guess?"

"The most powerful? I really don't know." Van raised his hand, and after a moment of awkward silence, William continued.

"Well, tanks are meant to support infantry, so mounting a field cannon on the tracked chassis proved rather challenging; plus, every nation had a different idea of what the tank should do. To put a gun on a tank, you need to customize it. We are now getting into the muddy waters, but from my right, you have a wide range of calibers." William stepped aside, revealing a row of different cannons mounted either on wheels or suspended from the ceiling by steel cables.

"But why 75mm? And how come our tank has 57mm?" TH created another file in his CPU.

"Seventy-five is a healthy balance between a fire rate and damage. Anything higher and your cannon will shoot slower with lower velocity due to the weight of a shell. Going the other way will fire faster, but the damage won't be as significant. I have greatly simplified the decades of tank development. It's called living with trade-offs," the more welcoming voice of William had changed to an annoying tone.

——

"Why didn't we go? There was so much to learn." James stopped Gio, who was about to put on the black goggles and lose himself in the simulation again.

"Because there was nothing for us to see, and Curator won't tell us where to shoot the Centaur or the Sherman. Simulations are our best bet. The only thing he would say to us would be a logline, which TVG created for us." Gio took a deep breath before he unlocked his tablet.

This medium-sized-heavy Italian hitter is a serious contender and threat to any opponent trying to cross its sights. Named after the famous Italian polymath Leonardo Da Vinci, will this tank shine in all areas like the renowned inventor?

"When did you get to name our tank?" James nodded. "I mean, Da Vince, Vinci is the last name I would think of, but hey."

"The answer is simple. I didn't. They carried over the name from the Interwar Exhibition match." Gio waited for everyone to be seated and then scrolled down into the Recording section and found his feed.

Moments later, all six pairs of present eyes were glued to

the TV as Giovanni explained everything.

"They gave my crew a 38T and told us to figure it out, since we would fight for real in three days. I assumed command and learned everything on the fly. Driving, gunnery, spare parts, everything was terrible. We didn't have the simulations yet, so training wore out my tank and crew, for that matter, and when the big fight arrived, we ended up second and somehow alive." Gio took a sip of water.

"So, why are you concealing the fact that you did this before? This gives us the upper hand!" Mark shouted. "You've already done this! We can win!"

"Because I'm not the only one who has done this before. Klemens, commander of the German team, and Zanai, leader of the American crew, are just two who we need to worry about. To add a cherry to the sweet cake of my misery, I'm marked!" Gio rolled up his sleeve, and his crew gasped in terror at the black barcode. "I might as well be homeless. I have no access to public transport or the Internet; nothing is available to me. So, this Tank Royale is my only chance. If I win, I get my freedom back. And I'm worried that I'll have to kill Mason and his crew to get there."

"You think you are the only one with a barcode on his forearm?" Adam also rolled up his sleeve. "Aren't we all political prisoners here?"

"We are," Mark, one of the twins, also revealed a barcode, "that is what Adam and I get for speaking up, and I'm confident that August and his band are due for their trial."

"Why didn't you say that before?" James turned towards Adam.

"Why didn't you, James? Why didn't you, Gio? Same reason as you." Mark threw his hat into the ring. "Who would?"

"So, you think that Mason and his band are also marked?" James turned towards Gio, who took a deep breath.

"A ninety percent chance that they are marked, but what would humanoid be doing there?" Gio scratched the back of his head. "Maybe Van seems to be one who volunteered. He is so happy to be here."

As the clock hit 23:45, Dema rolled on her bed thrice, trying to fall asleep. She tried again and gave up. The Curator seemed familiar, but then his face made Dema hide her head underneath the pillow, attempting to conceal the tears. *What was his constant mumbling about? WFV or FVW? VFW?*

As she sat on her bed, Dema couldn't close her eyes. She put on her uniform, closed the door, and slowly exhaled. Moments later, she descended the stairs and grabbed a water bottle from the kitchen. She looked around the garage and found open doors to the simulation room.

Before entering her cubicle, Dema leaned against the wall and thought: *It's so real out there. One shot will send us to kingdom come. What madness is this? How can we, as humans, enjoy a blood spectacle? Wasn't the War enough?*

When Dema put on her goggles, her eyes closed momentarily, and she waited for the tune to pass.

Oh, Dema. What brings you here this early in the morning? I would advise you to get some sleep. Agnes's soothing voice whispered in Dema's ears.

"I just can't fall asleep. Can we go over my position one more time?"

Sure, no problem. You selected the co-driver and radio/machine gun operator. As a co-driver, you will be helping Van and be the first *to replace someone if one of your crewmates perishes. You will read maps and communicate with your squad and team via the radio to your right. Below you, there is an escape hatch. For your information, Commander Knight logged in an hour ago.*

Dema looked around her position. There were two radios on the shelf to her right—one for internal communication and a radio for communication with the platoon. In front of her, she had a machine gun and storage for the magazines. She found Van's projection to her left, but he didn't look at her. Then, her feet hit a collision box on the ring that opened the escape hatch.

"I wanted to ask, why is this tank so cramped?" Dema adjusted her goggles.

Didn't you learn that in the Tank Museum? That was the reason for your visit, right?

"Let's say that each of us got a different experience. I wonder, will we fight against some of the tanks in the museum?"

The answer to your question is yes. There is a high chance of encountering several machines you see in the Museum and Tank Parks.

To answer your previous question. There are a few factors to consider, but you trade comfort for protection with the angled plates, which take up internal space, and if you look to your right, you can see these tubes. These tubes are part of the tank's suspension. Soviets had to outproduce the invading Germans, so decisions were made which affected the production of the tank. For example, there was no radio; only command tanks had one. Fear not; this tank was equipped with an internal communications system and a radio for external needs. It seems so simple, doesn't it?

"You are right. It is simple, but I don't mind." Dema looked through the sight. "Was there an attempt to correct the cramped space problem?"

Yes, there was. Five hulls and two completed prototypes of the T-34M were built, but it was discontinued due to the mentioned invasion. In front of you, you have a DT 7.62mm machine gun. While here, you will be fighting tanks and...

"Yes?" Dema shook her head just as Agnes cut out for a moment.

The machine gun will be useless, but you can harass the enemy, forcing the enemy to stay in the tank and not repair it. If anything happens, as I said, you are next to take the driver's position if Van is knocked out or TH, the loader's position. Do you want to proceed with the extra training?

"No, I do not wish to proceed with extra training." Dema shook her head.

Dema, I would highly advise you to do so. Are you sure?

"I am one hundred percent sure."

In that case, you have already completed your simulation training at one hundred percent, earning your team a thousand credits. Do you have any additional questions for me? If you require extra help with something, please don't hesitate to go to the museum website and learn more.

"I do actually have a question. Why are we the only mixed team?"

Unfortunately, I don't have an answer to that question, Dema, nor can I tell you why that is. I wasn't programmed to make up answers.

"Are you sure you cannot tell me?"

Unfortunately, I don't have an answer to that question, Dema, nor can I tell you why that is. I wasn't programmed to make up answers.

"Thank you. Can you link me to Mason's simulation? Please and thank you." Dema shook her head, seeing that Agnes wouldn't budge, and thought to herself: *Why can't they just tell us? Why?*

As Dema's simulation vanished after a tune and was transferred, she observed Mason punch the gun breech three times.

Everything all right, Commander Mason?

"I can't remember the shell signals. So, if I show fist, that means TH must load High Explosive, right?" Mason rolled his eyes and punched the breech again. "Or is it a first?"

An open hand means a High Explosive round. A fist means an Armor Piercing round. You show TH your fist two times; he will have to load Armor Piercing Composite Rigid round. If the armor's angle is too big or the armor is too thick, you use this round to pierce it. Keep practicing, and if you need my help, say my name. If you remember that, you will complete the tutorial and earn your team a thousand credits.

Mason closed his eyes briefly, but he noticed Dema standing on the other side of the breech when he looked to his right.

"You need to get some sleep. That stare of yours in the museum worries me." Dema tapped Mason's projection on its right shoulder.

"I'm fine; I have to be Dema, but thank you for caring." Mason smiled, but his rendered face hid the pain.

"If you have medications, take them," Dema said. "It helped me."

"I think that the medicine is the problem, Dema. I'll be fine." Mason took a deep breath. "It's not helping me, only poisoning me. On top of that, I feel like an addict who needs his fix constantly. I don't want to be..."

"Is there anything I can do?"

"If I were to burst with anger, just bear with me. I'll never mean to yell at you. Or Van and TH. Can I count on you?"

"Absolutely! Or as we say, loud and clear!"

"Can you help me with these shells? I'm trying to remember the hand signals, but I keep losing it. Please?"

"Let me find you another one." Dema grabbed a new one from the crate under her feet.

"If it is a high explosive, what is the hand signal? I believe in you. You got this. Think about it now, so you don't have to later."

"Open palm!" Mason did the required signal, and his projection smiled. "Open palm!"

"Are you sure?!"

"Yes! Wait! Yes, I'm sure! Open palm!"

"Good job, dear." Dema smiled. "Now imagine that the radio is out, or I become deaf. You fire at the tank and realize you haven't penetrated the armor. What is the hand signal?"

"A fist! I think that I'm ready to finish this!" Mason turned around and looked through the gunsight. "Agnes, I am ready to continue! Thank you, Dema!"

"You would do the same for me, Mason. When you finish, get some sleep, so tomorrow we can function at a hundred percent. All eyes are on us, and we need that reputation!"

"Will do!"

CHAPTER SEVEN

TALKS OF MANY

Thursday morning slowly arrived, and the entire complex was already blistering with action. Again, Mason was first downstairs, but Dema sat by his side this time. Van peeked from his room and looked at the two sitting there, waiting for him and TH.

Damn, they look good together. Speaking of together, why isn't Ember answering my calls?! This is slowly pushing it. Van grabbed his tablet and redialed the number for the fourth time in the morning. Again, he got directed to the voicemail. After, for the fifth time, he decided to leave a message.

"Ember, listen. What is happening? Why aren't you answering my calls? You can see me on TV, and I know you are watching me. Come on! I want to hear your voice! Please!"

Van hung up the call and joined the trio downstairs just as Benjamin appeared on the screen, grinning from ear to ear.

Good morning, Gasoline Cowboys.

Today is Thursday, June 10th. Before I say what you are doing today, I have news to report, as promised, to keep you in the loop. After five years of traveling, humans and an android will land on Pluto, thus completing the challenge set out by United States CEO Kevin Hamilton. Human/ Android kind has officially landed on each planet in our Solar System. Where will we set out next? A new space station no.58, collaborating with Orion Luxury Hotels, has just begun orbital construction. Now, there have been a few changes to our Royale, so everyone listen carefully.

A Chaos mode has been added to the simulation, where only the strongest will survive. A hundred thousand dollars will be added to the final pool. The choice is yours. Also, we will pop in for an unscheduled interview today, asking you questions provided to us by the viewers, allowing you to get additional exposure!

Tomorrow, Friday, instead of Saturday at 16:45, your newly acquired skills will be tested in the simulation, where there can be only one winner. But, no pressure, the entire world will be watching. Get ready for a spectacle that will surely be remembered for generations to come! Steel on steel, blood and oil, everything ensures that your names will either echo into eternity or be lost in the mundane.

A screen momentarily flashed with a Stand-By title, and Benjamin appeared again, resuming his announcement as if nothing had happened.

My name is Benjamin Bell, and this is Tank Royale of 2145, brought to you by TVG and Orion Entertainment Systems.

"You heard the man, people. This is it!" Mason said to his team as they finished breakfast in the garage lounge.

"And after that is done, we're going home, my friends!" Van whistled. "While I definitely love the energy that we have going on here, nothing beats my home. Of course, all of you are invited to crash for a few days so we can collectively return to reality."

"I'll take you up on that offer, Van." TH made a thumbs up.

Mason looked around the table and noticed Dema's head in her arms. As he was about to speak again, TH straightened up.

"Van, let's do the simulations." TH stood up from the table. "I need to practice as your co-driver when Dema is at my place."

"All right, TH. We'll see you soon." Van glanced at Dema and understood TH's intention.

As Mason watched them leave, he sat beside Dema, who still didn't acknowledge his presence.

"Everything all right? We're almost home." Mason tilted

his head just as TH closed the door to the training room. "Listen, I wanted to say thank you for your help. The fist is the armor piercing, and open palm is high explosive!"

"I am happy, Mason, I really am." Dema looked up. "Do you think this was fate?"

"I'm not following." Mason scratched the back of his head. "What?"

"Yesterday, the Curator. I recognized him. He was the CO of the surviving US forces in Europe. Our plane crashed in the Alps and had to reach the Gaeta Naval Base in Italy on foot. Scavs, locals, and nature attacked us. We barely made it there. But he did not recognize me." Dema shook her head.

"I mean, with all due respect, there must have been so many people in the group. He could have missed you."

"There were four of us." Dema folded her hands. "Four, and I was the only female in that group."

"Oh." Mason leaned back and blinked. "But you're in Ukraine territory, not the Alps. So, how did you meet him, if I may ask?"

"I guess I have to paint you the larger painting before I dive into my survival in the Dark Zone. What?"

"Here we say to paint the picture. While we paint the painting for sure." Mason smiled, and Dema tapped her thumbs. "But, please continue. Tell me more."

"Okay, so to paint a picture. In the aftermath of the War, new organizations and groups rose from the ashes and cut half of Europe for themselves. Scavengers or Scavs, the largest group, created this sort of a nation-state, but Orion Group wasn't there yet to rebuild, so mayhem ensued. I joined several survivors, hid, and traveled across Eastern Europe. Somehow, after many days and sleepless nights, we ended up in Bratislava, a former Capital of the Slovak Republic. From there, we could see the Wall, built by the EURO Group to keep Scavs and others out. Scavs ran the entire sector and kept a watchful eye on the crossings. They caught a few of us trying to get to the other side." Dema looked at Mason, who nodded.

Dema silently looked away, and Mason realized she was reserving many details for herself, but curiosity pressed him.

"We lived like this for two years, when suddenly, we heard on the radio that Orion Corporation has switched their focus on Europe and clean up has started. There was a full-scale invasion into Eastern Europe, and again we got caught in the crossfire. As we ran through the frontlines, I swam through the Danube, found a hole in the Wall, and ran for it. A few days later, I got captured by the US forces, and we found the plane with William and his men on board. After we crash landed in the Italian Alps, we traveled South towards the last US naval base on European soil. There, a last ship awaited us. Not all of us made it. I ended up on the streets of Norfolk. I found a low-paying job in an antique shop. It burned down last year, so I was on the street again. I was broke, hungry, and thirsty, and my savings were bleeding dry daily. It got to the point when even dumpster diving wasn't enough, so I decided to end it once and for all. When I was about to jump, I saw an ad on one of the ships, and that is how I learned about this Tank Royale."

Dema squeezed Mason's hand, holding her tears. "Thank you for listening. As I am talking, I think that was a sign from God. Not what I expected, but still a sign."

"It was a first step, Dema." Mason looked at the tank and then back at her. "First step of many towards greatness."

"Yeah, you are right. So, I prepared a plan. The closest office for the registration was in Atlanta, so I bought a train ticket and made it to Atlanta with my last dollar. I got registered, and I am here. So that is my story." Dema looked at Mason. "How about you?"

Mason felt his heart tear to pieces as he considered telling Dema the truth. *I don't want to lie to her, but what if she speaks the truth and doesn't have to deal with IC? I think that the best course of action would be to walk in the middle and omit certain facts.*

"Are you all right? Where are you?" Dema tapped Mason's forehead. "Hello?"

"Sorry, it's just there is a lot to unpack. Well, after the War, my brother and I, from my last savings, moved to Pampa, Texas, with our aunt. All things considered, my aunt was doing well, but then my brother Ail..." Mason gulped, but was able to suppress the memory just as the Spider was about to calm him down. "The car accident took our parents and left him in a wheelchair. And that wasn't the only thing. Migraines, my hand was broken, so medical bills went up. After my hand got better, I made a deal with my aunt. We split the bill. She would pay the utilities, gas, and food, and I would cover the insurance, medical, and other things."

"In Europe, well, before the War, we always laugh at how US healthcare is so expensive, compared to our public...." Dema scratched her knuckles. "How could you afford it? Pardon my..."

"Dema, it's all right. In Florida, Orion Corp. started a Clean Air Initiative, repairing the atmosphere with some science magic or something like that. It is an impressive feat that needed a lot of workers to function, so last year, I finally got a schedule. I traveled to Florida on Monday, which took about four hours by train, and I would stay there till Friday when I would go home. I had therapy sessions on Saturday, and a paycheck would arrive on Sunday. Repeat."

"That is so nice of you. Listen, if we win, I will give you some of my cut. It seems like you need it more than I do."

"Thank you, Dema, but don't worry about it. To answer your burning question, one of my colleagues told me about this Tank Royale ad he saw. So, I boarded the train home, waved goodbye, went through the process, and ended up here. Tell me, how did it feel when you found that hole?"

To his surprise, Dema smiled, briefly flashing her front teeth. While it wasn't a complete smile, she was almost there.

"It seems like desperation brought us together. Mason, when I found that hole in the Wall, I couldn't believe my luck.

I took a deep breath when I crossed it, but I was alone when I looked over my shoulder. I felt a cold wind blowing all around, but I had to keep moving as I still heard gunfire all around me. It was midnight, and I did not know where to go. Suddenly, I noticed a firefly lighting the way, so I followed it. I was in the wonderland."

"I wish I could have seen it." Mason stood up and hugged Dema. "You know what? Let's take a walk. Just two of us."

"Thank you." Dema grabbed Mason's hand. "Where do you want to go?"

"You choose." Mason smiled when Dema clutched his elbow, but before they could leave, Mason's wrist tablet vibrated, and a moment later Ail's face appeared, awaiting him to accept the video call.

"That's your brother?" Dema looked at the screen. "Well, accept it!"

"He can wait." Mason took a deep breath, but Dema accepted the call, and Ail's jaw dropped to his lap when his face appeared on the screen.

"TH, can I ask you something?" Van removed his VR headset and looked at TH, who gently placed his headset into the charging station.

"No, you cannot," TH replied, and Van raised his eyebrows.

"Oh, never mind then." Van scratched his chin, but then TH tapped his knees as the awkward silence was about to settle in.

"Of course, you can ask Van; I'm pulling your leg." TH gave Van a thumbs up, who slowly exhaled.

"I was about to say, TH! You said a few days ago that you are an experimental machine of war, but what else can you do, if you don't mind me asking?"

TH remained silent for a moment and even looked away.

"Can you keep a secret?" TH looked back at Van.

"Of course I can!" Van launched towards his metallic colleague.

"Then so can I." TH tapped Van on his left shoulder. "Don't worry, I'm kidding! I'll tell you!"

"Come on, TH!" Van threw his hands in the air. "Please don't do this to me!"

"When the project got shut down, I didn't have a choice, and I apologize for omitting this fact from everyone. I was immediately shipped to the scrapyard, as the Glitch made me incompatible with the rest of my brethren, well, all but one. But as they were about to process me, I got hotwired. I don't know who or when, but I woke up buried and had to crawl my way out."

"I'll stop you right there." Van coughed. "Hotwired?"

"Before that, I was mute, but then I could speak. My first word was, 'What?' As I went through my memory, I found many programs I didn't have before—Handshakes and Social Interactions, to name a few. I left the scrapyard and began looking for an individual or a group that hotwired me to get answers to my questions. The best chance of them seeing me would be here, so I stole and broke into shops. However, my doing that caused a grave injury to an individual, and I finally got caught. It wasn't moral, but the ends justified the means for me. When Internal Control learned who I was, they shoved me right here. Can you keep a secret?"

Van didn't speak this time as he slowly processed what TH just said. Finally, after what seemed to be an eternity, Van looked at TH.

"I don't know what to say." Van walked around the room. "Thank you for telling me."

"I only need to hear yes from you." TH also stood up.

"Yes, I'll keep your secret, brother. But it's only fair that I tell you something in return." Van rolled up his sleeve and showed TH his barcode. "I'm not here by choice. My family's farm is the last surviving privately owned farm on the East Coast, and we fight hard to keep it this way. However, a few days ago, we got shafted, and let's just say a sacrifice was needed to keep the Corps and Internal at bay. A bribe, offering, whatever you like to call it, to keep the farm in our hands. Well, I am the lamb."

"So, you think Mason and Dema are also here by force?"

"I'm one hundred percent sure that Mason is. He strikes me as the type to cause trouble, but not for his pleasure."

"Then out of what?"

"He is like me, unhappy with this new way of life that was thrust upon us. However, I don't think he is lying about his brother. He wanted to but didn't, but he also didn't seek any pity for his situation. So, I assume Mason is here because he wants to protect him. Dema, however, I'm not sure. Our hot babe might be here willingly." Van looked at the empty stations. "But I might be wrong."

"Speaking of women, your girlfriend, Ember. Were you able to reach her? You're trying hard to reach her." TH tapped his thumbs.

"I don't know what is happening! We've been together for three years now. I'm worried TH," Van gulped, "do you think she went with the nuclear option?"

"Does she have nuclear warheads?"

"No, no, TH, it's a saying, not meant to be taken literally." Van laughed momentarily. "In this case, the nuclear option is that she had already buried me and moved on."

"Well, you are alive, right? I can see you, and I can touch you. And she can too, right?"

"I don't know, TH." Van looked at his boots. "I don't know."

"Have you considered the nuclear option?" TH tilted his head. "It's a moral risk."

"I'm not going down that route. Once I go, there is no coming back. However, I've faith that my girl will contact me sooner or later. It must have been a shock. My family, too, it took them a moment to finally respond to me." Van looked at TH. "Thank you."

"Well, good job, everyone!" Gio removed the goggles and dried the sweat from his forehead. "And just in time to rest and get ready for another round."

"Why are we not doing the Chaos?" Adam tilted his head. "You heard Benjamin, people will watch us live, and we need all the help we can get. And a hundred thousand dollars to the pool. A hundred thousand!"

"Adam, let me ask you. What is happening tomorrow?" Gio turned towards Adam. "Go on, say it."

"We have that simulation match!" Gio nodded as Adam figured out the answer.

"I need to have all of you rested for tomorrow. So that you know, this is Chaos #2. I went through the #1; trust me, we don't want to do it. This is how TVG is messing with us."

"But a hundred thousand dollars is a hundred thousand dollars!"

"Adam!" Gio raised his voice. "When we win, you'll have more money than you can ever imagine. And that is only a tiny thing compared to the fame we will have! So, we'll sacrifice a hundred thousand now, so we will have millions later!"

"Yes, Sir!" Adam exhaled and walked away.

"All right, but we still need to go to the Tank Museum anyway." James scratched his chin. "At least give us a quick tour. And you must explain yourself to Mason."

Gio whistled, and the bulldog ran up to him. "All right, All right."

"Was it a good idea to adopt this dog?" Adam stared at the dog for a moment. "Really?"

"You want to eat?" Gio decided to ignore Adam's comments. "You seem to be hungry!"

Sharik stretched his head and sat on the floor, his tongue flailing left and right.

"Are we going to dine in?" James stood at the door, awaiting the rest of the crew to join him. "Or we can order."

"We're going; and so is Sharik. I believe that his owners

will be back for him."

"Four tankers and a dog." James looked at Gio and then at the obedient bulldog. "But he seems nice."

Gio clapped his hands. "We got a long way to go and a short time to get there!"

———

At precisely five in the afternoon, Mason and his team stood in front of their garage, observing the staff preparing their main floor for an interview with four chairs staring them down. Drones were already in position, silently hovering there like hummingbirds.

"So, how do you guys feel?" Mason looked at the silent team and smiled. "Come on, this is not an execution."

Only Dema chuckled while Van and TH remained silent.

"Hey! What questions are we to expect?" TH waved at a man with headphones, who gave them a quick look and then turned toward his staff.

On his jacket, the large title in the white of Producer reflected the afternoon light, and Mason tapped his thumbs.

TH received the answer to his question five minutes later, as they were prompted by the man in the headphones to take their seats; however, as they got to their seats, the man raised his hand.

"I'll need Mason to sit all the way to the left. Next to him, Dema, followed by TH and then Van Bryant. Assume your positions; Benjamin will be here in two minutes. Smile and wave. He'll ask you a couple of questions, and we are done! Afterward, you are to return to your whatever."

"How many people are watching us?" Dema raised her hand.

"A billion people tuned live into a last segment with the Power Platoon, so we're expecting more or less the same." The producer nodded and walked away.

"A billion people!" Mason looked at his crew. "I don't know what to say."

"To put it into perspective, imagine the entire population of India before the War watching us." TH momentarily stared at the woman struggling to untangle colored wiring.

Mason tapped his chin as he thought to himself. *Wow, I haven't needed the pills for several days. I might finally be off! No triggers yet. After I win this, I'm getting that Spider removed, no matter what. I don't care that I wasted the money, but I really don't need it now. What am I going to say to the billion of people? Ail? Aunt?*

"Mason, we are on!" Dema nudged Mason on his shoulder and grinned from ear to ear.

In front of them, Benjamin's holographic projection rendered from the rig below and immediately waved its hand at the invisible audience. Then, like a conductor, he turned around and opened his palms.

"Good afternoon, everyone, and welcome to the interview with Team 28. We have a crew of four operating Crusading Angel. It is a well-balanced tank with good armor, a decent gun, and overall good mobility. The questions I'm about to ask you were submitted by both premium and standard viewers. Mason, you're up first. This is a question from one of the TVG staff. How do you feel commanding this armored chariot of war?" Benjamin turned to Mason, and the hologram grinned from ear to ear.

For a second, Mason couldn't talk, but then he collected his thoughts.

"It's an experience. But I cannot do it alone. My team also worked hard to understand the complexity of this competition. It roars, and as you said on the first day, our Angel has a character of its own. As we're learning about it, Angel learns about us." Mason decided to walk down the vanilla answer road, and Benjamin nodded.

"Thank you for telling us, Mason. Van, this question is from a viewer from Alaska. She is asking if you are single."

Mason watched Van raise his eyebrows, but then Van smiled into the camera, saying, "Girl, I'm already taken, but good luck next time!"

"Short and to the point. Faithful people are hard to come by these days." Benjamin pointed at Van and turned towards TH. "This question has been submitted by a clinical psychiatrist from Corporate City-State of Hong Kong. He is asking if you find it enjoyable to be working with humans? If not, what can we do to improve this relationship?"

Now, all eyes were on TH, and for a moment, Mason noticed Giovanni and his crew peeking through the windows. TH took his time to answer to the point where the producer with headphones began tapping his wrist and waving his hands. Mason thought that was a loaded but interesting question, as he was the only one to look around.

"For God, the magnum opus was mankind. For mankind, it is artificial intelligence. And for artificial intelligence, we are. So, I am thankful for all parties involved, and I think that overall, we are all doing a good job. Nobody is perfect, and everyone has their moments. Concerning my friends in flesh and bones." TH pointed at every single one of his teammates but pointed twice at Mason. "I'm honored that I can join forces with the best of the best in this strange Battle Royale concept. We don't have much time on this Earth, one way or another, so spending every minute with people and animals is worth it in my eyes. We can live in harmony after all."

"Wow, thank you for an insightful answer, TH. Dema, it's your turn. This question is from one of my interns. Being a member of All-American Platoon, how do you find working with the other members?" Benjamin looked at Dema and back at the camera.

"Why are we the only mixed group in the entire lineup? Is there a reason behind this decision?" Then, Dema broke her calm and smiling character and went on the offensive. "Where are August and his team? Why do you keep raising prices for needed equipment?"

Mason blinked, awestruck by Dema's direct questions, unable to form any thoughts as his mind kept processing what had happened. Van also looked at Dema while TH continued facing the front.

"Okay, so a different question, then." Benjamin played it off. "How about...."

"Why are we the only mixed group in the lineup?" Dema asked again.

Benjamin's smile vanished and showed the Producer sitting behind the control panel, thumb and index finger. After a short nod, Benjamin slowly exhaled.

"Dema Bella Balakin, what do you think you're doing?" Benjamin shook his head, and Mason realized that this was the first time he heard her full name. "Just answer the question, please, so we can move on."

"I want to know the answer to my question. Why are we the only mixed crew?"

"Dema, I cannot answer that. Even if I knew, does it matter?" Benjamin walked up closer. "Please, answer the asked question. I have nine other crews to talk with."

"Is this all live?" Van turned to his team. "Let's just answer the question so we can move on."

"No, it isn't. Currently, your AI-generated models are answering the questions based on the collected data," The producer said from behind. "For cases like these. Dema, why are you tanking your chances? Currently, around eight hundred million people are watching live. This exposure can only help you as, by popularity, you are pretty much cannon fodder, and your chances of survival are decreasing by the minute. All of you are here to gain something. Do you want to throw it away?"

"Dema." TH turned towards her. "Benjamin cannot help you. For the sake of Mason's brother, please, just answer the question."

"Okay," Dema raised her hands, "forgive me for asking

questions during an interview! More like an interrogation than an interview, but hey."

"Thank you." Benjamin joined his hands and gave the producer the nod.

"All right, thank you for answering our question. Now, I have a few more before we wrap this up."

————

Following the departure of the interview staff half an hour later, Dema shook her head and wordlessly vanished upstairs, leaving the crew in a confused silence. After a while, the one to speak was Van.

"They had AI models of us talking while Dema asked her questions. Can anyone even comprehend that fact?" Van threw his hands in the air. "Anyone? Hello?"

"Yeah, that about checks out. Our speech patterns are just data that can be fed to artificial intelligence. It's effortless for me to master if I was gathering these patterns, which I'm not, I promise."

"What worries me more is Dema." Mason looked up. "We have a simulation match tomorrow, and I cannot afford to lose focus. I need us on point, ready to go."

"Forget Dema; she'll be all right. Do you understand what they just dropped on us?" Van threw his hands in the air. "Hello? I'm talking to the brick wall here. Anyone?"

"And you need to understand that 3D-generated models of us are the least of our worries. Yes, it is scary, but do you...." Mason slowly exhaled. "Van, first, we need to survive, then we can focus on identity. Survival takes priority over everything else."

"Van, Mason is right. If we lose our cool now, especially tomorrow, our public support is gone in the wind, and so are we." TH tapped his thumbs. "Please."

"I understand!" Van raised his voice for the first time. "But do you understand the greater implications? Possible fraud, identity theft, malice, just to name a few things."

"Van, why are we getting worked up about it now if this was already happening? I feel that this is a test, purposely trying to derail us. Like that Chaos simulation."

"I am sorry," Van relaxed his stance but looked away. "I failed."

"No, you haven't. But I almost did." Mason took a deep breath. "I just need to ensure that...."

"No need. I was an overt moron who almost tanked our chances at getting any help we could get," Dema stood on the staircase, "and I cannot have on my conscience you two arguing because of me or worse, something down the line. Yes, having a computer pretending to be us is scary, but there is nothing we can do about it now. So, Mason, my head is in the game, and I am sorry again for my behavior. It's just...."

"Dema," Mason raised his hand, "welcome back, and apologies accepted."

"How about a group hug?" TH grabbed his tablet. "And then group picture?"

"TH, that second is my department. I am the one with the camera, after all!" Dema smiled. "But yes, a group hug would be nice."

"I'm hungry," Van tapped his growling stomach. "Let's speed this up, please!"

CHAPTER EIGHT

SHOTS FIRED

Mason opened the commander's hatch and took a deep breath. The newly installed hardware blew his and his team's minds as gasps of the new reality filled the simulated interior of the tank. Instead of chairs, they had multi-directional treadmills with sitting support, beefed-up hardware, and fresh black suits with white lighted lines, and now, they were in one large room instead of their own cubicles. When Mason looked around, he couldn't believe that he was inside the state-of-the-art mil-simulations. Friday morning came and went, and so did lunch as Mason and his crew decided to sleep in. Then, after a late brunch, the day's main event arrived. Now his eyes ate the eye candy of the HD graphics, and Mason thought to himself:

In the Bootcamp, we had something similar, but oh my, this is amazing. Focus now, Mason! Get your shit together, as billions watch your every word and move! It would be good to have Team 6 back, but we have to do without them now. Sooner or later, their absence will be explained. It better be! Crap, I should have got the pills, just in case. Well, no time for that now.

He could feel the cold steel as his hand touched the handle on the side of the turret. Other tanks rendered into the view and immediately rolled down the hill before them, leaving behind a cloud of realistic dust and smoke particles. As Mason looked up, he found instructions, and a countdown posted on the skybox.

PRE-GAME LOBBY

Please drive down the hill to the Staging Grounds and pre-pare your tank for the action. When the countdown hits zero, you will be transported into battlegrounds. Think before you load your tank. This is your time to shine and show your fans and the world what you are made of. Remember, there are no assists, only kills.

You must complete objectives to progress to the next stage apart from killing each other. In the meantime, watch the interview with Hwang Jeong-Min, a former South Korean Tank Commander callsign Bear 698. Platoons are disabled during the first round.

Requirements to count the kill:

If the crew count drops below two, ignoring the state of the tank, the final shot will be credited to the last shooter.

If the tank has damage beyond repair, regardless of the number of surviving crewmembers, it is considered a kill, and a score will be awarded to the last shooter.

Stage One: Crews will compete for the radio stations placed all around the map, and radio operators will have to leave the tank and upload the artillery coordinates. It will be primarily one-on-one engagement. If a radio operator is knocked out, the commander is required to upload. After stage one, there will be a ten-minute intermission.

Stage Two: Survivors from the first round will evade the Hunter while fighting against other teams. Platoons will be allowed, but friendly fire is on. The crew that destroys the Hunter first receives an additional two hundred thousand dollars to their pool.

Stage Three: If the winner is not decided in stage two, a race against the clock will force the survivors to evade certain zones and reach points of interest before they blow up. Good luck, and may the best crew win.

Countdown showed they were around an hour before the match, so Mason closed the hatch, plugged his headset into the side, and looked at his crew, more precisely on TH, who tapped the breech, awaiting orders.

TH immediately picked up on the look. "I'll perform to the best of my ability, and so will Van and Dema."

"Where to, Commander?" Van's voice cracked in the internal comms.

The software realistically rendered the T-34 to the smallest detail, including the sounds, interior, equipment, and scratches.

"Down the hill to the Staging Grounds!" Mason opened the squeaky hatch again, realizing that there was no danger yet.

Mason looked at his shaking hands and squeezed the drive-fly wheels, attempting to relax. He took three slow breaths, trying to calm his racing heart and the Spider inside him.

"Will do!" Van said as the tank rocked itself, roaring the engine in the process.

"Is there a silencer for this racket!?" Dema shouted, and TH also opened his hatch, leaning on his left hand.

Due to the cramped conditions of the Angel, the engine sound filled up the crew compartment, and moments later, Mason gave the nod to TH as they cleared the hill and came across the Staging Grounds.

Staging Grounds were made of stations for each tank, and already crews ran around, loading their tanks with shells, magazines, camo nets, and other equipment. Mason thanked God as more tanks were rendered and drove to the Staging grounds.

What would it look like if we were to arrive last? Well, let's see how the interview helped us. Mason slowly exhaled and adjusted his headset.

The stations were filled with ammo crates, gas pump, and other things.

"All right, team, let's get this, W..." Mason pressed himself against the hatch and jumped down from the tank. "We got this!"

A transparent wall appeared as they parked, blocking other

teams from joining them and giving them privacy in the simulation. Mason found a hovering note above his head. As he reached for it, the text was rendered into the simulation. *Gasoline Cowboys, this equipment was provided to you by the premium plan users who have watched and judged your interview performance. Enjoy!*

As everyone got out, Mason slowly exhaled as their station wasn't filled with more equipment than other teams, with only bare essentials awaiting them in wooden boxes.

"I am sorry again. I wish I would have known that my outburst would have consequences," Dema said in a shaking voice, but Mason gently rested his hand on her shoulder, telling her with his eyes: *It's all right.*

"Crew, I need to say something before we load up." Mason turned to his crew, who dismounted the tank as well. "We've a real fight to look forward to, despite it being a simulation. When we die, we die. Bring it in, everyone!" Mason raised his fist in the air, followed by the rest just as extra ammunition boxes rendered next to them. "We'll pull through, and we will lead the way!"

TH took the first box and gently opened it. The squeaking cover made Mason reach for the volume control. *My ears will not survive this.*

TH examined the shells. Reflective bronze body with a nasty-looking head topped off with a redcap. On the side, TH found an AP inscribed. For a moment, they all stared at the cylindrical object in TH's hands, with the first one to snap out being Mason.

"Okay, TH, let's load up." Mason clapped, prompting Van and Dema to get moving.

"Our tank can carry around seventy rounds of different shells, but I would carry around forty. The fewer shells we carry, the less of a chance of ammo detonation, but we need just enough to get by." TH flipped the shell around and tapped the tip. "Let's make it forty-five. We might need several shots to finish the deed."

"TH and I'll load the tank with ammo while Van and Dema look for practical necessities we can use to survive. Once we are done, we should think about what to do next, seeing that we have around fifty minutes." Mason looked at Dema, who observed the nearby crew wrapping the long barrel in a camo net. "Dema?"

"Oh yeah!" Dema turned around. "My apologies, I am on it!"

————

Sitting inside his bunker-like studio in a suit and tie, Benjamin Bell felt that his clothing didn't mix well with the setting of the Tank Royale. Still, the contract required Benjamin always to wear a suit, even though military attire would be better suited. His red-brown eyes looked around the studio as the door opened, and a man of Korean descent, clad in a green and black uniform, entered, followed by Benjamin's broadcasting staff. Finally, the guest was here, and Benjamin felt shivers of respect on his spine. He fixed his tie, stood up, and invited the man to sit. Moments later, the camera light turned red.

"Good afternoon, viewers and Gasoline Cowboys. Soon, we shall see how our gasoline cowboys can ride and fight for the first time on the big screen! We highly encourage you to tune in and let others know about the greatest show of your life. I have a special guest with me today. Please welcome Corporal and Gasoline Cowboy himself, Hwang Jeong-Min, call sign Bear 698! He is a big media celebrity and influencer in Corporate South Korea. How was the flight?"

Jeong-Min looked around, smiled, and his eyes fixed on Benjamin first, then into the camera.

"It was a smooth flight, thank you for asking. I got to read the Tank Royale data you sent me. I look forward to co-hosting these Tank Royale with you, but I have a few questions."

"Sure, sir, but before we start, how should I call you? Do you go by rank? Mr.?" Benjamin looked into the camera, then at his producer, and then back at Jeong-Min.

"Jeong-Min or Min will suffice." Jeong-Min leaned back in the chair.

"Thank you for the clarification; please call me Benjamin or BB. Now, tell our viewers about your background."

"I grew up next to the Cheorwon County Tank Base. Both of my mother and father served in the South Korean military. In South Korea, all males between the ages of eighteen and twenty-eight must enroll in compulsory military service, after which the individual has a choice to stay. My parents wanted me to join the Air Force, but once I got accepted to the Black Dragon platoon, the elite tank force in South Korea," Jeong-Min smiled, "they changed their minds. Our job was to stake-out the DMZ; however, it was cut short due to the War, during which I became a recruitment liaison and was given a custom T-145 SKM MTB, which is a South Korean-licensed version of the Russian T-145. While we had our domestic build tanks, the T-145 was easier to build and scavenge parts for. After the worldwide integration into Orion Network, I became Chief Social Media Officer for the New South Korean Corporate Army. While the North Korean Government has changed, there is still tension on our border. I'm still staking out the Demilitarized Zone with my platoon and border guards every now and then. Yet, even with a united world, tensions are still there. Maybe Korea will be unified one day, but I think we have a long way to go."

"Thank you for telling us; that was very insightful, and thank you for your ongoing service to keep the peace. I'll make one more announcement, and we will be on track, pun intended."

Benjamin scanned the new script, took a deep breath, and grinned from ear to ear.

"Welcome to the Pregame Show. Viewers who purchased the premium plan don't forget to utilize it fully and use the in-simulation cameras for a better view. As for the rest, you have to stick with the main footage, but no worries, after the game's end, you'll be able to download the footage and use the in-simulation camera to relive the top moments or analyze the game for yourself, but of course, stay here for the post-game analysis. Now, Jeong-Min, what would you like to ask ?"

"Which tank do you think has the highest chance of winning this simulation? I've to say, TVG has been fielding a rather diverse line-up ever since its inception," Jeong-Min looked at the large screen behind him, where twelve 3D models of the tanks had just finished the idle animation. Some's turrets turned a hundred and eighty degrees; others' engines spurted a black smoke with a roar.

"To the point, I like it. Wanna make a bet?" Benjamin pulled out his tablet but did notice a surprised look on the face of one of the producers.

"How much?" Min opened his Bank App and looked at Benjamin.

"Fifty dollars," Benjamin said.

"All right, fifty dollars ready to go. I better win because my wife will kill me if I don't. Let's talk about the lineup." Jeong-Min shook hands. "From the data, I'm betting on the Panzer IV G Hydrostat."

"Are you sure?" Benjamin looked at the highlighted tank model, which aimed its turret at Benjamin.

"I'm sure BB. Never been more sure in my life."

"Give our audience a reason for your pick," Benjamin smiled, "and then I'll tell you mine."

"All right, let's talk uniqueness first. The Panzerkampfwagen IV Ausf. G Hydrostat is a one-off experimental tank with a pet-rol/hydraulic engine, which would increase the forward and reverse acceleration, giving Panzer 4 a slight tactical advantage on the battlefield regarding maneuverability. Now, the fire-power," Jeong-Min closed his eyes for a moment as he looked for the official name, "L/48 7.5cm KwK40, one of the accurate guns with powerful shells in the lineup. However, there is a significant downside. The armor, compared to other tanks, is weaker all around."

"Interesting. My choice is the Australian Cruiser 4 or AC-4. This chariot of war comes with a 17-pounder gun, but that is not why I chose it. AC is one of the smaller, which isn't much, but still, tanks in the line-up, allowing its crew to play with the terrain and give them many tactical opportunities, which tanks like Sherman don't have. While the 17-pounder is godsent, it's an inaccurate cannon at long range while using APDS. However, one shot is enough to liquify anything when it connects. Plus, it looks good."

"So, my Hydro against your Aussie Cruiser." Jeong-Min smiled for the first time, receiving a thumbs up from one of the producers.

"With picks out of the way, let's talk about the battlefield where this simulation will occur. Before that, we have an announcement from the CEO of the United States, Kevin Hamilton." Benjamin looked away as the red light on the camera vanished.

"Are you all right?" Jeong-Min looked at a sweating Benjamin, who exhaled deeply as they entered the break, and the red light vanished.

"Yes, I have to be." Benjamin took a sip of an energy drink. "Three days without sleep, and I haven't seen my family in weeks."

"Once this is over, you'll see them,"

"After this, my team and I have to gather the footage, and with the studio, we must decide if to make this into a movie or series. TVG demands that everything be recorded and stored, then turned into a digestible medium to repackage and sell again."

———

Three, Two, One. Time to roll out! Get out there and win!

The screen turned black, and after an orchestral tune, it

changed into a dense pine forest. Mason first felt adrenaline rush into his body as he pressed his face against the vision slits of the commander's cupola.

"Van, follow the road, TH, load the gun." Mason took a deep breath as he issued his first orders. "Dema, anything on the radio?"

"Will do, Commander," replies came moments later as Angel started advancing, and soon, it picked up speed.

Mason bent forward; he noticed his crew also grasping their surroundings. *It would definitely make for some nice pictures,* he thought as Van steered the tank right, avoiding a fallen tree that blocked the pathway.

"Dema?" Mason asked, and this time he got a response.

"I am not getting any signal. Once we clear the forest and the hill, I should be able to receive." Dema scratched the back of her head.

"Van, do you see that hill in front of us?" Mason poked out of the hatch as his eyes followed the paved road, surrounded by the dense pine forest, and found the hill.

Angel's suspension with large road wheels worked as intended when the tank came across large potholes, keeping the tank mostly stable and Mason's late lunch in his stomach.

It could have been a beautiful stroll through the forest, the silence, enjoying nature, and the sound of birds, but our loud V12 is killing the vibe. Can actual reality be this gorgeous? Mason scratched his chin. *Hmm, so, is this where we will die? Hope not! Ail is waiting for me, and I won't fail him.*

"Yes, I do." Van's reply woke Mason up from thought land.

"We have a long fight ahead of us. Everyone, keep your eyes peeled. We will fight, we will prevail, and victory will be ours! How is everyone feeling?"

"This is amazing! I don't have to work out while I'm driving!" Van screamed into the radio, but the engine's sound was cut off.

"What happened?!" Mason shouted into the comms as the

Angel almost flipped when it drove into the ditch.

"The engine will stall if I don't switch gears on time. Sorry guys! I'll keep it in check!" Moments later, Van brought the almighty Kharkiv diesel V-12 back to life, and Crusading Angel cleared the ditch.

"Tanks are advancing, and the audience is cheering. So, what should we expect from this simulation, Benjamin?" Jeong-Min placed his tablet on the black table and looked at Benjamin as the camera's red light started to blink again.

On the screen behind Benjamin, the studio saw the battlefield and tank movement color-coded based on their performance in the test simulations. In addition, there was a list of tanks, crews, vitals, and boxes to track the progress. Finally, there were several points of interest marked as well.

"Tonight, ladies and gentlemen, we will see it all! Heroic fights, cunning exploits, explosions, leaking oil, the tension between contestants, everything is to come. Dear viewers, thank you for tuning in, all two billion of you."

"Two billion people? I'm out of words." Jeong-Min shook his head.

"Don't be; we'll be sitting here for a while. In the meantime, we'll take questions sent to us by the premium viewers. If you want to see your question answered live or in a dedicated Q&A, consider purchasing the premium plan with an ongoing sale on all perks and packages. Since two billion are watching us, this program is automatically translated in near real-time to all the viewers, depending on their setting and location. Jeong-Min, do you wish to take the first one?" Benjamin clapped his hands, and the screen rendered a new window with the list of questions and the system randomly highlighting the first one.

"The first question comes from a viewer in Berlin, Germany.

How big is the simulation map? I think you can answer this question, Benjamin," Jeong-Min passed the question right back.

"The simulation map is a hundred times fifty square miles with diverse playgrounds ranging from ruined cities to hills and open fields, which we can shrink or expand at will. This gives the advantage to everyone to fight on their terms. Of course, we have a few things in place so that the game won't be twelve hours long, and there are two stages with an optional third one if need be. Okay, next question! Does the loader have any other responsibilities besides reloading the main weapon? This is for you," Benjamin muted his microphone.

"Additional loader duties include doing the inventory, servicing the main gun, and being handy in quick repairs. Nowadays, the loader has been replaced with the autoloading mechanism, but on older tanks, they are still present and ready to go."

"That was insightful. We have time for one more. Why not give everyone the same tank for equal opportunity? I'll take this one." Benjamin coughed. "Because it would be boring. What makes fighting interesting is the asymmetry between different tanks. Our contestants come with different skills and training, which also influence the flow of these games. We already leveled the playing field as much as possible."

"Indeed, Benjamin is correct. Each tank is its own character in this match, making for a better viewing experience for all." Jeong-Min threw his hat into the ring. "Hope you all understand."

"All right, this is the place. Dema, can you receive?" Five minutes after the start of the match and after two unsuccessful attempts, Van got hold of the timing for the gear change, and Crusading Angel finally made it to the hill's top and cleared the forest.

Now, balancing on the top, Mason slowly opened his hatch and scanned his surroundings. As he reached for his binoculars, a message popped up saying *Binoculars not available*. Mason cursed between his teeth.

In the distance, a ruined city rendered into view. There was a lake and a horizon sprawling cornfield; to their right, a military outpost, a massive river with three long bridges and hills, but several tall antennas stuck out, giving a sense of direction, and distant shots started to blend into the background noise.

"I feel exposed, not going to lie," Van beat Dema in reply as both looked at each other, expecting a shell heading their way.

Dema's hand froze on the radio knob as she picked up chatter, pointing her towards the military outpost.

"Yes, I can receive it now. There should be a radio station from where I will send the coordinates. It should be half a mile away to the right in that outpost. Orders?" Dema wanted to continue, but an explosion halted the tank, which echoed in the distance. "It seems like Nahuel just exploded into a million pieces. One tank down, ten more including us remaining," Dema reported as a radio message confirmed the kill.

"All right, Van, steer right and head to the base." Mason took a deep breath as Van slid the tank down the hill. "Everyone, keep your eyes peeled. This is it!"

"Time to see some action!" Van whistled, but the roaring V-12 drowned his further conversation with Dema.

———

"Well, this is interesting. Agnes, zoom at the outpost," Benjamin said to the AI, and the camera moved to the outpost, where Crusading Angel and another tank had just entered the base and headed for the radio set up in the middle, hidden behind the crates and barricades, forming a rectangle of pain.

"Hmm, Benjamin, pull up the stats of the T-34 and Delat," Jeong-Min focused on the T-34, which parked behind the bunker during the Delat Torn's advance.

"So, who do you think will win the encounter?" Benjamin switched the camera view onto the one mounted on the tank itself, and the statistics for both tanks appeared on the second screen.

"Well, it depends on a million factors, Benjamin. The simplified rule here is that whoever spots the enemy first usually wins, but things like positioning or a clear line of fire are just a few things to consider." Jeong-Min pointed at the contested outpost. "But this is in the real world. While mil-sim realism bleeds into simulation, it is not as straightforward. For example, you may shoot first and certainly destroy the enemy, but by shooting, you reveal your position to the other enemy tanks that are looking for you. Sometimes, not taking the shot might be a good call, but not always."

"Well, Delat Torn has a five-shell magazine," Benjamin said as a brief reloading animation of the Delat Torn appeared. "For those interested, Delat Torn means split turret in Swedish."

"Crusading Angel has a longer barrel, allowing the shell to retain much penetrating power and accuracy. Also, their loader is humanoid, so Mason has an autoloader. This is going to be interesting."

"I swear I saw another tank entering this area, but I don't know where it is." Mason turned 180 degrees as he looked through the vision slits on the commander's cupola.

The only things he saw now were black containers and tank barricades; the tension rose with every second. Finally, Mason squeezed the rail on the breech and breathed deeply.

"I'll do a recon; all of you stay frosty. TH, man the gun; Dema, take the loader's position; be right back." Mason counted to three and opened the hatch.

"Be careful!" Dema said just as Mason unplugged his headphones and climbed down.

Mason looked back at the Angel, smiled, and vanished behind the boxes as his eyes lay on the square. The radio station sat in the middle, surrounded by barbed wire and black crates. Still, the enemy tank was nowhere in sight as all sounds melted into one. Mason crawled back to the T-34, and moments later, he plugged in his tanker hat.

Okay, Mason. Dema will be covered when she is at the station. Reposition or wait them out. Mason considered his options.

"So, do we drive in or wait them out?" Van was the first to ask the question after a moment of silence.

"The problem is that the enemy tank is not there, but once someone enters the square, there is a clear line of fire, so..." as Mason was about to tap the breech, a loud ringing filled the tank.

It took a moment to recover, but nobody could hear anything for half a minute, and Mason threw his hat on the ground, crying out in the process. But unfortunately, his team was inoperable as the ringing and vibrations picked up in intensity, and Mason felt the Angel falling apart.

"Where did it come from?" It was hard to determine who said it, but the hearing returned moments later.

"Did you turn off the engine?" Mason squeezed the ear flaps on his helmet.

"I heard you say to turn it off, so it is. Wait! I see them. The tank just pulled into the square," TH shouted as he slid down his loader's hatch.

Mason looked at the tank's antenna through the vision slits on the cupola as it drove behind the crates. As his shaking hands cranked the flywheels, Mason spotted the gap between the black containers. Immediately, he spotted the problem. The barrel wouldn't fit unless he rotated the turret all the way around, where the opening would allow the barrel to pass.

"Why are you not firing? They are right there!" TH tapped Mason on his shoulder, but he had to move with the breech instead of reply.

"I don't have a good firing angle, and shooting through the containers will be pointless. Is it loaded up?" Mason felt adrenaline going through his veins as he finished cranking the turret.

"Yes, it is. We haven't fired yet." TH placed his hand on the following shell as furious cranking ended.

Mason leaned to the gunsight and aligned the cross with the Swedish flag painted at the side of the box turret. Moments later, he observed a crewmember jumping out and heading for the radio to relay the coordinates. Then, the Swedish tank started rotating its turret, scanning for targets.

"Firing!" As Mason said it, he pressed the left pedal trigger, and a loud bang echoed in the tank.

The shell nailed the tank, and the turret stopped rotating as TH ejected an empty shell and loaded a new one like a hot potato.

In desperation, one crew member manned the commander's machine gun and started spitting lead blindly all over the square.

"Up!" TH tapped Mason three seconds later, who swung the gun and aimed at the front, where the driver would sit, but Mason sought a bit lower, between the roller wheels.

"Away!" Another loud bang echoed in the tank, and TH had another round in the breech.

Mason fired again, hitting the ammo storage below the turret, and the enemy tank went out in a blaze of glory.

"We did it! Our first kill!" Dema shouted, and Mason exhaled.

"All right, let's finish this. Van, get us closer, and Dema, prepare to relay the coordinates," Mason closed his eyes and took a deep breath, trying to calm his shaking hands as TH rammed a new shell into the cannon.

It's only a simulation; you don't need the Spider. You don't need it! You don't need it! Mason opened his eyes.

"Commander, that is a confirmed kill. Team 12 is out of the game," Dema reported.

———

"All right, then. I wonder what happened to Team 12? Why did they push out?" Benjamin leaned forward as the red on the vitals of Team 12 confirmed yet another team out of the game. "They had everything going for them!"

"I can only think of one scenario. They advanced, believing the other tank was immobilized after the shot, but drove right into the trap. Speaking of the shots, the 17-pounder from the AC IV grazed the T-34 beforehand. Remember when I told you that 17-pounder is inaccurate at the longer ranges?" Jeong-Min sipped his blue energy drink on the table from the start. "Well, it is accurate, just the ammunition it uses isn't."

"I think they learned that early WW2 Sabot rounds and 17-pounder don't play well together, and now, they would have to play it close to the body, seeing that. But, dear viewers, 17-pounder can still annihilate anything it sees." Benjamin looked at the screen, where more red flashes appeared. "With this, the first stage is officially finished, and we are onto stage two. Let's get a quick peek at the board with the remaining tanks. Tanks in red are out, tanks in yellow are damaged, and green are good to go."

"What is happening with Team 20? Why both red and yellow? Is it critical?" Jeong-Min looked at Benjamin, who zoomed in on the Ram II.

"Looking at the vitals, only two crewmen are alive, and the tank is in a bad state. It is their choice, either give up or try to make it to stage two." Benjamin zoomed in on the heavily damaged tank in the streets of the town. "In my opinion, they should call it. Just look at them."

The track had been blown off, the turret had holes everywhere, and the engine emitted a black smoke while two tankmen tried to get the right track together. Then, on the left side of the turret, there was a large hole; moments later, a tank exploded, sealing the fate of Team 10.

"Benjamin, aren't teams 16, 18 and 22 together?" Jeong-Min connected the dots.

"Indeed, they are. It seems like TVG has its favorites, so it is up to teams 14, 26, and 28 to fight and take the win." Benjamin smiled into the camera. "Well, this will give a breather to our remaining crews. The tankers have completed the first stage in thirty-five minutes. At the same time, I explain stage two; however, our guest will be playing as well." Benjamin looked at the teleprompter, smiled into the camera, and then looked at eyes wide open, Jeong-Min.

"What do you mean by I'm playing as well? I wasn't notified." Jeong-Min took a sip of water as Benjamin leaned toward the camera and pressed the button on the table. "So, what about our bet?"

"Attention, all remaining crews. Now that stage one is over, I would like to congratulate our surviving contestants. You have a ten-minute break before stage two, so use it wisely. The second stage is our tank version of Cat and Mouse. Our guest will select his tank and will hunt you down. You can kill each other during this stage, but I highly recommend working together to defeat him, and trust me, Jeong-Min will not be playing around. Good luck, and we are going into a short commercial break." Benjamin closed his eyes briefly as the camera turned off.

"So, what am I bringing to the fight? I should have figured that the setup in the corner would be for me." Jeong-Min pointed at the human-sized glass box with a black VR treadmill.

"Yeah, it just appeared on the teleprompter, but I believe in you. No pressure, two billion people are watching live." Benjamin laughed.

"Thank you," Min said as he put on the black suit and stepped onto the treadmill in the corner of the studio.

Benjamin leaned back and looked at two tank models on the screen, awaiting Jeong-Min to pick up his tank, and five minutes later, they were live again.

"Good afternoon, everyone, and welcome back to the Tank Royale. Jeong-Min, one more thing. Since today is your birthday, we at Tank Royale have a special gift for you. You'll be linked and fight with your mates from 689 crew, lag-free. Good hunting, and to all the viewers, five minutes remaining till stage two. In the meantime, I'll take a few more questions from our viewers."

———

"Isn't that Gio and his crew?" Mason came to life as his crew rested and tried to calm down after the thrill of the kill kicked in.

As Dema uploaded the coordinates, their screen went black and transferred to the map's new part. They were surrounded by the dense forest, which seemed to go on forever, with ridges in the distance. Their moment of silence was disturbed by the P26/40 rolling down the hill towards Mason, who opened the hatch and waved. Mason spotted deep scratches and two holes next to the driver's viewport on the front plate. Jerry cans on the side of the tank were riddled with bullets, and where the commander's machine used to be, there was only a brown stick with an attached magazine.

"That was," Van exalted, "fun! I felt alive for a moment! I think we can do this, my brothers!"

"Me too," Dema closed her eyes, "our first kill and many more to come. Then, we are going home."

"All right, squad, let's get out," Mason said as Da Vinci parked next to them and turned its engine off.

"Well, good thing that all of you are alive." Both teams embraced each other, but Gio's team wasn't gasping for air as much.

"That was tense, but I can tell that you guys made it without a scratch." Gio walked around the T-34. "Uhh, never mind. Mason, look here."

Mason joined Gio and covered his mouth as he found the leftover shell from earlier still stuck in the frontal plate.

"But your tank got hammered; whom did you fight?" Dema joined the twins, who vanished without any response, leaving her with raised hands and a surprised face.

"They had a little beef before the simulation, but they are fine." James joined Dema, who stood aside, observing the never-ending tall pines.

Even though goggles and the tank hat covered his worn face, Dema could still feel his eyes piercing her soul.

"All right, so whom did you engage?" Dema tapped her thumbs. "We want to know everything!"

"Are you sure you want to know everything?" James grinned, but Gio waved his hand.

"Centaur III, my love, but we survived thanks to Gio's sixth sense. They fired at us, not checking if they scored the kill. Thinking that they killed us, they drove past us, forgetting that Gio got his bearings together and blasted them into the engine, reloaded the gun by himself, shot the side of the turret," James tapped the pierced jerry-can, "knocked out track just to BM. The final shot rendered the tank beyond repairable, giving us a kill."

"What is BM?" Van scratched his head. "I don't remember learning this term in the sims."

"Bad manners is a term primarily used in sports and video games. Think about it like adding salt to the injury," James was first to respond. "Gio can get intense sometimes."

Mason and Gio stared at the stage two map in the back, which, as the first stage, featured diverse elements, from the ruined city to hills and wide-open flats.

"See this spot?" Giovanni pointed at the red X on the hill.

"What about it?" Mason shook his head, growling between his teeth as he felt his forehead turning red. "X marks the spot, right?"

"Red X marks Hunter's spawn location. Now, for a hundred percent, it will be a tank destroyer, and it will be either German or Russian, with a big enough gun to ignore any armor or angle and mobile enough to stalk us. So, the blue cross is where we are, and the green is the Power Platoon. But, hey, can anyone tell me who is still alive?" Gio shouted at the rest of the band.

"Only the Australians!" Dema shouted back, and Gio gave her a thumbs up. "Where are they?"

"They must be somewhere here, but let's look at this. Your tank prefers flat open grounds, while mine could use a flat road, so hills are out. So, this leaves us with the forest, flats, and city."

"We can cross out the open as well, leaving us with the city and the forest areas." Mason slowly exhaled when Gio halted him.

"Everything all right?" Gio changed his tone again. "I hear you growling like a trapped animal."

"I don't know. I'm having the ride of my lifetime, but again, one mistake and my crew will go out in flames, and the weight of that knowledge is crushing me. Every night, I turn on my bed. Plus, my head hurts. I drank water, but it burns!"

"Brother, give wings to your triumph. You and your crew scored a kill and survived stage one. Half of the line-up didn't make it here, and you guys did, thanks to your leadership. Remember, wing your crew as well." Gio smiled as Mason nodded his head. "So, are you thinking what I'm thinking?"

"You're right. A little boost of confidence goes a long way. But how is it that you know everything?"

"I read, and I know things. Simulations helped as well to somewhat level the playing field. So where are we going?"

"Well, the forest is out of the question, leaving us with..." Mason didn't have to finish the sentence since both of their eyes met, and both pointed at the city.

———

"All right, welcome back, and stage two starts in three, two, one, go! All hands on deck and guns ready to fire!" As the camera went live again, Benjamin said, "I have to briefly talk about the choice that Jeong-Min made."

Benjamin pointed at the two models on the platforms, which were rendered into view.

"Now, Jeong-Min has selected a Waffentrager, or Krupp-Steyr Waffenträger with an 8.8cm or 88mm anti-everything cannon. In World War Two, only a few tanks, like Sherman Jumbo, could survive and fight against this mighty German cannon. Now, Jeong's friends trained in the simulations, just like our contestants are using, so they will know what to do." Benjamin looked at the battlefield map. "Both surviving platoons and Team 14 flocked to fight in the urban setting. Time to see what they have to offer,"

Benjamin turned around and watched the Waffe render inside the simulation. After the crew shook hands, Benjamin smiled as Jeong-Min climbed into the commander's seat and pointed at the ruined city before them.

———

"They are reusing the city from the first stage!" Dema removed her headphones just as Crusading Angel and Da Vinci parked by a ruined house with a crushed car in front of the open garage.

"Well, then we should be good to go!" Dema relayed the response from Da Vinci, but Gio had already opened his hatch, so Mason followed suit, shouting, "Lead the way!"

"You didn't sound very convincing." Mason waved at Gio, who leaned on the roof-mounted 8mm Breda machine gun.

"Well, I'm not. Another tank drove by us a moment ago, and I didn't even notice it,"

"Who was it?" Mason scanned his surroundings but only saw ruins. "Let's hunt them down!"

"It could be the Australians, but I'm not sure. They had a camo net on the tank, but I could make out a long barrel, which doesn't help, but that narrows it down to a Power Platoon."

"I smell a huge advantage for the Power Platoon." Mason rolled his eyes. "But again, we fumbled that interview, so we only got essential gear!"

"Best everything from tools to gear; I heard those pesky Germans got NV, but working for the corporate means that strings are attached. Now, let's blast them to kingdom come. You all right, Mason?"

"Yes, I am all right." Mason took a deep breath. "It still hurts like a mothertrucker. Have to be!"

"All right then, follow us then to victory!" Gio gave Mason a thumbs-up as the hatch closed behind him.

"Will do!" Mason closed the hatch and plugged in his headset. "Van, follow Da Vinci. Everyone, let's keep our eyes peeled for the Power Platoon. We've another tank in the vicinity!"

"Will do!" Replies came moments later, but Da Vince abruptly stopped as Angel moved again, and Mason punched the breech. *What the hell is happening again? Those morons!*

"Well, tanks are about to enter the city, but hedgehogs are blocking the path for both Platoons. Jeong-Min is currently targeting the stranded AC-4, which means he will win the bet. Damn." Benjamin looked at the screen and swiped to the right, where the camera showed Waffentrager in full flight.

"Look at this, ladies and gentlemen, that is smart. Jeong-Min had ordered fire from the backside so the hull could serve as a recoil compensator. However, tests showed that this Waffentrager could only fire from the front or back. Otherwise, the platform would flip." Benjamin looked around when he heard the thunder in the studio, and two seconds later, AC-4 exploded as the camera showed the kill shot, nailing the tank underneath the turret and blowing up ammo storage.

Then he heard an exchange in Korean, followed by loud shouts. Benjamin smiled as Jeong-Min ordered his driver to turn right at the crossroads.

———

Mason felt his eyes twitch as Gio found the street suitable for both tanks to enter the city. The ruined houses, a small empty square with a damaged fountain, burned-out trees in the park with demolished benches, and the streets riddled with holes. *I should have taken those pills. Fuck me! Ahh!*

"Everyone, keep your eyes peeled. They can be hiding anywhere." Mason opened his hatch just enough so his eyes could poke out.

And while looking through the bulletproof glass on the vision slits that would provide him with protection, Mason, after weighing his options, decided on a much clearer but dangerous view. Clouds of black smoke coming from the main square and demolished church tower showed them the way. Growling again, Mason tapped his right hand against the goggles. *So help me, God. It burns!*

"Van, you are doing a good job." Dema touched Van's shivering left shoulder.

"Thank you, Dema. I miss the gear change or brake too late, and we are out." Van took a deep breath.

"It is just a simulation," Dema tapped the pan magazine on top of her machine gun, "but it must be pretty close to what I had to crawl through. They know how to make it real."

"This is a warzone! Blown out houses around us, walls riddled with holes; this is scary," TH swung his periscope around, "this is terrible! You must feel bad for the people who live here!"

"Can humanoids get claustrophobic?" Mason closed the hatch and looked at TH over the gun breech, but the roar of Angel's engine muffled TH's answer.

"They're slow, aren't they? I don't like revving our engine only to keep it in second." Van tapped the brake levers, drawing TH's response.

"All right, Van, stop the tank now. Dema, radio Da Vinci that we're stopping, preferably now. I should have told you this earlier, TH, but something is wrong with the coaxial machine gun."

As Mason said this the tank halted, but TH tapped Mason on his right shoulder.

"Are you all right? You are white as the chalk in our garage and a bit more aggressive. Dema and Van know what to do, so there is no need to use 'preferably now.' We understand what to do!"

"Let me worry about the crew; you check on that machine gun." Mason shook his head. "Move it!"

"Machine gun works perfectly; it is not jammed or empty. Are you all right, Commander Knight? How can I help you?" TH wanted to continue, but Mason had already unplugged and climbed out of his hatch.

Moments later, Gio emerged from Da Vinci with a what the hell is happening look on his face, simultaneously throwing his hands in the air. For a moment, Gio shook his head left and right, frantically scanning his surroundings, keeping his profile lowered.

"I think we need to split up. You can continue down the road while we turn here." Mason walked up to him and pointed at the fork.

"And why would we do that? If we split, they'll pick us up one by one." Gio tilted his head. "It's three vs. two vs. one vs. Hunter. We are staying together!"

"We can cover more ground, plus our radios are working." Mason shook his head.

"I can see your point, but we need to stay together," Gio looked around him again, "but there is a lag as our radio operators are relaying back and forth."

"No, we need to split! There is no time." Mason took a deep breath. "Sooner we kill them all, the better, so I can finally go home!"

"How do you know? Have you done this before?" Gio picked up on the vibe. "What is the matter with you?"

"Don't you dare." Mason closed his eyes again.

"Our best chance to deal with the Power Platoon and whatever Hunter is coming up against us is to stick together. Splitting is the stupid idea." Gio tilted his head, reading Mason. "Are you all right? Unfortunately, this is not the Mason I know."

"First TH, now you! Can you people catch a break? I am fine!" Mason formed a fist with his right hand, forcing Gio to step back.

"All right, then. Go wherever you want to go. I shall see you in the garage." Gio raised his hands and turned around. "Don't cry when you get blown up to kingdom come. Time to find these Australians!"

When Mason rejoined his crew, he felt six eyes staring at him despite only seeing TH holding a shell in his hands.

"So, what is the plan?" Van's voice cracked in the comms.

"Turn left here and follow this street." Mason looked through the vision slits on the commander's cupola. "Let's get this over with."

"What about Gio and his team? Should we not stick together?" Dema coughed.

"We are on our own. Turn left, and let's get this done and over with!" Mason almost shouted into the comms, but he halted himself as Da Vinci vanished behind the corner, leaving only dust clouds and tank tracks behind him.

———

"Whoa, did you see that? It seems like the All-American Platoon is about to snap in half, but the tension is also rising between the Power Platoon members. Both Platoons are about to run into each other," Benjamin pointed at the city map, with five tanks closing in on each other, carefully navigating the city grounds, "and Jeong-Min is holding down the Main Street. Who will go up in flames next?"

Benjamin stood up and walked around the table momentarily, but his eyes were fixed on the screen.

"All right then, let's look at the most potential engagements. Oden will clash with Jeong-Min, while Crusading Angel will collide with American Made, leaving the Da Vinci Tank to fight it out with Tomoe Gozen. Italians and Japanese had a little tank version of hide-and-seek earlier, so they're ready to end this. The finale is here, and I recommend watching it because things are about to go down! This is the final charge up the mountain, and fatigue has started to hit already."

"Where are they!?" Mason's eyes twitched again, and he felt his focus leave him.

Why does everything have to be the same! Ruins there, ruins over there, a small park there and there. There is nothing original here. Just ruins!

"They're around here somewhere for ninety-five percent." TH looked through the periscope. "The silence is killing me."

"Van, turn Angel to the right, but not completely. We'll wait them out here." Mason quickly weighed the options. "Extra angle should provide us with better protection."

"Will do." This time, Van's voice missed the excitement and drive from earlier; moments later, they were in the position.

The ruined house partially covered Crusading Angel and provided a perfect overview of the street and crossroads where the enemy should cross. After another ten minutes of nothing,

Mason was about to open his hatch for a better view when he spotted a reflection between the buildings to his left.

"Van, drive out; I need a clearer line of fire." Mason shook his head. "It seems like the enemy is to our left."

"Are you sure? I feel that they are aiming at us!" Van shouted, but to no avail, as Mason had already decided.

"Just drive!" Mason's eyes focused on the spot as Van drove out.

A long barrel poked out from the window of the ruined house, and soon, most of the rounded turret came into view, including the turret light, which gave their position away. Mason started cranking the turret to target the barrel, but strength started to leave him, and his vision blurred. Finally, with his last remaining strength, he got the gun pointing at the enemy tank, but before he started to shake violently and his world turned black, he pressed the trigger, and the last thing he felt was hitting his head.

———

"Mason!" Van was first to remove his goggles when he spotted Mason shaking violently on the ground, bleeding from the head.

Van tore his suit apart and almost collided with Dema, who had just entered the real world after the sign GAME OVER appeared. Dema blinked and looked around, trying to process her return to actual reality. Then she stepped aside, but her eyes caught Mason on the ground as well. Her eyes widened, and her breathing increased, but she couldn't move. Next to the door to the simulation, there was a red button for emergencies. Only TH's voice snapped her out of the shock.

"What are you waiting for!? Press it! Mason needs help now! I'll try to stabilize him." TH looked at Dema as he gently turned Mason to the side. "What are you waiting for?! Press it!"

"On my God! Oh my God!" Dema sprinted towards the door and pressed it, shutting down all the simulation systems and engulfing them in flashing red and blue lights.

CHAPTER NINE

DOWN AND BAD

"Is he all right?" TH tapped the glass, prompting one of the doctors to turn around momentarily.

The way to the four-story hospital went quickly, and now they were stuck without any information in the empty hospital hallway. Due to the hospital's location, the rush of the Battle Royale complex wasn't present here, but still, many injured Filler contestants passed by them, either in wheelchairs or body bags.

"TH," Van tapped TH's left shoulder, "TH, calm down, brother. He is there, and he'll be all right."

"They always say that! I have seen it a thousand times. It seems like they are arguing and pointing at sleeping Mason. Something is happening. Hey!" As TH said it, Dema joined them and looked at the doctors pointing at Mason, and then one scanned the body with his tablet while the rest prepared the tools and systems.

One of the men in white put on the VR goggles and linked himself to the robotic arms that hovered above the operating table while a woman checked her watch and pressed her palm against Mason's sweaty forehead.

"What are they doing? Hey!" TH tapped the glass again, but now, he noticed his reflection as they blocked them out. "You bastards!"

"TH, I'm confident that Mason will fight through whatever he is going through, and our job is to be there for him, so we'll go home together," Van said to no avail as TH continued tapping the window. "TH, please. You're not helping his or our situation."

"Van is right." Dema touched TH's forehead, calming him for just a moment.

"But what if he doesn't? Statistics and math never lie! Eight out of ten contestants brought into this hospital will never make it." TH raised his voice and pounded the glass again, but he held onto Dema's left hand.

"TH, he will make it, no matter the math. You said eight out of ten cases would never make it. What about the two that do? Mason will be one of them, mark my words." Dema attempted to push TH away from his reflection but gave up halfway.

Minutes passed, and nothing changed, and silence started to get to everyone on the team. Even Van began patrolling the eerie, quiet hallway, with his footsteps echoing around them. As Dema looked at the digital clock on the door, she slowly exhaled. It had been four hours since they arrived from the Simulation match, and darkness from outside started to take its toll. *Come on, Mason, I need you. I cannot imagine what I would do without you. Please, God, if you are listening, help Mason. He prays to you all the time, even more than me. Don't forget him at his darkest hour. I love him, and I cannot lose him. His brother cannot lose him. Imagine what would happen if Ail learned that his older brother flatlined alone on the operating table. We are this close to going home.*

Little did she know that Van also tried to formulate a prayer in the adjacent hallway while drying his tears into his sleeve. Finally, he looked up as a nurse rolled a body in a black body bag and vanished into one of the rooms.

Mason, you better pull through, because I don't know what we would do without you. We got this far, and we'll go home together. God, if you are up there, you know that I never asked for any help, but now, please ensure that Mason will pull through. We need him. I need him. Mason has shown me something, something that I haven't ever seen. A determination to fight, despite what he is going through because he is going through something, yet he leads us into the fray, Van thought as the clock ticked life away. He turned around and walked back to the lobby, where Dema got seated. A moment later, TH joined her.

"Team 28?" Another doctor appeared from behind the corner, holding a black tablet.

The mask covered his face, and only his green eyes were visible. Then, dressed in a white coat with a black tie, he invited the team to sit with him in the adjacent lobby, away from the main entrance. When they got seated, he removed his surgical mask but didn't rush to deliver the news.

"Do you have any news for us?" Van broke the silence first. "How is Mason?"

"Contestant Mason Knight is stabilized for now. However, he is staying with us for the time being. I advise you to return to your station to resume your duties. Please..." Doctor slowly exhaled, "don't worry, we'll take good care of him."

"No, we'll wait here!" TH tapped his index finger on the doctor's tie. "You'll have to remove us by force."

"If it comes to that, I will call security. You did your best and acted fast. Now, thank you for your service. I'll make sure that someone will pick you up." The doctor stood up, put his mask back on, and vanished into the hallway.

"We heard the man!" Dema clapped her hands, but TH shook his head, refusing to move for a solid minute, ignoring what the hell look that Dema gave him.

Then, as TH finished counting to fifty, he walked on his toes to the corner. He slowly peeked into the hallway, like a commando operative on a secret mission, and pressed onward, hugging the wall.

"What the hell?" Van whispered, and Dema scratched her head. "What do we do, sister?"

"Let's follow him." Dema lowered her voice as well, and

soon, they caught up with TH, who pointed into the hallway where the doctor talked with a nurse who also had a tablet.

"Maria, after I send you the data, ensure they have left. While it might be easier to just say he didn't make it, TVG is breathing down my neck to keep contestants like Mason and his modification alive. The last thing I want to do is a six-hour surgery to remove it." Doctor shook his head. "What's wrong with the Internet in this building? Why is it so slow?"

"What modification? Is he in danger?" The nurse leaned forward. "IT is looking into it. They say it should be ready before the surgery.

"Are you aware of the CMA?" The doctor switched screens on his tablet, and after two beeps, he typed something.

"CMA? I don't remember this," The nurse said.

"Clear Mind Act, which outlaws all modifications to the brain and nerve system, permits mechanical limbs and organ replacement," Doctor calmly explained. "Mason has a Nerve Spider MK2, if I am correct. It is an illegal modification bought by suffering soldiers with PTSD since the VET program wasn't operational then. The Spider lives with a bearer and learns what triggers PTSD, and then it numbs the system, but it needs pills to survive. Depending on the modification, when it doesn't receive food for two or three days, it gives a user a seizure and attempts to gather its food supply, damaging the body in the process. After a while, it will become an addiction, and it seems like Mason has attempted to fight it."

"How do we know when it is activated?"

"Long-stares, complete numbness to the violence around the individual and suppression of feelings like tears and laughter. Individuals may be in deep depression or lose their sense of direction, just things we know about. A hundred thousand Nerve Spiders have been deployed, and we can only guess when the next individual malfunctions."

"Who did this?" The nurse picked her jaw from the floor. "How is this humane?"

"Don't know, but it costs around ten grand, plus monthly food supply makes it a pretty expensive option and deadly. Five thousand deaths were recorded, but it could be way more. There is an entire underground industry that IC is fighting. Mason, like others, must have been extremely desperate to take this fix, and only they know what they are going through. Do you have any questions? If not, I must return and prepare for the operation; I am taking the point on Mason, and that Spider will be difficult to locate. It might get ugly because if we fail to extract Spider on time, he will take Mason with him to the other side." The doctor looked over his shoulder. "Okay, this is getting ridiculous. Here is my tablet; transfer the data. Then check on the contestant in room 280 or that gasoline cowboy from that IS-2 tank. Alexander Gordon. If he is nearly dying, send the harvesting crew to get his organs. We need the liver, heart, and both of his kidneys. Tell them to store everything else for a rainy day."

"Yes, Sir! I'll go to IT first." Nurse bowed her head and jogged away while the doctor slowly exhaled, tapped his forehead, and entered the operating room.

"I think the coast is clear, guys," Van whispered, and Dema allowed herself to breathe. "What the hell!?"

"So, what do we do? We don't have much time," Dema looked around her, but the hallways remained empty, "and I need to use a restroom."

"Okay, this is what we'll do. I and TH will check up on this Alex guy while you do your deed and then try to stall the nurse as much as you can. We'll see you outside." Van looked at TH, who gave him a thumbs up.

———

Unlike the white hallways of the hospital, the restroom was painted navy blue. The mirror above the sink forced Dema to look away as she cried. She closed her eyes and took a paper towel, but the flushing toilet sound caused her to look down.

"I'm sorry to hear what happened to Mason." Dema looked up as she finished cleaning her face and noticed another woman by her side. "You guys stood your ground in that fight. Very impressive."

Her long black hair matched the tank uniform, and her blue almond eyes measured Dema, trying to read her. The first thing that jumped out was a patch on the woman's shoulder. The white O and underneath, number 18 forced Dema to look away momentarily—*the House favorites. Be careful.*

"Well, the doctor says he will be alive, but they will keep him for the night. My name is Dema."

After a moment of hesitation, the woman shook hands with Dema, relieving the tension in the air.

"My name is Wang Xiu, Commander of the Chi-Nu-Kai or Imperial Year 2603 Medium tank Model 10 Prototype and leader of Team 18."

"That is a long title, not going to lie," Dema chuckled. "Wow. So, you are..."

"Yes, I'm from the Power Platoon. Well, not by choice."

"Really? I thought that you were one of those who came willingly, seeking glory or whatever. So how is it up there?"

"Up there? I'm not following." Xiu looked around her. "Please explain."

"Well, you guys have the best gear and stuff. Night vision, camo nets. Or the fact that security does not kick you out or points tasers at you."

"You think we have an advantage? My tank is a paper tiger. Yes, it looks scary, but we have little to no armor, miserable speed, and a cramped interior. We're in the same boat, Dema. Germans got a night vision to set them apart. Americans have possibly the best all-around tank, and what do I get? A camo net. That is my uniqueness! A camo net. And all-female crew because of representation. Do you know how hard it is to coordinate five women in a box on tracks under fire?" Despite the outburst, Xiu chuckled, and so did Dema. "You four are more in sync than we are. That is a compliment."

Dema pondered for a moment about the new revelation.

"I didn't mean to launch at you like that. It is just..." Dema hid her shaking hands in the deep pockets of her pants.

"Mason, right? I believe in the guy. When I first saw him grabbing lunch in the cafeteria and learned that he was here to pay the medical bills for his brother, my respect increased tenfold. Do you know why I'm here?"

"Not by choice, I reckon. Please, go ahead." Dema stepped aside, and Xiu slowly exhaled.

"I'm here because there is a friend I haven't seen in ages. I hope that I get to catch up with him soon."

"That is nice. Nothing high stakes. That is what friends are for, right?" Dema tapped Xiu's right shoulder. "If I may ask, who won the simulation?"

"By Platoon or by the Team? Well, of course, Team 16 with their Hydro tank or however you call it, then it was Gio," Xiu halted herself, "I mean Team 26."

"You know Giovanni Smith?" Dema moved closer.

Wang Xiu looked around the bathroom, awaiting someone to jump from behind the corner.

"How do you know him? You are from Japan, right?"

"Well, it is complicated. I was born here in the US, but then we moved to China because my dad got a job offer. One day, he went on a company fishing retreat. Somehow, the Chinese Navy didn't spot them sailing into naval wargames they played that week. According to official sources, the computer failed to recognize them as a civilian vessel and launched a missile at them, ending their lives in an instant. So, after burying an empty casket, I moved to Japan, and now I am back here."

"I am sorry to hear that; I truly am. How do you know Gio?"

"His name is Giovanni Smith, or as I called him, Gio, my best childhood friend. We grew up on the same street in the now-gone New York, but his family moved away. We kept in contact, but during the War his trail went cold, and I couldn't believe it when I saw him here." Xiu dried her tears, and Dema handed her another paper towel. "I don't know if he recognized me or not. Maybe he did, but he likes to keep many things to himself on the other side. You have to press Gio to open him up."

"It sounds like you two are pretty close." Dema went for a hug, and Xiu accepted.

"Ten years we played together on the dirty New York streets with rats and the homeless before they were wiped out. Now, we are together again in this." Xiu grabbed her wrist. "We are on the same edge together, yet we are miles away from each other."

"Everything all right?" Dema tilted her head to the right.

"It's just this barcode." Xiu rolled up her sleeve, and Dema covered her mouth. "You seem surprised. Wait, you thought that some people are here willingly? Nobody is."

"I have the same one!" Dema also rolled up her sleeve, and Xiu nodded. "That means that TH, Van, and Mason..."

"Yes, they did something and took the offer. What are you in here for?" Xiu said and looked at the mirror once more.

"It's complicated." Dema's face turned red as she looked away.

"It isn't, Dema. Like you, I am a political prisoner." Xiu shook her head as her hand rested. "You have that belief. The belief that you want to make the world a better place. I remember the First Amendment. Freedom of Speech. Oh, how we took that right for granted. Dema, promise something. If we meet each other on the battlefield again, we won't shoot at each other."

"Me promise? I cannot do that. Mason is the Commander, not me." Dema pointed her index finger at Xiu. "What do you mean by again?"

"I need to hear it. The only way we win, one way or another, is to defy what they want from us. Dema, do you think that this simulation was it? TVG is going to milk the cow till it dies. We'll see each other again for sure."

"I should have figured that when they said the ride never ends, it truly never ends. You know what, my friend, I promise." Dema embraced Wang. "I promise to defy the order if I can."

"Thank you. Now, if you excuse me, I need to leave. Good night, and I hope that Mason pulls through."

Xiu left before she finished the sentence, leaving Dema alone in the bathroom. She stood motionless until the lights turned off but refused to move, her thoughts racing, processing what she had just learned. She covered her mouth again and turned around, prompting the lights to turn back on. *Oh no! God, if you exist, please show us the way out. Please!*

———

Thomas Askarov exalted when the loading bar finished, and the following 3D model was sent into production. His "burrow," which he nicknamed Bureau of Tank Research and Development, sat on the factory's second floor. On his door, Askarov Entertainment's digital sign hung. He looked at the clock to his right and closed his eyes as he thought about the next task. Even with the dark mode on, Thomas looked away from the screen every now and then to rest his eyes.

A birthday present for the love of my life. Rendering the next model into the testing simulation only took a moment, and as he was about to launch it, approaching footsteps forced him to look over the monitor. *Everything needs to line up, from size to movement.*

"Well, good evening, love. I hope you didn't forget that you have a flight tonight at 10:00 PM to Great Falls." Like Thomas, his right hand also had blue-greenish eyes, but this time, she trimmed her long blonde hair. "And shower; you smell terrible."

"Thank you very much, Adriana." Thomas hid the window, stood up, and stretched.

"Are you all right? You haven't left your office for two days; you still have the tracksuit from our dinner. You're whiter than the wall behind you."

"Yes, I finally got this Semovente da 105/25 done, and I'm now onto the L3/33 CC."

"Semovente? Is that Italian? I thought that we had to deliver a lot of German tanks?" Adriana raised her eyebrows.

"The overhyped German-Engineering. While I admire the rekindled flame for World War Two technology, we are getting paid by the batch no matter what, so I figured we could use some diversity. Look at this thing." Thomas pointed at the screen where a tank had rendered.

"That's L3?" Adriana sat behind the computer and zoomed in on the tank. "It's so small."

"Officially, it is called a tankette, but you can call it Lil Tank. Only 4 or so feet wide and 5 feet tall give or take. Happy Birthday," Thomas smiled and pulled up the data from the machine.

He watched Adriana attempting to hide her tears, followed by the kiss.

"You remembered?"

"I always do, my love." Thomas pressed the Enter and loading bar and began rendering the blueprints to the 3D model. "This one is just for you. It took two days to render it. Would you like to have it with machine guns, the anti-tank rifle, or the flamethrower?"

"Lil Tank? I would take one with the flamethrower. From the front, it has a face. Look!" Adrian pointed at the screen, and Thomas nodded his head.

The headlights angled the front plate and barrel of the 20mm anti-tank rifle, creating a sort of face as Thomas swapped out the gun for the flamethrower.

"Engineered to perfection. Would you like to have the

flame fuel stored in the trailer or on the backside?"

"Thomas, it is already perfect as it is; you don't need to bother yourself with such details," Adriana smiled, "but can you put it on a trailer?"

"For you, everything." Thomas looked down at the unfinished hulls in the workshops.

"Why is it so quiet?" Thomas looked around him. "Time is of the essence. I don't want to tell the TVG morons that we are behind on the shipment!"

"Well, the simulation match is happening. They're at the final stage," Adriana said. "That's why nobody is here, all home watching."

"It's Friday already? Let me guess; the Power Platoon is at full strength with some stragglers trying to regain their composure."

"Well, not exactly. Both Crusading Angel and American Made traded shots, while the Italians knocked out the Japanese but got destroyed by the Germans, who then secured the win by blowing up that Waffen-thing. I am sorry that I cannot pronounce that name."

"It ended?" Thomas switched the rendering program to the simulation footage. "Did Waffentrager fire at the G?"

"G?" Adriana tilted her head.

"Panzer IV G Hydrostat, love." Thomas felt his heartbeat increasing as he waited for the footage to load.

"Yes, they fired." Adriana tilted her head. "Everything all right?"

"Did they survive the shot?" Thomas began biting his nails. "They couldn't survive. Math cannot lie. Did I do something wrong?"

"Yes, they did." Adriana looked at ventilating Thomas. "No, you triple-checked it. I'm not following."

Thomas brought another office chair and rewound the footage, which went live with an audible beep. Then, bypassing the post-game analysis and the awards, Thomas held the rewind button like a trigger on the machine gun.

"Oh my!" Thomas shook his head and closed his eyes.

"I don't understand. What did you find?" Adriana attempted to analyze the frames but gave up halfway.

"I need to make a call." Thomas launched from the chair, but Adriana grabbed his hand.

As Adriana pressed play, she covered her mouth, and her eyes almost jumped out.

"How did they bounce that? Eighty-eight can penetrate... one shot would liquefy any target, especially all the tanks in this lineup."

"What? How? Oh," Adriana tapped the screen, "I think I'm following."

"From the front, even with the spare tracks, there is no chance that round bounced. Someone must have coded the armor value and given them a bit more. The alarming thing is that they only did it for the Hydro." Thomas walked around the office. "They said that my numbers are final!"

"Thomas, calm down. I know you are a perfectionist, but..." Adriana grabbed Thomas's right hand.

"But what?! In order to preserve the historical data for each tank..."

"Thomas, listen. No matter what we do, TVG will ignore it, just like ignoring our requests for more time. New tanks are being rushed out and sent out God knows where. Like that KV-1 with the Panzer 4 gun. I couldn't even finish testing when we had to ship it." Adriana raised her voice. "We need to do something about this."

"So, did you even do some QA?" Thomas slowly exhaled and then tapped his thumbs. "Tell me that you did."

"Barely, but I can safely say that tank will shoot and move around. For how long? I don't know. They didn't even bother to take spare parts."

"Well, it is a good thing that we are going together. Why Asia, of all places?" Thomas stood up. "Prepare the car while I shower. Please and thank you."

"Already done and waiting. Don't forget to lock the doors." Adriana waited for Thomas to copy data on his laptop.

"Go away! If you brought me more pills, get the hell out!" a man wrapped in bandages cried into the room when he heard the door open as his life support started beeping.

"Did you hear me!? Let me die in peace!" Then, as his eyes focused, he noticed a humanoid and man emerging from the darkness, dressed in the same uniform that hung in the closet next to his bed.

"We're not medical staff, Alexander. However, we would ask you a few questions." A humanoid brought two chairs.

"Questions about what? And who are you? Reporters? Media Influencers? Fans?"

"Is there a difference between those nowadays? My name is TH, and this is Van. We compete in this Tank Royale and would like to ask you for insight. Any tips and tricks?"

"Oh, God! I knew it! They are going to milk this." Alexander rolled on his bed. "Like you had a choice."

"Is there a trap?" Van tilted his head and looked at TH.

"Always is. These games are rigged from the start, so get out while you still can. I thought I could survive more than two games, but I was mistaken." Alexander coughed. "They changed it, didn't they?"

"Two games?"

"Yes, the Heavyweight Royale and the Interwar Match; I was promised my freedom afterward. One more, and that is what put me here. The ride never ends! Once you are in, there is nothing you can do."

"You were in the Interwar Match?" Van pretended to know, and Alexander nodded his head.

"Yes, I was. But, since I don't have much time, you are

the only ones who need to know this. I'll let you in on a little secret. Some of us were here from the start, leading into a final showdown for the world to see. It wouldn't be a fun time when TVG favorites would roll over everyone, so they sprinkled others all around to give you some sort of a chance unless you figured that out already. In that case, you know everything there is to tell you."

"Why did they have a break while you didn't?" TH continued making notes on his tablet.

"I'm marked as a corporate political prisoner. I have no rights, but I could have reclaimed them if I had won, but I didn't like all of you. We are just cogs, and people will cheer us on to move the TVG gears. Nothing more, nothing less. You flatline, they replace you."

"So, others are prisoners as well?" In his mind, Van looked at his barcode through his sleeve.

"Aren't we all prisoners in this corporate pyramid, where we are valued based on our raw output?" Alexander coughed up blood. "But it felt good when we gave the finger to the corporate machine. Bouncing shots, blowing up others, trash-talking the system, those were the days before they tightened their grip on us. I am not saying that the system is terrible. I am saying that we need to be better."

"Can you tell us their names?" Van said, and Alexander coughed up blood on white sheets. "Names of those who have already done it?"

"Me, Klemens Neufeld, Zanai Collins, Wang, and Gio." Alexander coughed up blood, and machines started to beep.

"Who?" Van leaned over Alexander, but he only made out blurbs.

Alexander pointed at the TV with his last remaining strength, where Team 26 was shown receiving the award. Van wiped the blood from his face and pressed his hand against Alexander's burning forehead.

"Giovanni!" Alexander cried as machines began beeping

again. "Please pull the plug! I am already dead! Please!"

"I will do it." TH walked up to the central switch while Van gave Alexander a thumbs up.

"Thank you!" Alexander squeezed Van's right hand.

A moment later, a grave silence descended on the room, and both Van and TH looked at each other with shock and awe in their eyes. In five seconds, the medical staff shoved them out, bringing a large black body bag, and wrapped Alexander's body in it. In the hallway, they ran into Dema.

"So, what did you boys learn?" Dema raised her eyebrows. "Everything all right? You have blood on your sleeves!"

"That there are contestants who were in the grind before, one of them being a man named Giovanni."

"You mean Giovanni Smith?" Dema raised her eyebrows. "I just met someone who knows him. What about the blood? Have you killed anyone?"

"Well, we helped." TH tapped Dema's right shoulder. "It was better for all parties involved."

Thanks to Adriana's charm and a phone call, both Thomas and Adriana boarded the 10:00 PM flight to Great Falls, Montana. Only a few other passengers were present on board, watching the evening TVG highlights, including the Simulation Match, reliving the moments once again. The small jet had wheels up at 10:15 PM, and a two-hour flight was ahead, which allowed Thomas and Adriana to catch up with the madness of the Tank Royale.

"So, I have been analyzing the footage and am now ninety-five percent confident that something is fishy." Thomas looked at Adriana, who raised her eyebrows.

"Thomas, I told you already, nobody cares at this point, but maybe it was a HEAT round? That might have explained that non-penetrating hit," Adriana kept her voice down, "it went through the fence."

"No, it wasn't the HEAT for sure. Look here." Thomas pointed at the round and pressed the slow-mo play. "Look how it flies.

No objects in its path, no wind, nothing, straight head-on shot."

The capped shot hit the spare track and left a large hole, but the frontal armor plate remained untouched.

"Did they deflect any hits before this engagement?"

"Yes, they did, but those shots were in the realms of possibilities. The steep angle of fire and one hit." Thomas reviewed the footage again. "Here. The 41M shot too low, so yeah."

"These are TVG-chosen tanks and crews. Oh, how time flies. I still remember when they shipped them to us to begin the testing."

Adriana lowered her voice when an older gentleman eyeballed them, and moments later, he slowly strolled toward them.

"At least that's what they want us to think. TVG just raised the prices in the Tank Shop yet again. Do you remember the first live testing at Little Rock State Park? We were both standing at the observation deck, watching our RC 38Ts battling in the mock-up battle. Then, that phone call moved us right to the live testing."

"It was a sight to behold. It was a lot simpler, but again, the budget for this venture was five dollars: no simulation training, not as many spare parts, and two workshops in our small factory. Now, we are a giant, and from what I heard, we'll expand upwards and to the high seas."

"So, what is the purpose of your flight?" The older man sat beside Adriana, who smiled while Thomas worked on the model.

"Business meeting. How about you?"

"I am traveling to see my son. Apparently, he got into this Tank Royale, and I haven't heard from him since. I recently got a screen, so I don't know if he fought yet. The last thing he said to me is that he will win."

"What is your son's name?" Adriana steered the conversation while Thomas clicked away on the 3D model.

"Alexander Gordon." The older man returned the smile.

"Then we wish him all the best." Adriana nodded, and the older gentleman looked at the man leaving the airplane bathroom.

"I must get going; the bathroom is finally available. Pleasure talking with you." The old man stood up and strolled down the corridor.

Adriana ensured the older man closed the door behind him. Then she turned towards Thomas.

"All right then." Thomas looked back at his laptop display and logged into the TVG Network.

"Do you know something that he doesn't?" Adriana whispered as a stewardess walked by.

Instead of saying anything, Thomas pressed the alt-tab, and the rendering model changed to the medical report and highlighted the dreaded name, *Alexander Gordon*.

"He died around thirty minutes ago. It was only a matter of time before Medical pulled the plug."

"How do you have access to such data?" Adriana shook her head. "Where is my access? And we should tell the older man when he comes back! He needs to know."

"Let's just say that I know a guy, who knows a guy—all-around access to everything my heart and mind desires." Thomas waited for the program to open. "When we land, we need to talk about Bell Entertainment."

"We need to tell him." Adriana folded her hands.

"We don't have to tell him anything. He doesn't have much time anyway, and telling him that his son flatlined won't help him. It will be better if he finds out on his own."

"Sure, why not? Why did TVG keep him alive? Look, there is even an MP4 file." Adriana touched the screen, and after a moment a file loaded up.

"Oh my!" Thomas looked around to ensure nobody saw the footage. "That is gross!"

———

"Gio goddamn vanni, what the hell! Do you know how dangerous this is?" Zanai Collins almost punched Gio when he emerged from the darkness of the tank park and sat down on the bench. "This better be important."

"You didn't see the second text?" Gio widened his eyes, and Zanai raised his eyebrows. "And don't be hard on yourself. Come on, nobody saw you anyway. I almost didn't."

"I'll pretend that I didn't just hear that."

"How many times have you mocked my hand movements and insisted that I should get a pizza? And I cannot make a joke about how you blend well with the night?"

"You are right. I am being a sensitive moron. I miss the good ol' days. Now, I feel like a mockingbird, just repeating what our handlers tell us." Zanai shook hands and embraced Gio. "Okay, what is happening?"

"We have a problem. Alex is dead. Oh yeah, almost forgot. Happy birthday, Zanai, right?"

"What?" Zanai sat on the bench. "Impossible! He was the best of us! I thought that he would pull through!"

Gio gave Zanai a moment to recover before he spoke again. Zanai stood up and walked around the bench two times before sitting down again, taking time to regain his composure.

"It is up to us then to finish." Gio took a deep breath as his eyes followed the long barrel. "Or they end us."

"Impossible!" Zanai pounded the wooden bench. "Tell me that you are kidding!"

"He was the only survivor after the JS-2 got blown up sky-high. A friend sent me a message with a brief summary of the medical report that came in an hour ago."

"Alexander and his crew literally stomped everyone, but it seems like the game was rigged from the start. Nobody cares how many tanks you killed; all that matters is that you won. I'm not even mad that we traded shots with that T-34 in the simulation." Zanai shook his head. "I still cannot believe it."

"You're not?"

"I'm tilted but impressed. It went through the coaxial machine gun port and blew up a shell, which my loader held in his hands when he was loading up the ready rack," Zanai went silent, "fireworks soon followed. God damn!"

"I do not think that Alexander's match was rigged. You cannot predict the placement, and as much as I hate this, Alexander got sloppy. They got flanked, just like the Cologne Tank Duel. You all right?" Gio sat down next to Zanai.

"Nobody was sloppy at Cologne. It was a combination of limited intel, quick decision-making, and a bit of luck. This entire setup is bullcrap. They dragged us to interviews and talk shows, making us these faces of the new entertainment, and we barely even had a chance to set up shop. We got back to the garage just three hours before the live simulation. While on that subject, I'm tired of the constant tokenism on top of being a political prisoner," Zanai finished ranting and looked at Gio, who folded his hands.

"Well, I am marked as well." Gio rolled up his sleeve, and a black barcode appeared.

"What are you in here for?" Zanai's eyes were wide open. "Gio, you never said anything! I thought you were insane going into the TVG meat grinder on your own accord! The one who came willingly!"

"I expressed moral concerns about TVG and their viewing catalog and followed it up with the system itself, so they marked me. And then, I found myself on the briefing, having no recollection of my arrest or how I got there."

"Brother, there is something you need to know. We'll be airdropped into Mongolia." Zanai leaned back on the bench. "Why couldn't we fight here? I would rather die on US soil than somewhere in Asia, pretty or not."

"Of all places in the world, why Mongolia?" Gio quickly traveled in his mind over the map of Asia and landed in Ulaanbaatar.

"Think about it. Two million or so people are living in the

area of Western Europe. On average, that would make it two individuals per square mile if my math is correct. It is diverse in geography and will work in whatever they have in store for us."

"The Zanai I knew from day one never guessed!" Gio was still processing the fact that the main fight wouldn't be in the United States.

"My white stepbrother scored an excellent job in Miami HQ, and now I regret speaking out. He kept his mouth shut. Plus, Klemens has a hard time keeping his crew in check. They think that they can boss us around."

"What is the matter with Klemens? That is not him."

"Nobody is himself now. Klemens is an engineer who likes to be left alone with his charts and numbers, not go on a week-long tour to talk with people. This is it. One winner will walk, and everyone will leave in body bags or not at all. Klemens vanished before he could tell me, but from what I decoded today, meaning yesterday, when he was fighting in the simulation, the nukes leveled Berlin to the ground eight years ago. Then, two days later, when we are deployed, nukes hit Washington DC."

"I didn't know that!" Gio raised his voice. "No wonder! That explains it!"

"Well, now you know. As much as I liked this venture, I preferred it when it was small and we all acted like ourselves. In that, we were together, trying out this new thing, but now, TVG primed us and turned us against each other."

"Tell me about it. It was bound to happen sooner or later. Why even bother with platoons in the first place? I mean, I respect Mason, but..."

"I don't think 28s know that the fight for life or death begins now. You know why we didn't have to bother with platoons, but we did it anyway? Social media traffic, sponsors, and control. You at least didn't have a scripted interview. I don't have much time, Giovanni, but I wanted to ask you something.

Where did the rule of two survivors come from?" Zanai stood up and stretched his legs. "Always wondered that, but Agnes cannot answer it, and this is probably my only chance to ask the certified tank nerd. No offense."

"None was taken, Zanai. Well, you need a driver to drive and a gunner to shoot the gun. It comes from the French Renault FT, which was considered the first *conventional* tank with a rotating turret. The driver drove the tank, and the commander commanded and shot the gun."

"Thank you for telling me about Alexander, brother Gio; he'll be missed." Zanai shook hands with Gio, but looked over Gio's shoulder when he heard footsteps. "If the situation was different, we would raise a glass to his health. Do you think his father knows? His wife?"

————

"Van, do you have a moment?" TH halted Van as he was about to close the door to his room.

"I'm not exactly in the mood to talk, but what is it?" Van yawned.

"This just arrived." TH handed Van his tablet. "It was sent to me by accident. It's Ember."

"What? Why would Ember send you a message, but not me?!" Van swiped up and found a video message awaiting him.

From the thumbnail, the face of Ember appeared, and with shaking hands, he pressed play.

TH gave him a thumbs up and went downstairs. He put his foot on the roadwheel and climbed the Crusading Angel. When he closed the hatch behind him, TH opened a new note in his CPU.

I don't know if anyone will ever have a chance to read this, but I need to say something. I would never imagine that humans would use others' deaths to entertain themselves. The question is, why? Wasn't War enough? Half of the world's population was lost over the five years. Four billion people. Four Billion! Why? One life lost is too many, but four billion? At least we have a coffin ready for us.

———

Dema was about to sit on the bed when a loud cry from the hallway forced her to run out. To her right, Van pounded the wall like a battering ram, trying to hold himself together and beeping tablet with the cracked screen balanced on the edge of the floor.

"Van, what is happening?" Dema grabbed Van's right hand, but he didn't reply; instead, Van twisted his arm out of the lock and continued pounding.

"Hey! What is happening!?" The rage and pounding didn't stop any time soon, so Dema pulled Van towards her.

"Are you all right?" Dema choked Van for a moment before he tapped out, finally calming down.

Dema looked at his bleeding knuckles and pressed his hands together.

"Yeah, Dema. I'm doing positively great! Just smile and wave, right?" Van said with a sardonic smile as he gripped his hair and slid down the wall in agony.

TH poked out of the loader's hatch, and Dema nodded. Then, after a thumbs-up, TH walked outside and vanished into the night.

"This day couldn't get any worse!" Van reached for the tablet but gave up halfway. Instead, he lay on the floor and took a deep breath.

"I know that we lost, but so what? It was just a simulation," Dema said. "Hopefully, we learned something that we can use in the actual fight. And Mason is in good hands. He will be back soon."

"Dema, it is not about simulation or Mason. It turns out

that the people whom I valued the most have ditched me. I wanted to propose to her next month!"

"Who? Why?" Dema sat beside Van, who hugged her like a weeping kid. "Ember?"

"Ember, my girlfriend. I should have figured that when I said goodbye, it was the goodbye forever."

"But what made you so furious? We're going home soon!"

"I didn't want to be called the Lover Boy of the Tank Royale, so I lied about why I was here, but I guess that didn't matter anyway. Ember lost her right arm in a factory accident two years ago. Sturdier prosthetics are expensive, but we were denied everything because of our farm. I put a target on my back and went underground, looking. And I almost found what I needed, but then they tagged me. So, I pressed the pedal to the floor by posting anti-corporate posts, and in two days, an unmarked van pulled into our farm, and I was transferred here. Farming is not exactly a money maker. It turns out that her new boyfriend has what I don't have. Money, and to rub salt into the wound, she sends me a video of her rock climbing with that money boy." Van took a deep breath as his hands started to shake again.

"I am sorry to hear that. How long have you been together?" Dema shook her head and touched Van's red forehead.

"Five years, Dema, with that bitch! We did and survived everything together. So why am I even here now? Dema, I wanted to propose to her and marry her!"

"I do not know what to say. I do not know. Well, do you have your own dreams on top of yours with Ember? Do you still want to open the distillery? There must be something that you want." Dema nudged Van on his left shoulder.

"Distillery was just smoke and mirrors, Dema." Van took a deep breath. "A cover-up story for the world to leave me alone, but now?"

"Think about it," Dema leaned back, "I am confident there are things you always wanted."

After a moment of silence, Van looked at Dema again.

"I guess I always wanted to own an S560." Van smiled sadly and closed his eyes. "Yeah, the S560."

"What is that?" Dema felt tension easing.

"A heavy-duty pick-up truck would be beneficial at the family farm. Roads around my family farm are ideal for such a car. It is a perfect mix of formula and pickup. That is the best of both worlds. And while the mileage suffers a bit, it's a truck."

"I meant to say something for yourself. What do you want?" Dema tapped Van's right shoulder.

"What do I want?" Van looked at Dema. "What do I want? Dema, what do you desire?"

"What do I want?" Dema scratched the back of her head. "Hmm. The house is nice and all, but I would be alone in it. Well, unless I found someone."

"Like Mason?" Van shook his head. "I can imagine you two living in a small house with a garden. Little Knights running around. Two kids minimum is my rule."

"Stop it!" Dema laughed. "But I guess you are right."

———

As TH entered the World War Two section of the Tank Museum, he spotted a man dressed in a gray and black uniform sitting on a bench, surrounded by sleeping war machines. A patch with O and the number 16 jumped out upon closer examination. Unfortunately, it was hard to make out facial features because the hands covered the man's face, and soon TH could hear words of desperation in German.

"Sir, are you all right?" TH sat down next to the man, who didn't respond at first, but then the man finally looked up, and red eyes greeted him.

"And who are you?"

Many emotions today. I wonder what the matter with him is. TH scanned the man from head to toe again.

The man also had a long beard, spreading wisdom and seriousness in the empty hallway.

"My name is TH. Team 28, Crusading Angel." TH extended his hand. "And who are you?"

After a moment of hesitation, the man shook hands.

"They call me Klemens, Commander of the Panzerkampfwagen IV Ausf. G mit Hydrostatische Antrieb and Leader of Team 16," Klemens said it with a German/American accent without dropping a sweat.

"English, please? I have no idea what you just said." TH nodded.

"My apologies. Tank Mark 4 G with Hydrostatic Drive. Funny enough, I am the only one who can say in my team."

"How so?"

"Well, I am the only one born in Germany; the rest were born here in the States. I want to apologize for the fake beef between us made by my crew." Klemens took a deep breath. "I have nothing personal against you or your crew, and I wish we would have met under different circumstances. How is Mason?"

"No harm done, my friend. My Commander is stabilized, and that is all we know. On the contrary, it brings views, right?"

"Yes, that is true. For me, my life was numbers, charts, and coding in a small room. Not this stage lights, scripts, or interviews. Do you know what saddens me the most?"

"I'm all receptors," TH said, and Klemens smiled, "or ears, I should say."

"My tank is supposed to represent a sovereign country that no longer exists, and people living there don't recognize the achievements and history of the German people. My Oden is just a prop. Berlin is just a settlement, located twenty miles from the original Berlin, just a crater, and Oktoberfest is a shadow of itself. The beer here is shit, but these days, even in Germany, it has dropped to unacceptable levels. It used to be world-class. Team 20 represents Canada, right? Toronto and Vancouver are still standing. While they don't ride on mooses," Klemens chuckled, "they have something to fight for. Canada has never won a Battle Royale, so they are motivated."

"Klemens, plural of the moose, is moose, but your point stands. Canada has always been four major cities anyway, so that is not a fair comparison."

TH tapped Klemens on his left shoulder, and he even laughed. "You are right. Thank you. Imagine being French in Canada and being ruled by the British monarchy. I mean, pick the lane."

"Not anymore, they aren't. Well, it is a free-for-all, right? So, everyone is against each other?"

"It's a joke, TH. In the end, yes. There can be only one standing, after all. No offense, TH, but how can you differentiate between good and bad as an android?"

"I really cannot, but I know this. Everyone is a cog in the large machine, and we have a part to play, whether we like it or not. I am technically a Nomad because humanoids have no citizenship whatsoever. I have no culture to fall back on; I only have my skills programmed into me, which I learned during my service life. And next time, do not put me into the same category as androids and robots. I don't want to be associated with them."

"I understand TH, but grow a pair. We're about to blow each other to kingdom come, and your only concern is words? We are cogs; you said it yourself. TH, sticks, and stones may break your bones, but words cannot hurt you." Klemens shook his head. "They called me Nazi at one point, just because I am proud German, raised in Berlin."

"Yet the words are the ones that hurt us the most when we are most vulnerable." TH folded his hands.

"That is a fair observation, but in the grand scheme of things, a 75mm shell will hurt you more than someone calling you a robot."

"You're right." TH relaxed his stance. "So, which tank here is your favorite so far?"

"My Oden is currently my favorite because it showcases our ingenuity. It is an all-around balanced and rather innovative tank from the era. Did you know that yesterday, eight years ago, nukes leveled Berlin to the ground?"

"I'm sorry to hear that. Did you see it happening?"

"Thank you, TH. I was returning from Norway when the news arrived. I glued my face to the screen, watching what had happened, and a few hours later, we flew above the crater. It was estimated that the nuke had landed on the Brandenburg Gate. My family waited for me at the airport, which also got targeted. Erased at that moment." Klemens bit his hand.

TH tapped his knees as he made a note in his CPU and tapped his forehead, thinking about the magnum opus of humanity, the WMD.

———

As the Saturday hit eight in the morning, the alarm forced Dema to evacuate her dream. She cursed between her teeth and turned over. Moments later, she heard Van's alarm, followed by loud grunting and silence.

"Van, you all right?" Dema shouted as she reached for her old music player.

"No! Everyone, leave me alone for ten more minutes!" the response echoed in the garage, and then silence.

"All right, but don't be too long." Dema fixed herself, and moments later, she joined TH, who stared at the garage door.

"Good morning, Dema." TH invited Dema to join him, and she quickly wrapped the cable headphones around the music player.

"Do you also need ten minutes?" Dema looked upstairs. "And why are you staring at the door?"

"Waiting for Mason to come back so we can all leave together."

TH looked at silent Dema. "I am sorry about what happened to Van, but I sadly couldn't feel what he was feeling, so my apologies for thrusting it on you. I forgot to account that you have your problems. It won't happen again."

"It actually helped me as well." Dema placed her hand on TH's right shoulder. "I needed that moment, same as Van."

"How can the pain and sorrow of Van help you? Please explain." TH touched his head.

"Well, he made me realize that I have feelings as well. I had to suppress most of them; this, TH," Dema waved the tablet. "And for the first time, I feel that I can love again and truly see what I want from life going onward. Clear as day, I can see it."

"Mason, is that right?" TH gave Dema a thumbs up. "Unless there is someone else I am unaware of. Van? He has a girl-friend!"

"Yeah, it's Mason. There is something about him. Something that I love, but I cannot pinpoint what exactly."

"Don't look at me; I don't know." TH raised his hands in the air. "I wonder, Dema, what will it take to stop TVG from killing people?" TH nodded.

"Something needs to be done, TH."

"But how can people sitting in front of the TV eating fast food help us?"

"We will figure it out, TH," Dema grinned from ear to ear, "but we need to start somewhere."

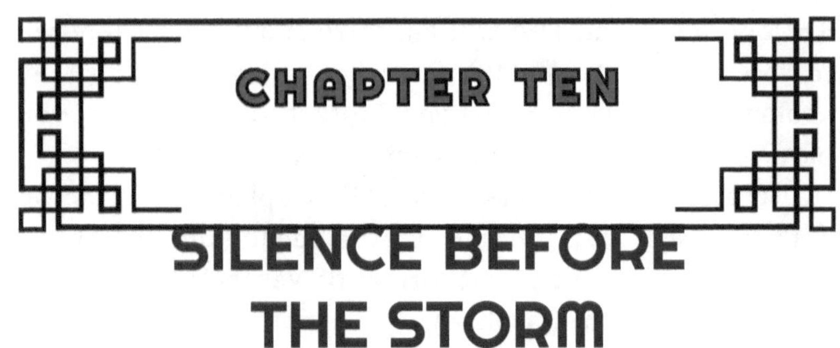

SILENCE BEFORE
THE STORM

"Benjamin, are you there? We are on air in five minutes! Hello?" Jeong-Min pounded on the gray door, which bore the *Benjamin Bell* sign.

Around Jeong-Min, studio personnel ran around, carrying lenses, tablets, and a large trophy covered by a white cover with large black letters. Still, no response from the room.

"Benjamin, get your ass up! We are live in four minutes, and two billion people await you." Jeong-Min pounded on the door again.

"Sir, my apologies, but Benjamin is currently on sleeping pills and won't be airing today, but will join you tomorrow." The young female coughed behind Min. "Please, this way. We'll have the teleprompter ready for you. Do you prefer English or Korean?"

"Well, all hands on deck then," Jeong-Min joined the intern. "He didn't look well in the first place. Good to know that he is finally resting."

"I can only tell you what I heard, which is that we are behind the broadcasting schedule. Other programs complain about their run-time," the intern said, "thank you again for being here."

"Pleasure is all mine." Jeong-Min looked at the door one more time. "Script in English, please."

———

"Good morning, Van. How are you feeling?" Dema waved at Van, who slowly descended the stairs, leaning against the railing.

"I needed those ten minutes, and now I'm ready to emerge into society again." Van, dressed in his pajamas, saluted. "Not going to lie. I'll miss this place. There is a weird charm to it. While I can't quite put my finger on it, I like it here, but home is waiting. My brothers, Mom, and Dad, they must be worried. I tried to reach them, but to no avail. Anyway, how're you all?"

"You don't have to put the mask on for us; we all understand what you are going through, but glad to have you back. We're just waiting for Mason and the announcement for today, and then we're going home." TH gave a thumbs-up, and moments later the corporate tune played, and the face of Jeong-Min appeared on the screen without Benjamin Bell by his side.

"Where is Benjamin?" Dema leaned forward, with Van and TH peeking from behind her shoulders.

Good morning, Gasoline Cowboys!

It is precisely 10:00, and we have a long day ahead. Benjamin won't join us today, but don't worry; he will return soon. All right, I would like to congratulate the simulation winners, and now it is time for some news. As of 09:40, three billion people tuned in, and a million purchased a premium plan, which we are all grateful for since it helps fund our future seasons. From the world news, the Clean Air Initiative has fully restored the ozone layer, and they are not stopping any time soon, so please do your part, install a small air filter today for better sleep and brain activity for only c$35.99, and enroll in the Clean Air Initiative today to support the ongoing efforts!

An earthquake hit South Korea; more details are to come as the situation develops. I wish my countrymen and brothers in uniform all the luck and, for those affected, a speedy recovery. Yeah. Continuing the news, I will have special guests in the studio at two o'clock, who will show us the process from blueprints to the real deal.

This is Commander Jeong-Min, and I will be here after the commercial break to review the highlights from yesterday or whatever I'm told to do. So, I do apologize; I haven't done this in a while.

"So, are we going home? They don't seem to be rushing us. Hmmm." Van's loud 'hmm' filled the garage. "My thinking hmm is unable to figure this out."

"All right, team. Let's pack our luggage to be ready when Mason comes." Dema clapped her hands and made a fist.

Actually, my sincere apologies; I made a mistake.

Everyone glued their eyes to the screen as Jeong-Min appeared on the screen once more. Van touched Dema's shaking shoulder, and TH looked away momentarily.

You'll be picked up tonight at 22:00 and will be deployed tomorrow on the battlefield, where the real fight will begin soon. Cowboys, listen to me! This is what you trained for! Like tanks, you must be in sync and on point. Think before you load up. You should have received a standardized packing list, and feel free to customize it to your needs. Ammunition will be loaded when you board the transport. You'll also need to refill your fuel tanks. Don't forget anything of value here.

Everything will influence your combat prowess, from terrain to the state of your tank and equipment. Remember, the decision to fire or not fire, stay at a long distance or close the range, drive out or remain hidden are the choices that can save your life or cost you victory. Everything comes with advantages and disadvantages. Remember your training and you'll make it far! So, heed the call of your intuition; your mettle is upon you! Good luck!

"What the hell?" Only Van could speak as the screen changed to the primary desktop. "I thought we were going home! They are kidding, right? They must be! No, I don't believe that!"

TH looked at the Crusading Angel while Dema sat on the wobbly chair, and her head vanished in her arms. Next to them a tablet beeped, and Gio's face appeared, but Dema hung up and took a deep breath. The bright light in the garage vanished, and darkness settled in for a moment.

"Where is Mason!?" TH touched the front headlight as he said, "Where are you, brother?"

———

"Absolutely perfect, you're a natural at this." The entire studio applauded Jeong-Min right after the announcement. "The correction at the end, just perfect! Chef's kiss!"

"Thank you, everyone, but only for today." Jeong-Min waved and leaned back in the chair. "Benjamin is the true face of this Tank Royale. I'm just an honorable guest."

"All right, sir, we have a commercial break for now, and after that, we'll hit the live feed into the Tank Royale sector. Do you need anything else?" A man with a tablet walked up to Jeong-Min and attempted to salute.

"At ease, soldier." Jeong-Min smiled. "Can you give me the data for our contestants? I would like to check something."

"No problem; you should be able to see it on the board behind you. So, what exactly are you looking for?"

Jeong-Min smiled again. "Just wanted to make sure that at 14:00, I'm live again, right?"

"Yes, sir, that will be correct. At 14:00, you're meeting with Chief Designers Thomas Askarov and Adriana. Anything else?"

"Not really; I shall let you know," Jeong-Min said, and the man nodded.

Jeong-Min randomly touched the screen, and Team 10 began loading. After a short moment, a 3D model of Centaur Mark III was rendered. Five faces jumped out at him, and soon, the diversity started to jump out. While they were all Caucasian, each young man came from different parts of the British Isles or traced his origin. In this case, George Adams–Commander from England; Cadell Evans–Gunner from Wales; Anderson Steward–Loader from Scotland; Michael Doan–Driver from the Isle of Man; and Niall Byrne–Codriver/Radio

Operator traced his ancestry to Ireland.

"What do you think? The most diverse Battle Royale this Season," the man with the tablet said. "We always deliver on our promise. Everyone can find their favorite, no matter who and where they are!"

Instead of saying anything, Jeong-Min touched Team 18, and five female faces appeared, all with Asian features, and a similar story jumped out, except for the Commander, who was US-born but lived in Japan. He hovered over the 3D Model of Chi-Nu-Kai. Gunner from Indonesia, a Loader from the Corporate City of Hong Kong, a Driver from Corporate Mongolia, and a Co-Driver/Hull Gunner from the Corporate Islands of the Philippines.

"You're right, but I'm missing Africa. No African countries made their tanks during World War Two?" Jeong-Min finally spoke up.

"TVG presents an all-black crew that rides on the mentioned Sherman for the complete diversity circle. Commander Collins's ancestor fought in World War Two on an M3A3 Stuart light tank, and of course, all contestants are from the US." The man with the tablet nervously looked around.

"So, tokens then. Hm." Jeong-Min looked at the screen, where the Japanese Tank aimed its barrel at the viewer in the idle animation. "But Chi-Nu-Kai is a Japanese tank, so why is it not crewed by the Japanese crew only? Why did I even ask? Tokens again."

"Sir, this is above my paygrade; I'm just here to make sure that you are comfortable and know what you say for the broadcast," the man shook his head, "but I can take a guess that I won't be responsible for."

"If answering my hypothetical question is a liability and could result in you losing your job, then don't answer it. Are there any questions from the audience that I can answer?" By then, Jeong-Min noticed the hornet's nest of internal politics. "Might be an excellent filler in the meantime."

"Oh, yes, there are a lot of them. Do you wish to go live in five minutes?"

"Yes, we can go live now; that will be perfect." Jeong-Min stood up and stretched his neck while the crew prepared for the next live broadcast.

———

"Gio, what are you doing!" James tapped Gio on his right shoulder, and sparks stopped flying from the top of the turret.

"I'm cutting this single hatch in half so Mark and I can open and close our flaps separately, and then I'm reinforcing joints on the hatch itself. Once finished, I'll need you to hand me the roof-mounted machine gun to attach it back to its original place. It's on the shelf, next to the spare tracks."

"Ready when you are!" James walked up to the shelf and momentarily played with the empty magazines.

"Have the twins prepared the tools yet?"

"No, not yet. After the morning news, they vanished to grab breakfast." James turned around and slowly exhaled. "Tonight, we're leaving!"

"Do the inventory before the twins return," Gio shrugged his shoulders, put on his goggles, and soon sparks started to fly again, "and also, start welding as many spare tracks to the frontal plate as you can."

"You are not hearing me. We are leaving tonight!" James raised his voice, but Gio shook his head.

"James, does it matter? We knew the wind's direction. Look, I'll ensure that I'll take care of you all. It is upon us now, and we must adjust. We can sit here and cry about it, but that's not going to help us."

"You're right. Will these tracks actually help, or is it just for the feeling?" James took the spare track link and placed it onto the frontal plate.

"Might help, might not." Gio smiled and returned to the

cutting. "After this, we should talk with our remaining platoon members."

———

The mood in the garage had dropped below zero, and with three rucksacks, a gym bag, and a smaller bag on the table, Dema was the only one looking towards the garage door, awaiting Mason to come back. With each minute ticked away on the digital clock above her head, she heard Van slowly breathing behind her. TH walked around the kitchen, occasionally stopping to look at the door, and then continued walking.

"Guys, do not worry! He will be here soon!" Dema attempted to raise the down spirits. "And while we are not going home yet, I believe that with Mason, we will."

"About that. Isn't this a little messed up? I don't know if you remember," TH said, "but there were glitches in a few announcements. Do you remember the screen glitching and then resuming like nothing had happened?"

"I think I saw it too," Van scratched his chin, "like flashes or something?"

"So, any guess where we might be heading?" Dema continued to string the conversation.

"Dema, I just want to go home." Van rested his head on one of the backpacks. "I want to see my family! My bros, mom, and pop."

"Van, do you remember how you screamed at us for not caring about AI replacements?" Dema turned away from the door, and even TH stopped walking briefly.

"Yes, I do. What are you getting at?" Van raised his head.

"What if they are trying to destroy us psychologically before the fight, so we make mistakes?" Dema pointed at Van, and TH immediately picked up on the idea.

"What Dema is trying to say is that video Ember sent, well,

might have been fake!" TH nudged Van, who took a moment to process what his partners had discussed.

"Do you guys think it's fake!? Please, don't play with my emotions because now I don't know what to think!" Van sprung from the chair and pounded the table. "If it's just an edited video, I swear to God, I'll kill everyone at TVG."

"Alright, calm down, my friend." Dema stood up as well.

"Do not friend me, Dema!" Van pointed his shaking index finger. "I'm sorry for yelling at you. I couldn't even sleep yesterday!"

"Guys, look!" TH waved at a figure standing in the doorway, concealed by the glass from the kitchen and a shadow. "Who is that?"

"My children! Daddy had returned!" a familiar voice echoed in the garage, and a moment later, Mason entered with a wide smile.

"Mason, you are back!" Dema launched towards Mason, who extended his arms.

"Hell yeah, I'm back! Are we ready to go home?" Mason hugged Dema and felt her tears watering his right shoulder.

"So, what did I miss?" Mason waved at TH. "One of the nurses told me you were with me until the operation. Thank you for sticking with me."

"What would we do without you?" TH gave Mason a thumbs up.

"You would go on with your lives, live for me and remember. I would do the same for all of you. Van, you all right there?" Mason looked at Van, who continued staring at his boots. "Hey, come here. What's up?"

As Van explained the video and the aftermath of what happened, Mason embraced him as well, like a mother goose with her gosling.

"Van, you're with Ember for how long? Three years? Do you still trust her?"

"I, I don't know Mason. Would you?"

"My answer will differ from yours. Answer this question for yourself, all right? Now, what did I miss?"

"Tonight, we are being deployed. So how do you feel?" Van tapped Mason on his right shoulder.

"Wait, tonight?" Mason stepped back and widened his eyes. "Hold on a moment. Tonight?"

"Yes, tonight."

"Well, I'm not saying that I'm surprised by this development. Now, the words of the doctor finally make sense. He instructed his assistants and nurses to do the bare essentials on me because everything else would be a waste since I'll die soon, which told me everything I needed to know."

"You're awfully calm about this!" TH raised his hands in the air.

"I made my peace with it. All right, no time to waste then! Dema and Van will focus on mobility-related matters, while I and TH will focus on firing-related matters. Before we start packing, I would like to apologize for concealing my problems, which could and probably will cost us in the real fight." Mason sat on the box. "And I promise I'll try to overcome them and lead you to victory."

"Mason, look here. We all have our demons to fight." TH looked around him. "Our tank might not be perfect nor powerful, and we might break down, but under you, we will make it."

"Thank you, TH; I value it! And I'll keep saying my thanks to you for standing by my side every chance I get, and I'll praise the big G for keeping me, well, us alive just a bit longer."

"I would like to say something if I may. As the time approaches, I think I need to come clean in front of all present." Van stood in the middle of the group and rolled up his sleeve, revealing a black barcode. "I apologize for not disclosing this earlier. Now that genie is out of the bottle. I feel much better."

"You're not the only one, Van." Mason smiled and rolled up his sleeve. "Like you, I'm marked, and so is everyone competing. That goes for our Gio and his crew."

Mason extended his arms for a group hug, and everyone stood silently for a moment.

"Guys, the barcode doesn't make us inferior, nor does it change my perspective about all of you. We are who we are." Mason watched Dema gulp while TH raised his hand.

－－－

When the clock showed 13:50, Jeong-Min stood up to greet Thomas and Andriana, who had just entered the studio but were immediately taken to the next room by a man in a black suit. Jeong-Min tapped his foot underneath the table, awaiting the guests as he reviewed the prompt with questions. *This is all too scripted—it's time to do something about it.* As Benjamin warned him, the prompt was politically correct and diverse in its language, with certain words and questions highlighted.

"Why are these words in red?" Jeong-Min raised his hand.

"That is for Benjamin to know where to stop. Sometimes, he likes to go on a tangent, so the red is his cue to return."

Jeong-Min nervously looked at the backroom, when 13:58 appeared on the digital clock, where Thomas and Adriana still hadn't left. He tapped his foot under the table again and looked around the beehive.

"We are live in a minute and thirty seconds; where are they?" Jeong-Min stopped one of the interns, who shrugged his shoulders.

"Corporate wants a word, and we already announced that the talk will be delayed. Apparently, it has something to do with the simulation, or so I heard?" One of the producers waved at Jeong-Min.

"What exactly happened in the simulation? Did I miss something?" Jeong-Min looked at the man, who vanished behind the camera.

No response as usual. Don't question; go with it. As Benjamin said, entertainment business.

When the clock hit 14:15, Thomas and Adriana left the backroom and joined Jeong-Min at the table. After their hands were shaken, Thomas prepared a chair for Adriana. The producer counted down, and all the cameras lit up red.

"Good afternoon, viewers; we are glad you can join us for the first and probably the only Making a World War Two Tank segment on Battle Royale TV. Today, we have special guests, and while many of you are going to see them for the first time, they have been with us since the beginning." Jeong-Min ditched the prompt and, in return, got an angry look from the Producer but thumbs up from all the interns. "Thomas, Adriana, glad to have you on the show. How was the flight?"

"We arrived yesterday since most of the work was done, and we just played around, awaiting new data," Adriana said. "How do you like this Tank Royale?"

"It is a rather interesting entertainment concept, and it is better than what my wife watches. I love you, honey, don't be mad at me." Jeong-Min smiled at the camera. "So I decided to ditch the teleprompter and get right into it. But I always wondered, what tank was the most difficult to resurrect from the ones in this lineup?"

"All tanks give us a healthy challenge, but probably the Hungarian 41M III Turán with the long 75mm cannon. I only had two pictures of the interior, one from the side and a spreadsheet from the Hungarian Archives dating back to 2045."

"So, what is the next step once you gather data?"

"Well, the next step is to put it into a 3D program, where I import all the data available. After that, the program renders it in 3D, and I play with the details, starting with the interior. Once the tank is finished, I improve it with historical guidelines. For example, the T-34 tanks are famous for their poor visibility, so in the late '44s, a new commander's cupola was added to the older T-34 models. Also, instead of polished steel used in periscopes, we used glass." As Thomas talked, the screen behind him showed him working in the office, with peeks at the displays. "Every tank gets the same treatment. On some, we add some flavor like the RP-3 rockets on the Centaur."

"So, what happens now?"

"Now, once I submit the model, I go straight onto the next one. As the model goes through the system, the machines generate and spit out related parts, starting with the hull, and after four hours, the kit is ready for assembly. After everything is piled up, a workshop takes over, assembles the tank, and does the first tests, and this is where Adriana comes in." Thomas looked at Adriana, who waved at the camera.

"So, what is your job?" Jeong-Min turned toward Adriana and smiled.

"Well, I'm the field girl. Once the tank is ready, I drive around our obstacle course and then to the shooting range to test the firepower. I and the computer gather needed data, and if something goes wrong, we return it to the workshop. It is ready to fight once it gets a 100 percent completion mark. Then we load it on the train, which brings it here. The workshop prepares the documentation, like a factory manual and others, for contestants to use. Once it is shipped, the computer updates the training simulation, where my job ends. The cycle repeats itself." Adriana pointed at the photograph of the Canadian Ram II late production being secured by the factory personnel on a railway flatbed.

"You mentioned the workshops. How many are there on the factory grounds?"

"Since we don't have the assembly line, six to eight workshops, depending on the workload, each with ten to fifteen engineers. We do not rush this kind of work, but speaking of rushing, please, whoever is sending the orders, please give us more time; we beg of you."

"I have one more question before we go to the official Q&A. How long does it take to have a tank combat ready?"

"Three to four days, depending on the machine, but add a day or two just to be sure."

———

"Well, this is progressing nicely!" Mason walked around the Crusading Angel with the list, checking off everything. "Good job, everyone!"

"I must say, it is like packing for a road trip. Are we taking this spare roadwheel?" Van rolled the large roadwheel and looked around the back of the tank, filled to the fullest with auxiliary equipment.

The tank's sides were also covered, and on the turret handles, TH finished placing spare tracks for extra protection.

"Everyone, stop what you're doing!" Dema clapped, gaining everyone's attention. "Let's think about this. On the one hand, yes, we need all those things, but on the other, let's not forget that we need to shoot occasionally."

"All right, so what do you reckon, Dema?" Mason carefully placed the toolbox on the ground.

"We should carry more ammunition, just in case. Each crew gets two to three boxes, and that's it, but I think that we can scavenge more from the combat area."

"I would like to object." TH raised his hand. "I'm standing on top of the ammunition boxes, so filling it up will not help. Mason and I are gone for good if we get hit there."

"So, what do we need?" Van climbed on the back of the tank.

"I got an idea," Mason walked to one of the boxes and pulled out the camo duffle bag, "each of us will pack our personal belongings here, freeing some space in the back. Now, we don't need four tents; we only need two."

"All right then," Mason tapped Van's right shoulder, "I'm putting you in charge of packing our luggage and, looking at the clock, we need to move our asses."

"You're the only one who isn't packed." TH pointed out the luggage in the kitchen. "And it seems like we got some guests."

"Well, well, look who is here!" Giovanni knocked on the open door, followed by the rest of the 26s. "You made it!"

"I did." Mason climbed down and embraced the group. "It wasn't easy. Good to see you as well. Any news on our friends?"

"Still nothing. Anyway, we'll head back to finish packing. Good to have you back," James said, and a moment later, only Giovanni stayed behind.

"Mason, I would like to apologize for raising my voice back in the simulation. But, if you wouldn't make it, I would never forgive myself that our yelling would be our last exchange." Gio extended his right hand, and Mason shook it.

"No, I'm sorry for yelling. You have nothing to apologize for. Withdrawals do this to a man."

"Water under the bridge?" Giovanni bit his tongue.

"Water under the bridge." Mason embraced Giovanni, who nodded. "Water under the bridge."

"Glad to have you back." Gio tapped Mason on his left shoulder. "See you soon."

"Well, I have to say, it looks much better." Mason clapped thirty minutes later and walked around the tank again as TH piled up the backpacks.

After rethinking, the back of the tank wasn't as full as the first time, and a quick peek inside gave Mason an odd satisfaction. *Packed and ready to roll. God bless them. They must have been terrified of me being gone. With August and his crew gone, I'm not surprised. I never really had a good friend or group of good and close friends. Van was right, there is that chemistry between us. The fact that they pushed through, I mean, I don't know what to say. God bless,* Mason thought to himself, looking down at his crew and smiling.

"The only thing we are missing is ammunition. Should we refill the tanks?" TH waved at Mason, gaining his attention.

"Yes, refill the tanks on our tank so that we can tank the

tank." Van grinned. "And then we can tank with the tank, so our tank can finally be the tank and tank us to victory."

"Will do, Commander. I meant Mason." TH saluted and grabbed the hose from the corner.

Mason walked up to the table, filled with power tools and plates, but the manuals were gone.

"TH have you seen..." Mason called out, but his eyes caught Dema sitting on the stairs, reading the comments underneath their pictures.

"Dema, are you all right?" Mason sat beside her and noticed her red eyes and wet spots on their STREETPAUSE Page, covered with photos and videos.

"No, I am not. I am not so sure about this fight." Dema dried her tears. "We might die!"

"Dema, we're backs against the wall, and the only way is forward. You know, even my faith won't help me here. I must pull the trigger, or we all die, and I cannot have that on my conscience!" Mason said just as Van joined them. "My faith doesn't permit me to kill human beings for sport."

"So, how can we win if you cannot pull the trigger? Well, at least, how can you win morally?" Van tapped his thumbs together.

"Simulation didn't really count, as I shot at pixels, but it gave me a lot to think about while I was on the hospital bed, waiting to be released. However, I have to shoot first. Then, if we survive, I can moralize my decisions." Mason slowly exhaled. "I agreed to this."

"I got an idea as I'm looking at the time. It's three in the afternoon, so how about we grab something to eat and just walk around? It should clear our heads and hearts." Van smiled as he steered the conversation. "And also a little celebration that you are with us, Mason. So, what do you guys think?"

"A day brightener will for sure help us. All right, Van, lead the way!" Mason stood up and gave Dema a hand, who happily accepted as the gray clouds above her head sailed away.

"You don't understand how good it is to have you back!" Dema smiled and hugged Mason again. "Even though it has been a few hours. I'll repeat it. TH would stand by your side if they didn't kick us out. He even decided to stalk a medical staff just to stay with you a bit longer."

"Thank you, TH." Mason tapped TH on his right shoulder. "It means the world to me. All of you!"

TH stepped aside. "You gave me something I couldn't receive otherwise. A purpose. A bloody one, but still a purpose, none-theless. I got an idea to add more brightness to our shining day. Let us find the ridiculous tank in the area."

"I think I have a serious contender to that claim," Dema said. "Right this way."

"What is it?" Van looked over his shoulder. "Don't tell me. I might have something as well."

"Hold your horses, both of you." TH gave them a thumbs up as they left the garage, "Also, how about a group picture? The band is back together! I expected Dema to take point on this one!"

"There is always next time," Dema grinned. "However, I will let that one slide to you."

"I agree!" Van looked around him. "I can already see the caption."

Mason clapped his hands, and his eyes found a complex employee who observed the happening. "Could you take a picture of us?"

The employee shrugged his shoulders and accepted the tablet. As everyone lined up underneath the large 28, the employee snapped several photos, handed the tablet back, and departed without saying a word.

"Thank you!" Dema noted, but the employee was long gone. "Okay, you just leave."

Dema took a deep breath as they walked and wrote at the bottom of the lovely post *To the TVG meat grinder we go. Wish us luck!*

Then, she locked the tablet and looked at Mason, who stared into the distance again, hands behind his back.

"They really don't care now, do they?" Van whistled at the employee, who continued walking.

"I am sure that there are some that do." Dema nudged Mason. "Is that right?"

"They're humans after all, like we're and definitely not perfect. But I guess that's what makes us human."

"Does that mean I am human as well?" TH tapped his thumbs as they walked, "Or at least honorary human?"

"You're more human than all of us," Mason tapped TH on his left shoulder.

CHAPTER ELEVEN

INTO THE FRAY

Mason watched Van park the Angel inside the heavily modified Galaxy Transport Ship. Seeing the Polish crew back after days of silence was somewhat surprising. Night had descended on the Great Falls International Airport, and three other Galaxies appeared from the darkness, consuming other crews with their war machines. Dema squeezed her duffle bag beside him, looking into the distance, where blue lights illuminated the runaway from which the first Galaxy took off. Behind them, Gio, with his P26/40, and August, with 14TP, dropped their anchors on designated platforms with their team numbers.

"I wished that we could stay one more day in the complex, but they are on the clock, so I don't blame them." Gio waited for the Galaxy's turbine engine to fade away before he spoke. "The sooner we finish this, the better for all parties involved."

Dema walked to Gio and touched his left shoulder, but he grunted something and was about to board when August and Zasada approached the group. The unmarked van that dropped them off drove away into the night.

By their shrugged shoulders and unsure steps, even Mason felt his heart saddened, but Gio's wild gestures forced him to shake his head, and the volcano erupted.

"You left us for days, not a single word from you. So, tell

me, why shouldn't we blast you to kingdom come when we land?"

"Yes, you have every reason to be angry at us, but we'll play fairly and honor the Tank Royale code if such a thing exists. We might have failed you, but there were more pressing matters." August shook his head, but James pointed his finger at Zasada.

"And what exactly were those pressing matters?"

"August, allow me to say it." Zasada came to the forefront. "It was about me. My stepbrother had been marked as the corporate hobo, and Internal dragged out my family and team for a *talk*."

"What is a corporate hobo?" Dema tilted her head.

"It is a hobo who is not registered at the Unemployment Center and abuses the corporate welfare system, and my stepbrother and his girlfriend have been doing it for the past year until someone snitched on them. Since I am related," Zasada rolled up his sleeve, showing restraining marks, "I do not defend or like what he did."

"Where is the rest of your crew?" Van crawled his way out of the driver's hatch.

"Home, possibly watching us. TVG allowed us to compete, but we will be two down, relying on Zasada's driving and my shooting." August looked over Gio's shoulder and found his cruiser.

"Well, all I can say is that we wish you all the best. But unfortunately, it seems like trouble is heading our way." Dema pointed at the approaching TVG operator with the black tablet lighting the man's face blue.

"Good evening, All-Americans. The Tank Royale Staff has already taken off, and you are scheduled to depart at 11:30. Now, we will fly to the Corporate Republic of Hong Kong to refuel. From there, you'll be airdropped to the fight. A ten-hour flight awaits you, allowing you to prepare yourself mentally. Corporate has been kind to all contestants, and the second floor of the Galaxy has been reworked to the living quarters, but don't expect luxury. Benjamin Bell will be live, and you haven't heard this from me," the operator looked around him, "they will be revealing many new things that might require your attention, so if I were you, I would run to the TV right now unless you are not finished packing."

Soon, only Gio and Mason stayed behind, standing on the edge of the ramp, looking at the last night on US soil.

"It's good that you are back," Gio said as he looked at Mason. "Again, my apologies for yelling at you."

"Water under the bridge." Mason looked at the bright lights of the Great Falls skyscrapers and dancing holograms in the evening sky.

"Let's be realistic here; August and Zasada will not make it. They are outgunned, outdated, and under-crewed. I admire their enthusiasm for dying in front of millions." Gio looked at Mason and paused. "I need to come clean with you."

"Please," Mason said.

"I have already done this before, as you know. However, I and a few others go all the way to the beginning, even before this went mainstream." Gio rolled up his sleeve, and Mason noticed the barcode. "I was one of the first political prisoners who were offered to compete. When the tests are over, I'm shipped back to the IC prison until I'm needed again."

"So that time we met in prison, you were...."

"Yes, I was waiting to be shipped to Great Falls for the actual games."

"Oh, Giovanni," Mason smiled, "no hard feelings, my friend. You played it well when we saw each other again."

"Yeah, I had to keep the appearance of the happy contestant."

"Dema met your friend, Wang Xiu," Mason pointed at Dema, who gave them a thumbs up as she climbed inside the tank, "and like you, my crew and I are marked for standing out of the line."

"No matter how many spare tracks I weld on the frontal plate," Gio looked behind the T-34 at his P26/40, whose front was covered by the spare tracks (barely visible to the naked eye due to the darkness), "someone will always know your weakness."

————

Another minute of silence passed, and as Mason was about to enter the Galaxy, he heard Giovanni say something, which prompted him to stop.

"Let's say it will be me against you in the final stage. Who will win?"

"Hmm," Mason pondered. "I never really thought about it."

"So, do you let me live? Or do I let you fight another day?" Gio slowly exhaled. "One way or another, one of us is not walking out of here. Last tank standing, that is the rule."

"Let's cross that bridge once we get there." Mason looked at the beeping red light. "I think we got to go."

"All right, one moment." Gio knelt and kissed the ground. "May I see you soon. If not, well, it has been nice."

————

Mason looked into the darkness again, but as he was about to walk inside, he heard a familiar voice cutting through the night. Next to the unmarked car was his brother Ail, sitting in a wheelchair with an airport employee.

"Well, someone is waiting for you! Go!" Gio shoved Mason off the ramp, and a moment later, Ail felt Mason's tears on his right shoulder.

"Brother! Brother! You don't understand what panic you caused!" Ail collected himself. "Aunt almost had a heart attack! When we saw you on the TV, well, it got slightly better. You went AWOL! And this is the first time I see you after weeks!"

"But didn't we call each other? I showed you everything: the tank, my crew, everything!" Mason slowly exhaled, but Ail shook his head.

"You never called! I called everywhere! Customer Support, local Congressman, everyone just to know where the hell you vanished!" Ail's face momentarily turned red, but returned to its original color when Ail noticed Mason gasping for air. "Hey! What's happening to you? Mason, are you having a panic attack? Talk to me!"

Mason slid on the ashplant, taking three deep breaths to calm his racing heart. *So, I talked with an AI? What a twisted world this is!*

"Mason, talk to me!" Ail nudged the airport employee. "Can you help him?"

"It's all lies! They used AI to trick me. I thought that I had called you! It was all lies." Mason gulped but couldn't hold a singular tear escaping his eyes.

"Mason, it's all right." Ail nodded as the man helped Mason to stand up. "It's all right, big bro!"

"No, it's not all right! They did the same thing to Van! What is a reality!?"

"Mason, I'm alive, and so are you. Let's keep it that way. Where are you going? I thought that you were heading home."

"I'm not coming home yet, Ail. The simulation match was just the training for the real thing. I'm going to fight for real this time." Mason tapped Ail on the left shoulder. "I made my peace with it, and now you must as well."

This time, Ail remained silent, scratching his chin while the airport employee checked his watch.

"Mason, I believe in you. All four of you. Van, TH, you and Dema. But, Mason, it's not about the money. I'll need you to return in one piece, preferably with that girl. Now, focus and come back. Aunt and I will be waiting." Ail looked at the ramp, where Mason's crew awaited them, and gave them a thumbs up. "The finest gasoline cowboys are waiting for you. Focus, and you'll come home."

"I will be back!" Mason hugged Ail, who nodded. "I promise I'll be back. Just tell me, did the date work out?"

"Yeah, it did, Mason. I think Claire and I got a good thing going. Focus and remember that it's not about the money! Don't forget that!" Ail looked at the employee who opened the door to the unmarked van.

———

On the second floor of the Galaxy, the All-American Platoon set up their corners as Gio waited for Mason and then closed the door behind them. While the beds weren't luxurious, James had already occupied the bed closest to the TV screen, followed by the twins. August and Zasada sat next to the door with Sharik, from which Mason and Gio emerged, and Van, TH with Dema sat in the middle discussing the factory manual but stood up when joined by Mason. Sharik slept in the corner on a white pillow, scratching his ear.

"All right, everyone, let's see what they have in store for us," Gio grabbed the remote and turned on the large screen, but the onscreen message said: *STANDBY; WE WILL BE LIVE SOON.*

"All right, that didn't work. Any ideas to kill a ten-hour flight?"

"Yes, I have a question that I wanted to ask you, Dema." James raised his hand like an obedient student in the classroom. "I don't want to be insensitive, but Eastern Europe is well known for strong apocalyptic literature. Were they close to the predictions?"

"James, all of them got some things right. Some lived in the metro, others at Lake Vongozero. And while there were no vampires among us, there were a few cannibals along the way. No aliens and picnics thou. Interesting that you know about Eastern Euro literature."

"Roadside Picnic is my favorite book of all time. I like a more philosophical aspect to it. Heavy smoking, though, but I guess that is a part of the course for that heavy Soviet depression."

"Now that I'm thinking about it, why don't we get more focused worldwide news in the US?" Van looked at the TV.

"I guess we don't care that much about other nations?"

"It is not that we don't care," Mason looked around him, "but I can assume that it has something to do with one corporation controlling the narrative."

"Are you telling me that *ALL NEWS, SOUTHERNSTATION, and SUNNYTV* are all owned by one company?" The irony in Van's voice made everyone burst out laughing, including Mason.

"Well, don't forget about *VIDPLAY, TRIDENTZ,* and *STREETPAUSE,* our amazing social media. AI replaced seventy-five point three percent of software engineers." Zasada grinned from ear to ear. "No wonder it's missing the human touch."

"You were the software engineer for the corporate social media?" James widened his eyebrows. "No offense, you don't strike me like a software engineer."

"Well, I'm no longer. I lost my job because they spun it around, saying I had made that loophole. And the AI too. So, I gave them the finger, took my paycheck, and now I'm here. Look, I know that we will not win, but we'll put up a fight whether the game is rigged or not." Zasada pounded his chest.

"Why didn't he tell us this sooner?" TH tilted his head. "Why?"

"And what would that do? It is not a good selling story for the public, so nobody will care about my family or me. When they said that this is the most diverse Royale, they weren't lying." Zasada scratched Sharik behind his ears as the dog made himself comfortable in his lap.

"They really got everyone here." Dema was the first to speak after several minutes of silence as she looked at the flashing tablet resting by her side.

———

"All right, so where are we going?" Thomas tapped Benjamin. "And why Asia? Don't we have space stateside?"

"How do you know that we are going to Asia?"

Instead of replying, Thomas handed him the flight plan, with a stop at Hong Kong International Airport.

"We'll not even leave the Galaxy. Just stop to refuel, and we'll receive instructions there. Is there anything I need to know before we go live?"

"Yes, you'll need to turn a blind eye to several contestants and not give them coverage." Thomas took Benjamin aside. "You need to notify your producers as well."

"Who? Why?" Now all eyes were on Thomas and Benjamin.

"You need to give coverage to the Power Platoon ninety percent of the time, and the rest can go to others. You must show the strong female leads in Team 18, the black power in Team 22, and an average viewer in Team 16. The man who took Adriana and me to the back room told me to give this to you when we take off." Thomas handed Benjamin a sealed envelope. "You are apparently not in good standing with TVG for reasons unknown to me. The only thing that saves you is the popularity of this show and your past achievements."

"Why would I do that? Everyone deserves fair coverage, which is what the premium plan is for, so everyone can see their favorite!"

"Well, read the letter you got." Thomas moved a chair for Adriana while Jeong-Min took his place as well, and as the producer counted down, Benjamin sank into the chair as he scanned the text. "The fact that they still send letters is kind of classy. Messed up, but classy."

Benjamin folded the paper and took three short breaths as the light turned red. Then, with a smile, pretending everything was all right, he turned to the camera.

"Good evening, viewers, and I would like to welcome you

to the info segment about this Tank Royale of 2145. We don't know where the battle will occur, but we shall learn once we refuel in Corporate Hong Kong City-State. Thanks to your purchases of the premium plans and individual donations, we prepared spectacular entertainment this season, and of course, my co-hosts are here. So, I was asked to make a bet between us," the camera shifted, "but first, tell our viewers about your favorite tank."

"Well, this is my favorite." Adriana pointed at the screen where the 3D model was rendered. "This is a 76 mm Gun Carriage M18 or Hellcat. While it may not have armor, the speed and power will get this Kitty from Hell up speed and score some hits here and there. Thomas, correct me if I'm wrong, but Hellcat was one of our first tanks to leave the workshop."

"Yes, indeed. It was our sixth tank destroyer, and I remember I had to drag you out of it at two in the morning," Thomas smiled as the screen changed behind him, "while my pick doesn't have the speed, it has power. I present to you Versuchsflakwagen, or VFW for short. Designed initially to shoot down American bombers, I made an executive decision to bring it here. Just give this machine an excellent open position to work with, and nobody will get through unless they pepper the almost unprotected crew."

"For me, it has to be an IS-2." Jeong-Min waited for the 3D model to load before continuing. "Big gun, good armor, ready to put Tiger back in the box, which it did. While they didn't use single-piece ammunition like their contemporaries, it got the job done, which is all you need in war. Nothing more, nothing less."

"So we have twelve tanks heading into the pit." Adriana waved, and the camera swung towards her. "Now, who is your pick?"

"I'm sticking with the AC-4 Namarrkon." Benjamin tapped the screen and highlighted the Aussie war machine. "Min, your pick?"

"I'll grab myself that Swedish Delat Torn, but I feel that Thomas and Adriana have insider information here." Jeong-Min turned towards the couple.

"I can read you the statistical spreadsheets, but the crew matters in my personal belief. So, I am betting on the Crusading Angel. Although, for once, I wanted to mix it up a bit, and this tank caused me many headaches, so I want to see how it shall fight." Thomas looked at Adriana as the screen showed the faces of Mason, followed by the rest of the team.

"I shall bet on the Chi-Nu-Kai. So how much are we betting?" Adriana closed, and the four tanks were highlighted on the screen.

"Each of us starts with fifty dollars, which we pool, and if one of our selected tanks is out of action, we add another fifty, and the winner takes it all." All the co-hosts shook hands.

"Excellent. Now it is time to explain the structure of this fight." Benjamin smiled and looked at the screen behind him, where three circles appeared with twelve Xs above unknown terrain.

"We have three zones, each getting progressively smaller, with the third one ending in what seems to be a town," Jeong-Min said. "Contestants can hear bearing information to the nearest point on their radios."

"You don't want to get caught outside once the zone closes. The Xs mark the landing spots for our Gasoline Cowboys. From there, they will have to fight and roll their way into the final location." Benjamin widened his eyes as more markings began appearing. "There are also points of interest with two repair chances awaiting the two lucky crews with small repair opportunities along the way. Or maybe not; we'll see how the situation goes."

"These points of interest are not just for them, but for us viewers as well." Thomas read the room. "We'll be providing a commentary on all events happening!"

"Yes, we indeed studied for this exam!" Adriana smiled

and looked at Benjamin. "They all start on a level field, but skill and positioning are the keys to winning here."

"That is right, viewers. In simple terms, whoever shoots first wins first, and that should leave one tank standing, or a minimum of two surviving tankers. So, let's get them down into the pit already!"

"And now, we shall see how our crews spend their time. Cue the music!" Benjamin announced, and the camera turned off, with the screen immediately switching to a sequence of plane shots.

———

After a two-hour stop for refueling in the Corporate Hong Kong City-State, six Galaxy transports had wheels up at 18:35, ready for the seven-hour next leg of the journey North, and tension rose by the minute. Still, a howl from Van from the cargo bay forced everyone to run downstairs.

"Dema! Where the hell did you put that hammer? I said, put it next to the ammo rack." Van poked out of Mason's cupola and waved with a folder full of papers. "Girl, we'll need it for the tracks and other things."

"I swear to God! I put it where you told me!" Dema looked up from the tablet as she continually edited older posts with tiny messages. "One moment!"

"Help me find it, or we'll regret it!" Van waved his hands, prompting Dema to place the tablet on the mudguard.

"Those sick bastards!" August shouted from the back, and soon, loud cursing, pounding, and howling filled the cargo bay of the Galaxy.

After another hour of desperation, Mason finished his walk around the Crusading Angel and joined his depressed crew and platoon members.

"How bad is it?" Van looked away when he said it, finding Sharik watching his every move.

"Do you even want to know? Well, I don't even know where to start. Someone drained half of the diesel reserves but left untouched auxiliary box fuel tanks alone, cutting our range in half. As a result, we lost most of the tools, a tent, and rations for four days, leaving us with one and for you, Dema, you have to mend the radio antenna. Do you want me to continue?" Mason looked around him and sat on the side of the tank, and his head vanished in his arms for a moment. "Gio, how bad is it with you?"

"Don't even ask," Gio pointed at the newly found countdown, showing exactly *03:25:16*, "we got work to do. "

"Well, we got things to do as well. Someone eased out track tension, removed the light, hid it somewhere, and don't even get me started on the missing camo net." August shook his head. "They really hate us, don't they!"

— — —

"What do you mean by tanks belong to you?" Benjamin tilted his head during the commercial break.

"When the contract was signed, Adriana and I put a clause in that gave us ownership of all the tanks produced, including the *corpses* which we are rebuilding. When viewers tire of tanks, they will soon be scrapped because they are entertainment props for TVG. Still, for Adriana and me, they are living kit pieces of history and hope for others as well." Thomas handed Benjamin back the tablet and left him to his thoughts.

"Well, he is right, Benjamin. They are pieces of history," Jeong-Min emerged from the bathroom and closed the door behind him, "and they'll be airdropped into China in ten minutes? Where are we?"

"No, Mongolia," Benjamin broke the news and watched three pairs of eyes widening.

"Mongolia?" Jeong-Min walked closer, and his eyes started to pierce Benjamin's soul. "Why?"

"Yes, Mongolia. The most diverse and editable battle-field in the world reminds me that an announcement must be made." Benjamin tapped the microphone. "All contestants, we are approaching the drop points in two minutes! So, prepare for the armor drop!"

Adriana looked at the screens, where tankers began moving like disturbed ants, some waking up their colleagues, others taking deep breaths.

They didn't even get to see the surprise visit of their loved ones. So, we are really pushing them. The surprise wasn't them but the news of the early deployment, Adriana thought as she watched a few crying individuals sit in their positions and check the equipment for the final time. *But, of course, the camera will not show the weakness, only the steely determination.*

Adriana now stared at the screens; her senses fully engulfed in madness. First, she found the camera focusing on the stoic Klemens. The man took a deep breath inside his Hydro and closed his eyes briefly, his hands resting on the vision slits of the commander's cupola. Then, the camera switched to the Sherman tank, and Zanai appeared, carefully and with reverence, folding the star-spangled flag, which would hang from the turret's side upon landing. Then, upon finishing, he ensured that his crew members tied everything up and were ready for the drop as the counter mercilessly ticked seconds away. The camera soon flashed on others, who also slowly got seated with the last hatches closed on the Polish 14TP tank. *The zero hour is upon us. May God have mercy on their souls.*

Adriana would almost miss the short transition sequence between the shots where Dema appeared, furiously typing something on the tablet. Adriana looked at Thomas, who continued talking with the staff and opened her tablet. After a short chime, she landed on the interconnected social media page of Team 28, formed out of all social media accounts created by the TVG department for the contestants. With interest, Adriana began swiping the liked images and was asked by the system to refresh as a new post was made.

Upon refreshing, Adriana raised her eyebrows as if no new post had appeared. She scratched the back of her head and opened one of the more recent posts, where a photo appeared, showing newly reunited Mason with his crew, posing next to the garage door. As her eyes scanned the text, Adriana picked up on several mistakes in the sentences, with some letters being capitalized. Again, she scratched her head, and it clicked as the capitalized letters formed SOMEONE HELP US.

Adriana looked outside of the plane window at the dark clouds. *So, this is it; our babies are going to the pit.*

"Everything all right?" Thomas walked up to Adriana, who nodded her head.

"Can you believe it? This is it! Look, my hands are shaking!" Adriana looked at her fingers, and Thomas smiled.

"I'm keeping mine in my pockets so they don't see it, but here we are. From a little welding project to the largest TVG Battle Royale, with millions in their seats, eyes glued on their viewing devices, cheering them and our dream on." Thomas held Adriana's hand as they looked outside at the silent night.

"Did you know that timing isn't on our side?" Thomas spoke after a long silence. "As TVG moved our schedule, we have to deploy our contestants in the middle of the night and start broadcasting tomorrow morning. It was all going so well, but the internal politics will kill us and the show's momentum sooner or later."

"I didn't even realize that. Why would TVG push their flagship show that fast?" Adriana pressed her forehead against the cold airplane window. "Love, I'm not feeling well."

"Everything all right?" Thomas took her hands in his. "Let's go to our room. We have been on our feet for a solid fourteen hours. We're all tired. Trust me; you'll feel much better tomorrow."

"It's just that everything is colliding with one another, and I feel that." Adriana bent forward. "We need to do something for these poor souls. We cannot just stand idle. Something, something, I don't know what, but we need to do something. Anything."

"Calm down." Thomas looked around him. "Deep breaths, Adriana, deep breaths. Inhale and exhale. You're tired, and so am I. It's not even healthy."

"But they are going to be..." Adriana looked outside the window.

"Adriana, please." Thomas joined his hands together. "I need you sound tomorrow!"

"But Thomas," Adriana slowly exhaled, "there must be something we can do."

"To remind you, you are the one who suggested prisoners." Thomas shook his head.

CHAPTER TWELVE

ARMOR DROP

"Five, Four, Three, Two, One, Zero. Good luck, everyone!" August's voice cracked in everyone's headphones. "Whatever you do, do not open your hatches. It turns out that the dossier is the instructions, so read them after we land!"

Moments later, Mason heard a screeching and loud racket coming from the back of the cargo bay. On the platform, T-34 was docked with a large green box, parachutes, and thrusters. A large red 28 was painted underneath him, and being first for the drop, Mason felt shivers on his spine.

"Good luck to you, too. I am sorry for my anger before we departed," Giovanni responded as he opened his hatch and waved at Mason.

"I completely understand, Gio, and as I said, no harm is done. See you on the ground. Good luck, Crusading Angel." Zasada saluted and closed the hatch behind him. "It seems like Sharik will be riding with you, Da Vinci. Keep him safe."

"Good luck, Da Vinci and Grom! May the best win," Mason said back and switched the internal comms on. "Internal radio check. Everyone report one by one."

"Dema reporting!"

"TH ready!"

"Van present!"

The voice in everyone's headphones was cut out as the

light turned green, everything went dark, and winds began to howl.

Prepare for the armor drop! Launching in three, two, one, you are away!

"This is it, everyone!" Mason had to hold himself as the T-34 launched toward the darkness and vanished from Gio's sight for good.

Then, as Mason opened his mouth, the platform leveled out and set sail across the dark sky, guided and balanced by the thrusters to the drop point. Van looked to his right and found Dema shaking like a wet dog, trying to hold on to the seat and the gear lever.

"First time jumping off a plane?"

"First time jumping off a plane in a tank, which is not airborne!" Dema cried out as the force of the wind was counterbalanced by the thrusters.

"Dema, we'll be safe! Here, grab my hand!" Van extended his hand, and Dema squeezed it. "Don't worry; if you do not look down, you'll be fine!"

We are landing in three, two, one. The Crusading Angel had landed. Dema heard the crack in the radio and then static as the platform leveled again in a moment and touched down.

———

Five minutes later, after the racket concluded, Mason was first to open the hatch with his shaking hands. The cold night wind punched him in the face, and moments later, frontal and gunmounted lights came to life, illuminating the hilly grasslands around them. One by one, the crew got out, but after a quick look, Mason clapped his hands, gaining everyone's attention.

"All right, we have no idea where we are, so I reckon we'll sleep here, and in the morning, we will figure out what to do."

"Shouldn't someone stay up and guard?" Van asked. "I would not like to be blown sky-high in the first hour. We all have come too far to lose it all in an instant."

"Any volunteers?" Mason started to play with his thumbs, awaiting a tribute with favorable odds.

"Mason, you are the Commander, so command us." TH walked up to Mason. "We cannot have a vote in combat. Your word is what matters. Your wish is our order. If you tell us to load the tank and get ready to roll in two, we'll do that. If you tell us to stay here all night, we'll do that, but you cannot be so indecisive. So, what is it? Do we roll out, or do we stay a night?"

TH's words silenced the little noise present as Mason took a moment to reply with noticeable hesitation in his voice.

"Dema, take the remaining tent for yourself; I want to see everyone lined up in front of the tank at sunrise. TH takes the first guard. If you need someone to switch, choose whoever you think can be next. Are we clear?"

"Yes, Sir!"

"Well, in that case, good night everyone." Mason shrugged his shoulders from the cold and climbed back into his position with red eyes and a racing heart.

We have landed. Holy crap! This is it! This is the moment! Wow, from drying swamps to IC prison, ending up in the TVG Tank Royale. I wonder, can Ail see me? I need to be strong and decisive for both me, my friends, and my Ail. Aunt too. I promise, when I make it, I'll talk more with her. For everything she gave us, from the roof over our heads and warm food, I don't remember spending much time with her. I can only imagine what she had to go through when my parents...

I don't think I ever had such a good group of friends. Well, I have some friends back in Florida, but we don't have a deeper relationship. Just hi and another day in the grinder. TH, Van, and Dema. Maybe from the beginning, we have had to work together. That is what friends are for. The fact that they went with me to the hospital and didn't move on, well, mere words cannot describe my thanks. I think we kind of found each other in this hyperactive, brave new world. I cannot even imagine myself in the USAC and working in a lithium mine, dying there alone.

Mason, you can reminisce when you win. Ail, I promise I'll get my head in the game and come home.

"Adriana, what the hell?" Thomas said as he placed his tablet into a charging station. "Please, do not tell me that..."

"Can we even fight the system? This Orion Network?" Adriana lay on the bed and looked from the airplane window at the bright stars shining through thin clouds. "Can we?"

"I'll entertain this exhausted train of thought for a moment. Why the sudden change of heart?" Thomas moved a chair closer to the bed. "I'm all ears."

"Why are we here, Thomas? Why are we traveling with this circus? Those who make the balls don't travel with clowns."

"We're here because... because this is the life we live now. It was bound to happen. They would drag us from our offices into the national spotlight. Sorry, into the worldwide spotlight. To answer your second question, the reason why we travel with the circus is that we'll have to clean up, gather data, and optimize our production for the next contract." Thomas slowly exhaled. "I didn't mean to launch at you when we talked beforehand."

"Truth may hurt, but I needed to hear it. I'm responsible for these people. At least I feel that responsibility," Adriana continued, staring at the ceiling.

"Look, love," Thomas took Adriana's hands into his, "you're giving them a fighting chance. Otherwise, well, you can imagine..."

"Why are you justifying this?"

"Why a sudden change of heart? Is it because of pleading messages from contestants? You're actually helping them to get out of IC prisons. While not all will make it, some will and will have a chance to start a new life. You're doing more for the inmates than anyone else. I meant to say we are. On top of that, we bring history back to life for the entire world, and well, we're making it mainstream. In return, we get paid handsomely."

"But," Adriana rolled to the side, "we're no longer Thomas

and Adriana. We're Askarov Productions. It seems corporate has become us, and we have become corporate."

"Adriana, you are tired, and so am I. One last question before we resume this conversation at another time." Thomas's patience slowly ran dry, but he saw the finish line. "Why would you want to bite the hand that feeds us?"

"Because that hand is also beating us with a metal rod. I want to take the metal rod away and change it for something else." Adriana looked at her flashing tablet and ignored the stream of messages.

"You can't have the cake and eat it too, right?" Thomas tapped his forehead.

"How can we retain our identity in this corporate machine?" Adriana turned toward Thomas, who remained silent.

"This was never about the tanks or TVG. It's about control. Did you know that I had suppressed a lot of data and pretty much rewrote the history because some suits were complaining about reality?" Thomas closed his eyes, remembering the board meeting as the first tanks rolled off the production line. "But hey, we got paid."

A conference room full of suits and ties, each lecturing about different diverse aspects of the TVG and its intended demographic, forced Thomas to shake his head, and the memory vanished.

"Adriana, we worked hard to reach the top of the food chain. Now, we don't have to worry about the next water or electricity bill with red overdue flashing at us. Do you want to go back to that life? You know what? I'm done talking about this for the foreseeable future."

"The higher we fly, the harder we will fall, Thomas. It's not about the money. It was never about the money. We proved ourselves in our eyes and to the world. Now, we need to do something with the voice we have. And this is a start. Where else can we start if not with the largest entertainment provider in the world?" Adriana looked at Thomas, who vanished into the restroom and dimmed the lights. "Sooner or later, Thomas, sooner or later."

———

"Mason, do you have a moment?" Van sat down next to a motionless Mason, who stared into the night, tapping his thumbs and humming a song.

"You need to sleep, Van. I'll need you tomorrow ready to go!" Mason shook his head and snapped out of the stare, storing the rosary in one of the many pockets of his uniform. "How can I help?"

"I had a nightmare," Van said in a shivering voice. "I watched myself die as the first from our group. I was out in the open when I got blasted. I saw the shell piercing my body, blowing me to bits. Organs, shattered bones, everything! Then I got run over by an unknown tank. Then, vultures…"

"Hey. It's a nightmare and therefore not real. You imagine the worst that can happen, and I don't blame you." Mason looked at the tent where Dema slept and then back at Van, who covered himself with a blanket to battle the chilling wind blowing by. "I cannot sleep either. One mistake, and we're gone—so many things to consider. I miss a small detail or a tank hiding in a bush, and we're done. It doesn't help that TH and I are standing on the ammo boxes."

"Well, if you spot them first?" Van tapped Mason's left shoulder. "You got this. I know that with the rosary wrapped around your hands, you…."

"Van, listen to me. I'm dammed either way. However, I'll be more damned if all of you die because of me refusing to fight back, and I cannot, cannot, have that on my conscience." Mason looked at the moon, partially concealed by the lazy clouds.

"Don't gaze at the stars for too long, brother. I never really believed in the big G in the sky, but could you send a prayer his way for me tomorrow? Well, for everyone, of course." Van smiled and climbed down from the tank. "I need to hit the bushes."

"Will do, however, one more thing. I'm sorry about Ember if that video is actually real. If that is the case, I'm sure you'll find someone better. I was a year into a relationship once and had to end it. I'm not going into the details, but it was better for both parties involved. If the video is fake, well, you could not ask for a more loyal person in your life."

"Thank you, Mason. Look, I'm shattered to the core, but I'll do everything in my power to stay on top of my game. When I, well, we, make it to the finish line, then I can learn if the video is fake or real."

"If you need anything, you know where to find me."

"Mason, on the bright side, Dema is taken by you, for which I'm happy. I think both of you found each other. I mean, it's a perfect fit. So, for me, TH would have to suffice." They both burst out laughing, with Van drying his tears into the left sleeve of his uniform. "Thank you for the words of encouragement. Time to heed the call of nature."

"You'll find someone else!" Mason shook his head as Van climbed from the tank and vanished into the night.

Moments later, Mason heard Van throw up. He shook his head and covered himself with the tarp.

"I have never been in a relationship with a human before," TH said out of nowhere, prompting Mason to jump on the spot. "I mean, he is a handsome man, but not my type anyway. No homo, as human men say to each other at the end of the conversation, that might have revealed a bit of an emotional side."

"Dude, you scared the crap out of me!" Mason slowly exhaled. "You were listening to us the entire time?"

"I may or may not have overheard someone saying my name, so I approached. However, I didn't mean to disturb the conversation."

"Not at all, but thank you. So, do you also have a problem sleeping?"

"I don't sleep, but I wonder what I want to do with my life. I hope that I can make it to the Moon Base one day. Just to see the Earth from a different point of view."

"And we'll go there. All four of us, when we make it to the finish line. Why didn't you say that you want to go to the Moon?"

"I'm a humanoid, and there are only a handful of things that bring me what you would call satisfaction. And seeing Earth is one of them. However, a stronger desire is to prove myself. I'm an expendable machine that never sleeps. Even when I'm idle, my eyes are wide open. And while I don't have enough time on this Earth…" TH gazed at the moon for a minute before continuing, "I know that…"

"Know what?"

"Never mind. Thank you for listening. Commander, I would advise you if… No, I advise you to get some sleep. We'll need you tomorrow on top of your game if we want to make it to the finish line."

———

As Da Vinci's crew went to sleep, Giovanni took a deep breath and sat on the turret roof, looking into the darkness. The cold wind howled as Gio closed his eyes. *Is this the end? A new start? God, if you are up there, help me, please! I know that I have been lacking in my faith, but please, show us the way.* He slid down Da Vinci's side and walked up to the rear of the tank, completely vanishing into the night. *Why Mongolia, of all places? Half of the continental United States is empty. I never imagined that I would die outside of the US. Hmm, it's kind of funny in a twisted way. Is this fight even worth it? Can we just drive away? I don't want to kill them—Klemens, Mason, and, of course, Xiu. I shouldn't have left her. I ran away like those rats in New York. God, why was I so stupid!? She was it, and there was nobody else that could have matched her. I chased that paycheck, forgetting the real deal. All right, Gio, focus now and get some sleep. Vincerò queste partite!*

Giovanni took a deep breath and walked around the tank, stopping in the front, and for the last time, he said: "Vincerò queste partite!"

Looking behind him, he noticed James standing there with his arms folded under the blanket.

"What is the matter?" Gio turned towards him, and the moon had come out of the clouds, fully illuminating the campsite with a bright white light.

"Twins don't speak Italian, Gio. Gio, Gio, Gio, the Gasoline Cowboy, is your head in the game?" James walked up to him. "Now, we don't have time to reflect."

"I need to get something off my chest, which I did. Now, I'm fully in the game." Gio looked into the night, breaking eye contact. "I'll get all of you to that finish line, wherever it is and no matter the cost. We will get to the finish line."

"But will we cross it?" James raised his eyebrows. "What are our chances? There are eleven other contestants to worry about."

"James, we will cross it as I said. And, we have to worry about ten."

"What if you are right after all, and we have to eliminate Mason and his crew? And what about August? Zasada?"

"August and Zasada are not going to make it. I wish they did, but they are not going to. Outgunned and outnumbered. Maybe they have speed, but that is not all you need in this fight. Sooner or later, you have to shoot back. They're dealt an unfortunate hand. A deadman's hand, James, and we'll be dealt one, too, if you don't rest. Good night, James. Let me worry about Mason when we get there." Gio climbed the tank, but as he was about to close the hatch behind him, he overheard James saying something as he entered the green canvas tent, flapping in the cold wind.

Odio l'oscurità!

"While you were able to help me calm down for a moment, still, I worry. Good night, Gio!" James smiled as Gio shook his head and opened the commander's hatch, just in time for Gio to conceal his raised eyebrows and shaking hands.

———

"How are you holding up?" August found Zasada pacing around the platform, stopping only when he flashed him with a flashlight.

"It is what it is," Zasada shook his head. "I thought you were asleep."

"Not with the adrenaline pumping through my veins." August lowered the light. "How are you holding up?"

"I already said it is what it is. I cannot afford to think about what happened there. I must look forward, block out all the emotions, and survive."

"Never took you for a stoic, Zasada. Open up a bit. Maybe it is the last time we'll have the chance to do so."

"So, you don't believe we'll make it to the finish line?" Zasada raised his voice. "Why?"

"I never said that, so, respectfully, don't put words into my mouth." August decided to play it cool as he realized that Zasadas' nerves were about to shatter from the thick air all around them and the weight of tomorrow. "I always believed in your leadership, even in the jail cell. We survived IC, and we'll make it. It's just we don't talk as much the actual talk."

"We're men, and we don't talk about our emotions. I have my weight to bear, and you have yours. That is how it always was and will always be. Now, go to sleep so that we can perform tomorrow. We're last in everything, so tomorrow, we must make up that difference."

"While that is the case, we can share the struggle, as we did in the jail cell, TVG, and beforehand. You can carry a bit of mine, and I can carry a bit of yours. Trust me, I learned that in therapy, and surprisingly, it works wonders."

"Wouldn't that even out the weight of our burden?" Zasada shook his head.

"Not at all. Quite the contrary, it eases a lot of it. So, let's hear it from you first, and then I will throw my cents in as well. So?"

ARMED AND DANGEROUS

The morning sun's heat and the loud cookware racket forced Mason to drop the blanket, and as he was about to roll over, he found himself staring at the slope. Luckily, he grabbed himself at the last moment. As his eyes adjusted to the morning light, his jaw dropped. The landing platform found itself on a grassy hill overlooking a giant sandpit. Down the hill, the clear border between the sand and grass was just the start, with vast dunes sprawling over the horizon. Moments later, Mason heard Van cursing as he attempted to climb out of the driver's hatch and hit his side on the spare track. Dema had already packed the tent as TH pulled two shell boxes out of the green crate, which landed with the platform. The straps were untied, and soon the first gunshots echoed in the distance.

"Morning, everyone!" Mason slid down the angled plate, cracked his back, and joined the crew.

"Morning, Commander! The tank is almost ready; I have to re-rack the ammunition. Dema is preparing breakfast, but it is not much. Then, ah, there she is!" TH rattled out what happened and pointed to Dema, handing Van a loaf of bread, dried meat, berries, and milk chocolate bars.

Then, with a firm stride and a big smile, she walked up to Mason and handed him the same tration.

"Thank you, Dema. It looks good! So, does anyone know

where the hell we are?" Van looked at TH, who remained silent for a moment.

"According to my GPS, we're in Mongolia, of all places. Although I have to say, it is empty." TH turned around 360 degrees, hearing only a gentle breeze whisper by.

"It looks like Day Three of the World Creation." Dema looked down into the sandpit. "I played with the radio for a bit, and there was not that much chatter, so I prepared breakfast in the meantime. TH found a map, compass, and a notepad in the box. Look here," Dema grabbed the map and handed it to Mason, who quickly finished his breakfast, "this is where we are and looking by these three circles, which are the zones, that are getting smaller and smaller until they end up in Ville, I am sorry I cannot read this. TH, can you help out?"

"Of course. That is Villers-Bretonneux. I have no idea why it is a final zone, but it must have its meaning. We are hundreds of miles away, and only TVG knows what awaits us. We have to head north, but first, we have to cross this sandpit, which stands in our way." TH pointed at the seldom-ending sandy horizon as the wind started to pick up. "This T-34 has a range of precisely 250 miles on full tanks, which we don't have, so I give us around 150 miles of range before we have to refuel. That is considering that we'll be on the flat-open road all the time, so let's go with a hundred miles for the operational range, and this is rounding it way up. Apart from that, we have twenty shells and six magazines for our machine guns..." TH wanted to continue, but Mason raised his hand.

"This is what we'll do. Our direction will be Villers, whatever the name is of the final zone while keeping our ears and eyes peeled for opportunities. Crew, double time. We got a battle to fight and the finish line to reach." Mason looked at the cloudless sky just as the final preparations were finished.

Villers. Why does it sound so familiar? Where did I hear it before? Okay, Mason, focus. This is it, the ultimate test.

"Guys, look at us." Van raised his voice as everyone was

about to climb inside the Angel. "Look at us good-looking cowboys about to travel into the unknown and herd that victory back home. If someone is doing promotional posters of us standing upright and looking heroically into the distance, all I can say is that I want my royalty."

"You are right." Dema turned her torso slightly to the left and twirled her hair. "Let us do it! Some poses."

"Van, one correction. We aren't just cowboys. We're gasoline cowboys!" TH said. "But I like it. The old hardware still has it in him!"

"I wonder, is there a female version of a cowboy?" Mason scratched his chin. "I mean, a cowgirl, right?"

"Well, yes and no." Van took the map into his hands. "The cowgirl is the correct word; however, even women on our farm prefer to be called cowboys. Apart from being a slightly sexually charged word, the origin of the word, at least according to my grandfather, is derived from the verb cowboying, which is a term used to describe work on a farm or ranch, especially herding cattle and so on. Maybe there are more educated people in the English language who know the exact answer to your question. To TH's point, we're gasoline cowboys!"

"I didn't know that." Mason looked at the slowly climbing sun. "We can share some trivia on the way. Come on, team! Double time!"

———

"Well, this is great!" TH opened his hatch and looked at the massive dune before him.

"I see it as well." Mason opened the commander's hatch and cried out, "God damn! That thing is huge!"

Dune skipping was fun for the first few hours but slowly became a chore, and the grasslands, which Dema mentioned, were nowhere in sight. Just more sand, dunes, and occasional overlook once the Crusading Angel cleared the dune, followed by screeching brakes and silent curses as the tank slid down the slope and tracked onwards. Trying to read the map with constant elevation changes made Mason's stomach act up, so he quickly folded the map and looked at the horizon to calm his breakfast.

"This is the largest one yet. I give it a solid twenty feet, and with that assumption, there is no way we are getting on top of that," Van's voice cracked in the headphones. "The slope incline is too steep for us to clear. This is definitely more than sixty if I remember the degrees correctly."

"Van, the only way is around it. Does anyone know what time it is?" Mason took a deep breath as he watched the dune before him.

"Time to see some action," TH tapped the gun breech, "but about what you said in the hangar, you can fire back if they fire first. How about you shoot them first, preventing them from firing at us?"

It took a moment for Mason to reply as the V-12 racket gave him a short window.

"So?" TH shook Mason's shoulder.

"Look, I have had a serious rethink since we boarded the plane. All right, if I honestly feel they have spotted us, I shall fire unless the better opportunity presents itself." Mason shook his head.

"That sounds way better, Mason. Dema, anything on the radio?"

"No, but there are these smaller circles with question marks, and one seems like it is just in front of us." Dema leaned into the machine gun sight. "There is a wooden shed in front of us. I think that is the question mark!"

"All right, Van, pedal to the metal." Mason pressed his face against the vision slits of his commander's cupola, observing the dunes around them.

"Will do!"

———

The Crusading Angel climbed a smaller dune a moment later to get to the vantage point, and Mason stopped breathing when the dunes opened, and an oasis appeared in front of him with a lake, grass, large bushes, and the mentioned old wooden shed. In front of it, a large black box sat, awaiting someone to pick it up. Van slammed on the brakes with a roar as Angel slid down the dune into the oasis.

"All right, everyone out of this oven, and let's see this package." A loud curse followed Van outside of the driver's hatch, and moments later, a cry of desperation echoed in the oasis.

"I have to say. This is the most beautiful desert I've ever been in. It is probably the only one I ever saw, but it still counts as the most beautiful one," Dema said with awe as the blistering sun picked up in intensity as everyone got out, "and the silence! Well, except the screaming."

"I don't know why we're angry. We should have expected this." Mason looked at the spare bogies resting in the black box. "Should we hide it? Destroy it?"

"I would say, leave it be for now. Dema, this silence is music to my ears." Van looked at one of the dunes when he spotted something glittering. "What is that? That doesn't look good! Hello?"

All eyes focused on the glint, and a moment later, the sound of the roaring engine soon answered the question, with Van quickly lowering his hand as he was about to wave.

"It's a tank!" TH took a step back. "Do they see us?"

Instead of saying anything, Mason pulled out his binoculars and focused on the approaching tank. The turret started rotating towards them, and the hatch opened. A man emerged again, holding binoculars and scanning his surroundings, escorted by a strong glint.

"Everyone, to your stations!" Mason shouted as he felt the enemy had laid eyes on them and found a red maple leaf on the white background. "Canadians!"

His eyes locked with what Mason assumed was the Commander of the Canadian tank and froze on the spot. Then, unable to move or react, Mason stood awestruck as the tracer rounds flew around him.

"Mason!" TH launched towards him and woke him up from the flashback, but a loud grunting drowned by the machine-gun fire forced TH to grab Mason fireman carry style and dodge bullets left and right until he reached Crusading Angel.

"What happened?" Dema shouted as TH lowered Mason into his station and closed the hatch behind him.

"Yeah, what happened?" Mason shook his head and found himself inside the T-34. "Oh snap, my Spider was triggered. Sorry!"

"You were gone while the enemy tank opened fire at us! Orders?" Van's voice brought Mason back, who poked outside of his hatch, but the tank vanished from sight.

"Turn right here, and we should be able to flank them. Why have they descended into the oasis as well? They had a clear shot at us!" Mason punched the breech and took a deep breath to collect himself. "Dema, any chatter?"

"Nothing, apart from the last channel looping the rules. There was another opportunity a few miles down the road, but it seems like the enemy tank blocked it!"

Everyone covered their ears when Angel's turret deflected a round, but then the quartet regained their composure as Van released the brakes, and Angel drove forward, throwing up large clouds of sand behind it.

"All right, everyone, keep your eyes peeled." Mason pressed his eyes against the vision slits of his commander's cupola, looking for the Canadian war machine. "This is it!"

———

"One thing I do not particularly enjoy about the Battle Royale Concept is because seventy percent of it is complete silence.

We get a lot of action at the start, and then small engagements happen all the way to the final stage." Adriana looked at the screen, where the movement of the tanks was displayed and color-coded, just like in the simulation.

"TVG has Filler content for that exact reason, Adriana. While they are on the move, other programs can shine. Of course, if you had purchased a premium plan, you have a choice," Benjamin smiled into the camera, "but this is also an endurance test for both the tanks and crews. Still, it seems like the action is about to start on several hot points, and we can make some assumptions about how this will turn out. Place your bets now with the Orion Betting Office; now or never! Remember, viewers, positioning is the key, and it seems Thomas is up first with his Crusading Angel against Canadian Peggy!"

"Both tanks lost sight of each other, allowing their commanders to hatch a plan. Crusading Angel uses the old shed for cover while Peggy hides in those bushes, but look at Da Vince. Why is it covered head to toe with spare tracks?" Jeong-Min zoomed onto the Italian tank, crushing everything in its path, carefully treading the line between the grasslands and the desert.

The leftover tracks covered the front plate, sides of the tank, and turret from both front and sides, creating an armadillo-looking object.

"Well, the riveting process is a unique animal. While it is the fastest production process, the rivets are not strong enough, like welding or casting, so Commander Smith attempts to mitigate the weakness by adding tracks. The reality is that it barely helps and adds additional weight, which increases fuel consumption. However, it improves the crew's morale," Thomas touched the 3D model and remained silent for a moment, "and maybe that is what he'll need to win."

———

"Where the hell are they!" Mason almost twisted his neck as he looked around, but the only thing he could see were the bushes and desert.

The heat of the blistering sun warmed up the tank, and soon Dema waved her hand as she touched the hot radio knob. Mason could hear their breaths quickening by the minute, and sweat drenched his uniform.

"I lost them as well!" TH turned his periscope left and right, scanning the bush line. "I think they have a jump on us. Can we count on you, Mason?"

"Well, they shot at us first, so I think it is time to send some rounds down the range."

"I think I see them! A barrel is poking out one of the bushes to our right!" Dema shouted while looking at the compass in her hands. "Bearing 080."

"I see it!" Mason looked at the circle with the degrees painted above his head, locked onto the target, but he lost it when moving to gunsight.

"Why are you not firing!" Someone shouted as Mason frantically scanned the edges of the sight, looking for a hostile tank.

"This sight doesn't have a strong magnification; give me a moment!" Mason's hands began to hurt as he cranked the hot flywheels, but then a loud ringing filled everyone's ears as another shot bounced off Angel's turret.

"Not again!" Dema cried out, but Mason didn't give in to the ringing this time as he finally found Peggy's barrel and pressed the trigger.

"Did we hit them?" Van shouted as the breech recoiled, but couldn't hear any response.

"Mason, you split his barrel wide open. Time to finish the job! Loaded!" As TH said it, the breech recoiled again, giving him the answer.

"Why is it so hard to breathe here!" Mason coughed as he sent down another round into the enemy, and moments later, another round left for the Canadian tank.

"I think we got them!" Dema shouted as she aimed her machine gun at the burning bush line and opened fire.

"Mason, it's over! They're out of the fight. Come back!" TH leaned over the breech and punched Mason on his right shoulder. "Mason!"

Mason waved his head left and right, focusing on the target and breathing slowly, his foot pressing the trigger, unresponsive at first.

TH looked around him and realized what was happening. The ventilation hatches on the turret weren't extracting fumes from the constant firing fast enough as the gray particles flew all around them. So, instead of saying anything, TH launched toward his hatch and opened it. Then, he climbed outside and opened Mason's hatch, allowing more air to come in. He grabbed Mason by the collar with his left hand and pulled him out.

"Van, open your driver's hatch!" TH shouted as Dema stopped firing and scrambled to reload her machine gun.

"Why would I do that? The enemy might still be alive!"

"If you do not do it, we'll suffocate!" TH raised his voice. "Fumes and heat, Van!"

"Shit!" TH held himself as Van angled the tank away from the bush line; gasps filled the air as two more heads poked out.

"Mason! Orders?" Van shouted at a recovering Mason while Dema scrambled out of the hatch like a scared cat, gasping for air.

"All right, let's go check them out, but keep your eyes peeled." Mason took slow and deep breaths of the almost fresh air, observing black smoke rising before them.

The wreckage of the Canadian tank soon came into view, surrounded by the blazing fire from the bushes. Mason noticed the name Peggy painted on the tank's split barrel, and the corpse of a dead tanker attempting to climb out of the side door; a cloud of black smoke coming from the engine would soon attract unwanted attention.

"This is horrible!" Dema looked away. "I need to get out!"

Van also peeked out of his driver's hatch, thanking God that fate hadn't met them, but the death and destruction soon got to all four tankers. A moment later, as they climbed another dune and the tank came to a stop, Dema sat on the warm side of the turret, looking at the vast dunes all around them, slowly taking in the slap of reality as the fires on the Ram continued burning high behind them. Van also remained silent, closing his eyes, hoping the burning wreck would disappear if he opened them, but it didn't. He quickly made a sign of a cross as he remembered the nightmare.

"TH, how many shells do we have left?" Mason turned towards TH, waving away the black smoke that the wind blew towards them.

"I would have to double-check. Do you hear it?" TH pointed at the two-prop cargo plane heading towards them.

"It doesn't seem to be armed. Look, it's dropping a crate!" Mason grabbed his binoculars and focused on the black crate slowly sailing across the noon sky, hanging from a black parachute.

"Should we go get it?" TH turned towards the Crusading Angel and noticed the significant dent on the side of the turret. "Mason, you got lucky! Look at that dent!"

Instead of saying anything, Mason's jaw dropped to the floor. Crusading Angel saved his life, and all doubts about the imperfections vanished instantly. *Wow*, was the only thing Mason could think of as he found his seat and plugged in his headset.

"Let's go get that crate. One down, ten to go! Remember, guys, this could have been us. I hope that we won't make that idea a reality."

"They are dead!" Dema's voice stuttered. "They are dead!"

"Dema, this could have been us," TH replied as Mason and Van remained silent, processing death in their worlds. "On top of that, we barely knew them, so, and I hate to be that human-oid, but..."

"Both of you, please! We're not out of the woods or desert yet. Do you think I feel good?" Mason silenced them both. "Please, we must press on, or we'll join them. Dema? TH?"

"Yes, Mason!"

"Understood Commander!" TH laid his hands on the periscope handles and swung left.

———

"Well, that went quickly. In the first thirty minutes, we lost Peggy and Gaucho." Benjamin brought up the screen with the platoons and crossed out the Canadian and Argentinian tanks. "Both nations were going for their first World Battle Royale Win, but good luck next time!"

"Look at him running." Adriana pointed at the tanker from Gaucho, limping away from the burning wreckage as the victor vanished behind a grassy hill.

Jeong-Min looked at the scoreboard and whispered something inaudible as the first zeroes appeared on the screen. Then, they faded into obscurity with the names of the knocked-out contestants.

- *Team 20 Ram II late (Peggy) Surviving 0 out of 5—OUT*

- *Team 8 Nahuel DL D3 (Gaucho), Surviving 1 out of 5—OUT*

"I have to say, Turan is performing rather well, but Nahuel's crew got caught with their pants down again. Apologies for the mess; we just landed and didn't want you to miss the action and my commentary." The camera swooped around, showing the personnel unloading the Galaxy transport plane. "We're almost done. Our brave staff pulled an all-nighter to set up the gear."

"After crates are secured, we shall observe the Power Platoon members briefly. I'm curious how the Hydro crew is feeling by dragging that fuel trailer behind them." Benjamin looked at the flat tire of the trailer, dragged by the Hydrostat, and one of the crewmen angrily pointed at the distance.

"Well, they need it to survive. At the Research Bureau, I had a problem figuring out the fuel consumption and range of that Hydro. I had to cross-reference several sources, and I still couldn't figure it out, so we are going with slightly improved original stats. Also, it is a risk as one shot to the tank, not that tank, but the one on the wheels well..." Thomas ratted out facts and remembered the dreaded sleepless night in his office, surrounded by energy drinks and oily pizza boxes.

"Jeong-Min, you have been silent so far; everything all right?" Adriana turned towards the silent tanker, who observed the incident.

"Yes, everything is all right, Adriana, but call me Min," Jeong-Min smiled, "but I'm surprised that Turan is doing rather well, and I just ate my words. They threw a track."

The camera flew over the heads of the androids who emerged from the Hungarian tank and commenced the repairs while the man with binoculars scanned his surroundings. With his left hand, he reached into the pocket of his uniform and pulled out a chocolate bar, biting away large chunks.

"That will be bad for them since another tank is nearby, just behind that hill. They will have to remove the wire mesh screens to repair the tracks, which is good for all things considered. Originally, Turan was fielded with 8mm spaced armor plates. Still, thanks to the German cooperation, we can assume that the Hungarians got their hands on the lighter mesh screens that offered the same protection as their full-plate counterparts but with less weight." Thomas opened the Note App on his tablet while the camera changed the angle. "So much historical trivia. I encourage all viewers to look up some interesting facts in the meantime."

"And we might read some live on air!" Jeong-Min pointed into the camera. "Send us something good!"

———

After restocking the ten new BR-271 rounds, Crusading Angel dived into the desert again, and dune hopping soon became a chore. As the analog watch showed a precise 15:00, Mason slowly exhaled. Unfortunately, the crew's mood dropped faster as the Crusading Angel slid down the next major dip in the desert, as the green hills hadn't appeared. Even with the improved ventilation, the sand dust, fumes, death, howling engine, and blistering heat were still issues, forcing several stops along the way.

"Dema, my guide in the night, are you sure we're going the right way?" Van turned towards Dema, who squeezed the stock of her machine gun, whispering a prayer in Ukrainian.

"According to the provided map, we should be at the edge of the desert, but if it continues, all of you can split my dinner." Dema opened her red eyes. "Please, greenery, be there, please, for the love of God. I would suggest finding an overlook."

"No one is splitting anything. I need all of you at your best, and an empty stomach is not a viable option. Van, pedal to the metal. I'm sick of dune skipping, and I do not want to see another desert ever again!" Mason coughed as he felt sand between his teeth. "No matter how gorgeous looking it is!"

With all hatches open for some sort of heat ventilation, it only worsened as the wind blew sand everywhere.

"Yes, Boss! Do not have to tell me twice!" Van steered left and led the Crusading Angel up the slope, but halfway the sprocket wheels couldn't move the tank forward, and T-34 slid down the hill.

"Van, let's try to find a less steep slope." TH scanned around, looking for a friendlier incline with his periscope first and then poked out for a better view.

"Steeper slope is the least of my worries. The engine is not as powerful as it was. My take is that we have sand in the air filters," Van reported. "Last thing I want is to be engineless in a desert."

"All right." Mason opened his hatch as Angel's engine stopped howling. "I think we should be good here. TH, Van, check the engine. Dema, I'll need you to join me up here and keep cool; we're not out of the desert yet."

"How are you holding up?" Dema said as she joined Mason, who rested his eyes from the blistering sun as TH and Van ran around, juggling the screwdrivers and wrenches.

"I'll be better when we get out of this desert. How are you holding up?" Mason shook his head and smiled.

"I am worried about you. We came close to losing you. Do not do that again, please."

"Look, Dema," Mason grabbed her hand, "I'm working on it, I promise."

"All of us are." Dema smiled. "I am just scared. When your only vision is the gunsight of a machine gun in the heat of combat, your imagination takes over," Dema said in a shivering voice. "Ricochets, revving the engine, everything is multiplied tenfold. Oh my!"

Instead of saying anything, Mason looked at Van, who swept sand out of the air filters and the top of the transmission while TH cleaned the bolts. In ten minutes, Dema gave a helping hand, and soon the tank's rear end was screwed together.

"As I said, Mason, the air filters were the issue. We did what we could, but our Angel could use a pit stop." Van waited for TH to pack everything and then reported to Mason, as he ensured everything was tight and ready to go.

"All right, let's get out of this desert. TH switched with Dema so that she could look around for a few hours and get acquainted with the shells. Should the worst come, we will all rotate our positions from now onward."

"I was about to suggest that. I do not mind staring at the angled plate for hours." TH waited for Dema to get out, and then he effortlessly slid into Dema's place as Van climbed into the T-34 via his driver's hatch.

"Everyone in?" Mason plugged in his headset. "On the first rotation, we'll rotate clockwise. I'll drive, Van will work on the radio, and so on every two hours. The first leg of our journey is almost behind us! We'll need to push a bit more! Just a bit more. When we find green, we'll know we have reached the threshold! Clear?"

———

"Thomas, do you have a moment?" Jeong-Min took the crate with camera equipment from Thomas, who nodded.

After spending another six hours in the air, all but one Galaxy aircraft departed for home. However, as staff ran around, all presenters decided to give a helping hand during the commercial breaks. In a few hours, the plane was unpacked, just in time for the first fight, but as another downtime occurred, the unpacking continued, with one of the producers navigating the traffic like a police officer.

"Yes?" Thomas looked up from his tablet.

"I would like to ask you: How did you join this venture?" Jeong-Min sat down at the box.

"Hmm. That's a long story!" Thomas stood silent for a moment.

"I don't think we are rushing anywhere?" Jeong-Min shook his head. "I'm just trying to meet people and learn about their corner of the world."

"Well, my corner of the world is nothing special. I grew up poor in the Little Rock, Arkansas suburbs. After finishing high school, I enrolled in a trade school and became an engineer. Then, I helped my father expand his consulting and blueprint development firm. However, my mother passed away, which took a toll on my dad. I took over the business, but I knew he and I needed something fresh to do, so one day, four years ago,

I somehow waltzed into the flea market, just thinking and not paying attention. I really don't know why I went there, but as I strolled the long street, my eyes laid on a little box."

Thomas found his backpack and pulled out a glassed tank model.

"What tank is that?"

"BT-42, a light-artillery tank, captured and modified by Finland during WW2 from the Soviet Union. So, I bought all the documentation and told my dad, 'Let's build a life-sized one.' He initially hesitated and asked for a day to think about it as I stockpiled the necessary tools. The next day," Thomas dried his tears, "he handed me over the calculations for the real-life-sized model on which he worked the entire night. After the Purchase, we lost our consulting company to Orion Umbrella. So, with a lot of time on our hands, we started welding the parts together. Sadly, my dad didn't get to see the completion since that bitch cancer got to him, but Adriana moved into the neighborhood. We both found our passion and love together for us and the tank sitting in my backyard. One of our neighbors called a local TV station, giving us the opportunity. I got a call from TVG that day, expressing interest. So, we submitted the details, went through the process, and here we are. How did you get here?"

Jeong-Min took a moment to reply as he handed Thomas the tablet with an image where Min and his squad posed for the photograph next to a T-100 SKM South Korean MBT.

"Military service, Thomas. I sometimes have second thoughts as I imagine a different life as a civilian. But the train had already left the station, and pulling the emergency brake would make much-unwelcomed noise, threatening my already established foundation."

"Thank you for your service. I considered joining the military, but ultimately, I decided to use my brain elsewhere. No offense."

"None taken, and I understand that. While it may seem

that the military is for everyone and they want you to see it that way, only a few will make it out unscathed when push comes to shove. There is no glory to be found in any war, and whoever tells you otherwise is a liar." Jeong-Min looked into the distance and shook his head. "I heard that the United States finally ran out of Purple Hearts that were minted for Operation Downfall."

CITY OF FIRE AND BRIMSTONE

After another three hours of begging the desert to end, Mason wept with joy when the grassy hills appeared in the distance, and soon, all four lay on the grass, praising God that the dunes and dips had finally ended. Crusading Angel roared again as Mason steered it right and made a quick stop to change his place with Van. A moment later, a silence had descended on the grasslands, and the tank hid underneath the green camo net. A minute later, Mason handed out lunch rations. Bread, dried meat, and water were on the menu, followed by crackers and one bar of chocolate split three ways. The silence all around helped Mason to collect his thoughts after a rumbling drive.

Well, the desert is behind us. I'll miss it, though, in a strange way. I think this was the first time I actually saw a desert. Gorgeous, yet deadly. Now, we have grass to look forward to. And while hills seem to break it up, it will be a monotonous drive again. Damn!

"Mason, I saw spaghetti in the ration box, so why on Earth are we sticking with bread and dried meat?" Van took a bite and looked at the unopened wooden box.

"Sorry, what?" Mason shook his head. "I was away for a moment."

"Why not spaghetti brother? I'm getting a good work-out with my hands," Van flexed his biceps, "and I need the calories to feed my two children. And not just my kids; we all need to eat!"

"Because I want to save them for dinner. Once we finish that box and stick with the plan I crafted, we'll run out of food in two days at lunch, which should be enough to get us to the final zone. But again, I could be completely off, so we must scavenge something along the way."

"How about a little celebration of surviving the first day so far?" Van exhaled. "Come on, you are killing my muscles here."

"My friend, the best I can do is my third of the chocolate bar. I'm already splitting the MRE bags as best as I can."

"Keep it, Commander. Hey, Dema, why so silent?" Van turned towards Dema, who used the back of the T-34 as the stand for the provided map.

"Well, we should make it to the second zone just in time. The problem is that there is a large town just over that hill, and the entrance to the second zone is five hours of drive away, give or take, depending on thousands of things."

"All right, so we have to cross the town no matter what." TH moved his finger across the streets. "It seems like my memory is corrupted, but some 1s and 0s tell me this town seems to be familiar."

"So, this is what we'll do. Van, TH, we have time before we advance into the pit, so I was hoping you could inspect the T-34 and clean the air filters again. We need all the ponies we can get out of that engine. Dema and I will scout the outskirts. We should be back soon, and then we're rolling again."

"Did you just say ponies instead of horses?" TH tapped his chin. "Was it intentional?"

"Yes, TH, Mason is trying to keep our spirits high." Van and TH saluted, and a moment later, the banter between the two vanished into the wind.

"Would you like to race on top of this hill?" Dema readied herself, but when she looked to her left, she found Mason sitting on a large rock. "What is the matter?"

"A few hours ago, I killed four or five people. People with families awaiting them home." Mason looked at the clear afternoon sky. "I feel their angry looks on the back of my neck. We could have teamed up or something."

"It was either them or us, and by them opening fire on us, well, they were not looking for battle buddies." Dema took a deep breath before saying anything more, trying to walk the line. "Then you would be responsible for our deaths. Imagine your brother discovering that you got blown to pieces in Asia, of all places, with no chance of getting your body home, if he would ever find out. The last words you said to him would be the ones you said on the tamarack."

"When you put it that way, Dema," Mason sadly smiled, "I didn't have a choice."

"Mason, I do not care how you justify this. We are all counting on you, and we know there is a question of morality in everything. It was either us or them." Dema took Mason's hands in hers. "Please, don't forget that. I do not want to give you a lecture. You bear the most weight of us all, and adding more pushes you to your limit."

———

"Well, look at that. Most of the crew are scouting ahead, which did happen. Commanders would hide their tanks and scout ahead for potential obstacles in the way, and if possible, they would radio in for intel. All tanks are about to converge in this mock-up city one way or another," Benjamin smiled at the camera, "we have some significant action awaiting us."

"Warfare had changed a lot, and while I do not desire to call these tanks primitive, the technological advancements certainly helped out. But, I wonder, do we get to see CAS?"

Jeong-Min played with the screen momentarily. "It's an all-out urban war!"

"What is CAS?" Benjamin looked at Jeong-Min, who scratched the back of his neck, thinking about the highlighted tanks.

"Close Air Support," Thomas and Adriana said simultaneously and pointed at each other. "We have a wide selection of birds on stand-by, ranging from the infamous Hs-129 to a lesser-known Piaggio P.108 Artigliere gunship." Thomas showed off several models on the screen, crowning the brief presentation with a colossal four-engine plane with a long barrel poking from underneath the fuselage.

"I have to say, you are more prepared than I am." Benjamin turned towards the camera and pointed at the viewers. "Now we're going live in the city, which is the central part of the first area. The city itself is a random German periodically correct city, turned into a warzone. We have a few elements to make this engagement memorable, and we'll see how our contestants are ready to handle the all-out warfare. Nerves will be shattered, the oil will leak, and steel will fracture! All of this is to come."

"And you even get to see Tank Museum come to life." Thomas nodded his head. "For all the premium viewers, I hope that you have been eavesdropping on your favorites because I just got the news from the top that there might be a blind spot where your nano drones won't be able to fly, so bear with us."

"So, how many nano-drones are flying out there?" Jeong-Min turned towards Benjamin, who swiped left with two fingers.

"There are five hundred million premium users registered, currently flying in the first area, while the rest of us stick with the main camera."

"Doesn't that create problems?" Min tilted his head.

"Absolutely no problems. Nano drones fly in orbit and have strong magnification with 16K resolution. When I first heard it, I thought it was some science fiction."

"So, someone is watching us?" Adriana looked up at the scattered clouds slowly sailing through the afternoon sky. "Is it safe? I want no Peeping Tom problems here."

"Someone is always watching, Adriana." Thomas lowered his voice, "Always watching. But I think our location is off-limits. However, I'll bet that someone will try to get here."

"What a voice! Have you considered being a voice actor?"

"Nah. This is a better gig, but when I run out of money, I'll see what I can do." Thomas grinned from ear to ear. "Back to tanks, I presume?"

"You presume right, Thomas." Benjamin looked into the camera. "We got a few minutes before we go to a commercial break. Afterward, we'll be answering some questions from the audience. How is everyone feeling?"

"Excited," Adriana said between her teeth and then smiled into the camera as well, "Glad to be here. Thomas and I worked hard. Right, love?"

———

"Everything all right, Van?" TH handed Van the kit with packed tools.

Van nodded and sat at the turret, looking into the fading desert behind them. He turned his head when he heard wild horses galloping towards them, free as the hawks flying above them.

"Look at that harras, TH. We used to have horses when I was little." Van lost himself for a moment as the horses passed them by. "Racing across the walked-out forest paths; those were the days. The best 4x4 vehicle you can ask for in any terrain. I remember our dad taking my brothers and me on mountain rides before Alzheimer's got the better of him. We rode for about two days, camping in the wilderness, hunting and skinning the game. Trust me, if I could do it again, I would without any hesitation."

"I have never ridden one of these in my life." TH extended his arm and touched the forehead of one of the more curious members of the harras.

Van smiled when he observed a child-like curiosity waking up inside TH as the machine examined the living. *These are the moments you live for.* He shed a singular tear of joy as the horse galloped away to join his brethren.

"Then we shall ride together when we get out of here." Van packed the toolkit and shut the lid with full force. "And we wait for Dema and Mason. Brother, I am scared."

"Did you know that I get stage fright?"

"Get out of here, really?" Van raised his eyebrow. "Really? You get stage fright?"

"One of my brains belonged to a human." TH tilted his head. "Yeah."

"Wow. That is metal and kind of disgusting at the same time. However, that is something my youngest brother would do. He always has a knack for putting things together that shouldn't be. Once, on Cinco de Mayo, he presented us with a hardshell taco and peanut butter inside. It was one of the tastes of all time; I tell you what, TH. So, the human brain. Your processing power must be insane."

"I'm kidding. The last thing I need is another processing power to drain my limited battery. What are you afraid of?" TH watched Van nervously laugh. "You can tell me."

"I'm scared that I'll die. I saw myself die in a nightmare. Mason told me that it's just a dream and not real." Van's face turned a shade of pale, and he looked at his shaking hands, which he immediately hid in the pockets of his uniform to calm down. "I'm scared that I won't see my brothers, family farm or home. I fear I won't find another woman to love me. And that I'll never taste tacos with peanut butter and jelly, as my bro promised."

"Brother," TH tapped Van on his left shoulder, "as Mason said, we'll cross the finish line, and you will have everything back in no time, plus a lot more."

"Thank you, TH." Van embraced his metal brother. "I promise we'll ride on the horses when we get home. It will be one of the best experiences you'll ever have."

"We shall do that and much more." TH looked up when he heard another engine sound, and a moment later a tank with a yellow cross on a blue background appeared.

———

Van and TH immediately dived onto the ground, but they could only hear the rumbling engine. For a moment, Van decided to peek out, expecting the lead heading their way.

Instead, only two crewmen were visible, waving their hands. The turret was turned the other way, revealing an autoloading mechanism loaded with shells.

"They seem to be friendly!" Van waved back as they parked next to them a moment later. TH grabbed the wrench, but Van lowered TH's hand.

"Good afternoon. We need your help." The crewman from the turret dismounted, followed by his companion. "Could we borrow some of your tools? In return, we can spare a few chocolate bars or the entire ration. Or both."

"Is this a trick?" Van tilted his head. "We'll fight tooth and nail!"

"Stay back!" TH raised his wrench against the two men, who immediately followed his order.

"No, one moment." A short exchange in Swedish occurred, and a moment later, Van stood with two chocolate bars in his hands.

"Can borrow the tools now?" the tanker said with a strong Swedish accent. "We'll give you the ration after we finish."

TH turned towards Van, who gave him a thumbs up. Two men began juggling tools between each other; one screwed in the lightbulb in one of the road lights while the other cleaned the gun barrel with the rod.

"I think we should do the same," TH found Angel's rod, and momentarily, the long rifled barrel started smoking black clouds. "No harm in a little preparation before a big fight."

"Thank you again! I hope that we will be able to unite forces for the next part," one of the Swedes shouted. "Our platoon completely ditched us."

"Sure, why not? Where is the rest of your crew?" Van approached the Swedes, hands behind his back,

"Over there." Both Swedes pointed toward where Mason and Dema had left ten minutes ago.

"Well, isn't that lucky? Some of us headed that way, too. So, what brings you here?"

"All four of us were caught running a smuggling op of blood diamonds from Africa to Swedish Elite. Politicians, CEOs, and even Royalty. We made the mistake of trusting the government. If we win, we get our freedom back. How about you two?"

"I'm a political prisoner for my beliefs. Both of us are. It was said that the United States was one of the freest countries in the world, yet they still jailed people with different opinions that didn't suit the government. Our new world just cranked it up to eleven," TH rambled on.

———

"All right, Dema, what do you see?" Mason whispered as they hid in the bushes overlooking the ruined city.

"I see tank hedges, trenches, auto-cannons, and soldiers. They dressed old androids into periodically correct uniforms and gave them weapons." Dema handed Mason back his binoculars as she looked at the sentries patrolling the streets, flashing their rifles and anti-tank weaponry.

As Mason looked back and forth between the city and a map, he took a deep breath, but the quiet before the storm made him stand up. As he looked around, he noticed two other tankers observing the situation, pointing at the map and the nearby hills. He saw the yellow cross on their shoulder patches and immediately lay on the ground.

Dema fixed her hair as the two tall, blond-haired, blue-eyed men with bright white teeth looked around them, and one began closing the distance, showing his empty hands. Soon, his companion followed.

"What is happening?" Dema nudged Mason, who pointed at two tankers to their right. "Oh crap!"

"I think they want to talk. What can we lose?" Dema took a deep breath as they found them and began waving at them. "And they are handsome."

"Dema, I do not think that is a good idea." Mason watched Dema fold the map and wave back.

"Look, we have no chance of getting through that city alone, so maybe we can unite for a moment." Dema took a first unsure step toward the two.

"And then what? It will be a race of whoever shoots first. I'm not sure." Mason weighed all the options for the moment. "I guess I'll have to worry about it later. "

"What can we lose from talking with them? Anyway, it seems like Van and TH have made up our minds for us." Dema pointed at their Crusading Angel driving alongside the Swedish Delat Torn, and moments later, both crews stood facing each other with their backs to their machines.

With a blistering afternoon sun above their heads, Mason thought to himself: *We have nothing to lose working with them, but why would they work with us? We blasted them in the simulation, so seeking a revenge kill is not out of the question Okay, play it cool, and don't get us killed!*

"Well, it seems like the loneliness got to us." Mason smiled and regretted opening the conversation this way as he felt ten different sentences sitting on the tip of his tongue. "So, you want to team up?"

Like Crusading Angel, the Swedish Machine had four crewmen, with the name Carolus Rex painted on the turret side instead of the gun barrel. The tank seemed much more modern, with perfectly defined lines and none of the visible rough edges that were all around the Angel.

"It seems like our crews have already made a deal, so we shake on it?" The Commander of the Swedish crew extended his hand, and after a bit of hesitation, a truce formed.

"What is the deal?" Mason replied and looked at his crew, and his eyes found Van, who stepped forward.

"We agreed to a cease-fire between us and attempt to pass through the city and fight alongside each other. However, if we were to make it, we would part our separate ways and not shoot at each other," TH reported. "They seem to be honorable."

"All right, we can work together," Mason said with his arms folded, "but I still don't trust you."

"That is fair; we don't trust you either, but is that healthy tension that should allow us to work together? If you are worried about revenge for a simulation match, we couldn't care less. Where are my manners? Ludvig Akerson, Commander of the Carolus Rex, and my fellow Swedish American brothers. Who are you?"

"My name is Mason Knight, and this is..." An engine sound cut out Mason's introductions as a smoking large four-engine bomber flew above their heads and crashed into the city square, followed by the bark of machine guns and autocannons from both pursuing aircraft and ground anti-air stations.

"I think this is our cue! Radio on at all times!" Ludvig shouted, and moments later both tanks rolled down the hill and engaged the perimeter defenses.

— — —

Crusading Angel was the first to achieve the breakthrough in the city's outer defenses, just as the analog clock inside the tank showed 03:47. Carolus Rex followed closely and attracted fire, ranging from rifle shots to anti-tank cannons, and soon, strafing airplanes joined the battlefield. Finally, Van slammed hard on the brakes, allowing Mason to lay the gun on the other anti-tank cannon nest.

"Firing!" Mason felt the wind next to his ears as the breech recoiled, and a moment later, the shell had split the barrel in half.

"I am sorry to report, but they tracked us. Commencing repairs now!" Ludvig's voice came to life in TH's headphones, and after TH relayed the message to Mason, another tank, covered by debris and tank tracks, came into view as its long gun started to rotate towards the Crusading Angel.

"Dema, is it loaded? I need to kill it!" Mason looked at Dema, who, with shaking hands, pushed the round into the breech, and among the gunfire from nearby soldiers, explosions, and the rattling of the machine guns and autocannons, Mason heard a screech and then an empty click.

"What do I do!? It's jammed!" Dema punched the breech. "I am sorry! I do not remember!"

"Van, reverse to that back alley!" Mason shouted, and a moment later, the tank began reversing, its tracks crushing everything in their path.

"Dema, there is a handle on the breech, which should help eject the shell," TH shouted over the sound of the V-12 engine. "You got this! Mason, should I switch with Dema?"

As Angel reversed, the tank in front of them fired, and soon, loud ringing filled the T-34. The shot glanced from the frontal plate and found a target in a nearby building.

"They have been mishit. Their driver is gone, and the horizontal turret drive is out. They are requesting immediate assistance!" TH reported the status of the Carolus Rex. "Commander, did you hear me? Should I switch with Dema?"

"Our breech is jammed! Give us a moment," Mason shouted. "Tell them that!"

"Yes, Sir!" TH's response was drowned by the gunfire and whistling bombs. "I have static!"

"What? Static?" Mason slowly opened his hatch, and after waiting for a moment for the dust to settle, he poked out and waved at the Carolus Rex.

"Hey! Park in the street behind you!" Not sure if they heard him, Mason pointed at the corner of the street as the Rex came to life and started reversing.

"That was stupid, charging head-on!" Van let go of the gas and engaged the brake as he rear-ended the wall behind them, prompting Mason to close the hatch behind him and press his forehead against the rubber cover of the gunsight.

Soon, more shots either ricocheted off the Angel or were absorbed, sending shockwaves and spall all around the interior.

When Mason looked at the torn and bleeding sleeves of his uniform, he bit his tongue, and at that moment, his eyes found steel fragments all over his body. And while his hand was about to pull the first one out of his body, his mind overruled and focused Mason on the battle. Another glancing shot and Van's scream drowned in the roaring of the engines and gunfire.

———

"I go it!" Dema wrestled with the gun breech, and after another minute of struggle, she heard the click, and the ejected shell hit the tank's floor.

Attempting to grab the shell with shaking hands took her several tries, but she hugged it, lifted it, and shoved it into the breech.

"Loaded!" Dema shouted with tears in her eyes as Mason pressed his eyes against the gunsight.

"All right, where is this tank?" Mason rotated the turret left and right, using only a large window to move Angel's barrel. Still, another glancing shot prompted Mason to press his hands against the earflaps of his helmet, praying to God to silence this madness just for a moment. He couldn't even formulate a singular sentence as the world slowly closed in on him.

"Does anyone know what tank is engaging us?" someone shouted as the ringing finally ended, prompting Mason to use the vision slits on the commander's cupola to scan his surroundings.

In the hull, TH cocked the charging handle on the machine gun and mowed down a group of soldiers that emerged from the rubble and smoke, followed by another tank. The long cannon with a muzzle brake was first to peek out of the smoke.

"Not just the tank; look to your left; there are soldiers with rocket launchers looking for Carolus Rex or us!" TH swung his machine gun right, but he couldn't reach the rocket man, who fired but missed the track of the Crusading Angel in front of him. "Van, are you all right?"

TH looked at weeping Van, squeezing the levers, his bleeding hands trying to hold on to something.

"Van, you are bleeding!" TH shouted but couldn't get his attention as Van continued staring at him, riddled with spall of varied sizes, piercing his protective clothing.

The sound of yet another airplane engine forced Dema to cover her ears, but looking through the periscope, the ground attacker leveled part of the street to the ground. Behind them, it sounded like the entire armada was about to close in on their position. Mason flipped the switch two seconds later, and the co-axial machine gun forced soldiers to seek cover, buying Mason time to rotate the turret back.

"I move, I'll give away our position," Mason shouted this thought out loud and opened his hatch to ventilate the fumes.

Dema shouted something in Ukrainian and dropped the shell on the floor. As her hand searched for the source of pain, Dema bit her tongue when she felt a fragment stuck in her right side. She looked through the periscope and froze for a moment.

"Mason, another tank is in front of us, and it's big! Luckily, it doesn't see us yet," Dema stuttered as she reported the finding.

———

"So what tanks are they facing apart from each other?" Jeong-Min shook his head as he spotted tracer rounds cutting through the air.

Due to the large amounts of rising smoke, all screens changed to thermal vision, attempting to find the contestants hiding among the rubble.

"Well, let's look at the Crusading Angel for a moment. There is a Jagdpanzer IV/70 V to their left, an underappreciated workhorse of the German Army during World War Two, overshadowed by its big brothers Jagdpanther and Jagdtiger. Jagdpanzer means a hunting tank in German. A Soviet heavy called KV-1, the star of the early Soviet Armor, but this is a unique variant called KV-1 C 756(r), a merge of German firepower and Soviet armor," Adriana summarized the situation. "And that is just a tiny sample."

"Well, Thomas and Min, your tanks are surrounded from three sides," Benjamin parried the strike and looked into the camera. "For all of you betting out there, we currently have the most volatile chances of all TVG programs, so we're doubling the payout on all current bets and tripling the money for guessing the final two tanks standing!"

"I hope for my Swedish meatballs," Jeong-Min smiled as he watched his favorite barely making it behind the cover, followed by an explosion, "but Ludvig's leadership will get them out of there. The man seems to know what he is doing. They're already a man down, and reloading the autoloader will take a bit longer."

On the screen behind them, Ludvig opened the commander's hatch and sprayed the lead at all sides with his machine gun while his tank turned around to target the incoming tank to its right.

"I can assume that you have fought in the urban environment, so can you tell us, what is the best chance for our contestants to make it?" Adriana turned towards Jeong-Min, who tapped his thumbs.

"Get the hell out of there; it is all I can say. With no infantry support, they are as good as dead. It happened to us during the War. We raced to the city of strategic interest with my platoon, and let's just say it was a slaughter. Tanks don't like urban combat. Armor and flesh must work together to survive." Jeong-Min scratched his chin. "Chechen Wars in the late 1900s is a good case study. Russian armor became easy prey in narrow streets, where Chechens had the high ground or hid in the basements with their anti-tank weaponry. From there, it was just like shooting fish in a barrel."

"Thank you for sharing with us," Benjamin smiled, "so much historical trivia to go around."

"Yeah," Adriana looked at the screen behind her, "So much trivia."

———

"Empty!" TH shouted as he heard clicks on his machine gun.

"Van, hit the gas and break through, as the enemy is waiting for the smoke to clear. So three, two, one, hit it!" Mason shouted, drying the sweat from his forehead with his left hand, observing the smoke clouds slowly disappear.

Van put it in reverse instead of advancing, and at a snail's pace, T-34 vanished behind the buildings. Another stray shot bounced off the frontal plate, forcing Van to bite his tongue. With every hole in the ground, Van tried to hold on to the controls, but the spall pierced deeper into his skin.

"Why didn't you go forward? Van, what the hell?" Mason shouted into the comms, "Van! Forward!

"I cannot go forward, brother!"

"Or how about we use that Cafe to get to the other side? We can flank the tank and get the hell out." Dema, with shaking hands, attempted to push the hatch open but gave up halfway.

"All right, let me think for a moment." Mason leaned his head on the breech.

"Come on; we don't have much time!" Van shouted as he felt tears coming down his cheeks, trying to keep his shaking hands on the levers. "I'm sorry!"

"Okay, this is what we'll do. TH, take the loader's position, and Dema, check out the Café. Double time!"

"Will do!" TH waited for Dema to open the loader's hatch with her shaking hands and tears in her eyes.

Mason climbed out and helped Dema to open the other hatch. "Girl, you got this!"

"Oh my!" Dema hugged Mason for a second, and then he watched her vanish among the rubble.

However, as he was about to close his hatch, he felt a cooling wind blowing the clouds of battle away, and at that moment, time froze for Mason. He could see the box turret of the Carolus Rex flying out of the hull in the blaze of glory. More burning tank wreckage lit the way. Empty casings of various sizes and large holes littered the ground all over. Soldiers either laid face down or were blown all over the place, some crying and begging their mates to end their suffering. With his eyes twitching, Mason sat back again inside the turret, taking three deep breaths to calm his racing heart. He looked through the vision slits at the place where Dema vanished from his sight, biting his nails. *You got this, Dema. I believe in you! We all do! God protect her if you can. Please!*

Then, as he rotated it to ninety degrees, he noticed a tank destroyer firing at their position, hitting the driver's hatch with full force. A loud ringing and screams from below prompted Mason to lay the gun on the driver's hatch of the low-sitting tank destroyer. He took a deep breath and pressed the trigger pedal, blowing the tank destroyer sky-high.

"Van, you all right?!" Mason pressed his hands against the ear flops, picking up on a whimpering.

"... Mason, I'm not! Where... hell... Dema?"

"Van! Repeat it!" Mason's intuition prompted him to look through the gunsight again, finding another man with a bazooka crawling out of the rubble.

In a second, Mason dispatched the man into the afterlife with the machine gun, then scanned his surroundings for more targets.

Dema climbed back into the tank a few moments later and shut the hatch behind her, shaking like a wet dog. TH already sat back in his new seat.

"Mason, I don't think I can take this anymore," Dema's whimpering voice sounded in the comms. "Get us out of here!"

"Pull yourself together!" Mason shouted. "If we fail, we won't make it! What is the status? Can we get out?"

The only response he got was muffled weeping.

"Dema, if we don't get out now, we die! Now, pull yourself together!" Mason shouted again, but deep inside he felt his heart shatter with each word. "Please! What did you see?"

"Both ends of the street are blocked. Our only way is forward, turning immediately left so the demolished house can cover us from three anti-tank guns aimed at our position."

"Thank you, Dema!" Mason gently touched her shaking shoulders. "I'm proud!"

"I failed! I should have spotted that earlier!"

"You didn't fail!"

"I did! I am slow and weak!"

"You are not!" Mason shook his head. "You are not. Everyone! Please keep your eyes peeled for the enemy positions and call them out immediately. If they immobilize us, we are dead! Van, pedal to the metal! TH, switch with Dema." Mason pressed his forehead against the gunsight as the Crusading Angel roared out of the smoke, crushing everything in its path.

CHAPTER FIFTEEN

PANZER OF THE LAKE

"And just like that, the main event of the first stage is behind us." Thomas looked at the bombers leveling the mock-up city to the ground.

"My odds weren't favored today!" Jeong-Min pounded the desk, then took a deep breath as he looked at his bank account. "I guess that makes it a hundred dollars?"

"Did my AC-4 go out?" Benjamin looked at the Hydrostat vanishing into the forest, leaving a burning Aussie tank behind it. "Oh. Do we have any survivors out of the knocked-out tanks?"

"Well, we have from Gaucho, awaiting the flight. After that, there will be only one more extraction flight in this ring, and then flights will be suspended until the first ring closes. After that, contestants enter phase two." Adriana pointed at the screen, where a limping teen with the Argentinian flag on his shoulder finally entered the zone, illuminated by the green smoke, and lay on the ground, holding his right leg.

He cried out and closed his eyes. The man reached into his uniform, but the camera cut to the 14TP running over a soldier with a machine gun and vanishing behind the buildings, waved away by the falling rubble and tracer rounds.

"So, what is the plan now?"

"Now we will pull out surviving tanks one by one and shall see how they are doing on the crew count." Benjamin swiped right on the screen, and the remaining models started to render. "Remember, viewers, if the crew count drops below two, you are out of the game. One to drive, one to shoot. An extra number is parentheses marks the number of kills."

"This game is really testing our contestants. Long, monotonous drives, and of course, one bad decision can send you packing or to the grave." Adriana looked at Thomas, who shrugged his shoulders.

Team 10 – Centaur Mk.III (Boudicca) – Surviving 3 out of 5.
Team 16 – Panzer 4 G Hydrostat (Oden)(1) – Surviving 4 out of 5
Team 18 – Chi-Nu-Kai (Tomoe Gozen) (Adriana) – Surviving 4 out of 5
Team 22 – M4A1 76W (American Made) – Surviving 5 out of 5
Team 6 – 14TP (Grom) – Surviving 2 out of 2
Team 26 – P26/40 (Da Vinci) – Surviving 4 out of 4
Team 28 – T-34-57 mod.42/43 (Crusading Angel)(1) (Thomas) – Surviving 4 out of 4
Team 24 – 41M III Turan 75(1) (Horthy) – Surviving 4 out of 5

"Wait! There is a survivor from the AC-4!" Benjamin looked to his left and found one of the interns pointing at the camera.

All four hosts leaned forward as they watched a tanker in a brown Aussie hat peeking from the bush as the bombs whistled all around him. He held the issued map, looking around, attempting to find North.

"Good for him." Benjamin touched Team 8 and the burned-down Gaucho appeared on the screen.

"May he make it safely to the extraction point," Adriana whispered.

"Now we take a break as the Filler shall commence." Benjamin was about to stand up when Thomas halted him.

"No, we have eight surviving tanks, and we will give each one a dedicated five to ten-minute screentime before we go to the break. The last time I checked, there were more non-premium users than premium ones. Hey..." Jeong-Min clapped his hands and pointed at every single staff member, "keep the cameras running. We will be done once I say we are done!"

The shock and dead silence spread across the tent studio, but some personnel clapped.

"That is what I'm talking about. Ads can wait; we're still in the game!" Jeong-Min switched the screen and British Centaur rendered into view, dropping several smoke grenades to cover its retreat.

———

"Mason! Van is bleeding!" Dema opened the loader's hatch and found Mason staring at the bombardment of the city, through which they barely made it out alive. It took a few nudges to catch Mason's attention.

"Yes?"

"I said that Van is bleeding, heavily. You are also! It doesn't look good." Dema touched Mason's burning forehead and said, "TH is doing everything he can to help him. Get to his driver's hatch and pull him out from there."

A scream of pain forced Mason to jump down and rush towards the driver's hatch, ignoring his wounds for a moment.

"Pass him through here!" Mason tapped on the driver's shattered viewports, and a bloody hand allowed Mason to peek inside as he locked the hatch open.

His hands found Van's head, and a moment later Mason felt Dema and TH pushing Van out of the tank; Mason looked away as Van came into the full light. His bloody tanker's uniform was shredded to pieces, and black/green fragments of all sizes stuck out. There wasn't a single spot on Van's body not covered by blood, torn fabric, or chunks of steel. As he carefully placed Van on the ground, Mason felt a thousand needles piercing his skin. He slid beside Van and took a deep breath, fighting off his pain.

"Now, whatever you do, do not pull out the fragments yet. The only thing keeping him alive is adrenaline. Mason got me one of those blankets; Dema, check that constant beeping," TH issued orders as his eyes flashed two times. "I will find the biggest ones and assess the situation.

"What beeping? There is still a bombardment just over that hill." Dema poked out of the driver's hatch, feeling the shredded and bloody seat covering her back.

"All right, I will attempt to help him, but I need you to examine the tank completely, from brake levers to the gun-mounted light. Dema, bring the map and check where the next extraction point is. I can stabilize him, but we need to get him there," TH shouted. "Dema, did you hear me? We need to make this quick!"

Instead of listening, Dema kneeled to Van and took his hands into hers, fighting hard to keep the tears from falling.

"We'll not make it to the extraction point, no matter how hard we try," Van coughed up blood. "We only have around fifty miles left in the fuel tank, give or take. So, you need to use it to find more fuel and press onward!"

"I want you to be quiet! We will get you medical care since I can only do so much," TH silenced Van, who closed his eyes.

"I do not want to be a drag; you still have a chance to win," Van finally said as he coughed up blood on TH's knees. "I don't want to be the sole reason that you lose your chances of getting out of here."

"No, you are getting care." TH made a fist with his right hand. "It's my job to keep humans safe, and I will not change that anytime soon. Mason, help me pick him up. I will drive. Dema, where the hell is the extraction point?"

"Dema, Mason, I need you here for a moment." Van rolled on his side and waited for the rest of the crew to join him.

"We are getting you to that extraction point." TH looked

up at the afternoon sky, mixed with dark clouds and black smoke from the bombardment, with the sun slowly setting behind the horizon.

"All right, I'll make this quick since you have a long way to go. You have around fifty to sixty miles left before you run out of fuel. There is nothing you can do for me. I lost everything, my family, girlfriend, and any dreams I had. I only want one thing now. You need to win." Van bit his tongue from the pain but still smiled. "You owe me that. There is my lunchbox next to my seat. Please do not open it unless you need help. Now, get me to that tree to see the sunset before I die. Remember, fifty to sixty miles left to go. It has been an honor, my family."

"We are getting you to that extraction point!" TH didn't see the desperate punch coming in. "What was that for? I am trying to help you!"

"Drop me by that tree, drive, and win! Win! Win, for God's sake, if he exists." Van tilted his head and attempted to remove his uniform. "Get out while you still can. That is what I want. I want us, and now you, to win. Nothing else matters."

"Van, we are getting you there! Why don't you say something!? Dema? Mason?"

"TH, they did a bare minimum on me, so how do you think they'll treat him?" Mason looked at TH. "We did what we could."

"TH, if you remember me, I'll never die." Van reached for TH but gave up halfway. "If you remember me, I'll never die."

"But you'll die if you don't get help!"

"TH, Van made up his mind; let's do what he wishes." With tears in her eyes, Dema waited for Mason to help her as TH remained kneeling there, pounding the ground with his fists in a perfect synchronized movement matching the exploding city behind them.

As they got to the lonely tree on the hill, Mason gently rested Van against the trunk and wiped the blood from his eyes while Dema squeezed his hand.

"Thank you both. You were my best and pretty much the

only friends I had. Ones that stuck around," Van said as Mason and Dema walked away, holding onto each other.

When he heard the roaring V-12 slowly fading away in the distance, Van turned his head around and painfully smiled. The pain had blinded him, and his body felt a thousand knives piercing his skin. Thunder roared, and raindrops started to water him, soon showering his entire body, cleaning him of the spall and blood. All sounds had blended into one tidal wave, beating his remaining senses into submission.

So this is how I will go out? It is still better than getting shot on the street or run over by a car. I see Alexander on his deathbed, begging for death, and that would have been me. Stay strong, my brothers! Mom, Dad, you raised me right. Ember, wherever you are, I forgive you for your actions, even if you did the unthinkable and left me. If not, well, don't wait for me; I'm not coming home. Find someone else to be happy with. That's the least you can do for a man on the gallows.

Van coughed up blood and pulled several large fragments out of his right arm, but his mind was already finishing the eulogy.

Mason, Dema, TH, you were the best out of all I have ever met. You were pretty much the only friends I had. The question is, do I get to see the end now?

Van's thought trail was disturbed by an approaching vehicle, and moments later the sound of the moving tracks forced its way to Van's head.

"Why did you come back? I said leave me alone! You don't have enough fuel! Why?" Van looked up at the approaching voices, but it was hard to distinguish who that was as the colors slowly faded into black.

Whoever that is, they are not taking me alive or getting anything out of me! I'm not telling them anything!

Van bit his tongue, found one of the larger steel shards, and pulled it out of his weak body, crying out in the process. Before he could finish the deed, his hands gave out, and the shard meant for his throat fell by his side. Feeling life leaving his body, Van looked at the black sky and closed his eyes forever.

"Okay, we can take a break, but keep the cameras rolling on the contestants." Jeong-Min pointed at the terrified intern, who saluted and nodded his head.

Since the takeover, the number of non-premium viewers had doubled, and Benjamin had to agree that all three of his co-hosts were performing way better than him. As the hosts dispersed among the tents, Min looked at Adriana.

"Adriana, may I ask you something?" Jeong-Min invited Adriana to sit down.

"Please, how can I help?" Adriana smiled as she watched Thomas talk with the producer.

"I'm trying to learn more about people with whom I'm working here, and it just so happens that you're here. Just out of curiosity, how did you join this particular venture, and what did you do beforehand?" Jeong-Min noticed Adriana's face turning red.

"It was just a happy accident, I would say. Before this, I was a 3D artist and one of the first influencers after the War on the newly launched TRIDENTZ and STREETPAUSE, but as the years went by, I burned out. I needed to do something, and I still had a significant following. So, I got the idea to start my own TV show. I moved out of my hometown, Salt Lake City, bought an RV, and toured the US of A. I decided to video blog about post-war life. You probably heard of the blog show called *Ashes of the Freedom*." Jeong-Min nodded. "You actually see it? It didn't get much traction outside of the United States."

"I watched it on the flight here. It was a really moving experience. With few differences, Ashes of Freedom mirrored life in Korea and elsewhere, I assume. My apologies for the interruption; please continue."

"One day, I decided to stop doing what I was doing as I burned out again. I needed a complete one-eighty in my life, so I started to work in one of the diners on Route 66, but even that became dull work after a year. So, I randomly set my GPS to take me places. It directed me to Little Rock, Arkansas, where I saw Thomas building a tank in his garden. As I watched him weld day after day, my curiosity got the better of me, so I approached him, and we talked. And we talked for hours, like long-lost friends who had found each other after years of radio silence. As we talked, I made up my mind. I took gloves, which I found in the garage, and learned how to weld. Then, I got an idea, and soon, I ran the tank's social media account. A local TV station gave us a spotlight, and TVG approached us. We went through the submission process, got in, signed the contract, and here we are."

"Guys, you need to see this!" Benjamin called out to everyone, and in two minutes, the broadcasting tent filled to the fullest. "I just received this notification from TVG!"

On the screen, an email appeared, and the TVG signature headline confirmed that this was official.

Dear Tank Royale Community,

As President of TVG, I am honored to bring you this news. Firstly, I would like to invite you to the TVG Awards and Corporate Emmy Awards, where the Tank Royale has been nominated for the best TVG Show of 2145, the most viewed live show on Earth, and the Top Royale Show of All-time, introducing you to the Hall of Fame. In addition, you have also been nominated for the Diverse Voices Award and Most Diverse TVG Show. Finally, you have been nominated for the Corporate Emmy Award 2145, crushing most categories and leaving the competition in the dust. Please see the provided link for more information, and I look forward to meeting all of you personally upon your return from Mongolia.

Jeremy Horten,
President of TVG

"Didn't I say in the invitation that this will be the greatest show on corporate television?" Benjamin stood on a chair. "To all those who said I wouldn't make it, see me now! I made it, and you didn't!"

Moments later, a loud cheer and clapping erupted, and congratulations and phone calls poured in.

Thomas decided to step aside and look into the rainy distance. *Good for him. Ahh, Adriana, what the hell are you doing? We've got a good thing going on here, so why do you want to change it? We don't have to live from paycheck to paycheck anymore. What is it that you don't like? With us, even though we are not responsible for their deaths, at least they have a fighting chance. Is the current system perfect? Absolutely not, but it's much better than what we had before.* Thomas caught himself gazing into the distance, thinking about his creations battling it away, but then shouts of terror prompted Thomas to turn around.

"What is happening?" Thomas ran to the broadcasting tent, where everyone huddled around the screen, observing a kill shot replay.

"Horthy just nailed the Sherman. That wasn't supposed to happen," Benjamin's voice whimpered. "I'm done. We're so done. The TVG favorite just went out. Oh no!"

Thomas looked at the screen and noticed Team 22 flashing red with the camera flying over the Hungarian tank that drove up closer and observed the Commander staring at the burning wreckage, possibly expecting survivors. As minutes ticked by and the fire continued spreading, the man slowly exhaled, climbed back into his tank, and drove away. As the tank vanished behind the hill, one of the bodies moved, and moments later, Zanai looked around him and ran in the opposite direction.

The scoreboard came up a moment later, logging in the kill.

Team 22 – M4A1 76W (American Made) – Surviving 1 out of 5

"They should have asked for the different variant, but no," Thomas burst out laughing. "Well, that is what they get."

"How come?" Jeong-Min moved forward when he heard Thomas laughing. "Can you explain?"

"It turns out that TVG are total morons. The approval process goes like this," Thomas linked his tablet to the screen, and moments later, a spiderweb of tanks and their variants appeared.

M4–Type, M4A1–Type, M4A2–Type, M4A3–Type, M4A4–Type, M4A5–Type, M4A6–Type
M4(Composite Hull)
M4(105mm howitzer)
M4 HVSS (Horizontal Volute Spring Suspension)
M4 105 HVSS

"So many!" Benjamin swiped around. "Wow. How do you do it?"

"I created the list based on the guidelines provided by TVG, so in this example, I did a deep dive into the Sherman family and recommended the optimal tanks for the competition. I sent it and twiddled with my thumbs, awaiting the response. When that arrived, a process I explained a few days ago commenced. And I know that they didn't read the entire thing. They went down the list, passed the M4, and ended up on M4A1 76W. They saw a big, long gun, that was about it, forgetting about other aspects like crew comfort, armor, and other elements. I specifically highlighted the optimal choices, but they just skipped them. Their call, not mine, and my hands are clean."

"How many are there?" Benjamin looked up as he lost himself in all the variants, temporarily forgetting about the death of the Corporate's favorite.

"Well, just for the Sherman family in the World War Two Era alone, we're looking at twenty variations or so, if I remember correctly. These do not account for Sherman-based tanks like the M10 or Special Variants for engineering, rockets, mine clearing, or flame-throwing. Feel free to browse or ask me; I can name them all with my eyes closed."

"So, you modeled all the variants?" Jeong-Min nodded. "Impressive!"

"And guess who did a hundred percent test on them all?" Adriana raised her hand. "Yeah, I drove in all of them, fired them, and fixed them."

"If I may, you need to take a look at this." One of the interns raised the tablet in the air. "Some viewers are getting upset with the death of their favorites."

"Well." Thomas was first to read the posts, and inside him, he felt his heart smiling, "It is unfortunate that their favorite is out, but the show must go on!"

"Okay, what do we do?" Benjamin looked at the thread of angry posts, but as Thomas refreshed the page, the calls for ending the subscription or general sadness over the death of contestants vanished.

It showed only comments calling for more heart-pounding action and clashing steel. Thomas continued refreshing and scrolling, but the "bad" comments vanished as more and more blood-demanding ones poured in like a waterfall.

"They are gone! Lost in the sea!" Adriana widened her eyes as she witnessed the hand of corporate intervention first-hand. "We all saw this, right? They suppress them!"

"Indeed, we did." Thomas returned the tablet and looked at everyone with a burning question in his eyes. "Do we bring this up?"

"Let's focus on what matters," Benjamin clapped his hands, "the show must go on!"

"Of course, we must bring this up!" Adriana looked around her. "Am I the only one who sees blatant censorship here? They deserve to express their angry opinion! Their favorite just went out in a blaze of glory! Of course you would be pissed!"

"I'll need everyone to keep their eyes peeled." Mason's

voice was the first to break the two-hour silence since they left Van behind.

"Yes, Mason!" the unlively responses from the two remaining crewmembers sank the already bad mood even deeper, passing the zero-point mark.

And Mason didn't blame them. He had no energy to motivate or scream at them to keep focused. He sat there, hunched over in his seat, staring at the two switches and flywheels for the past half hour.

A moment later, a clap of thunder sounded, and the Kharkiv V-12 roared back as TH shifted the gears. The rain picked up intensity, beating the roof of the roaring Crusading Angel on its path.

Mason looked to his right and noticed Dema's red eyes, and for a brief moment, he spotted his bloody reflection staring back at him. Her shaking hands rested on the periscope handles, escorted by an occasional whimper.

"I could have saved him. We could have got him to the exfil point," TH's voice cracked in Mason's headset, "but no. Go on without me and win. What is this, a theater drama? I think that I'll never understand humans and their behavior. He could have gotten medical help and seen his family before he would pass away, surrounded by his loved ones."

"TH, there was nothing we could have done for Van. Never mind. Dema, get on the radio and listen for any broadcast and report if anything sounds important," Mason said in a shivering voice. "Please."

"Will do." Dema shook her head, and a moment later, TH watched her flip knobs on the radio.

As Crusading Angel cleared the ditch, TH opened the driver's hatch just as the shower turned into a mist. Mason followed suit, and a moment later he watched the sun peek from behind the gray clouds. *TH is correct; we could have saved him. Mason, you got a taste of the real deal, and it cost you, Van. Get your shit together and get them to the finish line. You can only lose one... No, I am not losing anyone! Nobody else will die under my watch. Never.*

"There are seven tanks, including us, remaining. The broadcast says that we are close to the second zone. The time is 19:37, and the sun will go down in an hour. There should be terminals, which we can use to restock if needed. One should be nearby, as it triggered a proximity notice in the chatter. That is all," Dema finished reporting and, a moment later, returned to the loader's position.

"There should be one then, just behind this hill." Mason pressed his face against the vision slit, hoping to see through the rain as the visibility dropped faster than Angel's fuel indicator. "At least, I think."

Moments later, TH silenced the mighty V-12 as he parked behind the small hill, only exposing the turret. Mason closed his eyes and rested his forehead on the padding underneath the vision slits of his cupola. When he opened the cupola and looked into the late misty afternoon, the tank's silhouette appeared, sinking Mason's heart even lower.

"We have an enemy tank right in front of us, facing sideways, which is ideal. The problem is that I cannot determine where its gun is, and I just lost them." Mason punched the breech and woke up Dema, who fell asleep standing, holding the shell like a newborn baby.

"I am sorry!" Dema shouted, and Mason unplugged himself momentarily. "Sorry!"

He waited and then plugged himself back in, slowly exhaling in the process. The last thing he wanted to do was to parent his friends.

"Dema, please, don't you fall asleep on me. We can rest once we find a suitable place to camp! TH, how much fuel we have left?" Mason walked the middle road.

"Around ten miles. Wait, what is that gunfire?" TH shouted, and Mason spotted green tracers flying before his gunsight, peppering his tank without any damage.

"Who would ambush them? There is no return fire. Dema,

wake up!" Mason tapped Dema, but without any response.

He gave her a little nudge but no response again, so Mason stepped on Dema's foot with full force, finally waking her up.

"Dema, get on the loader's periscope and look around. If needed, open your hatch."

"I am sorry for falling asleep." Dema shook her head and pressed her face against the periscope. Mason counted to three, opened his hatch again, and noticed that the rain had stopped falling and visibility had improved.

"Mason, Commander, stress can make people sleepy, and they can do nothing about it. I saw it once; one of the men in my unit just shut down as the enemy machine gun nest was hosing us down."

"Understood," Mason blinked as he looked at Dema, scanning the surroundings, "Dema, try to fight it, please. One shot, and they'll be collecting our burning corpses or, worse, body parts. If they would even bother."

"I will try." Dema nervously smiled and vanished inside the tank.

Mason pounded the tank's roof when he noticed a smashed terminal in the distance and cried out. The enemy tank was nowhere in sight. *Was it just an illusion? My head hurts!* Mason touched his hot forehead and took a deep breath. *Focus, find the enemy, and send them home.* He also closed the hatch behind him and dried the sweat off his forehead.

"Everything all right?" Dema looked over the breech at the slow-breathing, red-faced Mason.

"TH, drive to the terminal. Dema, can you fix it?" Mason shook his head, blinked, and looked at Dema. "Tell me that you can."

"Mason, I think I can fix that terminal." Dema opened the loader's hatch again and took a deep breath of the fresh air, now mixed with the exhaust fumes of their tank.

Ensuring the coast was clear, Mason watched Dema dismount the tank and run up to the terminal, with TH driving right behind her.

Mason observed Dema examine the terminal, but then he looked at the horizon, where once grasslands had turned into a swamp from the torrential rain, and thought about home.

Ail, I hope that you never have to do this. I cannot lose you to the gears of TVG. I know you are watching me. Mason momentarily looked at the gray curtain sailing above his head and rested his senses. While he almost got used to the howling engine, the emptiness around him pushed his sanity meter over the hours ever so slightly into the red zone.

"Mason, love, come here. I have good news and bad news." Dema whistled, gaining Mason's attention, who quickly snapped out of it.

"Yes?" Mason slowly climbed down the tank's side and walked up to Dema.

"Well, the good news is that the screen was shot, but everything else is functional. The bad news is that we don't have a tablet or screen that I can link up with the base."

"So, we need a screen," Mason looked at the Crusading Angel, "and they took everything electronic from us. Wait, do you still have that old music player, by any chance?"

"Oh," Dema took a deep breath, "my apologies. I will see what I can do. That's not going to work."

Dema froze on the spot and hid her shaking hands in the pockets of her wet uniform.

"What is the problem?" Mason sat beside her, and Dema rested her head on Mason's shoulder.

"I just feel like we are not going to make it. We already lost Van, and I almost fell asleep. I can still feel tiny steel fragments all over my hands and face, piercing my skin and soul."

"You're not the only one." Mason rolled the left sleeve of his uniform, and Dema whistled when a bandaged arm revealed itself to the world. "The sooner we fix this, the sooner we will get the help needed."

"And we can mourn once we win." Dema nodded her head, and Mason touched her shaking shoulders.

"Thank you. Wait! The plane!" Mason turned around when he heard a four-engine cargo plane flying towards them, and moments later, a large crate hanging from the black parachute gracefully landed next to them.

"TH, there is fuel, but I don't know if it is ours?" Mason walked up to TH, who opened the box crate, and they found four by six rows filled with perfectly packed green and black jerrycans. "Dema! We're saved! Well, for now, at least!"

"Well, that is gasoline, and we need diesel, but let me check the rest." TH separated three jerrycans of the group two minutes later. "Also, I would like to say that the tank is not responding as it should. It is getting even more difficult to steer it, and sometimes, the brakes fail. We need to get to that depot or find one of those roaming repairmen."

"TH, I have a message for you." Dema picked up a drenched paper note stuck in the ground next to the terminal. "TH, thank you for listening to me. Not that many people do. Best regards. Klemens."

"Thank you." TH accepted the note from Dema, read it one more time, and then tore it on the spot.

"Guys, you need to see this." Mason climbed a small hill, and his jaw dropped to the ground. "We need to get around that huge lake."

The trio looked into the distance, where an enormous lake sat, covering the horizon as the sun slowly set behind the mountains, turning gray clouds into dark orange.

"That is just huge!" Dema accepted the binoculars from Mason and scanned the shores. "There are like three rivers without any bridges to..."

"I'll start refueling." TH tapped Mason's right shoulder. "Don't be too long. We have a lot of ground to cover."

"We'll be there in a moment," Mason said, and TH gave him a thumbs up.

"Take a look." Dema handed Mason the binoculars back.

"What am I looking for?"

As Mason scanned the area, the clouds had lifted, and the sun illuminated the empty but gorgeous Mongolian grasslands for a moment. She turned around; just the rumbling sound of a tank made its way between the hills, and soon Polish Grom rolled into view, escorted by clouds of smoke. August waved his hands from the commander's cupola like an excited child, and Dema waved back. August vanished inside the tank, and it turned towards them a moment later. August was first to climb down ten minutes later, followed by Zasada. Like them, the Polish crew also patched themselves with bandages and extra wraps, looking like reanimated mummies that decided to drive a tank.

"Good early evening, everyone!" A moment later, the crews shook hands. "How are you guys holding up? Where is Van? And thank you for not shooting at us. We appreciate it!"

After exchanging words of condolences and hugs, August looked at Mason.

"I'm so sorry again for your loss. We have a lot of ground to cover. The sooner we make it to the second ring, the better our chances of ambushing other contestants are, but I doubt that we will make it today. Driving in pitch black darkness is not fun, to say the least," August said, looking at the silent lake below them, bathing in the last of the sunlight before the darkness engulfed them. "I wish Van could see this view. Why is it that the world's beauty always shows in the sorrow?"

TH only shrugged his shoulders and searched through bullet-riddled backpacks for food.

"If you don't shoot us in the back, we can team up and try to make it to the second ring together, after which I am not making any guarantees." Mason extended his hand, and Zasada shook it.

"That is fine by us. So, where do we pitch a camp?" August looked at Zasada, who talked with Dema and smiled.

"Let's crush a few more miles in the darkness." Mason whistled as his feet tried to find dry land or a rock to stand on. "We're rolling out in five minutes to find someplace dry."

"I wonder, what are Gio and his crew up to?" Mason looked into the distance, hoping to see his wish, traveling on like they were.

"We got some chocolate bars to share if anyone is interested. Moments later, Zasada opened one of the crates and pulled out a stack of chocolate bars taped together with a gray tape.

"How did you get this stack?" Mason asked.

"Both of us are allergic to chocolate, so TVG changed our rations. Take some."

———

"Why is there a submerged tank?" James parked next to the canal; moments later, all four P26/40 crewmen looked at the odd tank guarding the passage.

It was hard to determine what tank sat there, guarding the canal for eternity with only a squarish turret sitting above the water. Hatches were wide open; the only visible clues were a rusty barrel and a black German cross.

"Why would they sink the tank?"

"Interactive and diverse map, James. I guess this has a historical significance, but I am not sure, or they are just milking history until they run out of ideas." Giovanni took one more look.

"Oh, Panzer of the Lake, can you bless us with the victory?" James said, straighten his back and saluted to the poking turret.

"It's a river, James," Gio looked around him, "but it sounds better than Panzer of the Canal or River. What other oddities will we find scattered around, and what we missed?"

"Seeing that dusk is upon us, we should continue rolling until we have to pitch a camp, and we need to try to find some dry land." James looked at the fast-traveling sun, and moments later, the crew of the Da Vinci found themselves in the pitch-black night.

———

As midnight arrived, Mason leaned against the backside of the hexagonal turret and gazed at the stars as the clouds cleared. Thousands of silver stars shone upon the campsite, and Mason's right hand reached into the sky, hoping to grasp one and pull it closer. The only sounds he heard were the fire crackling and his breath. He gazed again, but then heard someone shuffling around. Immediately, he stood up and found Dema going through her backpack.

"Dema, get some sleep. I'll need you ready for tomorrow. We've much ground to cover and more fights to undergo. Please, get some sleep. Whatever you're looking for, it can wait."

"I am trying to." Dema extended her right hand, and Mason helped her climb. "Can you believe that he is gone? He is just gone! Now, my only memory of him is a torn cushion seat that drips blood. Even if TH sits there, I cannot unsee him."

"I think once this circus calms down, we'll find more fond memories of Van. Do you know what's worse?" Mason sat back down. "He told me about his nightmare and how he would be first to go. I told him it was just a nightmare and that he should return to sleep. We talked a bit, but I think that I only gave him a bandage and not the actual solution."

"You could not have known," Dema smiled as she fixed her hair. "Who would?"

"God knows." Mason slowly exhaled, playing with the rosary beads in his pocket. "His plan was amusing sometimes. On the other hand, you lose a friend. Conversely, you look up at the evening sky and wish never to leave."

"You are right. Still, there is that hole in my heart that I cannot seem to fill with anything at this point," Dema said as she tried to grab a star into her hands. "Remember the desert earlier today?"

"That was today? I felt that we've been here for at least a week. You don't just forget something like that—just an empty but gorgeous-looking place. I wish that Van could see this as well.

"Yep," Dema said.

They sat there silently, gazing at the sky, each in their own world for a moment. Mason looked at Dema and decided that his shot was now or never.

"I have something to confess to you. I may or may not feel something more towards you." In his mind, Mason facepalmed. "I don't think we'll get a silence like this again."

You moron! That is how you open? Mason, what the hell is wrong with you?

"What is it? Shoot straight with me, please." Dema raised her eyebrow.

"I'm in love with you," Mason had to force that sentence out of his mouth. "Yeah."

"Well, it may sound strange, but I also have something to confess. I have been eyeballing you ever since we first met." Dema shifted closer to Mason, who shook his head. "But promise me something. Let's wait with the dance till we win. I do not want our love to jeopardize our focus or chances to win."

"That is a deal I can make. I want to add my apology as well. I feel bad for yelling at everyone back there." Mason touched his racing heart. "I am sorry. I'm not used to barking orders at people."

"If you would not yell at us, we would end up like our temporary allies. Water under the bridge." Dema rested her head on Mason's shoulder again. "Don't worry, I don't have any nightmares. I haven't had any dreams for years."

"I never really asked. Do you have a family?"

"I am alone in this world. Mom left shortly after my birth, leaving my dad and me on the streets. Eventually, we found a house but didn't read the fine print, realizing that we would live in Crimea, a contested area between Russia and Ukraine. I don't want to go into the details."

"I understand."

"We got a letter a few years later explaining the departure. Apparently, I was a mistake; one night turned into a nightmare. My dad was responsible for me, not her," Dema shook her head, "and I hated my mom ever since, but somehow, after the world went mad, I forgave her. I have nothing bad to say about my dad. I apologize for dumping this on you, but I have no one else to talk with. Do you think that I am a mistake? That I am responsible for the split?"

"I don't believe that." Mason took Dema's hands in his. "Do you think your dad is watching?"

"I like to think that, yes, he is watching." Dema smiled. "Your brother must be going crazy over you. From what I saw at the airport."

Mason laughed. "I never even expected to have a brother to begin with. Then, one day, I wasn't a single kid anymore. And I'm happy that he appeared in my life."

Min took a deep breath as he looked at the computer screen and accepted the call from his wife, Harin, who had just finished folding the laundry as the camera turned on.

"Hey, how are you? Hope I didn't wake you up." Min ensured he was alone in his tent, ensuring the canvas flap was all the way down.

"No, you didn't. I went to drop off, but we need to talk. He said he wants to follow in your footsteps." Harin leaned back in the chair. "What are we going to do about it?"

"Why would you want to do that?"

"You didn't hear? There are talks of unification with the North, and they are recruiting volunteers for Reserves! Hello?" Harin snapped her fingers at the silent Min. "Are you listening to me?"

"Quiet! I am trying to figure it out. Unification is not going to happen any time soon; I am sure of that. We're too divided for that, both culturally and mentally. Whoever spreads those rumors is just a fearmonger; do not listen to him. If something like that happened, I would be the first to know about it." Jeong-Min slowly exhaled. "Oh boy, what are you doing? Can I talk to him?"

"He will be visiting his friend's beach villa for a couple of days. Can you even do anything?"

"I cannot falsify recruiting papers on a track athlete, ready to compete in the Olympics. What would it look like on me? You? Our son?"

"I don't care. Make sure that he doesn't go anywhere, please. I already lost one, and I don't want to lose another."

"We are not losing any more of our children, I promise you that. Get that thought out of your head now, please!"

Harin shook her head. "Alright, I trust you. When should I expect you?"

"Unless this ends tomorrow, which is highly unlikely, I'll be home later this week, Friday at least. As much as I love TV production, I would rather watch the final product at home than camp out in a tent next to the runaway of an old military base. This is the reality part of the reality show. Constant reshoots for optimal angles, everything just piles up, and you lose a sense of time, but this is what I signed up for. I promise I'll figure it out."

"I know you will. I need to sleep; it was a long day at the shelter," Harin shook her head, "much barking, one way or another."

"Any adoptions?"

"Few cats, four snakes, and I think that's about it. Are you sure you cannot tell me why you wander around Asia, record interviews, and other things?"

"I signed that NDA. If I break it, I can kiss my career and our future goodbye. TVG runs a tight operation here, and they do not take kindly to failure. Our Chief Presenter Benjamin is overworked like a mule." Jeong-Min looked away from the screen for a moment, resting his eyes. "Poor guy."

"Well, you take it easy then. Last thing we need is another workaholic in the family." Harin grinned from ear to ear, and Min tapped his forehead.

"When you love what you are doing, well, the fun never ends."

"While that is true," Harin sunk into the chair, "don't lose focus on the prize. Alright, I need to go. Now, I must bully our accountant to finish the ledgers for the shelter. When you return, I need you to do a promotional advertisement for statewide adoption or a public announcement about pets and associated responsibilities."

"I'll see what I can do. I will be home soon. Take care." Jeong-Min blew a kiss through the camera and caught one in return.

"Help Benjamin if you can. He'll need you sooner or later. He cannot go far like this. He needs help as soon as possible."

CHAPTER SIXTEEN

SOLDIERING ON

Mason was the first to wake up. He stretched his neck and emerged into the bright morning light from the small tent. As his eyes adjusted, Mason shook his head. *A new day, a new challenge ahead. God, protect us on this next leg of the journey ahead.* Mason made the sign of a cross and looked at the lazy morning clouds sailing above the empty lands.

Moments later, he plugged his headset into the radio and began flipping knobs, listening to the static void. Apart from the rules and directions, the waves were empty. However, as Mason was about to give up, he heard a familiar voice.

"Is anybody out there?" Gio coughed. "Anyone?"

"Who is this? Gio, is that you?" Mason tilted his head.

"Mason? Good morning, brother! How are you doing? How is the crew?"

"You don't want to know," Mason leaned back on the chair and closed his eyes, "We lost Van. Other than that, we were able to link up with Grom."

There was a moment of silence at the other end before Gio spoke again.

"I'm sorry to hear that. I, we shall remember him as well. I only met him briefly, but I could tell he was a proud man from a proud family, walking with his back straight all the time."

"Thank you," Mason turned around when he heard someone descending into the tank, "what about you?"

"We haven't lost anyone yet, but after the beating we took in the town, well, I'm praying to the Almighty that we make it. It doesn't look good. Listen, everyone is near the entrances to the second zone. Be careful."

"Thank you, and you too." Mason looked at TH and turned off the radio. "Good morning."

"Likewise. Who was that?"

"Gio."

"We need to talk." TH sat next to Mason and tapped his knees before continuing.

"Yes?"

"Mason, my battery has hit the red zone. I don't know how long I have." TH unzipped his overall shirt, and after fiddling in his ribcage, he showed Mason the damaged batteries again.

"I would like to request that I become a driver while Dema will stay as a loader. The less movement I do, the better for us. However, if you need me up," TH's eyes flashed again, "I am ready to serve,"

"TH, are you scared of death?" Mason produced a singular sentence as everything, from beeping to flashing lights from TH's eyes, it all made sense.

"I am an ultimately expendable hardware losing the second wind in its sails." TH's voice cracked for the first time. "I don't know if I can prove to the world that old hardware still has it! Or that I would make it to the Moon to see the Earth from a different perspective."

"You're my brother TH, and we care for each other," Mason made a fist with his right hand, "you'll prove your mettle to the world, and you'll walk on the lunar surface."

"Robot brother? Well, I am the handsome one then." TH gave Mason a thumbs up.

"You said robot! Don't you hate that word because it lumps everyone into one category?"

"Mason, sticks and stones may break my bones, but the

words will never hurt me. Klemens told me that back in the Museum when you were on the table. I wasn't expecting that he would leave me a note. It could have been anyone else; what are the chances?"

"Slim at best," Mason tapped TH on his right shoulder, "but I'm happy that you got it."

"Thank you," TH tilted his head when he heard a commotion outside, "guess it is time to go."

After another three muddy morning hour ride, the Crusading Angel, followed closely by the Polish Grom, finally cleared the grounds and climbed another hill. TH turned off the engine and shook her hands.

"Well, that will be a problem," Mason looked through his commander's cupola vision slits and took a deep breath, "but we made it!"

Down the hill, around a hundred yards or so, in front of them, the three lines filled with concrete dragons' teeth formed a solid defensive object to overcome, with only a few checkpoints to cross. Behind the defensive line were barracks, silos, and a small city, surrounded by the flat green steppe and several hills varying in size. *Just as Gio said, be careful.*

"Nothing is marked on the map, but it seems like this black line is the border of the first and second ring," Dema's voice cracked in the headphones.

"Guys," August threw a rock at the T-34's turret, "come here, you need to see this!"

"All right, give us a moment," Mason shouted back. "Team, I just wanted to say that we made it this far, and I wish that Van could be here to witness this. There is still a place for him on the podium."

"We all do, Mason, we all do." Mason had to press his tanker's helmet against his ears to hear TH's response.

"You all right?" Dema watched TH's eyes flash again.

"I'm all right, Dema; maybe it is something with my system. A little reset will do just fine. Old hardware still has it!"

"All right, do your thing once we enter the second ring." Mason unplugged his headphones, and moments later, five tankers stared at the solid defensive line.

"Those are two problems that I wanted to talk about. Firstly, what you are looking at is part of a Siegfried Line or the Westwall, a German defensive line during World War Two. It has heavily guarded checkpoints, which is our second problem." August pointed at the camouflaged tracked gun platform, which made its home on the small hill behind the defensive line, covered by the bushes.

"What is that?" Dema took the binoculars from Zasada and scanned the hill, finding trucks and androids in gray uniforms running around.

"That is what you would call a VFW, or Versuchflakwagen, originally an anti-air vehicle, but now it is pressed against the tanks since its all-around 88mm cannon can do quite a lot of damage. See, we did our homework," Both August and Zasada nodded their heads, "and it is an all-android crew, which has more negatives for us than positives."

"Next entrance is around fifty kilometers, but there is no way we are making that since our fuel situation is rather terrible," August pulled out a map, "should we clear this, there is a gas station."

"How on earth is your map way more detailed than ours?" Dema opened Angel's map, and their stark contrast immediately jumped out.

While it shared the baseline, like hills, forests, and water bodies, August's map had more points of interest.

"Well, we found a terminal and purchased a better map. Did you guys even hear the radioman? He said it all there."

"Well, next time, then. Now, it begs the question, who will get shot first, and who will make it to the safety of the buildings and blow the VFW to kingdom come?" TH asked the dreaded question.

"My stomach is rumbling louder than our engine," Dema

said, looking at Mason.

"Guys, the VFW just started rotating its cannon towards us!" TH pointed at the VFW.

Mason could hear the electrical motor of the VFW's main cannon cranking the long barrel towards their positions for a moment of total silence. Soon, both tanks slid down the hill and found a refuge behind another, just in time as the first shot echoed in the quiet morning.

———

"And there it goes. The Japanese crew ended the Horthy's streak and was first to achieve a breakthrough, but it seems like they suffered some hits as well." Adriana zoomed in on the Chi-Nu-Kai and two girls attempting to fix the track while Hungarian wreckage smoked in the background. "In their proximity are also two members of All-American Platoon, Crusading Angel and Grom. Maybe Japan will finally get payback for Manchuria? This and much more is ahead of us, dear viewers!"

Over the hill, the Siegfried line guarded the second ring menacingly as the tanks began to converge on several checkpoints.

"All right, let us look at the stats." Benjamin leaned back in his chair while Thomas gave Adriana a thumbs up again, and she nodded.

The scoreboard zoomed in on the flashing red letters, highlighting the demise of Team 24.

Team 24 – 41M III Turan 75 (Horthy) – Surviving 0 out of 5

"The good news is that all the tanks are near the Siegfried Line, but whoever makes it inside will be something to watch out for. Now, we need to go to the commercial break, and I shall see all of you in a moment." Benjamin waved and looked next to him, awaiting his co-hosts to say something, but only Min's cap sat on the table, staring into Benjamin's soul. "Where are they? They were just here!"

"Well, all of them are changing into the uniforms of their favorite crews and are waiting for you. Most of the film crew also joined in on the fun." One of the producers handed Benjamin a cup of water. "May I say you need to drop that corporate look and have some fun? We also began shooting behind the scenes, so I'll need you to be as presentable as possible."

"I can see your point, but I cannot leave the boundaries of my character. The suit has put me here, and it is what will keep me here."

"Benjamin, listen to me. This is a small victory against TVG, us having fun. They hate fun. They only look at optimizing their bottom line with performance charts and other bullcrap, nothing more, nothing less. Look, half of our crew will be disbanded the moment the winner is declared because they don't trust us, and with the pay cuts, they are ready to put us on the shelf."

"I'm going to make one phone call." Benjamin smiled, but the sadness in the producer's eyes prompted him to turn around. "They attempted to shut down Bell Entertainment; I fought through and kept you guys on the payroll. I'm not going to let anyone down again. No downsizing or cuts; we are going full steam ahead. The show will go on!"

"Benjamin, we have been working together for more than twenty years, and I think this is the end of the road. Of course, I'll always stay by your side, but even your mysterious friend won't pull enough strings to keep us floating." The Producer stepped aside as the cameraman swung to the right and followed Thomas in the brown and green Soviet uniform, Jeong-Min in stylish gray German, and Adriana in the Japanese, including the helmet made out of *waterproofed hemp with a leather liner.*

"They look good," Benjamin nodded as he loosened his tie

for the first time, "you're right. Goddamn. I need to loosen up a bit!"

"So, go ahead! Don't distance yourself more than you must." The Producer nudged Benjamin and vanished behind the empty crates.

Benjamin was about to put on the uniform when loud shouts from outside prompted him to poke his head out. A wind blew open the canvas on the medical tent, revealing two surviving contestants from the first ring on stretchers, with Zanai sitting aside, talking with one of the bandaged-up tankers.

"Hey, we have some action happening at the border!" Jeong-Min raised his voice and waved. "Come on!"

"Take the lead on this one while I ready myself!" Benjamin's voice drowned in the rush as he put on the pants.

Hiding behind another hill, closer to the entry checkpoint, Mason felt that the VFW had pointed its massive cannon at his head. Instead of thinking about it, Mason slipped into Dema's radio position and linked up with August.

"So, what do we do? How do we get across?" Mason closed his eyes and took a deep breath, attempting to level his racing thoughts.

"Well, if we rush now, one of us gets blown up to the kingdom come, while the other has a high chance of hiding behind those barracks and possibly taking it out. We don't have to blow that thing up; we only need to disable its gun. The question is, how?" Mason heard August pounding the seat.

"Mason, how about we check out Van's 0.50cal box? We are clearly in danger, and Van said, *only use it when in danger.*" TH reached out for the box, and Mason could finally read the entire sentence. *Do not touch my lunchbox.*

"Well, we have nothing to lose, so we might as well go for it. TH hit it!" Mason leaned, and the contents were revealed to the world.

Two protein chocolate bars, a torn picture of Van and his girlfriend, another picture of the crew, an M2084 auto-pistol with one full magazine, and what appeared to be a smoke grenade, but the words THERMITE appeared upon closer examination.

"That son of the gun," Dema laughed, "how did he smuggle a pistol and a thermite grenade?"

"Did someone say thermite? Or am I dreaming?" August's voice came back to life, but loud barking drowned his voice.

"Van had left us a present before he died. A loaded pistol and thermite grenade!"

"Okay, so it is not so bad after all. We need someone to cross the defenses, kill the crew, shove the thermite grenade into the breech of that VFW, and attempt to make it back here. It begs the question, who wants to do it? Let's get out of our coffins and talk outside. The cover is enough for us to talk without being shot at."

As all five stood by their tanks, TH looked to his left, scratching his chin. Then, he focused his attention back on Mason.

"Do you guys hear drums?" TH peeked from behind the hill and said. "The bridge! Look!"

The quintet collectively dropped their jaws to the ground as a colorful procession of around fifty people on stocky horses rode on the metal bridge—men, women, and even children dressed in traditional Mongolian clothing carrying banners and singing. Behind them were carriages pulled by horses, which followed, storing the building materials for yurts. Last to close the column was a lonely man with a majestic eagle on his shoulder.

Mason was first to snap out of the trance and immediately reached for the binoculars resting on his neck, scanning the VFW, but like them, the androids were confused, pacing back and forth.

"Isn't it beautiful?" Dema walked up to Mason. "What are the chances?"

"I don't know what to say." Mason lowered his binoculars, but to their surprise, the column stopped, blocking the entrance.

"How did they get there? This is an active warzone!" TH looked around him, "But again, many people, especially here, carry on their nomadic lifestyle."

"They don't seem to mind," Zasada tapped his chin, "is there like a religious significance? A cultural custom?"

"Honestly, I do not care. It is a privilege to witness something like this." Dema climbed onto the hill and got seated, observing the procession collectively singing an unknown song.

Mason looked at his hands just as a big man stood in the middle, and a moment later, the ground trembled underneath his deep voice. Soon, others followed, sending goosebumps to all who watched.

"What do we do?" TH looked at Mason, who shrugged his shoulders. "Should we attempt to make a breakthrough?"

"Let us enjoy whatever this is because I feel that this is the last time we will see such a procession." Dema closed her eyes, taking slow breaths as the tales of the foreign land spoke to them.

———

"Okay, what the hell is this?" Thomas looked at the screen, where an elderly man got seated on a chair and received a first gift from a little girl. "Was nobody tracking this?"

"How about we sit back and enjoy this cultural moment?" Jeong-Min kicked his feet up on the table. "We may not get another chance."

"I agree." Adriana looked at Thomas, "Some humanity in this machine will not kill us."

"BB, forget the phone." Jeong-Min looked at Benjamin as he was about to accept the call. "This is a once-in-a-lifetime chance. Come on!"

"You are right," Benjamin placed his tablet face down on the table, "but we will have to start shooting individual interviews soon. I got a call from the top that they also want an episodic release with backstage footage, which means putting all of you into my chair."

"No AI?" Adriana raised her eyebrow.

"No AI." Benjamin looked at his wristwatch. "The sooner we get it done, the better for us."

"We'll get to it," Thomas grinned from ear to ear as he found people dancing, and for a brief moment, he noticed two tanks hiding nearby. "Damn. They really could have picked a better place."

For twenty minutes, everyone wordlessly stared at the main screen, observing generational traditions, and for a moment, they also felt joy. However, as Thomas noted later in the interview about this event, things were about to go down.

———

The procession slowly walked away, and Mason took a deep breath. He looked at Dema, who sat beside him, while TH continued staring at the bridge long after the party left. *I am, wow.* Mason thought to himself. *That was something. God bless these people. Do they know what we are doing here?*

"Mason!" TH raised his voice and pointed at low-flying airplanes that dropped black canisters on the ground, and soon, clouds of black smoke surrounded them.

"What do we do!?" Zasada coughed as the wind began moving the heavy clouds toward them.

"The good thing is that we're still partially covered by the hill against that VF thing. Let's wait till the smoke clears. I don't want to see our tanks getting stuck in the ditch only to get picked off one by one." Mason looked around him as everyone else slid down the hill as well. "Any suggestions?"

"Mason, Dema, I'll destroy that gun." TH opened Van's

lunchbox, shoved the magazine into the pistol, and grabbed the thermite. "It's now or never. I know where the gun sits, and I am sure that this is the best way."

"So, I have an idea," August said, but then noticed TH with the pistol and a thermite grenade in his hands.

"Do you think this is a good idea?" Dema reached for the pistol, but TH holstered it in one of his pockets.

"I'm going to disable that gun. Any tips?" TH set his sight on the VFW, or where it was last seen, pounding his chest like a linebacker amping himself before a game.

"TH, what about your battery?" Mason stopped TH. "We need you!"

"I still have some juice, and I cannot sit idle. I couldn't save Van, so let me at least do this."

"How about we use our tanks to kill them?" Dema raised her hand, but August shook his head.

"Too risky. None of our tanks can afford to play peekaboo with an 88mm cannon, ready to send us to kingdom come. We don't have a stabilizer or have rangefinder that distance. We can be sure that VFW has a lock on us and is ready to fire when we show ourselves. I must agree with TH," Zasada beat August to his response as he climbed on the tank's turret and removed the roof-mounted machine gun. "You have to shove it into the gun's breech like you are loading a standard shell. Then, once you get it there, make a run for it; these VFWs have support companies with them."

"TH, this is a Polish Browning wz.1928. While it's not enough, it is something. We only have one additional spare magazine with thirty rounds." August handed TH the machine gun and stepped aside. "VFW has a crew of six, but I don't know how many are in the support company. You would have to kill them all to be sure. Remember, the gun is the priority. We will be ready to go when the smoke clears. Or what signal do we use?"

"Just use your binoculars to see me. I'll wave my hands."

"TH, if you do not make it back, it has been an honor." Mason shook hands with TH, who put the machine on his right shoulder and hid the grenade in the overall of his uniform.

"Honor has been mine, but I'll be back, I promise!"

"See you soon, TH." Dema hugged him and stepped aside, but August halted TH with his hand.

"TH, we'll see you soon." The moment August said it, thunder shook the ground. "That is your signal! Run!"

———

"As Thomas said, you morons at TVG are to blame. Look how many versions of the Sherman are available. We built them all, tested them, and provided you with data with the best choices highlighted. All you had to do was to pick ones in yellow," Adriana sat on the video call with TVG bureaucrats and rolled her eyes as the Director for Equality and Fair Play finished his ten-minute rant. And while she hesitated to mute his entire speech, she decided to play the long game.

"Adriana, where is Thomas Askarov?"

"Well, I'm here to answer all the questions as my lawyer and my boyfriend briefed me. Thomas is currently busy explaining to the audience that a bigger gun is not always a good solution. I suggest you tune in and listen, but I know you are trying to have all of us fired. Why? We did all the work, and you still bitch about it." Adriana shook her head. "If you want to be fair, please give contestants an actual in-person interview. The ten-minute one is not cutting it. The AI replacement might fool some, but it is disingenuous to us, the contestants, and all the viewers who care, as we don't hear their true selves. Equality and fairness, my ass."

"So, how did they lose?" Another Suit raised her voice, silencing her companion.

"Watch it for yourself; you have the premium plan. Anything

else? If not, I have run some errands while the interviews are underway."

"Adriana, we do not care if you are recording us. Trust us; we'll be the last laugh."

In the background, Benjamin took the livestream to a commercial break and ran up with Jeong-Min to Thomas, who continued slapping his right knee.

"What's happening?" Min asked as Thomas handed him his tablet.

"Just having a good laugh at the TVG pecking order." Soon, Min also cracked up, but Benjamin's face turned a shade of pale.

"Hey!" Thomas snapped his fingers before Benjamin's face. "Hello? Where did you go?"

"We'll go live in two minutes," the producer shouted at Benjamin, and nudged one of his subordinates.

"Are you all right?" Adriana helped a heavily breathing Benjamin to sit at one of many black crates littering the broadcasting booth. "Hey! Talk to us!"

"Sherman getting knocked out is a huge problem as it was TVG favored. Someone at TVG will do crazy mental gymnastics and have everyone see it as a violation of my terms. I am so screwed once this is over," Benjamin said in a whimpering voice. "Can you guys comment for a moment? I need to catch a breath."

"Anytime, my friend." Jeong-Min tapped Benjamin on his back. "Come on, people. The show must go on!"

— — —

TH threw himself into the ditch as he finally cleared the tank's obstacles and entered the outpost. Looking over his shoulder, he watched the smoke clouds dissipate into the calm afternoon. VFW still occupied its original position on the hill, but there was a significant movement around it as TH's kin carried large black ammo boxes. TH crossed the barbed wire as fast as he could, and after a moment of navigating the buildings, checking every corner or a possible hole, TH found himself at the foot of the hill and began climbing the rocks, which shook each time VFW fired. Just before reaching the ledge, he made a note in his memory. *Come back. They need you.* TH counted to three and pulled himself up.

The unsuspecting android crew had just loaded another shell into the massive breech when TH started spraying them from the side, and moments later, his BAR jammed. Quickly clearing the jam and reloading, TH dispatched several more, with a last round flying towards the ammunition storage that immediately went up in the blaze of glory. TH looked away as the shockwave rocked his body. After pulling the bolt on the BAR, TH found an empty chamber.

Tossing the BAR on the ground action-movie style, TH climbed onto the platform and ejected the loaded shell. As he was about to shove the thermite into the breech of the 88mm gun, he spotted five androids with machine guns pointing at him. TH pulled the pin and rammed it into the breech, but his left hand got stuck when he attempted to pull it out. Soon, his system screamed at him that his left hand was no longer responding. As the bullets flew around him, TH aimed the pistol at his brethren and opened fire, killing three while forcing the rest to seek cover behind a truck. Quickly assessing his surroundings, TH tossed the pistol away and reached for the fire ax. After the second chop, however, another notification beeped. The one that he feared the most. *Low battery! Seek the nearest charging station or replace it!* Looking into the distance, he waved his hand. Again and again.

Seeing the orange fire shoot up against the sky, Mason scanned the platform with his binoculars and found TH waving for the last time before vanishing into clouds of smoke. With his heart racing, Mason looked at Zasada and gave him a thumbs up. Zasada nodded in reply and shut his hatch as the Grom roared clouds of black smoke out of its engine. Mason quickly got seated in his seat and plugged in the cables.

"The gun has been destroyed!" Mason shouted into the comms. "Dema, floor it. We'll pick up TH on the way!"

The Crusading Angel rocked forward, but Grom was already in second gear, advancing towards the checkpoint, being the first to enter the bridge. However, as they cleared the hills, Mason felt eyes on him as the sensation of something wrong rushed in. And whatever that was, Mason only had one shot to do it, as he was alone in the turret.

Mason looked to his right, and his heart stopped beating when he noticed another tank overlooking the passage from the other side. For a brief moment, the rising red sun on the white background appeared. With fury, Mason grabbed the handle for the horizontal turret drive and almost broke his wrist as he swung the gun at the target. Then, as he switched to cranking the vertical drive, he felt pressure against his hand as it got stuck. With tears in his eyes and a scream forcing its way from his lungs, Mason could only watch the shell hitting the Grom's track, sending it into an uncontrollable spin. The 14-tonne tank's large roadwheels screeched with pain, and Grom fell into the ditch.

"Holy!" Dema screamed into the radio.

The answer came in a blaze of glory as Mason watched another shell hit the ammo storage, sending the tank's turret flying high into the air.

"Dema!" Mason cried out, trying to hold his tears inside him, but Crusading Angel had already passed the wreckage, closing onto the mock buildings in front of it.

Looking through the commander's cupola, he noticed the Japanese tank turning its turret away. Then, to Mason's surprise, he watched the cupola open, and the woman in goggles sent him a short salute. Awestruck, to say the least, Mason pinched himself, but he was wide awake.

Mason squeezed the turret controls with shaking hands. Dema's shouting slowly faded away, and the roar of the V-12 made its way into Mason's head again as Dema parked at the gas station.

"Why did it spare us? They had a clean shot at us, and even the damn weather was perfect," Mason said as Dema climbed to the loader's position and looked at Mason, who took three long breaths, and then she remembered the conversation in the hospital bathroom. Quickly squatting down, she found an open ammo box and reloaded the main gun with less of a struggle than before.

Mason opened his hatch and closed his eyes, feeling the cooling wind on his face. "Let's refuel and keep an eye out for TH. Then, we'll floor it out of here. We still have a long way ahead of ourselves."

"Mason, this is a mock-up, not an actual gas station," Dema said a few minutes later as she touched the gas dispenser.

"Just like this life," Mason said. "TH, where the hell are you?! We need to move!"

"I would not say so," Dema leaned her head on Mason's right shoulder, "it is just a stage from which we will move on soon into the next one."

"Guys, need help here!" TH shouted as he peeked from behind the corner of the wooden house to their right.

"TH! Thank the Lord!" Mason turned his head and sprinted towards the house with Dema close behind, looking over her shoulder for any enemy.

However, as they got closer, Mason realized that his robot brother lacked his left arm, with the only reminder being a waving armless sleeve.

"I report one gun destroyed, Sir! On top of that, I secured some gas to keep us moving." TH pushed two black jerrycans with his left foot.

"What happened to you?" Dema looked away as she also

noticed an armless sleeve, but then she hugged TH for a second.

"I was stuck, and the only way out was to chop off my hand." TH shook his head. "But I can still work the radio. I am all right, don't scrap me!"

"You are riddled with holes! Are you sure that everything is all right?" Mason looked at TH, who had begun mirroring the beat-up tank. "Okay, get on the radio while we refuel. Shout if anything important,"

"Yes, Sir!" TH nodded. "For a moment, I believed that I died, but now I'm here."

As TH overtook them, Dema tapped Mason's right shoulder. With his left hand, Mason kept Dema's hand on his shoulder, slowly breathing, trying to calm his racing heart.

"Do you know why didn't they finish us? That was Wang Xiu, right? The girl you met in the hospital?" Mason turned to Dema. "Just tell me, I won't be mad. I have no reason to be."

"When you were on the table, I ran into her in the hospital restrooms. We concluded that the best way to do something is to not shoot at each other the first time. However, she couldn't guarantee a cease-fire if we were to meet again afterward. I promised the same."

"All right, that is all I needed to know," Mason smiled and released Dema's hand from his shoulder, "thank you for saving our lives."

"I'm no stranger to backroom deals. I had to do many of them in the Dark Zone, some more pleasant than the others."

CHAPTER SEVENTEEN

UNBREAKABLE STEEL

"How big are the fanbases of our crews?" Jeong-Min tapped his foot underneath the table, awaiting Thomas to explain why M4A3 76W HVSS was slightly better than M4A1 76W.

Adriana, on the other hand, had a good laugh as she observed the blowing social media of the triggered individuals, each attempting to get their point across. *It's so easy to get people rallied on social media. Why haven't I done this sooner? How is it this easy? I don't get it, but I see a potential.* Adriana tapped the screen and grinned from ear to ear, celebrating a small victory.

"I'm done talking; you can find all the information you need at osw.TVG/tank-royale/2145/lineup-info.com and find your preferred option. Benjamin, feel free to take over," Thomas took a deep breath and stood up, "nature is calling."

"All right, let me pull up the current list as Min requested." Benjamin swiped on the screen. "And then, with the magic of technology, you should be able to see the answer."

Team 10 – Centaur Mk.III (Boudicca) – Fan Base: 110 million viewers

Team 16 – Panzer 4 G Hydrostat (Oden) – Fan Base: 550 million viewers

Team 18 – Chi-Nu-Kai (Tomoe Gozen) – Fan Base: 600 million viewers

Team 26 – P26/40 (Da Vinci) – Fan Base: 45 million viewers

Team 28 – T-34-57 mod.42/43 (Crusading Angel) – Fan Base: 100 million viewers

"Despite the current frenzy, Turan still has a significant fanbase, but they dispersed the moment it blew up. However, I believe that there are a lot of non-aligned users as well, waiting for the showdown. It's easier to pick a favorite out of two than twenty." Thomas played with the screen for a moment. "A lot of people cheering on."

"I wonder, why does Team 26 have the lowest amount?" Jeong-Min nodded. "Counterpoint to Thomas. Sometimes, we just don't want to think."

"Well, getting back on track, Team 26 is the only team that hasn't seen any heavy action since the drop, but they weren't hiding either. Being the only riveted tank from survivors, I'm not surprised that Commander Smith is rather careful, but he is no coward, and I would like to retract my previous statement. They just spotted Hellcat and there is Centaur lurking nearby as well," Benjamin smiled at the camera as the screen changed to a drone hovering above the P26/40, which set its sights on the 76 mm Gun Motor Carriage M18 and fired. "This will be the last fight of the day, it seems like, as our crews are now primarily interested in preserving their tanks for the next zone."

"We'll be right back." Thomas nodded, and Adriana followed him several tents away from the broadcasting booth.

As they walked, Thomas pondered how to tell Adriana. Then, in a few moments, they reached their tent and got seated. Thomas took a deep breath and looked at the woman who was with him from the beginning.

"What is it? You don't look well." Adriana touched Thomas's pale-colored forehead. "What's wrong?"

"I'll not sugarcoat this, Adriana, and I must be frank with you. I picked up on your, let's just say, suboptimal comments," Thomas said, tapping his knees. "What the hell are you doing?!

I gave you all the reasons for our existence, even gave you the rationale. Why are you like this? Why are you sabotaging our dream? Something that we worked hard for?"

"People are willing; you saw it!" Adriana said in a shivering voice. "This is the moment to do something good! Or moral, I should say!"

"Adriana, for the last time. I hate to say this, but you were the one who suggested prisoners in the first place. On top of that, we're giving them a fighting chance. That's enough!"

"I suggested inmates, yes, and I'm a terrible person for that," Adriana held on to her tears, "but don't deny me to at least remedy or amend my soul."

"Adriana, we build tanks. That's where it begins and ends. However," Thomas looked over his shoulder, finding the coast clear, "what would you change for these contestants?"

"Well, first of all, I would allow them to rest in peace. While you were asleep, I found the master key and got digging. What I found..."

"Adriana, you did not just use my access to stroll through TVG systems!" Thomas was about to scream his lungs out but decided to keep his voice down.

"I wiped your trace out. What I'm trying to say is that..."

"Adriana, that information is now somewhere. If someone finds out... I love you, but this is pushing all the boundaries. It's getting to the point where you must choose between me or your clear conscience."

"You did not just say that! You did not!" Adriana looked at her shaking hands. "I'm asking you to do some good for these people. At least let's fight for their final rest because the next TVG show will not do so. Internally, they call it BRZ. Do I have to elaborate?"

"If you continue down this path, I cannot protect you. What happened to you?"

"Time happened, Thomas. Our world turns madder and madder. If you don't want to do it for the world, do it for at least one person. Dema."

"Who is Dema?"

"At least have the decency to learn something about your favored team." Adriana walked towards the medical tent. "Tell Ben that I'll do my interview in an hour."

———

Finally, after a mostly silent seven-hour drive, Mason ordered to stop the tank. The empty plains, void of any human or structure, slowly but surely ground away at his already exhausted psyche. He climbed out and lay on the ground, taking three long breaths. Every time, he felt tears coming as he remembered Van and the life his friend would never get to live. The blistering sun had vanished behind the dark clouds, and all the colors around him turned gray. Then, a moment later, he heard Dema lying beside him, with TH sitting on the turret, staring into the distance. Mason could see Dema's face more clearly, not obstructed by the goggles or the fog of war for the first time in days.

"We did not even get to say a proper goodbye to them!" At Dema's shivering voice, Mason knew she was barely holding her tears together.

"I know!" Mason closed his eyes and breathed deeply. "There is nothing we can do about it!"

"How can you keep going like this?" Dema turned towards Mason, who opened his eyes and noticed tears coming down her cheeks. "Please, tell me your secret! Do I need to get a Spider myself?"

"I told myself that we will mourn them once we win. Now, I need to have an iron stomach and nerves of steel. Look how far we made it!"

"Dema, Mason is right. We have crossed the point of no return, and the only way is forward. This is not an optimal situation by any metric." TH looked at the hanging wires in the place where his arm used to be. "I am missing an arm, and my battery is in red. Both of you are emotionally tired, to say the least. But these are the cards we were dealt with."

"You are right; I am acting like a child." Dema shook her head as Mason gave her a hand. "I am so stupid! We must push on like the machines we are!"

"It's all right to express your emotions, especially after what happened," Mason hugged her, "and more is on the way. Can you understand the weight I am bearing? Seeing you strong makes me stronger. Seeing TH with us gives me hope. After all, we're still a team with a solid chance of winning. Last time I checked, other crews are doing as badly, maybe even worse than we are."

"I understand." Dema looked over Mason's shoulder at the slowly descending sun, fighting off the gray clouds. "We are the Gasoline Cowboys, and we must herd this victory back to the metaphorical ranch."

"Or the home with a small garden and orchids, if I remember correctly." Mason looked at the beat-up Crusading Angel. "I think we can rest for a moment, but we need to press on. The last time I checked the map, we had a lot of ground to cover. TH, how are you feeling?"

"I don't know how much time I have left, but I know that I'm now on borrowed time. I had shut down most of the advanced systems, so if I may sound blunt over a day or two, you'll know why."

"We are all...." Dema looked into the distance. "I forgot what I wanted to say. I know; however, I do not know if it is an appropriate time."

"Dema, maybe in the next few hours, we might not have this chance. Please speak whatever is on your mind," Mason turned towards Dema, "and I have something to say as well."

"I do not even know how to formulate my thoughts, but that AI shook Van to the core. Okay," Dema took a deep breath, "was your call with Ail also fake?"

"It turns out that, yes, I spoke with an AI imitating my brother. While my blood boils by even thinking about it, I have to compliment that complexity because it sounded like him, and I couldn't even pick out any difference that would give it away."

"I am so sorry that you had to go through that. I just could not stop thinking about it. What did you want to say?" Dema took Mason's hands in hers.

"I wish that Van was here to hear it as well, but it means the world to me that you guys stayed with me in the hospital. Hmm," Mason raised his eyebrow, "speaking of fake, did you guys find something off about the entire TVG Battle Royale Complex?"

"No, I don't think so. What are you getting at?" TH said first, followed by Dema a moment later with a similar response.

"It's just on the topic of AI and fake people. I think it was either my first or second day in the complex. I sat alone in one of the tank parks and chatted with an Aussie from Sydney named Harper. He said that the entire complex, especially people around us, felt like androids with human skin."

"Interesting, but I do not know. If it is true, well, I applaud them for fooling us. Wait, in that case, are our social media posts also not real?"

"Guys, I had shut down my advanced computing to preserve my juice. Are you saying that everything in that complex was fake?"

"I wouldn't be surprised. We're convicts, after all. Well, that is something I wanted to say. Anyone else? If not," Mason looked at the descending sun, "we need to move."

As darkness spread across the battlefield three hours later, Dema and Mason had difficulty keeping their eyes on the road, surrounded by pines from all sides, and momentarily, Mason felt Crusading Angel drive uphill yet again. Even the two-hour rotations didn't help, as the going got more challenging, forcing Mason to leave his station unattended for several hours. Finally, after a mostly silent drive, Mason ordered to stop the tank, which replied with everything screeching, from roadwheels to the bolts that held the tank together. TH was first to peek from the loader's hatch and turn on his flashlight.

In Mason's mind, the short sequence of Grom spinning out and exploding kept replaying, escorted by his screams and pounding of the turret.

"Is that light on the gun mantlet still usable?" Dema asked TH, who flipped the flashlight in his hand.

"Let me check." Mason looked at the switch to his left and found the one, but after several empty clicks, gave him the answer. "I don't think I can shed more light on our journey. With this dense forest, I can't even see the full moon. On top of that, we've been climbing for the past twenty minutes. I don't want to find the edge and tumble to our deaths. I don't even want to think about it."

"Mason, the light is shot to pieces." TH's head appeared right in front of Mason's face as he stood up.

Mason waited for TH to get out of the way, and immediately, the cold evening wind punched him in the face, but the darkness and V-12 completely blinded his senses.

"Dema, can you drive just for a bit?" Mason found Dema partially illuminated by TH's flashlight as she climbed out of the loader's hatch.

"I am sorry, Mason, but I cannot take this anymore." Dema's shivering voice prompted Mason to hug her again.

"Mason, I'll ensure that the perimeter is safe for camp. I shall be right back." TH waved his flashlight and vanished into the night a moment later.

Despite Dema standing right before him, Mason could barely see her, relying on his touch and sound to keep her in mind.

"I know that we talked about it several hours ago, but I cannot keep it inside me anymore." Dema touched Mason's right shoulder. "I cannot go on."

"Look here, Dema. We need to press on. Like us, our tank is about to give in, which we cannot have. I'll spare you all the pep talk because I cannot find any words of comfort for myself."

———

"Well, we have to win first." Dema sadly smiled. "All right, I think we can soldier on."

"That is the girl I know," Mason smiled. "If you want, I'll stay here with you, but we need to keep moving,"

"Rather stay a night. Can we eat?" Just as Dema said it, Mason heard his stomach rumble.

"I think we can, Sir!" TH's flashlight blinded both momentarily, prompting them to look away. "My apologies."

"I know that there is one more meal in our bags. Dema, TH, let's keep the fire low."

"Yes, Sir!"

Mason found the flashlight as he remembered, climbed back into the tank, and after a minute of relentless search, he found Van's 0.50 cal box.

He momentarily leaned back in the co-driver seat, pressing his hands against his burning forehead. *Mason, Mason, don't you dare throw it now! Remember what Ail told you. It's not about the money. It's about you coming home in one piece. Focus Mason. You are close to the finish line. When you win, you get freedom and everything else.*

———

"Careful, Dema." TH stopped Dema with his remaining hand and flashed the light on a snake slithering between the fallen branches and large rocks.

"TH, how do you do it? How do you stay focused?" Dema found one of the rocks and sat down, dropping the branches she found to her feet.

"I learned something over the years I spent with humans. We have goals, right? What is our goal?" TH lowered his light, but just enough so both were partially illuminated.

"To survive and win. Is there anything else?"

"I apologize, but I should have asked a different question. What is our milestone here?"

"Milestone?" Dema tilted her head. "I am not following."

"The thing about goals is that after we fulfill them, nothing happens afterward. With the milestone, we know there is something more awaiting us. What awaits us afterward if we change victory from a goal to a milestone? You? Mason?"

Dema pondered momentarily as her mind tried to comprehend what TH was saying. But as it all became clear, she gasped for the air.

"You are right! We were so focused on the prize that I did not know what I would do with it. A small house with a garden, while desirable, is still a small thing in the larger picture. Oh my! Where would I go after this?" Dema shook her head. "You are so right!"

"Exactly. That is why I think we are so close to going over the edge one way or another. We're so focused on the goal that even when we win, we'll be lost afterward."

"I guess one of my milestones is to figure out my feelings for Mason." Dema looked in the general direction of the Crusading Angel and then back at TH.

"Is there a third party?" TH raised his flashlight for a moment.

"No, there isn't. We partially confessed our feelings to each other, but I didn't want to lose focus. You know that if one of us makes a mistake, our Angel will become our grave." Dema stood up and began collecting the wood she dropped.

"Dema. You have a valid point. However, think a bit more about the future. Mason is a diamond in the rough; trust me, this is a one-of-a-kind opportunity for you. You won't find another human on this Earth with whom you can trust your life. He got Van and me this far and will take you even further. Don't throw it away." TH shone the light back on the Crusading Angel.

A moment later, Mason handed Dema the chocolate protein bar as TH got a small fire going. "Here is our entree, and I shall attempt to make a four-course meal with a dessert."

"How can you do this?" Dema laughed and took a bite from the protein bar. "I'm this close to flying over the edge."

"Maybe jokes and laughter helped me a lot. Well, the fear of getting blown to pieces has something to do with it as well. But I haven't actually laughed in ages." Mason climbed back into his position, grabbed the flashlight, and vanished into the darkness.

Mason stretched and turned on the flashlight, and the howl shattered the evening silence.

"Mason, everything all right?" TH shouted into the night.

"Take a look," Mason handed Dema the flashlight, sat on the tank's roof, and leaned back on the turret.

The damaged boxes, pierced tents, and one external fuel tank were nowhere in sight, and the box with food rations was riddled with bullets. Dema untied the ration box and jumped down from the tank as Mason vanished inside the T-34, but moments later, he raised a water bottle from the hatch.

"It is not all lost, and most of our duffle bags are intact," TH tilted his head, "but this is a problem."

"I think that two-course value meals will be enough."

"Hey, look, we're not the only ones!" Dema pointed at orange lights illuminating the midnight sky and reached for them.

"Would you like to say a prayer before food?" Mason was about to do a sign of the cross when he heard wolves howling around them. "I guess we're eating inside."

"And I thought we only had to worry about other tanks,"

Dema cried out at the night sky. "Well, they wouldn't be that easy on us anyway."

For some unexplained reason, Mason and Dema laughed, with Mason even drying his tears, feeling the weight on his shoulders vanish for a moment.

"Why the laugh?" TH scratched his chin. "You humans are unpredictable."

"Just laughing in the face of death. Being cocky in such situations can partially help," Mason slowly exhaled, "but I guess as a drowning man, I try to catch every straw I can."

"In that case, the problem with kleptomaniacs is that they always take things literally." TH looked at Mason, and Dema was first to catch up on the joke and laughed.

"Come on, Mason!" TH shook his head. "I want to hear you say something funny!"

"Okay!" Mason raised his hands. "I buy all my guns from T-Rex. He's a small arms dealer."

A moment of silence descended on the campfire, but Dema was first to laugh again.

"I don't get it." TH shook his head.

"Small arms like firearms, but they're arms! Double meaning." Dema looked at TH, who tapped his forehead. "My turn. A blind man walked into a bar... and a table... and a chair..."

"I like that one!" Mason giggled like a schoolgirl. "TH, your turn."

"Okay, one more. What do you get if you cross a robot with a rock band?" TH looked into the fire for a moment.

"Tell us." Mason tapped TH's right shoulder.

"Heavy metal!"

"That is a good one." Dema laughed and looked at Mason. "Let's hear one more!"

"Okay. Two goldfish in a tank. One turns towards the other and says: So, how do we drive this thing?" Mason growled. "Yeah, it wasn't a good one."

"Give it another shot."

"Okay. What did the shark say when he ate a clownfish?" Mason looked at his friends. "This tastes funny!"

"Good one! My turn! How much do dead batteries cost? There should be no charge!" TH looked into the fire again, observing the red hot wood.

"It'll be an interesting morning. All five contestants are in proximity to each other." Benjamin sat next to the campfire, joined by Jeong-Min.

"It definitely will be," Jeong-Min looked into the fire, "so you finally dropped that suit. Have you ever visited the United Kingdom?"

"Well, I have never been there, and I have to say that dropping the suit just for a moment feels like I dropped all the heavy chains that Corporate had placed on me," Benjamin finally smiled, and Min nodded his head, "where are Thomas and Adriana?"

"Last time I saw them, they vanished inside one of the medical tents, probably gathering information from the survivors. Hey, what is the matter?" Jeong tapped Benjamin on his shoulder as he pulled out a flashing tablet.

"I don't know; it is just this. It started to circulate on VIDPLAY, and apparently, it is a leak of the new Battle Royale, and even by TVG standards, it is rather disgusting. Look," Benjamin made sure that the coast was clear when he handed Min his phone, "I had to download to the SDD of the Main Server."

Benjamin watched Min's face change colors as the thirty-second clip played out.

"This has to be from a movie; there is no way someone's mind is this sick. They cannot even leave the dead alone." Jeong-Min returned the tablet to Benjamin.

"It isn't. I made several phone calls to learn more from my inside source, but she hasn't picked up anything yet. It was leaked from TVG, one hundred percent, which is now accusing me of the leakage and wants to shut down my company."

"Well, if that clip is…, that would explain why the zombies in the movies look real," Jeong-Min whispered. "How can they get bodies?"

"From what I heard, all TVG contestants sign a form allowing Corporate and TVG to use their remains for scientific purposes, but it turns out that they have been doing a bit more than that."

"Why am I not surprised? Speaking of Thomas and Adriana, I may or may not have accidentally walked in on one of their arguments."

"I also picked up on the fact that Adriana has made some comments during the broadcast. While nothing offensive, there is an underlying message."

"I mean, we're in the middle of nowhere, talking to the camera all day. I'm not surprised that she is frustrated. Honestly, I just hope that we wrap up filming as soon as possible."

"I understand that. While this nature is nice and all, it takes a mental toll on you. Luckily, we're done with most of the behind-the-scenes shooting. The big part, or big suck, is ahead. There will be a post-game interview, among other things, all of which will take time."

"So, where is the big suck?"

"This." Benjamin woke up his tablet from sleep and showed the screen where the names of the surviving tankers lit up with the models, showing the actual damage done to the tanks with the highlighted most critical elements. "They're more damaged than anticipated."

Team 10 – Centaur Mk.III (Boudicca)
Critical: damaged engine
Team 16 – Panzer 4 G Hydrostat (Oden)
Critical: damaged NVG and suspension
Team 18 – Chi-Nu-Kai (Tomoe Gozen)
Critical: damaged horizontal turret drive
Team 26 – P26/40 (Da Vinci)
Critical: damaged electrical equipment

Team 28 – T-34-57 mod.42/43 (Crusading Angel)
Critical: damaged brakes and transmission

As Dema opened her eyes in the morning, she found Mason's place empty. For a moment, her heart stopped beating, thinking that wolves had got to him, but when she poked out of the commander's hatch, she found him standing upright and saluting next to the silent Crusading Angel with its turret facing the rear. After she got her bearings together, Dema's jaw dropped to the floor.

All around them, on the nearby ridge, down in the wide alley, on the top of the hill, other surviving contestants lined up with their worn-out tanks behind them, and for the first time in what seemed to be weeks, Dema found Gio and his crew. Like them, most crews had lost fellow tankers, and only Gio's team was at full force. The German team also seemed to take several hits, as did the Japanese Chi-Nu-Kai, and on the ridge, the British Centaur stood, reflecting the morning light; soon, one of the crew members pulled out bagpipes, and the scene filled with the tunes of Flower of Scotland.

"How long have you been standing here?" Dema's voice fought with the shrill of bagpipes.

"An hour or so." Mason grabbed Dema's hand as she smiled. "We all stood, remembering our friends. Then, upon unspoken agreement, we turned our guns away"

As the first song concluded, Dema smiled and looked at Mason, who dried his tears and took a deep breath.

———

For the next twenty minutes, all the surviving contestants stood in silence as the songs from the other side of the world played in the void of the battle. Mason had trouble holding his tears back, while in his mind, the first arrival at TVG, eating the sandwiches, exploring the World War Two-themed complex, all memories hit Mason as a tidal wave.

"Where is TH? He is missing out!" Dema scanned her surroundings, " TH? TH!"

"TH. Where the hell are you? TH!" Mason looked at Dema, who nodded, and both sprinted back to the tank.

"TH! Where the hell are you?" Mason climbed into the tank while Dema stood on the engine cover, looking between the trees.

"He is not in the tank!" Mason's head popped out from the cupola. "TH!"

"I'm here!" TH emerged from the tree line, waving as he shouted, "I went to scout ahead a bit. I have good news and bad news."

———

As the contestants enjoyed the songs played by their peers, the broadcasting base was ablaze with phone and video calls. Jeong-Min sat alone in the broadcasting booth, engaging with the audience. Simultaneously, Benjamin, Thomas, and Adriana stood in front of the computer screen, taking hits from the TVG C-suite after the social media started to glow with more leaked footage.

"When was this leaked?" A commission of suits and ties bombarded the trio with questions and threats hanging in the air.

"President, I cannot access such media as the broadcaster. Thomas and Adriana were with me. Neither they nor I know when it was leaked, and just like you, I was notified about the leakage now."

"So, who leaked it? You haven't answered the question."

"What makes you think that we did it?" Adriana took a deep breath. "Just because your board cannot pick an already better version of the Sherman tank, you are going to throw it at us? Where was it uploaded?"

"The first leakage was traced to Utah, United States, while

the second leakage is from this region as someone attempted to shift it into China, but the trace came from Mongolia or Russia. That is what we know, and you are the only crew nearby."

"Well," Thomas rolled his eyes, "none of us have access to such data, but I have to say, since the secret sauce of making real-life zombies is a rather brutal way, even by TVG standards, Last Shooter Standing Reality Show's secret was finally exposed."

"Speaking of the schedule, why aren't the contestants moving but sitting and listening to music?"

"What music?" Benjamin shrugged his shoulders. "As long as they are making progress, we're good to go. It's not like people are watching this live."

"You are not watching it? All tankers are staring at each other, listening to some crappy bagpipes," voices from behind President unanimously agreed, and a few nodded.

"No, because we're talking with you," Thomas said, folding his arms, "and so what if they are playing tunes?"

"Wow. First of all, if they don't make it, it is up to them. Secondly, we're about to lose many viewers because of that statement, which goes against TVG Community Standards." Adriana moved forward and raised her fist. "The same rules you selectively enforce."

"We'll find whoever did this, and you will stay on the schedule, so get them moving." The screen went black, and the trio slowly exhaled simultaneously.

"This will be a long day," Thomas said, but Adriana had already switched the screen and felt her heart move as the song concluded.

"Stop right there," Thomas shook his head as Benjamin was about to leave. "Why did you say that nobody is watching this live?"

"Whoever leaked that horrendous and inhuman footage is ready to take us all down. Well, I might as well spill the beans. We have no live audience. For people out there, the fight ended after the simulation. We've been talking with bots and AIs this entire time."

"Excuse me?" Thomas pinched himself. "Is this real?"

"Yes. We're in the process of gathering the footage. After the games end and the winner is decided, we work on a TV show or a movie. The live audience is unpredictable, creating a liability for us all. So, like any other TVG Battle Royales, we are using bots and advanced AI to keep the numbers high, so when people watch this at home, the FOMO will kick in, prompting them to sign up for the premium plan. After the finalization of the two versions, TVG and their post-production studios turn this into an animation or grain it enough so it looks like a movie with a flip of a switch. This is then added to the TVG Cinematic Universe. The winners in the real fight get featured and become celebrities. Then we make them promoters for the new movie or the TV show, of course, kept under tight supervision." As Benjamin continued spilling the beans, Adriana's face turned pale. "Do you think I want you to talk with AIs all this time? I'm going crazy!"

"What? You are serious?" Adriana paced around the screen for a moment. "I must be dreaming!"

"That is why I didn't want to take this gig in the first place, but I was forced." Benjamin folded his hands. "I only know this because I have a friend working in the TVG guts."

"So, the TVG Battle Royale complex is just a marketing promotion?"

"Always has been. Do you recall a two-season show about The Last Sully? He was the two-time consecutive winner of the TVG Battle Royale, and they made a TV show out of him. However, as he learned what was really going on, Internal ensured that Sully would never speak again. He died in a car accident while intoxicated to the gills. Of course, as a celebrity in the fast-paced internet sphere, everyone mourned him for about two seconds and then moved on."

"This is insane!" Adriana howled at the sky. "This is not the reality!"

"I'm afraid, Adriana, that this is the reality," Benjamin said and looked at the approaching Jeong-Min.

"Why are you howling? And why is Adriana about to pass out?" Jeong-Min looked at Adriana and caught her as she was about to faint.

"Let's get her help; I'll explain in more detail." Benjamin whistled as the alarm sounded.

———

After a short break, the British tanker adjusted the pipes, took a deep breath, and Scotland the Brave resonated across the hills. As the performance concluded, the problems from yesterday started to force their way forward, so Mason broke out the map and pointed at the marked depot, a hundred miles away from their current location.

"Dema, how are we on fuel?" Mason closed his eyes as he said it.

"Well, the indicator is between yellow and red territory, so I can only make an educated guess, Mason, but there is something a bit more alarming because the brakes and gear shifting are increasingly difficult. I had compiled a list of everything we need to fix if we even want to have a chance to win."

"It seems like we'll be going mostly downhill, but since you mentioned the brakes, I'm suddenly not so sure." Mason looked at the beat-up T-34, which kept soldiering on.

"I could feel yesterday that my arms are getting bigger and bigger." Dema smiled and flexed her biceps.

"Same here, love." Mason looked at the orange ball slowly traveling upwards. "We got a long day ahead of ourselves. TH, how are you feeling?"

"No difference from yesterday."

"Glad to hear it. Dema, how are you feeling?"

"A lot better. Just this terrain will add additional miles to our journey, and let's not forget that next time, fellow contestants will blast us to kingdom come. This is it, Mason; it is all or nothing."

"And that is what worries me. So let us eat breakfast, inspect the tank, and get cracking." Mason was already one step ahead.

"You made the dinner; I shall prepare the breakfast." Dema waved and vanished behind the tank as Mason took a detailed look at the frontal armor plate and almost cried out.

The frontal armor plate had seen better days, riddled with holes of all sizes and scratches. The driver's hatch took several hits, shattering one of the vision glasses with its cover. The attached spare tracks were nowhere to be seen, and the blown wide open barrel of Dema's machine gun sent shivers down his spine. The turret ring and gun mantlet took several hits, shattering the mounted light and leaving large dents behind. One of the storage bins went MIA, and the other was covered with bullet holes from the right side. The remaining thirsty external fuel tank hung on the back, awaiting its drink.

"It could be worse," TH observed Mason staring at the tank, "we could be a burning wreck."

"Mason, can you come here for a moment?" Dema's voice called out from the back.

"Yes?" Mason said, and Dema waved with the last ration cardboard box.

"There are three bags left. We will have to share breakfast, then skip lunch, split the chocolate bar, and if God permits, eat dinner, which leaves us with the last bag when we enter the final zone." Dema handed Mason the cardboard plate. "I warmed up the rice and chicken chunks, and we have smoked almonds. Half for you, half for me."

While the plate wasn't pleasant to his eyes, Mason closed his eyes and rammed warm chicken into his mouth.

———

"All right, ladies and gentlemen, welcome back to the Tank Royale of 2145, and I have to say, it has been a wild ride, full of sneaky shots, the second-longest killstreak by the Horthy, and sacrifices of many. Surprisingly, the Italian tank hasn't sent the British to the scrapyard. Note that I and Jeong-Min get a second chance. This is our up-to-date standing:"

Team 10 – Centaur Mk.III (Boudicca) (Benjamin) – Surviving 4 out of 5
Team 16 – Panzer 4 G Hydrostat (Oden) (Jeong-Min)(1) – Surviving 4 out of 5
Team 18 – Chi-Nu-Kai (Tomoe Gozen)(1) (Adriana) – Surviving 3 out of 5
Team 26 – P26/40 (Da Vinci) – Surviving 4 out of 4
Team 28 – T-34-57 mod.42/43 (Crusading Angel)(1) (Thomas) – Surviving 3 out of 4

"Not exactly what I was expecting, but now, all tanks need maintenance, so we have an endurance race, and you don't want to break down this close to the finish line! Thomas, Adriana, give us a quick run-down on what each tank needs to fix if they are to make it?" Benjamin smiled, and the camera shifted towards Adriana, who shook her head, trying not to scream.

"So, let's start with the Boudicca. Its 410 horsepower Liberty Engine would like to have some lubrication. Oden is surprisingly holding up, but it needs to reattach several road-wheels. Our Warrior from Japan needs a new horizontal turret drive, as now, they play at the fixed casemate tank. Da Vinci is all right, but the electronics could use a new battery. Finally, the T-34 and I don't even know where to start, but their priority is to replenish their oil reserves since their V-12 drinks a lot of it and add more brake fluid." Thomas answered for Adriana and described each live shot.

Thomas smiled, and the graphic of the beat-up Panzer 4

appeared. "It's a race, and everyone needs to shed some weight one way or another, but again, that is up to Commander Klemens."

"That is fair. Mobility is what matters now," Jeong-Min said as thunder sounded in the distance, and moments later torrential rain began to fall, forcing everyone to scramble into their tents.

"This constant banging is going to drive me crazy!" Mason was about to open his hatch but stopped halfway when he imagined the water filling the turret compartment, and his hands slid back.

The rain heavily obscured the visibility to the point that Dema kept the tank running in second gear, which the massive V-12 rumbled about.

"Slowly, Dema." Mason scanned his surroundings through the vision slits and loader's periscope. "If you want, I can take over, and you can rest."

"Thank you, love." Dema slammed on the steering levers, but the tank continued forward. "Mason, I lost the brakes!"

Mason could only scream as the Crusading Angel fully tilted forward, and a moment later, the thirty-ton tank picked up speed. With Dema calling God to save them and Angel's gears squealing, Mason fired the main gun, hoping to slow down their descent. It worked, but only for a moment. The last thing Mason remembered was hitting his head on the gunsight as the tank spun out of control and hit something.

CHAPTER EIGHTEEN

DOWNHILL STRUGGLE

"Well, this is interesting, dear viewers; it seems like Russians are in a ditch, Germans are attempting to make an insurance claim, Japanese are drinking tea, and Italians are getting double-teamed by weather and British." Benjamin took a sip of water as all the presenters watched the screen. "How much is in the pot?"

And while on air, everyone smiled; Benjamin's revelation left a mark on everyone's mind, especially on Adriana, who decided to skip every other broadcasting session.

"Well, all of us put fifty, and then we added another hundred, but since we are betting again, we need another two hundred in the pot." Jeong-Min pressed send on his tablet. "My wife will kill me."

"Ohhh." Adriana looked away when the Hellcat took a direct hit from Da Vinci, and the camera flew right through the large hole in the front, revealing the destruction inside the tank. "My heart cannot take this. It's too much!"

"BB, I'm curious where the final ring is?" Thomas rolled up his sleeves. "It seems like the rain is finally stopping."

Thomas looked at Adriana and gave her a short nod. He understood she was trying hard not to explode from what they had just learned a few hours ago. Thomas gave her a thumbs up, and Adriana nodded, but the nod was without feeling or weight.

"It is right below us," Benjamin stood up just as the last raindrop hit the tent and raised his hands like a preacher during a sermon. "Please follow me, ladies and gentlemen!"

As the camera swung left and right, giving the audience a peek behind the scenes, Benjamin stopped at the cliff's edge and pointed at the village below them. Jeong noticed the tank obstacles on the outskirts, forming a protective circle around the fabled town.

"It took the TVG Architecture, collaborating with the Stage Department several months to build the historically accurate mock-up of Villers-Bretonneux, and we shall have a front-row seat. So, stay tuned, and now we're going to the commercial break," Benjamin explained to the audience and waited for everyone else, including the camera, to leave for an afternoon break. "Thomas, I know that it was you leaking whatever that was. I understand your intentions, but you are not only putting yourself in danger. Orion bugged my house, watching my wife and son's every step and there were only a few blind spots where we could freely talk. Can you understand that?"

"Time to get that gunship in the air." Thomas turned around and left Benjamin to his thoughts.

"Thomas, we need to talk!" Benjamin turned around and caught up with Thomas, who took a deep breath. "Answer me! Say something!"

"What am I to say? It wasn't me, but Adriana," Thomas smiled as he looked around, ensuring that the coast was clear, "and I believe this will stay between us."

"What is she even thinking?"

"She wants a better world, a naïve hope. An urgent need to do something, not thinking about larger implications."

"I can see that the two of you are currently in a rough patch. I get that. From experience, go easy on her, but put your foot down when needed."

"Thank you for the words of encouragement," Thomas

smiled. "Thank you. I love her to death, but..."

"My friend, as I said, I understand. You know what? I'll talk with her and see what I can do."

"She is all yours," Thomas walked away with hands in his pockets, "all yours."

———

It wasn't hard to find Adriana, as Benjamin immediately spotted her standing on the edge of the cliff, staring into the distance at a lonely cloud.

"May I join you?" Benjamin coughed, prompting Adriana to turn around.

"Please," Adriana turned again towards the edge, and Benjamin joined her. "Did Thomas send you to talk to me and come to my senses?"

"Not at all, but now that you mention it, is everything all right?"

"Oh."

"I only asked to join you, nothing else." Thomas looked into the distance. "What a nice day we're having."

"Sure." Adriana scratched her chin. "Sure, sure, sure."

"Look, while I don't want to pry into your personal matters and the relationship with Thomas, understand that all your actions that you do here reflect primarily on my performance review. Do you understand that? The last thing I want is a TVG board breathing down my neck. One misstep from me and I'm off the air for good. You at least get to build tanks for the foreseeable future. I have no gigs lined up after this, and we need money. I don't get paid the same as you."

"Point being?"

"Do you have children?"

"No, we don't. Why the question?"

"I have two, and the only thing that matters in the world is me being with them, as this is the time when they are growing up and need me to guide them. I need to be there and not in the middle of Mongolia talking to AI. I have a favor to ask you. Save your activism for when we come back home. None of you present have any real skin in the game. If I mess up, there is a high chance that my family will never see me again. Please."

"Alright!" Adriana threw her hands in the air. "I'll keep it to myself."

"Thank you for your understanding. Now, can we rerecord some interviews in like twenty minutes when you'll be in a better mood by then?"

As noon arrived and the sun finally appeared from behind the clouds, Mason heard the screeching of the winch as the T-34 pulled out of the ditch.

"Dema, can you hear me?" With a shaky head, Mason kneeled on the thin plate and found Dema bent forward, bleeding from her forehead. "TH?!"

"Dema!" Mason grabbed the small pouch after he shook her, and moments later, he stopped the bleeding with a white bandage. "Dema, I need you!"

The tank halted, and Mason opened the driver's hatch, allowing the fresh air to fly in. Opening his commander hatch, he found a resupply-tracked vehicle crewed by two androids. The vehicle had a T-34 hull filled with equipment, fuel, and a folding crane. Mason quickly dismounted the tank, ran towards the driver's hatch, and, after a bit of a struggle, Mason pulled her out.

"Sir, what do you need from us?" One of the androids approached and saluted. "Are you all right?"

"Please, just make sure that our tank can run." Mason slowly exhaled. "My partner is also in the tank. Can you get him out?"

"Yes, Sir!"

"Bring some water." Mason carried Dema to a nearby tree and leaned against it as the android left to assist his colleague.

Mason removed his jacket and covered Dema's body, protecting it from the elements, and hugged her again.

Come on, Dema! You survived the Dark Zone, for God's sake! I cannot lose you now! Please! Mason kissed Dema on her forehead and held her in his arms, slowly rocking back and forth. *God, please help me. I know I crossed the line, but please don't let her die on me.*

After a minute of despair, Dema opened her eyes and looked around her, disoriented, bringing tears to Mason's eyes.

"What happened? Where are we, Mason?" Dema folded herself on the ground, pressing the muddy ground against her forehead, attempting to cool off.

"I got so scared that I almost lost you. It seems like after the brakes failed, we crashed into a tree, knocking us both out, but luckily, we recovered. I have no idea where we are or how far we have to go. I'm happy you are alive," Mason said, leaning against the tree.

"My head hurts! That must have been one strong tree! Is our tank okay?" Dema reached with her right hand for the gray afternoon sky and closed her eyes momentarily. "Where is TH?"

"These two nice TH lookalikes are doing a quick maintenance." Mason felt Dema's head on his left shoulder. "How are you?"

"Considering that I just survived a crash, I am doing fine; thank you for asking. How about yourself?" Dema smiled and touched her burning forehead.

"Could be better." Mason tilted his head.

"Ignoring the muddy ground and the fact that we are fighting to the death, I would never imagine visiting Mongolia." Dema looked at the scattering clouds, and a moment later, the sun warmed up the wet tankers. "I, a girl from a small village in Eastern Europe, am driving a World War Two Soviet tank kit across Mongolia in a *reality show* in a life-and-death scenario!"

"We landed on the grass, crossed the desert, fought in the city, traveled across the steppe, and now we are in the mountains and pine forests." Mason laughed and closed his eyes for a moment. "I'm not going to lie; I would definitely come back and just wander."

"Our friends back home are not going to believe us. It is one thing to see it on camera, but experience it?"

Mason gently leaned Dema against the tree and stood up, waving his hands in the process. "Hey!"

"That is a good question. Do you hear that?" Dema stood up but immediately regretted it as Mason caught her.

"Just stay here and rest. I'll look for TH. Hey! Where is my partner?" Mason ran up to the two androids that continued servicing the tank with TH nowhere in sight.

"Your partner is gone." One of the androids turned to Mason. "We tossed him into that ditch right there, as he is no longer needed. His batteries have run dry."

"What?!" Mason picked up the pace and soon held another body in his hands.

As he pressed his palms against TH's chest, Mason realized that administering CPR on the robotic body was pointless. On his chest, however, in one of the pockets, he felt a rounded object, which turned out to be TH's coin.

"No, no, no!" Mason howled at the gray clouds slowly sailing away. "Why?"

"Mason, where is TH?" He heard Dema's voice behind him, and soon, she kneeled next to him, leaning on a stick.

"He is gone!" Mason sat on the wet ground., "Dema, he is gone!"

"Why, Lord! Why now!" Dema said in a shivering voice and pressed her forehead against TH's chest. "Just a few miles, and we would be at the finish line!"

"I am sorry, but your partner is ready to be scrapped. We can take him apart and use some of the components to patch up your electrical systems," one of the androids said from behind. "It'll be better that way,"

"Piss off!" Mason shouted. "We are not scrapping him!"

"All right." Android raised his hands and walked away. "Then don't complain!"

"Do you feel it?" Dema touched Mason's hands as the ground shook violently, followed by the trees rocking back and forth, and the first rocks began to fall from the cliffs.

But Mason didn't care. He sat there in silence, taking in Mother Nature's violent embrace while holding the body of his friend.

"Ladies and gentlemen, we're experiencing an earthquake. We'll be right back after the commercial break." Benjamin held onto his chair as the ground violently shook. "If this won't throw a wrench into this entire operation, then I don't know what will!"

"That's why we got the engineering vehicles." Adriana walked outside the tent, completely ignoring the angry Mother Nature.

"Adriana, what are you doing!" Jeong-Min shouted, but his words drowned in the noise of falling broadcasting equipment, beeping machines, and screams of terror.

"Sir, Ulaanbaatar reports total destruction; look!" One of the interns pointed at the still-turned-on TV, where another two skyscrapers hit the ground hard.

"Well, Corporate will just shove it into the evening news and keep this going." Benjamin looked around him when the violent shaking stopped. "Oh God! The final zone!"

Everyone currently in the tent rushed to the edge, observing the clouds of dust and collapsed buildings littering the surroundings.

"On the bright side," Jeong-Min looked at Benjamin, who slowly exhaled, "it will make for a much more exciting final round. Well, at least exciting for some."

"I guess so," Benjamin said, "I guess so. We still have to tape the final interview before discussing it with the winners. I'll go first, then both of you and Min last. All right, everyone?"

He didn't wait for an answer as another intern handed Benjamin a tablet with the statistics.

"What?"

"Sir, one more thing. Team 26 has destroyed both the non-contestant Hellcat and Centaur."

"Why me! Why do I keep losing these bets? And why am I learning about this just now? You just added another five hours into post-production. Don't let that happen again."

"I'm so sorry, Sir. You were on a call and the interviews. Won't happen again!"

"Well, you are out; we are adding another fifty to the pool." Thomas shook his head and stretched his neck.

"Thomas, look!" Adriana flipped her tablet around. "Team 28 just lost another crew member!"

"What? How?" Thomas rushed back into the broadcasting booth and began rewinding the footage.

In two minutes, he found what he was looking for. He gave a short nod to Mason kneeling in the mud, pounding his teammate's chest. Respectfully, he rewound the footage back to the original timestamp just as Adriana and Jeong-Min caught up with him.

"How did he die?" Adriana caught her breath.

"Does it matter? They're close to the limit, but they are not the only ones," Thomas pointed at the screen, "we got four remaining, and only one will go home."

Team 16 – Panzer 4 G Hydrostat (Oden) (Jeong-Min)(1) – Surviving 4 out of 5
Team 18 – Chi-Nu-Kai (Tomoe Gozen)(1) (Adriana) – Surviving 3 out of 5
Team 26 – P26/40(1) (Da Vinci) – Surviving 2 out of 4
Team 28 – T-34-57 mod.42/43 (Crusading Angel)(1) (Thomas) – Surviving 2 out of 4

"Commander Knight, we have filled up your tanks, changed the oil, and added oil reserves to the remaining auxiliary fuel tank. We adjusted the track tension and serviced what we could. Still, you will need a garage," one of the android engineers saluted as he approached Mason and Dema, "my partner will finish the bolts, and you should be on your way. Just keep following the road. Maybe you would like this."

The service android handed Mason a black box with disconnected wires.

"What is this?"

"That is the brain of your companion. Keep it or have us recycle him."

"Of course we're keeping him! How can you even ask such a question!" Mason lashed out at the android, but Dema grabbed Mason by his hand, prompting him to stop.

"Thank you very much." Dema smiled, then pressed her palm against her forehead.

"Ma'am, if I were you, I would seek medical help as soon as possible." the humanoid saluted again and climbed into his recovery vehicle. "You should have allowed us to recycle your companion."

"Are you sure that you can drive?" Mason gave Dema a hand and waited for her to climb inside the tank as the recovery vehicle drove away into the afternoon.

"I can, Mason. It was a little nudge, nothing too serious," Dema said, looking at her shaking hands. "It's just us now. I did not imagine that TH would go out that way, but I guess it is better this way for us."

"All right, start the engine as I rerack some shells." Mason pressed the lever on the breech, expecting a shell to fall into his hands, but only an empty click was heard.

All right then. We have a ways to go. Focus, and we'll make it. God, thank you for being here and protecting us, especially Dema. Mason opened the first ammo box, but only a void greeted him. Finally, after another six unsuccessful attempts, Mason found four shells. He rammed the first one into the breech, and as he was about to place the second one closer to his seat, he heard Dema curse for the first time.

"Come on, you!" Dema punched the lever. "What am I doing wrong!?"

"Try again!" Mason climbed underneath the breech and rested his hands on Dema's shoulders, attempting to calm her down. "I believe in you. You got this!"

"I am trying!" Dema took a deep breath and started whispering the starting sequence again. *Gear lever neutral. Foot on the brake. Accelerator halfway up. Press the starter.*

"See, nothing! Why won't you work?" As Mason looked around him, hoping to defuse the tension, Dema became a time bomb.

"Where is the manual?"

"Right here." Dema tossed the book at Mason, and her head vanished in her arms. She took three deep breaths.

Mason started flipping through the manual, but his ears picked up a quiet sobbing.

"Why won't you work, you Дурна російська машина! You have one job! One job! You have just been serviced!" Dema broke down in tears. "Why?"

"Dema," Mason turned towards her, "let me check something."

"Sure," Dema punched the levers as Mason climbed out of the tank, but all he found were tread tracks in the mud that the recovery vehicle left behind.

Still holding the manual in his hand, Mason began furiously flipping through the pages again as Dema's muffled cursing and crying continued.

"Gear lever neutral. Foot on the brake. Accelerator halfway up. Press the starter. Nothing! Why? The second way, use the air, same process, nothing!"

"Dema, I got it!" Mason found the page he needed and waited for five minutes.

Then he slid back into the co-driver's seat, finding Dema collecting herself.

"What?" Dema's wet eyes greeted Mason.

"All right, so is the gear lever in neutral?" Mason looked at the group of levers coming out of the black box.

"Yes, it is." Dema tapped it, and Mason nodded.

"Do you have your right foot on the brake?"

"I do." As Dema said it, Mason heard a squeaking noise as Dema applied the brake.

"Did you press the clutch?"

"Clutch, clutch. No, I didn't." Another squeaking noise sounded, and Dema's eyes widened. "How could I forget about the clutch?"

"Well, we hit a tree, which could have been worse. Put the accelerator halfway up and press the starter." As Mason said this, the mighty V-12 came to life but cut out before it could roar. "You need to press both brake and clutch as you turn the starter. Slowly, we're in no rush."

Dema repeated the sequence, and the V-12 engine now roared to life. With joy in her eyes, Dema kissed Mason, who plugged her tanker helmet into the internal comms, placed it on her head, and climbed into his nest, where he sat on his chair.

"Thank you, Mason." Dema's voice cracked in the comms.

"Anytime. Now, get us to the final zone. For Van and TH." Mason placed his tanker helmet on his seat, and moments later Dema drove out on the forest path.

"For Van and TH. Let's get this done!" Dema steered the tank right, avoiding fallen trees.

"That's what I like to hear! We're almost there, and then we're going home!"

"Yes!" Dema whistled. "We are going home!"

———

After another two hours, Mason opened his hatch for the tenth time, awaiting something to happen, but only the sound of the V-12 echoed in the empty valley.

While the hills and mountains were good-looking and filled with trees, there wasn't any opening to allow the Crusading

Angel to leave the bowl, and the river to his right didn't seem to allow them to pass either.

"Mason, my stomach is rumbling. Have we eaten lunch yet?" Dema almost squealed into the comms. "Have we?"

"Yes, we did. Don't you remember that sweet chocolate bar?" Mason lied to himself and Dema as he saved up the final package for the finish line.

"That is right, I completely forgot," Dema cried out. "I cannot hear the engine over the rumbling of my stomach!"

"Same here," Mason bent over when Dema said it, holding his guts. "On the bright side, this is a good diet. I promise we'll treat ourselves once we reach the final zone. Do you need the map?"

"Yes, I do." Dema smiled to herself. "Thank you for helping me back there."

"Anytime." Mason slid down next to Dema and opened August's map as she turned off the engine.

The massive rocks on their left provided them with cover, while to their right, the steep hills assured them that nobody could surprise them.

"How are you feeling?" Dema looked at Mason, who folded the map.

"I don't know how I feel as my senses or moral compass have been completely shattered. My heart wants to weep for TH, but my mind pushes me forward. Am I broken?" Mason leaned his head on Dema's right shoulder. "It feels like I am in a tunnel. The light at the end is in front of me, but I don't see anything else. Nothing else matters at this point. Just that light at the end."

"You couldn't describe it better. That is exactly how I feel. Just tunnel vision all the way." Dema looked at Mason and smiled.

"But how do we know if that light is the end or the approaching train, ready to push us deeper into it, away from the light we are marching towards?"

"Well, the only way to find out is to go forward." Dema turned on the engine. "Keep an eye out for me, Commander."

"Will do!" Mason nodded, and a moment later he peeked out from his cupola, observing the everlasting emptiness around them.

———

"It seems like our crews are slowly but surely making their way to the last area, and I have to say, it doesn't look bright at all. Speaking of them, are the winners receiving anything else apart from the money?" Adriana turned towards Benjamin, who played with his thumbs, awaiting some action.

While she smiled at the camera, her stomach revolved with every passing minute, playing pretend for the artificial intelligence.

"We went big this year since this is the greatest show ever to grace television. When the winner is declared, we give them this cup." Benjamin swiped left on the screen, and a strange contraption appeared.

Two roller wheels, packed in the track and on the top, seemed to be a commander's cupola with a short barrel attached.

"Also, they get this." Benjamin swiped left once more, and a World War Two style gorget appeared, bearing the Tank Royale 2145 Winner title. "I think the winners are properly sent away for their vacation before they are called back. They always are."

"Unless they aren't," Adriana said to her sleeve as Benjamin shook his head. "Where would they go on vacation anyway?"

"Dema, keep your eyes peeled; I don't like this place," Mason said as the Crusading Angel rolled into a small village after another three hours of a silent drive.

"Can't see much, but I will try!" the response came a moment later.

"I do not like this either." Mason halted himself before

opening his hatch fully, but, looking through the vision slits, his heart stopped beating as a massive machine rolled into view with a white inscription painted on the side *Beast Slayer*.

Looking like a green box on tracks with the large howitzer up front, Dema slammed hard on the brakes, and just before the massive tank could lay its gun on them, Crusading Angel vanished behind the row of buildings, allowing both Dema and Mason to catch a breath. The ground shook as the tank fired, and Mason observed one of the houses crumble, filling his surroundings with thick smoke. He thought: *Careful there. Don't rush; we're close!*

"That was wow! What the hell was that?!" Dema climbed to the loader's position and found Mason staring at something through the vision slits. "Mason!"

"Dema," Mason closed his eyes and said in a shivering voice, "tank in front."

Dema's heart stopped pounding as she looked through the loader's periscope and found the German tank hiding behind one of the houses. Their barrel was set on the Crusading Angel, and the menacing muzzle brake made Dema and Mason do a sign of the cross simultaneously. Life flashed before Dema's eyes, seeing her actions from the first steps to post-apocalyptic wandering to meeting Mason and the rest of the band, leading into the future. Then, slowly, her heart began beating again as a man emerged from the cupola and waved at the T-34. The menacing muzzle brake soon vanished as the turret turned around hundred and eighty degrees. Mason pressed his forehead against the gunsight, and his foot felt itchy momentarily. He pinched himself. *They could have taken us out, but didn't. The least I can do is turn the turret to the rear.* As he thought this, Mason's left hand found the fly-drive wheel and began cranking the turret away.

———

"Did it just throw a track?" Benjamin looked at the screen where three humanoids jumped out of the metal box on tracks and began servicing the heavy-tank destroyer.

"But the main gun is still operational, and trust me, in testing, nothing could stop it. It sent rivets flying, and two of our demolition experts were severely injured as the fragments from the tougher armor found their mark." Thomas felt shivers on his spine as the memories hit in full force. "It is called a beast killer or slayer for a reason—the ISU-152. I'm confident that it can even stand against modern tanks, and this design is two hundred years old. This package comes with three shells just for this occasion. High-explosive, long-range concrete piercing, and we threw in there a semi-armor piercing just for fun."

"Isn't that a bit of overkill?" Jeong-Min leaned forward. "Concrete piercing?"

"Well, if you want to send someone out with a bang, this is the machine to do it." Thomas smiled but then covered his ears when the ISU-152 fired, tearing the speakers to pieces. "I think we'll need a sound guy."

"All set to decide the last two contestants for the final fight. Two tanks in the village and the other two playing peeka-boo."

"And on top of that, P.108 A, the Italian gunship, had set its sights on the Germans and Russians. It is in their best interest to work together, but hey, let us see." Adriana tapped the screen. "This thing was originally designed to sink merchant ships, so it should have a field day against the tanks. But hey, someone might shoot it down because it is pretty slow."

"I think they'll work together," Jeong-Min looked at the screen, where Mason climbed down from the tank and folded his hands. "It seems like that for the Beast Slayer; someone will take the hit with a freaking anti-concrete round that will liquify them, while the other gets the kill shot. Unless they whiff it."

"Makes for interesting television for sure. And then, well, the final zone, and we're getting out of here." Adriana sank into her chair. "I want to go home. It's nice, but I miss home."

"I can only guarantee that we'll not fire at each other until that ISU is destroyed. After that, I'm not making any promises." Klemens extended his hand, waiting for Mason to decide, "It's the best deal you, hmm, we get in this scenario. There is also that big plane ready to take us out."

"Why didn't you shoot us when you had a chance?" Dema moved forward, holding a wrench.

"Love, taking on that thing alone is suicide, but two have a fighting chance, and this late in the game," Klemens's eyes began to twitch as Mason thought about it, "there aren't many choices left. The final ring won't open until two remain, and conveniently, we two are here, and somewhere else, my former colleague is about to take it up with someone."

"Why won't we just wait you out?" Mason flipped TH's coin between his fingers, and Klemens laughed.

"I would do the same, but I bet they have something to force us out on the open field, like that plane. Mason, you or I don't stand a chance alone. Sooner or later, something will hunt us down."

"All right," Mason shook hands, "so what now?"

"Now we need to bait the beast to fire, and one of us will get it while it reloads. The question is, who will be the bait?" Klemens looked at his crew. "There are only two of you?"

"Maybe we have a third one aiming at you right now," Mason felt the tension rising, but then the ground began to rumble as a massive four-engine plane flew by.

Painted black with an Italian flag on the rudder, it commanded fear as it slowly turned around. Time seemed to stop, but after another flyover, Mason realized that the plane didn't have bombs; instead, it mounted a massive cannon underneath the cockpit. Klemens's tank backed into the alley, covered by the shadows of the houses, leaving a dark green tank with an exposed crew clinging to the side of the ruined house.

"Mason, orders?" Dema had already turned on the engine when Mason plugged in his helmet.

"I have never shot down an airplane in my life." Mason looked around the turret, but then a loud bang, followed by the crumbling building, reminded him of another problem. "Dema, we're engaging the tank first."

"Look at this, Mason." Dema climbed to the loader's position and tapped Mason on his shoulder as she placed the map over the breech. "Did you ever hear the story about a dragon guarding its treasure and a knight set out on the quest to claim it?"

"Yes, I heard, but how does it connect to here?" Mason watched the massive four-engine plane flying over, attempting to reacquire the target.

"It turns out that there is no depot in the final zone, but right here. The problem is that the beast is guarding it, and there are two knights."

"God damn it!" Mason opened his hatch and focused on where Panzer 4 parked, and his fears were confirmed. "It seems like they also figured it out."

"Orders?" Dema looked up when thunder echoed between the houses.

"That is our cue to go. Dema, pedal to the metal!" Mason grabbed one of the shells from the storage and squeezed it between his legs, attempting to save time reloading the cannon.

Mason held himself when the T-34 launched forward towards the street. Turning right, Mason laid the gun on the tank destroyer, and as he was about to pull the trigger, a pothole rocked the almost stable cannon, sending the shot flying above the roof of the ISU. The heavy machine gun mounted on the top barked bullets toward the Panzer 4, whose barrel poked out. Seeing sparks flying as the shell bounced off the ISU's gun mantlet reminded Mason of sparklers on New Year's Eve. He slid out of his seat, grabbed the shell from between his legs, and rammed it into the breech, as Dema hid the tank behind a pile of rubble.

Sitting back in his seat, Mason flipped the switch and pressed the trigger on the coaxial machine gun, sending lead into the smoke, looking for the potential sparks that would give away the position. Then, with his heart racing, Mason leaned his face against the periscope, frantically scanning the battlefield for the German tank and the tank destroyer.

"Mason, I don't see them!" Dema screamed, but Mason could only watch as his hands froze on the fly-drive wheels.

For a moment, Mason could observe the massive shell heading toward his tank and closed his eyes as the shell exploded behind the Crusading Angel, its shockwave almost slamming the T-34 into the nearby building. Mason pressed his hand against his left ear and felt warm blood. After sending a few more rounds into the smoke, he observed several sparks. Immediately, he switched back to the main gun and fired into the smoke.

"Dema!" Mason quickly slid into the co-driver seat, and Dema pressed her palms against her ears, trying to hold back tears.

By her moving lips, Mason realized that she was screaming but couldn't hear what exactly as ringing in his ears continued. Climbing back to the loader's position, Mason grabbed the shell with shaking hands, but dropped it. *Come on, pull yourself together!* Mason stopped the rolling casing with his foot, and after another attempt, he shoved it into the breech. As he leaned against the gunsight, Mason had to blink and hold his head, screaming in pain.

Mason leaned back, covered his ears, and looked down at his legs, where the spall shattered his uniform and skin. Then, biting his tongue, Mason pressed his face against the gunsight and found the target. The German tank rammed the ISU at full speed like a bull charging the torero. The last thing Mason saw through the gunsight was the giant explosion, sending the

Panzer 4 turret into the air and splitting the tank's hull into several pieces. The howitzer was out of action, and the barrel split open like a bouquet of flowers. Moments later, androids swarmed out, assessing the damage, but were mowed down by the coaxial machine gun from the Crusading Angel. Mason pulled his foot all the way down, sending the shell toward the ammunition storage. Time stopped, and Mason believed that he had missed. Then, like fireworks on the Fourth of July, Beast Slayer exploded to pieces, engulfing its humanoid crew in the blazing inferno with cooked ammunition flying everywhere. Mason looked away, closing his eyes in the process. He took a deep breath and slowly exhaled.

"Mason!" Dema's voice forced its way into Mason's ears, and when he looked to his right, he found Dema slowly breathing, holding her chest.

"Dema, are you all right?" Mason took her hand into his as she finally let the tears flow, watering the cannon's breech.

"I am ready to get out of here!" Dema shouted. "What about the plane!"

"Could you repeat that?" Mason leaned back. "My left ear! It's constantly humming. I can still hear with my right one. Now, we can talk once we park in that depot, which should be somewhere around here."

"Can you drive?" Dema climbed into the co-driver's seat and slowly exhaled.

"Sure!" Mason bit his tongue when he felt a thousand needles piercing his skin. "Gear lever neutral. Foot on the brake. Accelerator halfway up. Hold the clutch and brake simultaneously as you press the starter."

For a moment, the engine roared but immediately cut off. The second try yielded the same result. Finally, after the third try, Mason's blood began to boil.

"Why won't you work?! Help is right there! We did everything together. Cross the desert and steppe, fought in the city, witnessed two of our friends die, and you do not want to make the finish line! Why?"

"Mason, I think I have an idea." Dema looked away as Mason punched the frontal plate. "Take a deep breath."

"No deep breaths. The Depot is right there, so pull your shit together!" Mason repeated the starting sequence, but nothing.

"Try the air start."

"Done already, not working. We're so close to winning here. Only one enemy tank remains, and then we will win our crusade. Come on!"

"Where to start? You throw a track, your fuel tanks are pierced, and your oil is gone. Also, add a dead battery and three missing road wheels. Good thing that you crashed right next to us," a familiar voice called out from outside, and a moment later, Thomas peeked inside the tank and shook his head. "Wow, you two look like crap."

Dema and Mason widened their eyebrows when a man they only saw on television poked inside through the driver's hatch and smiled. Then, for a moment, their hearts stopped beating.

"Well, you weren't in the trenches for the past; I don't even know how many days," Dema said and closed her eyes from the pain.

"That is true, but I'll need both of you to get out so we can service your tank, somewhat patch you up, so you can be on your way. Hey, are you all right?" Thomas looked at Mason.

"His left ear is out of action, and so is our tank. Does this mean that we are out?"

"No, the rules say that you are out of the game the moment crew count drops below two, and if I can still count, I see two tankers in front of me. The damage I see is also not beyond repairable. You're in luck, both of you."

"But what about beyond repair?" Mason said, but Thomas climbed the tank, opened the commander's hatch, and slid inside.

"That is the second, not the well-defined rule. We'll patch you up." Thomas stepped aside as two androids attached the towing cables to the hooks up front, awaiting Thomas's command, while the two trucks pulled up closer, pushing away the wreckage of the German crew.

"Where is the depot? And that giant plane?" Dema lay on the ground next to Mason.

"There is no depot. We'll service you here, and that's it. I'm sorry for your loss." Thomas stepped aside as the team of androids got to work. "Concerning the gunship, the Beast Killer was enough."

———

"What a fight this has been! Unfortunately, we're in intermission because both tanks need serious maintenance, and action will resume soon. After a commercial break, we shall be back with a recap of the entire deployment, from landing to all the way here!" Benjamin waved at the camera, and the red light vanished.

"You're right; what a fight. We're so close to the finish line! Well, we're on it, pretty much," Jeong-Min smiled at the camera, ensuring that any lag in the broadcast wouldn't give him away.

"And it is not over yet. I wasn't expecting these two to rise, but," Benjamin looked around, "their favorites went out in the blaze of glory!"

"With Xiu, we got five survivors, one of which, the Argentinian guy, is in critical condition. So, who is your final choice?"

"Tough choice," Jeong-Min scratched the back of his head, "Crusading Angel it is. Did we have to get rid of those depots?"

"Not my idea. I was all for it during the pre-production, but it got shut down immediately. Glorified lure, nothing more, nothing less."

———

Just as Mason and Dema finished sharing the last ration pack an hour later, Thomas whistled at them, holding two energy drinks. His android crew had packed their tools and awaited Thomas at the trucks.

"I have good news and bad news. The good news is that your tank is ready to go, filled to the fullest with ammunition. The bad news is that you're not out of the woods yet. There is one more opponent to face. Drink this, and good luck to you. I'll see you soon, hopefully."

Thomas walked up to the Crusading Angel and slowly exhaled, tapping the mudguard.

"You gave me the biggest headache out of all your kin. Do not disappoint me, Crusading Angel. I have money riding on you, and I want to see a return on my investment. Do you understand?" Thomas walked around the beat-up tank as he spoke. "Good that we understand each other. God damn!"

"What was the trouble?" Mason tried his luck as Thomas was about to climb into the cabin of the leading eight-wheeler.

"Find out when you win, gasoline cowboy," Thomas grinned from ear to ear, "good luck!"

Mason gave Dema a helping hand with the bags, and moments later, the V-12 roared to life as the T-34 rode out into the sunset.

Passing by the two wrecks, Crusading Angel stopped for a moment. Mason opened his hatch and saluted the fallen. *Why can't this nightmare be over already? Why Lord!? Is this a part of your plan for me?*

"What is the feeling?" Dema said when Mason sat beside her, pressing his forehead against the sloped armor plate. "You can tell me. What is it?"

"That my nightmare is about to come true." Mason turned on the radio, flipping the frequencies knob. "Well, two nightmares, knowing the fact that we have a full ammunition load. One shot below my feet and we're done."

"Well, they have to ensure the fireworks for the winner."

CHAPTER NINETEEN

VILLERS-BRETONNEUX

"So, this is it," Jeong-Min said in Korean, looking at the screen when the broadcasting went for the commercial break for the day as his co-hosts were already in the food tent, eating dinner.

"This is it?" one of the interns walked by. "Are you leaving, Sir? There are quite a few things to do in the post-production!"

"No, I meant the showdown." Jeong-Min looked at her and smiled. "Two of the most skilled or the luckiest contestants are about to clash. You know that if you told me twenty years ago that I would sit in Mongolia, co-hosting a Battle Royale game, I would laugh at your apparent lunacy. Times are changing fast, I guess."

"Oh." Intern raised her eyebrows. "Okay. I don't know what to say."

"To answer your previous question, this is my last broadcast. After this ends, I'll immediately board the plane to South Korea. Family matters."

"I understand," the woman smiled, "so will your favorite win?"

"I hope so, but I don't know what to think about these games the longer I stay here." Jeong-Min leaned back in his chair. "This is right on edge, where the excitement ends, and an actual war begins."

"With all due respect, I can assume that this loss is much

smaller than the standard Royale, where one out of a hundred survives, but I feel your pain. I prefer the simulations, but emotions in this line of work are not helpful."

"Well, people demand games and bread, Orion listens, and TVG gives," Jeong-Min scratched his chin, "it hurts my soul when I see a good potential being wasted."

"Or maybe utilized? I think we can sit here and discuss the Battle Royale and its impact on our culture, but they are here to stay. Maybe if we lobby for more simulation matches, we can save a life or a hundred. You have way more influence than I do."

"So, this is a call to action, then. I shall see what I can do." Jeong-Min shook hands and was about to leave when the young woman hugged him.

"I just wanted to say thank you for talking to us after the earthquake. It was a shaky experience."

Even stoic Min grinned upon hearing the shaky experience line.

"You'll go far, my child. Remember, a good and authentic nature will get you far in life. Anywhere really. Keep it up."

———

As the sun was about to descend behind the horizon, Dema steered the Angel towards the entrance to the final zone. Mason slowly opened his hatch and scanned the surroundings with binoculars. The house, gate, nearby bushes, and bridge were copies of the last entrance without a massive gun platform overlooking the crossing. It was all eerily quiet, and Mason thought to himself. *It feels like we are late to the party.*

"Dema, I think we're clear to go—pedal to the metal! Let us cross the barrier, and we should be safe!" Mason closed the hatch and slowly exhaled.

As Mason said it, Angel rocked and advanced, slowly picking up speed, and a moment later, they found themselves on the bridge. Mason scanned the surroundings once they entered the final ring and screamed when he heard an explosion behind, almost flying out of the hatch when Dema slammed on the brakes.

"Mason, what happened?"

"The bridge just exploded." Mason took three deep breaths before replying, observing the remnants of the bridge collapse onto itself.

"So, that was the point of no return. If I remember from the map, another village should be behind this hill. The question is, where do we want to spend the night? There is a wide selection of houses to choose from. Also, they didn't fix the radio,"

"All right, park on that hill for a moment so we can get a detailed look before we descend into the pit," Mason pulled out his cracked binoculars and scanned his surroundings, "I don't think we'll be sleeping tonight. This is it, Dema. Our future will be decided tonight."

"Why did I even ask? Will do!"

Moments later, when Dema parked the Crusading Angel on the hill, the sunlight showed Mason everything he needed to know. On top of the massive cliff, and with binoculars, he could make out individuals with what seemed to be high-magnification cameras and a few drones hovering over them. The ridge continued to his left and right, forming a protective circle around the village with enough steep slopes to prevent them from climbing out once in.

"Good evening, and I am glad that you could join us. This is a recorded message; there is no need to reply." A blue hologram walked up to the tank and invited Mason and Dema to join him. "First, congratulations on making it to the final zone. We are thrilled to see the best make it to the finals! The village you are looking at is Villers-Bretonneux, the final battlefield of Tank Royale of 2145. On April 24th, 1918, three

British tanks clashed with three German war machines, marking a page in the historical documents of the first tank-on-tank engagement, so it is more than fitting to conclude this spectacular venture here. Once your opponent arrives, look for the blue beams, officially launching the final battle. Only two of you will be in this pit, but additional vehicles are on standby if needed. There won't be any close air support, only tank-on-tank combat! When you win, leave your tank and follow the green smoke, which marks the exfil zone. There are two billion viewers and counting cheering for you, so no pressure. This is the end of the message; get ready to go!" The hologram saluted and vanished right before them.

"Mason! The Museum Curator mentioned this!" Dema covered her mouth. "It's kind of poetic."

"And just like that, we're at the end. The question is, do we stay here waiting for the blue beam or drive down?" Mason gave Dema a hand, and a moment later, she lay against the turret.

Mason watched Dema reaching out for the evening clouds, only to retract her shaking arm as Mason slid beside her.

"So, we made it."

"In a kind of messed up way, I want to stay here just a bit longer." Dema turned towards Mason.

"I understand," Mason took a deep breath, "and I kind of feel the same way."

"Let us wait just a bit longer." Dema took a deep breath. "Whom do you think we will be fighting?"

"I hope it is not Gio and his surviving squad." Mason placed his head on Dema's right shoulder. "It is a nice sunset, not going to lie. Mere words cannot describe it."

Dema and Mason stared at the horizon momentarily, observing the last light before it gave way to darkness.

"My jacket is torn to pieces, so I'm not even trying to think about what will happen the moment the sun vanishes." Mason felt shivers on his spine. "Where is yours?"

"Oh, you are right, that..." Dema froze. "Mason, we have a problem."

"What is it?" Mason stood up and almost cried out when he noticed two blue beams illuminating the evening sky as the last light vanished behind the horizon and night claimed the throne.

"Orders?" Dema also stood up. "I think it's time to go."

"No need to prolong this any longer! Let's get this done!" Mason waited for Dema to enter, looking over his shoulder again, trying to identify the potential opponents, but the darkness began to settle in the arena with a first flare launching into the night.

Okay, Mason, this is it! The final! You either leave in the body bag or as a free man.

—— —— ——

Only the moonlight illuminated the dark street as Crusading Angel pulled into the village. Mason's need to stay vigilant overrode the need to find a dry place. Passing by another cafe with demolished tables, tossed chairs, and cracked pottery, Mason felt Angel crushing something underneath its tracks.

"This is scary! Can we not go there?" Mason heard Dema's shivering voice in the internal comms.

"Come on, Dema! You survived the Dark Zone! And we, of all people, we made it here. Why are we going so slow?" Mason could see a snail passing them in the darkness and shook his head again.

"Mason, I am not going anywhere." As Dema said this, Mason held himself as the T-34 came to a complete halt, and moments later silence descended on the dark street.

"Dema, we need to move." Mason nervously squeezed the

handle of the horizontal drive flywheel.

"Nobody else is moving except us. Just listen," Dema responded, and Mason looked around him, gently opening the hatch.

It was too quiet even for Mason's liking, as his heart began beating faster and faster. Doing a quick 360-degree scan, Mason slid back to his turret controls and turned off the turret light, engulfing them in total darkness. The inside red light, mixed with the light from two flashlights, reminded Mason of a camping trip with his brother, but he shook his head, trying not to think about the past.

"We are giving our position away, and on top of that, transmission is acting up again. Like us, this is the end of the line, and our tank, while good, is having trouble responding to my commands. On top of that, I can see the shredded plate in front of me, just waiting to pierce my heart with fragments or spall, or however it is called." Mason heard Dema breathing slowly in the intercom. "Thomas, or whatever his name was, only made sure that the tank could run, nothing more, nothing less."

"Not just that. I'm standing on the full ammo load. All right, let's park somewhere for a moment, then we'll talk. I feel that someone is watching us." Mason held himself as Dema backed into the tailor's shop and shut off the engine.

Making sure he didn't hit his head on the gun breech, Mason slid into the co-driver seat and looked at Dema, who stared outside the driver's hatch, not realizing Mason had joined her.

"Dema?" Mason gently tapped Dema's shaking shoulders.

"The entire world is watching us," Dema nervously laughed, but Mason noticed her shaking hands, squeezing the brake handles.

"Spit it out." Mason took a deep breath.

"I had never imagined that I would come to this point. Any mistake I make tonight or tomorrow can cost us the tank and, worse, mine or your life, and bearing that thought keeps crushing me. How do you feel?" Dema looked at red-faced Mason and noticed his right eye twitching.

"I don't have any words of comfort to tell myself or you, and I don't think prayers will help here. I feel like God has decided to sit this one out. We got this far, and so did the other team, whoever that is."

"Can we at least try to pray?"

"Sure." Mason reached into one of the pockets of his uniform and pulled out the rosary.

With reverence, Dema took the wooden cross into her hands while Mason held onto the beads.

"Dear God, if you are listening to us, please allow us to see us tomorrow," Dema opened the prayer. "Heavenly Father, you have protected us this far; shield us just a bit longer. Mason?"

"Mary and all the saints, please, offer this prayer to God, so he may answer it and see if it's just. Allow the souls of the fallen that came before us to enter heaven and sit by your side. Consider adding humanoids to the list of the chosen ones as well."

A light giggle and a short grin appeared on Dema's face.

"So, help us, God!" Mason made a sign of the cross while Dema gently kissed the wooden cross and returned it to Mason's hands.

The temporary peace that settled in Mason's soul immediately vanished as Dema squeezed the brake handles and looked before her.

"Mason, I feel that we will be facing Gio and his squad. Must be them!" Dema cried out. "There is no other way!"

"We don't know that yet." Mason felt his stomach revolting. "We have to work with our cards." Mason tapped the hull-mounted machine gun.

"What are you trying to say? Again, we will have to kill them, or they will kill us, and this time you have to be the first to pull the trigger! On our friends!"

"I know!" Mason realized he was about to start screaming at the shell-shocked Dema.

How did we make it? Through blood, mud, and steel, but was it worth it? Dema has to be right; Gio and his crew made it like he knew that this would happen! He said it at the airport! God, did you really decide to sit this one out? Please tell me that you didn't!

When Mason climbed back into the Crusading Angel ten minutes later, Dema handed him a water bottle wrapped in a canvas cover. Then, after a moment of silence for Van and TH, Dema turned on the engine and slowly rolled the Crusading Angel from the coffee shop. The rain had also stopped falling, and Mason opened both hatches for better ventilation.

The breath of fresh air brought a needed strength as Mason felt he was coming alive again, his heart beating steadily, and when he held onto the cupola, his hands didn't shake. He closed his hatch behind him and ensured under the flashlight that all boxes were opened, and ammunition was at hand.

What was in that energy drink? It's not helping! I am still tired. Mason remembered Thomas's drink and shrugged his shoulders. He heard Dema's voice as he scanned his surroundings through the vision slits.

"Look in front of you; something just drove down from the sidewalk, and it is about to cross the street." Dema shook her head, forcing herself not to fall asleep. "Why did he call it an energy drink? It tasted like water."

Mason opened the hatch, and his eyes focused on the small, tracked object crossing the street. Partially concealed by night, Mason made out a black cable trolling behind it. Mason tapped his ears, feeling the hearing somewhat return.

"We saw it in the Tank Museum! Goliath, the tracked mine?" Dema's sudden remembrance prompted Mason to make a sign of the cross.

"Oh, God, you're right! How much explosive did it have? Two hundred pounds of the high explosive ordinance?" Mason took a deep breath. "Dema, forward and park behind that pile of rubble. That should give us a clear shot, after which I'll need you to drive behind that building on the other side of the crossroads."

"Understood!"

"Dema, we got this!"

"Yes, we got this!" Dema responded. "We got this!"

Going three miles per hour, Mason could lay the gun on the Goliath, but after thinking, he switched to the coaxial machine gun and pressed the trigger. Both could see the tracer rounds hitting the Goliat's track briefly, sending it into a spin, but no explosion followed.

"What now?"

"Watch, Dema," Mason said, awaiting whoever held the controls.

Sure enough, a few nail-biting seconds later, three individuals dressed in black uniforms rushed out, holding repair tools, but froze the moment they got to the open as they looked around for the shooter.

Hiding behind the corner of the building, the perfect line of fire presented itself as he flipped the switch, engaging the co-axial machine gun.

"Nice to meet you!" Mason pressed the foot trigger, sending rounds down the streets, and moments later all three individuals lay in a pool of blood.

After a few more empty clicks, Mason opened his hatch and smiled.

"Mason, are you thinking what I am thinking?" Dema's voice echoed in Mason's head.

"No, what are you thinking?" Mason poked out of his hatch again, trying to examine his surroundings. "Dema, I need your help out here!"

"One moment," Dema said from below, and after a silent grunting and pounding, Dema's head poked out of the loader's hatch. "Yes?"

"Is there something in front of us?" Mason pointed into

the darkness, which engulfed the street in front of them.

After a few moments of silence, Dema was about to return to her position when whistling white flares illuminated the moonless sky, and Mason's heart stopped beating. An enormous tank destroyer blocked the road in front of them, approximately a hundred yards away.

With her eyes wide open as the flares slowly descended, and darkness again took over the battlefield, Dema could only say, "That is a big ass!"

"I would never have imagined you saying that," Mason laughed with visible terror in his eyes, "but I can see the guy with a machine gun guarding the rear. We need to circumnavigate his position and kill it."

"Or we don't have to," Dema pointed at three more Goliaths slowly driving from their cover, closing in on the tank destroyer's location.

"And with that, we'll take a short break, but don't worry, the battlefield camera is still on." Benjamin smiled, and when he received the signal from the cameraman, he turned towards Thomas.

"What is the matter?" Thomas looked around him, but Benjamin tapped the table twice before continuing.

"A tracked mine will level the odds and make this fairer. This should be about them, not them against something else," Benjamin gulped when he spoke.

"You mean three, right?" Thomas pointed at the screen with the live footage.

"Indeed," Benjamin smiled, "let's observe these little Goliaths going to work."

"Rather a big name for such a small machine, but then again, Maus exists, so I'm not even surprised." Thomas closed his eyes as the tracked mines pressed onward.

On the screen, the man with the machine gun shouted and opened fire just as the flares relaunched. The street was too narrow for a 72-tonne war machine to turn in time. Benjamin bit his thumb as a massive explosion rocked the place, turning damaged houses into ruins, while the fire from the blast continued jumping from rooftop to rooftop.

Seeing the massive shockwave from the black, Dema closed her eyes and held herself but pressed into her seat like a roller-coaster was about to dive. After a moment of defining silence, Dema blinked her red eyes.

"Almost went deaf, but holy moly, that was glorious. They fired beforehand, meaning we were close to either Gio or another tank. Which one, I have no idea." Dema took a deep breath as she felt all her organs returning to their original places.

"What did you say? My hearing is not fully back yet," Mason said as he flipped the switches, turning off the coaxial machine gun and the turret-mounted headlight.

Mason slid underneath the breech and ejected the empty magazine from the machine gun. A quick look around the turret for a spare didn't yield any results, including looking at the co-driver's position.

Mason climbed back into his position, scanned the surroundings for potential targets, and froze when he heard an engine sound nearby.

Through the ruined house to his left, Mason noticed a tank silhouette, and moments later, the Da Vinci drove by, barely illuminated by the burning wreck and flashing lamp posts.

"Dema, do not move," Mason whispered, and Dema froze in her tracks as the Da Vince rolled out from behind and drove right up to them.

Da Vince drove by without noticing another tank hiding in the shadows next to them. Mason pressed his face against the vision slits on his commander's cupola and watched Gio appear momentarily, scanning the surroundings. Finally, Mason could see Gio's tired face when he leaned on the roof-mounted machine gun, covered by blood, dust, oil, and debris. Mason slowly sat in his gunner's chair, looked through the gunsight, and gently put his foot on the trigger. Gio took one last look, closed the hatch behind him, and a moment later, the only memory was a cloud of dust sailing away in the cold wind.

"Who was it?" Dema was first to break the silence. "Mason?"

"Giovanni Smith and his Da Vinci, Dema." It took a moment for Mason to reply. "It's them! God almighty!"

"Are you sure?" Dema covered her head. "I knew it! "

"They look like crap."

"You look like crap, as well." Dema leaned over the breech, "I do not think that you finding a mirror right now is a good idea. I can almost see the gray hair underneath your helmet." Dema placed her palm over Mason's sweaty forehead.

"I would like to return a compliment as well. You look like crap, too. Not a good idea to be looking into the mirror at this time."

"Haha. When will this nightmare end?"

"I was so close to ending it, but I couldn't! The ship had sailed, and now, I have put us in danger. Don't tell me that there is another tank nearby." Mason punched the breech when he heard another tank engine.

"There is no way that they will miss us. So, you have to take the shot, no matter who that is." Dema grabbed the loader's periscope. "Mason, please do not hesitate next time because Gio will not."

"Are you sure?"

"He got this far, and we must assume that our platoon is as good as dead. No safety," Dema said between her teeth. "Yes, I am sure he will not hesitate to pull the trigger."

"Your intuition was right, so I'll take your word for it. If we could win without spilling blood."

"Mason, that is wishful thinking, and you know that.

There can only be one tank left standing, not two."

"I tried, oh God, I tried!"

"Hey, where is Adriana?" Benjamin waved at Thomas, who sat beside him and looked at the final zone below, illuminated by new flares hanging in the air like cotton watts.

The cameras were rolling, showing the action as the rest of the staff started packing up, and the first crates were already stored in the Galaxy.

"She didn't feel well, so she called it a night. Where is our tanker?"

"He is on an urgent call, didn't elaborate. From my intuition, it sounded more like a family matter."

"That is fair. Beer?" Thomas handed Benjamin a bottle, but he refused.

"I wonder why they didn't fire at them. Team 28 could have won, but...."

"Well, it is pretty hard to shoot at your former platoon colleagues. Why did we decide to do platoons in the first place?" Thomas decided to continue to pretend as cameras continued rolling, and Benjamin understood.

"Because drama, nothing more, nothing less."

"TVG will milk this Tank Royale to the teeth, and then they'll move on. It's like a parasite. Do you think that this Tank Royale should have been virtual?" Thomas tapped the beer bottle. "Are you sure you don't want one? Wasted on the live broadcast? Or you'll drink once the winner is crowned?"

"I won't drink either way, but thank you for trying."

"I don't want to alarm anyone, but that fire from the Jagdtiger is spreading." Thomas pointed into the distance, where the fire began jumping from house to house.

"I was on a call with TVG representatives, and they told me to keep the fire burning. Adds to the drama." Benjamin stood up and stretched his legs. "No more commentary until the winner is decided."

"But that might compromise the winner! We need to put

out that fire immediately."

"Thomas, the sooner they end this, the sooner they get home. TVG will ensure that the winner will be safely extracted." Benjamin knew that Thomas was not buying it. "That Jagdtiger was a start."

"Well, that somewhat helps. But it doesn't change the fact that a third tank is on the prowl. This was supposed to be a one-on-one duel." Thomas stood up. "I need to go and talk with the surviving tankers."

Thomas waved and vanished into one of the tents as Benjamin's eyes laid on the uncrewed recovery hover vehicle, prepped by the crew.

———

Dema carefully drove through the streets using only the weaker headlights, navigated by Mason and his trusty wrench. Two hits on the side of the turret meant a halt, while one meant to go. He used the full moon, which finally decided to leave its blanket of clouds and the slowly spreading fire, to see ahead with occasional flares launching against the night sky. As she steered right, a shell out of nowhere ricocheted off the tank's side, sending it upward. Dema slammed hard on the brakes, but the follow-up shot nailed the Crusading Angel from the rear just as Mason got seated and began cranking the horizontal drive flywheel.

"Dema, stop!" Mason shouted and immediately held himself as Crusading Angel abruptly halted.

He took a deep breath, laid the gun on the crossroads, and waited for the tank to appear. Seconds went by, and Mason took a deep breath as the light from the moon and flares dropped rapidly due to the black smoke covering the narrow streets.

"Turn off the engine, Dema!" Mason ordered, and a moment later, he could hear the engine of the other tank fading to the rear.

Mason shook his head and immediately began cranking the turret as he heard the enemy tank steer left.

"Dema, grab the shell and get ready to load the gun!" Mason said and pressed the foot trigger, sending the round down the street as the low-riding tank appeared.

Ventilating, Dema quickly opened the breech, ejected the empty casing, and rammed in a new shell.

"Up!" Dema shouted, catching her breath.

Two seconds later, both Mason and the enemy tank fired simultaneously.

Mason sent the turret of the enemy tank sky-high in a blaze of glory while the shot from the enemy tank nailed the Crusading Angel once more, setting it ablaze. The shell sent vibrations around the tank, prompting Mason and Dema to cover their ears and scream.

"Dema, we've got a problem," Mason coughed as he scrambled for the fire extinguisher.

As the smoke made its way into the turret, Mason finally found it, and a moment later, he put out the fire. Mason opened the hatch and sprayed his surroundings with white foam, putting out all the fires. Then, he quickly shut the hatch behind him and tossed the fire extinguisher on the ground.

"I think we're going to stay here for a while." Dema dried her tears. "That was quick thinking on your part. I almost gave up!"

"Dema, it's all right," Mason said, opening his hatch in the process. "Let's make the best of this situation. One down, one to go."

"Can we identify the tank?" Dema swung the periscope around but failed to find the burning wreck as it got stuck in the alleyway.

"I don't want to risk it."

"I am right behind you," Dema tapped Mason's right shoulder, "I am right there!"

———

While Dema continued talking to herself, Mason turned on the flashlight and quietly climbed out of the tank. Then, crouching, he got to the rear of the Crusading Angel. He readied his fire extinguisher and sprayed the back. Not daring to peek out, Mason sat on the ground and leaned against what used to be a kitchen wall. Dema carefully climbed down a few minutes later, and Mason got on his feet. Upon ensuring no tank was in sight, Mason first looked at the large smoking hole in the rear and the right side.

After Mason held the flashlight in his teeth, he and Dema pried the rounded rear access port open after a silent curse and grunting; a disintegrated transmission greeted them.

Dema looked at Mason, who began pounding the side of the tank with a wrench.

"Mason, that will not help the situation; you only attract unwanted attention." Dema grabbed Mason's hand.

"We're so screwed! Why did we get hit where we needed it the most!" Mason dropped the wrench to the ground and threw his hands in the air.

"What is done is done, but let us work with what we got; you said it yourself. We got stuck at the crossroads, which is good, right?" Dema looked at the three streets converging at their location.

"That is true." Mason took four long breaths. "I don't even feel I know myself. I want this to be over!"

Mason collected himself, straightened his back, and assessed the situation. "The turret is hand-cranked, so the loss of electricity will not affect us as much. So why do I get a feeling that this will get decided right here?"

"Doesn't have to," Dema said and climbed onto the engine deck of the Crusading Angel. "I think we can still fix it. We have the manual, right?"

"I don't know, Dema." Mason tapped the large hole and blinked. "What time is it?"

"Can you believe that we have only been here for an hour?"

Dema shook her head, "It's eight twenty-five."

"Oh wow." Mason stepped back and unintentionally flipped the coin between his fingers. "I wonder..."

———

The loud shouts from the medical tent prompted Thomas to run inside and find beeping machines. The field doctor exhaled and removed his surgical mask. Thomas looked away when Adriana ran inside the medical tent.

"I'm sorry to say, but contestant Toli Garcia died as the backup generators failed to keep him alive." The doctor tapped Thomas's shoulder. "If I were you, I would notify his family before the official numbers come out."

"Thomas, the third tank is knocked out, leaving only Crusading Angel and Da Vinci close to each other once more!" Benjamin shouted from outside. "And they're converging on each other!"

"I'm on my way!" Thomas nodded, and the doctor folded his arms. "What?"

"Also, tell it to the surviving contestants. They deserve to know."

"Will do," Thomas ran outside, and his eyes immediately found the surviving contestants looking through binoculars at the action below or staring emotionlessly in front of them.

Thomas felt his heart move as he looked at the four survivors about to have a front-row seat at the final duel. For a moment, Thomas wondered if they imagined themselves down there.

"If you guys want, you can come to the tent, or we can get you a screen here to watch. It is hard to see them after all," Thomas said as new flares launched; but he got no response. "Okay, the screen is in the broadcasting tent."

———

Zanai looked at Xiu, and both agreed without saying a word. *Da Vinci, it is.* Harper removed his Aussie hat, and his eyes found the Commander from the Centaur, George Adams, a slim man, and they agreed. *Crusading Angel.* Hands were shaken, and prayers were whispered.

———

Holding down the T-shaped junction, Mason heard the explosion and found a burning wreck of a sneaky tank destroyer, missing the Da Vinci hiding behind the ruins of the city hall.

"Dema! Focus!" Mason snapped his fingers, and Dema shook her head. "I believe it's almost over. Gio is in front of us, somewhere in that rubble."

"Huh, what?" A shell slipped from Dema's hands and clanked on the floor, reverberating inside their tin can. "Sorry!"

"The problem is this: Do they come from the front? Or from the side?" Mason first looked through the vision slits on his commander's cupola and then poked his head out.

———

Utilizing the light from the burning wreckage, launched flares, and the full moon, Gio and James found the Crusading Angel ten minutes later, sitting menacingly on the T-shaped junction, aiming at the burning wreck of Jagd 38T.

"Look at them." James pointed at Mason, who scanned the eerie, quiet street and closed the hatch behind him.

"It seems like they're not moving anytime soon due to their transmission." Gio looked at the open hatch on the back of the T-34 with parts and tools lying all around it. "Good news is that they are dead in the water. James, we're going to hit them from the side."

"Will do, but you only have one shot. Like them, we have a full ammo load! If they hit us, we're toast!"

"What have I become?" Gio slid back, and his head vanished in his hands. "This is not who I was supposed to be!"

"Who were you supposed to be then? Because I cannot imagine you doing anything else."

"This tank will become my metal grave, and I do not want it to be yours." Gio dodged the question. "Go, and I'll ram them. It should knock them out, which I'll use to blow them up for good. Find that green smoke and get the hell out of here!"

The long silence had descended on the ruined house as James's face darkened before answering.

"I'm your driver, so I'll drive you wherever you order me. Honestly, I wasn't expecting we would make it this far after we're crippled. No matter what happens, one of us, I hope, will get to tell the tale."

"I hate the fact I was right on that tamarac. All right, let's make sure that both of us can tell the tale. Both will be in the turret, so one shot there, and we're there. The end is here." Gio smiled as James gave him a hand, and a moment later, Da Vinci vanished behind the buildings.

The Italian heavy-medium picked up speed as its V-12 diesel engine propelled the Polymath, soon leaving behind the burning wreck of the Jagd 38T.

Entering the dreaded parallel street, Gio and James counted every yard and every second. There were a few bumps on the road and potholes here and there, and as they got halfway, Gio began rotating the turret on the right side, with the barrel almost scraping the houses. Another two minutes passed when Giovanni heard James talk in a shivering voice over the internal comms.

"Gio, prepare to fire; we're coming up to the end of the street. Should I speed up or slow down?"

"Speed up. If anything happens, it has been an honor." Gio pressed his face against the gunsight, but James slowed down to a crawl.

"James, what did I say!?"

"One bump or hole in the road will throw off your aim!"

"Speed up! Now!" Gio slowly exhaled. "Let's get this over with!"

"Will do, will do!" James hit the gas pedal and changed gear to second.

———

Both Giovanni and James held their breaths as they entered the junction. Moments later, Gio gasped in terror as he found that Mason had guessed correctly and turned the turret towards the other road. The full moon illuminated the long barrel without the muzzle brake, piercing the night.

James pressed the gas pedal to the floor as the Crusading Angel fired. Gio saw the muzzle flash instantly and the spinning shell flying toward him as time slowed.

"It has been an honor!" Gio halted himself as his life flashed in front of his eyes; just as the shell touched the side armor, where behind it, Gio had stacked the ammunition for easier reach moments before.

They really made sure that one of us would die. Full ammunition load. They really needed fireworks for the winner! Gio thought as he pressed the trigger. His world faded to black, and the last thing he heard was a massive explosion inside the tank as Crusading Angel sent another round down the range finished the deed for good. Da Vince was engulfed in the flaming inferno, just as the white flares illuminated the battlefield. In that bright light, Sharik ran out of the rubble, barking momentarily at two tanks before vanishing into the ruins forever.

CHAPTER TWENTY

IN THE END

"Headshot!" Dema shouted as she watched the turret of Da Vinci flying sky-high, but her shouts of joy stopped the moment she realized that a burning body had somehow climbed out of the driver's hatch.

"Mason, we need to go and help him!" Dema pressed the hatch to open it when she looked at Mason, who leaned back, his head vanishing into his arms.

Not waiting for him to reply, Dema climbed out, slid down the side, and ran towards the burning wreck. With a terror slowly settling on her face, she closed the distance between the two tanks and found a live body ablaze, rolling on the ground, attempting to put out the fire; but as she reached out, the fire had completely consumed him.

Dema slowly sat down on the debris, watching the cooked machine gun ammo sending fireworks into the dark sky. She gazed up at the rising clouds, searching for an answer she knew would never come. Then, as tears began to roll down her cheeks, Dema heard Mason ventilating behind her, and a moment later, she felt a rug on her shoulders.

"So, what now?" Dema leaned her head on Mason's shoulder as he placed Van's ammo box at her feet. "What now?"

It took a moment for Mason to reply as he watched the flares slowly descend. Finally, Dema picked up the ammo box and broke down in tears.

Mason took a deep breath and shouted into the night, "It's over, right? The nightmare is over! Right? Hello? Can anyone hear me?!"

Mason looked back and forth between the burning Da Vinci and Crusading Angel and closed his eyes.

"Mason, you did what you had to do. It would be either them or us." Dema walked up to Mason, who stared at the Crusading Angel and handed him Van's box.

"What am I supposed to say? I had to kill our friends." Mason wiped his tears away.

"I do not know, Mason. Everything feels so gray." Dema dried her tears as well. "The sooner we find that green smoke, the better."

"I do not think that my nightmares will leave any time soon. But, on the plus side, we can do therapy together." Mason looked at the dark sky while Dema opened Van's ammo box and pulled out TH's black box and the coin. "What do we do with our robot android friend? Is TH coming home with us, or does he stay here?"

"Let's take him. I think that is the best we can do for them. What's your take?" Mason flipped TH's coin between his fingers.

"Let's give our friends and Crusading Angel one last goodbye." Dema imagined somber orchestral music playing in the background.

She placed the box on the ground, removed the rug from her shoulders, and covered James's burned body.

"Is that Gio?" Mason kneeled to the burned corpse, taking deep breaths in the process.

"Does it matter now?" Dema looked at the now barely illuminated Crusading Angel. "Let them go face down if they must die. It will make it easier to say goodbye."

"I swear I heard that somewhere before! Who said that!?"

"Van said it to me." Dema shook her head. "Van, Van, Van, I can still hear your voice!"

Mason looked over his shoulder for the last time. The Crusading Angel sat there, and Mason felt the tank waving goodbye to the two surviving crew members. Then, for the last time, he walked up to his tank, touched its side, and felt the towing cable, just as he did the first time when he arrived at TVG. There, covered by night, the mighty T-34-57 mod.42/43, grazed and riddled with holes, looked like it was about to fall apart, held together only by the steel will and welding, contrasted to the burned wreck of the Da Vinci, Angel's Italian cousin.

Mason saluted and turned towards Dema, who silently awaited him at the Da Vince's wreckage, hiding her shaking hands in the pockets of her uniform.

Mason gave Dema a hand, and they walked down the destroyed street together, not looking back at the destruction. *Let them go face down if they must die.* Dema remembered Van's words of wisdom. *It will make it easier to say the final goodbye.* She rested her head on Mason's right shoulder as the flares illuminated their way forward towards the green smoke outside of the village, while Mason felt the weight of Van's ammo box filled with TH's black box. Mason took one last look over his shoulder, finding Sharik running into the night.

———

"Wow, what a ride, dear viewers! Mason Knight and Dema Balakin are the official winners of Tank Royale of 2145." Benjamin leaned back, and everyone inside the tent clapped, including the co-hosts.

"See Thomas," Adriana held Thomas's hand, "the tank that caused you to lose most sleep has won!"

Jeong-Min finished clapping and looked at the four surviving contestants. Harper and George continued jumping with their hands in the air while Zanai comforted Xiu, who broke down sobbing.

"It's going to be all right," Zanai said, but Wang Xiu pried herself out of the conversation and looked into the distance.

"What am I going to do? I am the only survivor and ended up in fourth place," Wang said. "Life has no sense anymore without Gio."

"Don't even think about making that jump to your demise!" Harper joined them. "All of us have much to live for. I didn't even know where I finished, and honestly, I couldn't care less. I'm alive, and so are you! Both good and bad memories will stay with us. They'll never fade away, and sooner or later we all will learn how to live with them."

"Also, count yourself lucky. Six out of forty-eight made it. We traveled to one of the most gorgeous places in the world, and all of you got to listen to Flower of Scotland echoing the mountains and vast forests of this battlefield. We should remember these moments," George sat down next to Xiu, "but we shall not forget the fallen who traveled with us and either commanded us or were commanded by us. We fought to the best of our ability."

———

Leaving the last crumbled houses behind, Mason first approached the green smoke. Then, Dema stood by his side and took him by the bicep, staring at the star-filled night sky. Then, she rested her head on Mason's left shoulder. However, as they stood there for ten minutes, nobody showed up, and the green smoke vanished into the night as well.

Then, twenty minutes later, Mason turned his head when he heard rumbling engines all around, and soon, the bright vehicle lights blinded them both.

"Both of you, get slowly on your knees and put your hands behind your heads!" An amplified voice from one of the cars prompted Dema to look at Mason, who dropped the box.

"Get on the ground now! Boys, get ready to light them up in three, two!"

"Yes!" Mason knelt and locked his eyes with Dema. "Get on your knees!"

As Dema knelt, men in ceramic battle armor emerged from transports and shoved them on the ground. Mason grunted as he felt cold steel locking his hands behind his back, and then a familiar voice cut through the night.

"Mason Knight! You actually made it, thus saving yourself the beating! Load them up! Overwatch, this is Alpha 0-1; the package has been secured!" Mason could only see a black boot talking to him. "And you even got a plus one. She looks good! If you think you are going home to your cripple, you're surely mistaken!"

——

A few hours later…

Benjamin took a deep breath as the screen came to life and found himself looking at Mason and Dema, sitting next to each other and smiling. Their faces bore no more sign of struggle. Instead of their uniforms, Mason was dressed in a blue three-piece suit and tie, while Dema sat in an elegant red and black dress.

"Well, Mason and Dema. This will be brief as you're tired. So, how are you feeling?" Benjamin opened the interview, pondering whether he talked with AI or the real Mason and Dema.

"We're tired but happy that we're going home," Mason said first. "Ail, I missed you, brother. Aunt, I said that I'd make it home!"

"Wow, what a man! Dema?" Benjamin scratched his head. "How are you feeling?"

"Same as my Mason. Tired but happy that we're going home. It was a long road, I tell you."

"But it flew as we had each other. Van and TH, you'll be

remembered. Both of you are our family. Time may pass, others will forget, but we'll remember you." Mason touched his forehead.

"Alright, last question. Actually, this will suffice for now. I want you to be rested before an in-depth interview. Do you have any questions for me, or we'll call it a night?"

"Dema, the microphone is yours." Mason smiled and looked at Dema, who coughed.

"How are you feeling? Like us, you came a long way!"

"Yeah, I'm super excited about everything! It was a long road indeed, but I'm looking forward to meeting both of you in person! Mason?"

"Is this the end, or we'll be back for more?" Mason looked into the camera. "Will there be more tanks?"

THE END

(Please see the THANK YOU and BONUSES)

As promised, Thank You, Jung Ju Hwan (Instagram @is_2.1944), for first bringing the T-34-57, aka Crusading Angel, to life.

Thank you, Mylan Isbell (Instagram @pendit_art), for collaborating on this project, bringing the world and tanks of the Crusading Angel to life.

Thank you, Sydney Allen, for the editorial expertise on my manuscripts.

Thank you, Muhammad F. Adiputranto (Instagram @hylobates_moloch), for digitizing the artwork and worldbuilding of the Crusading Angel.

Thank you, Atmosphere Press and the good people working there, for finalizing my idea and putting it out there.

Lastly, thank you to all who decided to read my story and give me constructive feedback.

If you have made it this far, dear reader, I have bonus content available. Please continue reading.

TANK OPERATING MANUAL

Please see the Instagram of @pendit_art and @hylobates_moloch for the more images. This section is dedicated to the main medium tanks with extra historical background. Consider doing your follow-up research as well.

AC-4 (Namarrkon)

The Australian Cruiser Tank Mk.4 (17-pounder) was a termi-nated successor of the AC-3 Thunderbolt, the only home-pro-duced Australian tank in WW2, which had never seen active combat with the Australian Armored Divisions as preference was given to the British and American tanks.

Thomas Askarov had brought the AC-4 back to life. With the available documentation, Thomas finalized the project, and the tank underwent testing and was approved by Adriana to participate in the TVG Tank Royale of 2145.

TVG Promo: AC-4: Long-barreled Aussie from the other side of the world had been blessed with the might of the 17-pounder while retaining a "low" profile for the medium tank. Named after the Australian aboriginal god of lighting, will Namarrkon ride the storm's clouds to final victory?

Centaur Mk.III (Boudicca)

Centaur (A27L) is a WW2 British medium tank, almost identical to its more famous relative, the Cromwell. However, the Centaur had a weaker engine, 410 horsepower vs. 600 horsepower, and a few structural changes. The Centaur was used for training, but several engineering variants had seen combat in Europe from D-Day to Northwestern Germany in 1945.

Thomas had decided to bring out a lesser-known tank of

the Cromwell family, choosing the Mk.III variant, which came with the QF 75mm gun and a special treat for the viewers, a 152 mm RP-3 rocket attached to the rail, mounted on the side of the turret, fired by the wire from inside. The tank underwent testing and was approved by Adriana to participate in the TVG Tank Royale of 2145.

TVG promo: *Fueled by tea, biscuits, bagpipes, and red fury, this Brit bears the name of Boudicca, legendary Queen of the Iceni during the Ancient Era. Will this Queen bring the final victory to the British Isles?*

Ram II late (Peggy)

Canadian Ram II Cruiser Tank was based on the M3 Medium chassis, a homemade tank developed for the Canadian Armed Forces during World War Two. Like many Commonwealth tanks, like Centaur, only the engineering variants had seen combat in Europe.

Thomas had selected the Ram II Late variation after an internal poll between Canadian employees. Utilizing the better Mk. V QF-6 pounder gun, 57mm, Thomas had finished the final model after two days, allowing Adriana to rigorously test this tank and approve it for the TVG Tank Royale of 2145.

TVG promo: *Named after Francis Pegahmagabow, the "Peggy" and its crew have a worthy challenge, as they are the first All-Canadian crew to attempt to bring the first-ever Battle Royale Win to Canada. Will the Canadian nature, power of the wind, and 57mm gun be enough?*

Panzer 4 G Hydrostat (Oden)

The only German tank to be produced and actively serve to the end of World War Two, the Panzerkampfwagen IV and its variants became the workhorses of the Wehrmacht. Originally designed to support infantry, they were up-gunned to replace the outdated Panzer III, starting with F2 variants; all IVs had received the infamous long-barreled 75mm KwK 40 gun, which carried this tank to the end of the hostilities in Europe.

Thomas had chosen a unique prototype of the G variant, referred to as the Hydrostat variant, which attempted to solve the low mobility aspects of the Panzer 4. After finalizing the project, Thomas carefully observed Adriana's testing and had to redesign several aspects of the hull and turret mechanism to participate in the Tank Royale of 2145.

TVG Promo: *Hailing from Germany, this Panzer IV underwent a modification of its powertrain while retaining the signature long barreled 75mm gun. Commanded by the hands-on German Doctor of Engineering, will this machine of war blitz it's way to victory, or will it break down halfway?*

Chi-Nu-Kai (Tomoe Gozen)

Development of the tank being able to counter Shermans in the Pacific came across several problems and delays, so the stop-gap project was created, named Chi-Nu, sporting a new long-barreled 75mm Type 3 Gun. An improved Chi-Nu-Kai project was constructed and tested, but never passed the prototype model. Both tanks never left the Japanese Home Islands and were given to the Home Defense Front.

Thomas mistook the Chi-Nu-Kai model for the Chi-Nu and sent it to production. However, this small mistake soon turned into an opportunity. Adriana pointed out that Kai's gun satisfies the contract, and the tank was shipped in the second batch as Adriana greenlighted Chi-Nu-Kai to participate in the Royale of 2145, providing viewers with an exciting tank to cheer for.

TVG Promo: *One of the more exciting tanks out there, which possesses a hull of the original Chi-Nu and a turret of Chi-To, giving it an increase in the firepower department. Arriving from the Land of the Rising Sun with the all-female crew of the most dedicated tankers and warriors, will they be able to win these games honorably?*

M4A1 76W (American Made)

The famous workhorse of the American Military during WW2, the M4 Sherman, and its consecutive variants became one of the most produced tanks of the war. It carried the United States to victory in both Europe and the Pacific. Also, Shermans were Lend-Leased to several nations, including Britain and the Commonwealth, France, the Soviet Union, and China, to name a few. M4A1 76W was the first Sherman variation to receive a long-barreled 76mm gun with appropriate benefits and trade-offs.

Thomas had to navigate the political and bureaucratic minefield of the TVG. While the result proved to be a good design, with a powerful 76mm gun and reliability, the better variants were on the table. Adriana greenlighted, and the tank was shipped with the third batch.

TVG Promo: *Rightfully named "American Made," this reliable machine is a crowd favorite and one of the most famous tanks of the World War Two Era. Armed with the mighty 76mm cannon, will the signature reliability, a powerful gun, and the name be enough to bear the stars and stripes at the final stage?*

14TP (Grom)

There are a lot of conflicting rumors and secondary sources about the Polish 14-tonne cruiser tank, 14TP, ranging from its very existence to even the purpose of this tank, but one can only wait till the Polish National Archives releases the primary sources. However, it is believed that only one engine-less prototype was created to advance the Polish Tank Research and Development further.

Thomas faced similar problems as, in the contract clause, a requirement was written to include the best homemade Polish tank. Upon data analysis, the 14TP was chosen, and Thomas, with Adriana, brought 14TP to life and greenlighted it with hesitation to participate in the Tank Royale of 2145.

TVG Promo: *Surrounded by mystery, this 14-ton medium cruiser was brought to life and crewed by an ace crew of Polish patriots who always know what they are doing. Will this tank be able to create its legend, or will it be shoved in the back of the Tank Museum?*

P26/40 (Da Vinci)

Resembling the Soviet T-34 medium tank, the Italian P26/40 was the next evolution of the Italian Tank Research and Development. Due to the state of Italian Industry and missing resources, only a few were produced. After the Italian Armistice, several factories fell into German hands, providing us with spare combat accounts of this tank.

This was a standard procedure for Thomas: found, recreated, and printed. Adriana tested this tank and provided feedback that the diesel engine would be a better choice, so it was fitted, and P26/40 was greenlighted to participate in the Tank Royale of 2145.

TVG Promo: *This medium-sized-heavy Italian hitter is a serious contender and threat to any opponent who dares to cross its sights. Named after the famous Italian polymath Leonardo Da Vinci, will this tank shine in all areas like the renowned inventor?*

T-34-57 mod.42/43 (Crusading Angel)

The legendary medium tank of the Soviet Armor, the T-34, served from the start of Operation Barbarossa to Berlin, spawning countless variants and licensed productions post-war. It remains one of the most produced tanks to this day, each variation improving on the rugged design.

Thomas's head-scratching had found an interesting variant of the T-34 called the T-34-57 mod.42/43, the tank destroyer.

Upon improving the tank with the historical guidelines, like giving the commander's cupola for better visibility, Adriana greenlighted the tank to participate in the Medium Tank Royale of 2145.

TVG Promo: *While it might be rough around the edges, do not let this Crusading Angel fool you. Being the jack of all trades and a master of none, this tank is a hard-working unit that will surely get the job done; but is it enough to be an all-rounder in this Royale?*

Strv m/42 Delat Torn (Carolus Rex)

It is a rare sight that someone can say that Sweden had an actual tank force during World War Two, as they weren't active participants per se, as most of the focus was on the more prominent players. Nonetheless, the Swedish Tank School is one of the more unique ones out there, and by the 40s standard, the Swedish tanks were modern machines with no combat record.

Thomas knew there was more to the Strv m/42 than meets the eye. This search resulted in the Delat Torn variant, a one-off modification with a special semi-automatic clip loader. Adriana greenlighted the tank for the Battle Royale of 2145.

TVG Promo: *This modern Viking will surely turn everyone's heads as one of the more modern tanks of the WW2 era. Crewed by the battle-hardened Caroleans, will the 22nd-century Carolus Rex bring shine again on the world stage?*

Nahuel DL D3/43 (Gaucho)

It is rare to mention the Argentinian Tank development during World War Two. Attempts were made in the Nahuel medium tank, heavily inspired by the early M4 Sherman and M3 Lee. There are even a few speculations about its name origin, but this Jaguar was ready to fight.

Thomas knew he struck gold in terms of rarity, but just like 14TP, this tank would have troubles on the battlefield. However, a contract is a contract, so Thomas recreated the project, and after final testing, Adriana approved the tank to participate in the Tank Royale of 2145.

TVG Promo: *While it may seem that Argentinian engineers were scavenging for leftovers, this Argentinian Cowboy packs firepower with*

41M III Turan 75 (Horthy)

The tank that had fallen behind the sofa of history, the
Hungarian Turan, could have been great if the Hungarian
World War Two situation had been different and allowed its
Tank Development to be fully embraced, which had partially
happened. Unfortunately, only one fully operational Turan III
with the long 75mm gun was produced.

Thomas and Adriana faced many challenges in bringing
this tank to life. Limited documentation, even a few images,
was just a start. Eventually, Thomas ironed out most of the
problems, and with hesitation, Adriana approved Turan III to
claim the place in the sun among its brothers in the Tank
Royale of 2145.

TVG Promo: *Tank Royale Research Department found this tank
behind the sofa of history, and after an arduous task, it roared to life,
showing an untapped potential with its powerful gun and decent armor.
Will this Hungarian underdog shine among its more renowned brothers?*

OTHER INFO

Want to collaborate with one of my IPs? Fan Art?
Fan Fiction (might be introduced as cannon)?
DM me on Instagram: @chalstoriesofficial

ABOUT ATMOSPHERE PRESS

Founded in 2015, Atmosphere Press was built on the principles of Honesty, Transparency, Professionalism, Kindness, and Making Your Book Awesome. As an ethical and author-friendly hybrid press, we stay true to that founding mission today.

If you're a reader, enter our giveaway for a free book here:

SCAN TO ENTER
BOOK GIVEAWAY

If you're a writer, submit your manuscript for consideration here:

SCAN TO SUBMIT
MANUSCRIPT

And always feel free to visit Atmosphere Press and our authors online at atmospherepress.com. See you there soon!

Florida-based author and creator **CHRISTIAAN A. LECKY** is the designer of the CHALstories platform, an ever-growing collection of literary works of varied genres spreading across three primary timelines. A mixed background of interests in business, history, and enjoyment of technology and culture provides the reader with unique world-building, writing, and execution. Christiaan hopes to pull from his backlog of ideas the right one for his next writing campaign and is already working on the sequel for *Gasoline Cowboys*.